REVENGE PLAN

ALSO BY LINZI CARLISLE

Village Lies
Graphic Lies
Old Lies
Nocturnal Lies

REVENGE PLAN

LINZI CARLISLE

For the girls

EMMA'S PLAYLIST

Just For fun

Tracks listened to by the characters in the story, or for inspiration as I wrote and imagined a soundtrack as events played out. Search Spotify playlists for Revenge Plan by Linzi Carlisle, and have a listen.

Haven't Met You Yet – Michael Bublé
The Flood – Take That
Believe – Cher
I Will Survive – Gloria Gaynor
Love Is All Around – Wet Wet Wet
Spice Up Your Life – Spice Girls
Sexcrime – Eurythymics
Come Undone – Robbie Williams
Fuck you – Lily Allen
Cloudbusting – Kate Bush
We Are Family – Sister Sledge
Girls Just Want To Have Fun – Cyndi Lauper
Vogue – Madonna
Can't Get You Out Of My Head – Kylie Minogue
Never Ever – All Saints
Better The Devil You Know – Kylie Minogue
The Sign – Ace Of Base
No Regrets – Robbie Williams
Girls & Boys – Blur
(I Can't Help) Falling In Love With You – UB40

She's The One – Robbie Williams
Saturday Night – Whigfield
Fastlove, Pt. 1 – George Michael
Mambo No. 5 – Lou Bega
Stars – Simply Red
Firework – Katy Perry
It's The End Of The World As We Know It – R.E.M.
The Passenger – Iggy Pop
Way Down We Go – KALEO
Under Pressure – Queen, David Bowie
Mad World – Tears For Fears
Back To Black – Amy Winehouse
Un-break My Heart – Toni Braxton
Killing Me Softly With His Song – Fugees, Ms. Lauryn Hill
I'll Stand By You – Pretenders
Confusion – Electric Light Orchestra
Never Tear Us apart – Paloma Faith
Don't You Want Me – The Human League
Unchained Melody – Robson & Jerome, Dave Ford
Don't Let It Bring You Down – Annie Lennox
Beautiful Girl – INXS
Antmusic – Adam & The Ants
Everybody Hurts – R.E.M.
Perfect Day – Lou Reed
Set Fire To The Rain – Adele
Why Does My Heart Feel So Bad? – Moby
Suddenly I See – KT Tunstall
Angels – Robbie Williams
The Show – Lenka
One – Mary J. Blige, U2
Don't Stop Me Now - Queen

MAIN CHARACTERS

Abigail – married to Martin; narrator

Lauren – married to Paul

Emma – separated from Craig

Hayley – married to Ross

Fiona – divorced from Danny

Jenna – divorced from Shane

Claire – married to Adrian

BEFORE

Haven't Met You Yet

I never thought that anyone would end up dead.

It was just another drunken girls' night, one of so many over the years, but that night was the catalyst for everything bad that happened afterwards. As we threw back shots, laughed, and posed for photos, we had no idea what was about to happen in the near future, or how our lives would be changed forever.

We'd met at the school gates, young mothers dropping off our kids outside the local primary school, our first tentative steps towards friendship being a coffee at the local coffee shop where conversation centred around our children. At some point, as our children had transitioned to junior school, and we'd found ourselves with a little more time on our hands, our friendship had progressed to lunch – a toasted sandwich and a cup of tea – and our conversation had moved on to other aspects of our lives such as our husbands, holiday plans, the best place to buy wallpaper to decorate the spare room, or the cost of having a conservatory added to the house.

By the time our kids made the move to one of the three secondary schools in the area our friendship no longer needed them as the common denominator and we began to dip our toes into the couples friendship pool, gathering at one or the other of our houses for the odd Saturday afternoon barbeque, delightedly encouraging the burgeoning friendships between our husbands and finding out, much to our surprise, that a couple of our husbands had gone to the same school and that one of them had even dated one of the other wives when they were both young.

Around this time, we began to venture out for the odd girls' night – an innocent evening at a local restaurant where we'd enjoy a meal and a couple of glasses of wine while we lamented our husbands' inattention or our latest failed attempt at dieting. We shared secrets, sympathised over marital problems, and discussed with dread our rapidly-approaching forties. We had our first girls' weekend away together, promising to make it a regular thing.

Fast-forward a few years and our children had left school for college, university, or a job of some kind, and we were empty nesters with too much time on our hands. Two of our group were now divorced, another was separated, and we had morphed into that dreaded group of middle-aged women who planned, with great excitement, a night out at which we would admire each other's newly-purchased outfit or freshly-highlighted hair as we threw back glass after glass of wine and shrieked raucously at the Michael Bublé tribute act.

We were bored housewives attempting to recapture a youth that existed only in our memories, desperate to show the world that we were still relevant, still attractive, still worthy of attention – which we sought with every photo posted by one or the other of us on our various social media pages.

It was around this time that someone mentioned a dating app they were on. The shock wasn't about the actual use of the app, it was about the fact that the friend in question was still married.

I suppose that's when it all really started...

1

The Flood
Believe

The room fell quiet after Lauren told us, the only sound being Take That playing from Emma's speakers, and we looked around at each other, waiting to see who would speak first.

Emma was the first to break the silence, uncurling her long legs from the settee and walking over to the kitchen counter to fetch another bottle of wine. Twisting the cap off, she expertly topped up our glasses before sitting back down. 'Well, I don't blame you, we all know Paul can't keep it in his trousers. If he's going to play away then you should too. I say go for it.'

'Emma, how can you say that?' I took a gulp of my wine. 'Two wrongs don't make a right, and maybe, if he only did it once, and he's sorry, then...'

'Then that makes it alright?' Fiona slammed her glass down on the coffee table. 'You're being naïve if you think he only did it once, Abigail. They're all the bloody same, look at Danny – by the time I kicked him out he'd slept with half the female population of Bromley and was busy planning to bed the other half before Christmas – which was three weeks away at the time.'

We all laughed – Fiona was known for her exaggerations, which increased in direct correlation with her intake of wine.

'Fiona's right, they're all a bunch of cheating bastards. Be honest, can any one of us truly say that our husband has never cheated on us? Exes included, of course.'

I stared at Jenna, flustered. The thought had never occurred to me. 'Martin would never cheat on me,' I said firmly, secretly trying to calculate when he'd last shown an interest in me in bed. He'd appeared distracted lately, and I was struggling with feelings of inadequacy. It didn't help that we'd been arguing a lot as well.

'Oh, yawn...' drawled Jenna, pushing her long dark hair back from her face as she stretched her legs out, her brightly-painted toe-nails a flash of fuchsia as she curled her toes up inside her bright pink, sparkly flip flops complete with little tinkly bells. 'You'd never know, that's the point, it's too easy these days with all these dating apps.'

I dragged my eyes away from her feet, glancing down at my own boring white flip flops. That was typical Jenna – vanity over practicality, every time – she must have tutted and reached down to untangle the little bells from under the straps at least ten times this evening.

'That's not true,' I said. I think I'd know if Martin was going on dates with another woman.' I laughed. 'He's hardly getting dressed up and disappearing off for the evening to wine and dine someone else, and he certainly never spends the night away, so how exactly could he be cheating?'

Emma looked at me sympathetically. 'That's not how it works, Abs. It's hook ups now – see someone you like, get a match, and meet up for a quick shag, it's that simple, any time of the day will do. Lunch hour bonking's all the rage these days.'

I stared at Emma, before turning to Lauren. 'Is that what you meant when you said you were on a dating app?'

A phone camera flashed and Hayley giggled. 'Gotcha. *Abigail having a confused moment – too much wine?*' She spoke out loud as she typed into her phone.

Jenna threw her head back, her deep-throated laugh making us all smile, and suddenly we were all reaching for our phones, taking pictures of each other as we lifted our wine glasses and grinned at the cameras.

Claire slammed an ice-cold bottle of flavoured-vodka down on the coffee table, yelling, 'Shooter time! Where are your shot glasses, Em?'

'She keeps them in the sideboard.' Fiona waved her hand in the direction of the dining area, puffing on her vape.

'I'll get them.' Hayley jumped up, returning with a stack of glasses and laying them out for Claire to fill.

The room filled with Cher's strident tones as her voice rang out from the speakers, the next track on Emma's playlist.

'Turn it up, Em, I love this one,' squealed Lauren.

'Oh, me too.' Hayley began singing along a little too enthusiastically, which made us grin.

'Down the hatch, girls. Here's to Lauren meeting the man of her dreams.' Jenna downed her shot, and we all did the same, crashing our empty glasses down noisily.

'Sod that,' said Lauren. 'I married him, and look how that turned out. No, from now on, it's all about the sex, baby.' She gave a dirty cackle as I looked at her in amazement.

'But... what if he finds out?'

'Little innocent Abigail.' Jenna reached for the vodka bottle and refilled our glasses, sloshing vodka over the table carelessly as I hurriedly grabbed a handful of tissues to mop it up.

'My little anal Abs, keeping everything perfect.' Jen winked at me.

'He'll never know it's Lauren. Hell, even I don't recognise you. Black suits you, and I love the hat, Busty Bromley Babe.'

'Give me that!' Lauren lunged at Fiona, grabbing for her phone as Fiona stood up, all five feet, ten inches of her

– more, if you included her heels – holding it out of her reach as she continued to study it.

'Hmm... he's hot... oh my... Dartford Dave's a looker... Oh, you've got a new message. Want me to open it? It's from Funny Man Mike.'

We were all staring at Fiona now, and trying not to laugh as poor Lauren jumped desperately, her hands falling short of her phone.

Claire crawled around, topping up our glasses again, and we all began drunkenly shouting, 'Read it, read it!'

'Fancy hooking up tonight? Am in your area.'

Jenna stood up suddenly, a match for Fiona's height, and grabbed the phone from her.

'Don't be a bully, Fi. He looks cute, I like a man with something to grab hold of.' She grinned, passing the phone back to a red-faced Lauren. 'I suppose that's why I got fed-up with Shane when he took up cycling and became the spitting image of a stick insect.'

'God, don't say that, I swear Shane became Adrian's hero when he slimmed down. He'd give anything to lose a few pounds. So would I, come to think of it.' Claire squeezed her ample stomach as she pulled a rueful face.

'You should come walking with me at Keston Ponds. I'm there every Saturday morning.'

'Maybe I'll just go on a diet.'

We chuckled – Claire wasn't known for her love of exercise.

'What time do you go walking?' I asked Lauren, wondering if it might do me some good. 'Where exactly do you walk? Maybe I'll join you.'

'I'll send you my route, I do the same one every time so it'll be easy for you to find me if you fancy it. Same time, same place, like clockwork.'

'God, not another stickler, you're as bad as Abigail. What happened to spontaneity?' Jenna faked a yawn as my phone whooped with a notification from Lauren. 'Can we get back to the far more interesting subject of whether you're hooking up with the funny man?'

'Well?' Emma spoke for all of us as we fixated on Lauren.

'But where's Paul?' I whispered. 'You're not– are you going to?'

Lauren smiled mysteriously as she typed a reply, checking the time on her watch. 'Might do... that's for me to know, and you to find out... or not. Who's got the bottle?'

'Here.' Hayley topped us up again, and we threw back the shots, a bunch of totally trashed middle-aged women looking far from our best. 'We should go for another walking weekend.' She clapped her hands excitedly. 'I loved our Dover to Deal walk last month, it's so beautiful down there. Can we? Please?'

'I'll second that,' said Lauren, giving Hayley a high five. 'It was fabulous, the views, the feeling of freedom as we looked out over the channel...' She sighed happily.

'Oh God, listen to Lauren waxing bloody lyrical,' groaned Jenna.

'Oi.' Lauren laughed good-naturedly. 'I was going to say it justified the amount of wine we drank later.'

'See? That's two of us already. So, is it a yes? Can we do it?' Hayley looked around hopefully.

We all nodded and mumbled, as someone said maybe we could go the following month, it might have been Fi, and Claire groaned, saying something about all these energetic weekends being hard work.

'Rubbish.' Hayley laughed. 'Remember when we stood looking over at France? And when we had lunch at that pub in St Margaret's at Cliffe, and–'

'And our phones said we were in France,' we all said, laughing.

It had been fun, Hayley was right.

'And then we drank champagne and spoke in French accents,' I said, smiling. 'You're right, Hayles, we should definitely do it again.'

'Do you promise?'

'I promise, we all do. Right?' I looked around at the others.

'Promise!' they all yelled.

'Hooray, group shot to seal the deal!'

She meant a photo, not a drink, and we clustered together as Hayley set the timer on her phone camera, all of us grinning like loons as we pulled silly poses for our traditional photo at every single one of our girls' nights together.

2

Fiona puffed on her vape, throwing it down on the coffee table. 'I need a real ciggie. Who's got one?' She looked at Lauren.

'Like I'm going to give you one now, after you pinched my phone.'

'Oh, come on, it was just a bit of fun, and you know we don't have secrets from each other. I'm impressed, you look hot and you're having a good time. What's the big deal? Besides, you're not doing anything Paul isn't.'

Relenting, Lauren pulled her cigarettes and lighter from her bag, dropping her phone on the chair. 'Come on then.'

'Me too.' Claire stood up, her knees cracking, and followed them out to the patio.

Claire always smoked when she was drunk, occasionally pitching up with a couple of packets to replace all the cigarettes she pinched from Lauren.

Lauren's phone gave a little beep, and the rest of us looked at it warily and then at each other.

Hayley grinned at me. 'I dare you, Abs.'

'No way.' I shook my head.

'Oh, for God's sake.' Jenna picked it up and clicked on the message. 'Lauren, he wants to see you at eleven tonight!' she yelled at the open doors. 'What do you want to do?'

'Tell him yes and to send his pin.' Lauren appeared in the doorway.

Jenna nodded, tapping away as I watched her.

'How are so familiar with it?' I asked, knowing the answer before the words were out of my mouth.

'How d'you think?' She winked at me.

'Am I the only one not on a bloody dating app?' I stood up, a little wobbly, pretending to glare at the others as they shrugged their shoulders and fell about laughing. 'Well? Who's on one then?'

'Hands up, girls.' Jenna smirked, lifting her arm. 'Abbie's got her school teacher act going.'

Emma held her hand up, her arm swaying slightly. 'Sorry, Abs, but Craig and I are separated...'

'Yes, well, I mean... I'm not judging anyone...' I looked at Hayley, who put her hand in the air and then collapsed in a fit of giggles.

'I'm not, I promise you, Abs. I'm just mucking around.'

I smiled at her gratefully, relieved to not be the only one in our group out of the dating app loop.

Her giggling turned into a coughing fit, and we looked on in concern as she wheezed, holding her chest.

'D'you need your asthma spray, babes?'

Nodding, Hayley pointed to her bag, and Emma rummaged through it, handing her the spray.

'Aren't you curious though, Abs?' Jenna looked at me questioningly, once Hayley's breathing had calmed down, her eyes watery, her words slightly slurred.

I was, but I didn't want to give her the wrong idea. 'I just... I mean... I get it if you're single, but Lauren? I thought she was happy with Paul, that is... I didn't realise he was, you know, more than once...' I didn't really get it, not the whole hooking up bit... just for sex... it made me feel uncomfortable... and I suddenly felt like I didn't know my friends as well as I'd thought I did...

'She was happy, babes, but Paul's destroyed that, he's a serial cheater so it's just tit for tat.' Emma weighed in. 'They're both just getting out there and having some fun.'

'But what if you want to meet someone and he turns you down? Isn't it embarrassing?' asked Hayley. 'I'd be mortified.'

Jenna was busy on her phone, smiling mysteriously, and my imagination ran away with me, imagining her arranging to go and meet some bloke for sex in half an hour. But then she frowned and I guessed I'd been wrong.

'I'll tell you one thing,' Jenna said as she put her phone down. 'I'd kill the bloody bugger rather than face rejection. Once in my life was enough.'

'A little over-dramatic,' drawled Fi, the actual queen of drama.

'Oh God, I'd give up Adrian in a heartbeat,' Claire joked as she walked back in, bringing with her a scent of freshly-smoked cigarettes.

'Could you even imagine Adrian having an affair?' Emma sniggered as we all pictured poor old, square Adrian with anyone other than Claire.

'Well, I'd never let anyone take Martin away from me, if I couldn't have him, no one could.'

'Not you as well.' Claire guffawed. 'What would you do, stab him with a carving knife? I'm not sure you've got it in you, Abs.'

'Didn't you know I was a serial killer in my younger days?' I said, giggling happily as they all laughed.

'As if,' said Fi, chuckling. 'Oh, she with the perfect marriage.'

'And it had better stay that way, otherwise Martin's in trouble.' I giggled again, enjoying the friendly banter. 'I'd off him and his dirty little bit on the side in one second. No one messes with my life.'

'I'd definitely kill Ross if he ever did that to me. I'd cut him up into pieces and keep him in the freezer and then... then I'd cook him on the barbeque.'

We all stared at Hayley. She always got a little too over-excited when she was drunk.

'No more going to barbeques at Hayley's, girls, especially if we haven't seen Ross for a while.' Fi spluttered into her wine as we all laughed hysterically.

Claire yawned, picking up her bag. 'Time for me to go, I'm knackered, and my cab'll be here any minute. See you all on Friday night.'

'Can't wait.' Emma grinned. 'A weekend away is just what I need.'

'I should go too, fancy sharing a cab, Hayles?' I picked up my phone.

'Sure, thanks.' She nodded. 'I wonder what time Ross will roll in.'

'About the same time that Martin does.' I laughed. 'Was Adrian joining them tonight?' I turned to Claire as we moved towards the front door.

'Yep, the whole bunch were getting together, I think.'

'Well, what do you know? Looks like I've still got it after all these years. Oh yes, I've reeled you back in at last, you couldn't resist, could you?' Jenna was murmuring at her phone as she smiled like the cat that got the cream. That's me.' She stood up. 'See you Friday, everyone. I'll pick you up at six, Abs, then we'll get Fi and Lauren.'

We all bundled out of the front door, me, Hayley, Claire and Jenna, leaving Fi and Lauren with Emma but, when I looked back, Lauren was on her way out as well.

'D'you think she's off for a hook up?' Hayley's question echoed my own thoughts as we sat in the cab on our way home.

'I don't know, maybe she was just messing around earlier... I feel a bit stupid, like I missed something changing in our friendships. I mean, when did they all become so... sophisticated? But... Lauren, though...'

'I meant Jenna.' Hayley slipped her arm through mine and gave a giggle. 'She looked... I don't know... like a woman on a mission?'

'Jenna? Really? She probably gets loads of offers... she's got that whole sexy woman thing going for her... Men can't resist her... If I was on a thing like that, I wouldn't even get one man interested in me...' I leant against Hayley, my voice wistful as I imagined a scenario in which I'd never find myself in a million years.

'Course you would, silly. But we're the lucky ones, Abs. You've got your handsome Martin, haven't you? And I've got my gorgeous Ross – who I'd never cook on the barbeque, obviously. We've got happy marriages so we don't need all that. Let them have their fun, they're not harming anyone.'

'I suppose so, unless they mess around with married men... or Paul finds out about Lauren...'

'But he won't, will he? Not from any of us anyway, we'd never betray our friendship. And it's not like he could say anything anyway. Oh, that's me coming up on the left.'

The driver nodded and pulled over.

'See you Friday.' I gave Hayley a quick hug. 'Who's driving?'

'Claire is, she's picking me up first, then we'll get Em.'

Our house was in darkness when I arrived home a few minutes later, and I switched the hall light on before pulling out my phone and texting Martin.

His reply came back almost immediately telling me not to wait up, that they were still at the pub. I noticed the absence of a kiss, feeling insecure, and went into the kitchen to fill two glasses with water, taking them upstairs and placing them on our bedside tables.

Once in bed, I picked up my phone, smiling at the photos we'd all put on of our night together. I glanced at the map Lauren had sent me, saving it in case I decided to join her for one of her walks, before bringing up the name of the hotel we were going to for the weekend and browsing the photos in the gallery. The images of the meals in the restaurant made me feel hungry and I deliberated over whether to go back downstairs to grab a biscuit but, glancing down at my stomach, I ruefully decided against it.

Feeling sleepy, I switched the light out, my mind replaying Jenna's words from earlier as I nestled into my pillow. *Martin wouldn't cheat on me, my inner voice reassured me, we were just going through a dry patch, that was all...*

3

I Will Survive
Love Is All Around

Where was Martin? I tried his phone again. It wasn't like him to be late home and not let me know, especially when he knew I'd be away for the weekend. I'd even told him what time Jen was picking me up.

Jenna hooted impatiently as I zipped up my weekend bag and looked around to make sure I hadn't forgotten anything. Satisfied, I hauled my bag down the stairs, stopping to fluff my hair in the mirror before rushing out and slamming the door behind me.

'Martin not home yet?' Jenna stared at our front door as I struggled with the seatbelt.

'Yes, he'd just got out of the shower so he stayed upstairs. We said our goodbyes there,' I added, wondering why I was lying – to Jenna of all people. But I knew why – I was upset with Martin and I didn't want Jenna to start mocking me and being unkind.

'So sweet, the perfect loving couple.' My window opened suddenly, and I jumped as Jenna yelled right beside my ear as she leant across me. 'Hey, Marty, not gonna say hello to me today?'

The window shot back up, and she pulled away from the kerb, grinning, as I smiled uncertainly at her and tried to decide if she'd been being sarcastic just now about the whole perfect couple thing – it was hard to tell with Jenna sometimes. But then I reminded myself that she was divorced and that it must be difficult to be faced with the companionship of marriage. That was probably why she was a little abrasive at times, I decided. Feeling sorry for her, I looked across at her, wanting to say something nice.

'You look nice. New top?'

'Thanks, I got it yesterday. Not too tarty, is it?'

It was a little… tight and low-cut and, together with her leather skirt, did rather give her a mutton dressed as lamb appearance. But still, I felt in awe of her, I always did, she had a sophisticated air about her, bold and filled with confidence, and beside her I always felt like an awkward school girl.

I glanced at the small flower tattoo on her shoulder, revealed as she reached up to adjust her rearview mirror. I'd never understood why she had it – she was the least flowery person I knew. The five tiny petals were white with a hint of pink, the stamens just fine strokes, the anthers merely darker pink dots. It was pretty, and I wondered in amusement whether I should get one, although I doubted that Martin would approve.

'No, it's perfect.'

She flashed me a grin, all deep red lipstick, and I smiled happily back at her, my own lips painted with the same baby pink shade I'd used for years.

'Shall I text Fi to tell her we're here?'

'No need.'

I looked up to see Fiona sitting on the wall outside her house, her long legs crossed, suitcase beside her, vape in hand and sunglasses obscuring her eyes.

The front passenger door opened, and Fiona looked at me over the top of her sunglasses. 'In the back, shorty, my legs'll never fit.'

I clambered out, hugging Fi before getting into the back seat. It was always the same, Lauren and I always got shoved in the back when we travelled with Jenna and Fiona.

'God, I'm looking forward to a large gin and tonic.' Fiona leant back. 'Today was a nightmare, first the milk was off, and you know how much I hate black coffee, so I had to send the cleaner off to buy fresh milk, which meant she was delayed making the bed, which meant I couldn't pack. And then, as if that wasn't all disaster enough, they mucked up my nail appointment. I had to wait for forty-five minutes. *Forty-five minutes.*' She gave an enormous sigh and took out her phone.

Jenna and I waited for more about Fi's disastrous day, with bated breath.

'Like I said, an absolute bloody nightmare.'

So that was that then, Fiona at her exaggerating best, a new achievement, considering she hadn't had any booze yet.

'Thirty-two minutes until I can enjoy a G&T.' Fi's freshly-manicured nails tapped on her phone screen. 'I didn't realise Eynsford was so close. I suppose I'll survive.'

Grinning, Jenna touched her own phone's screen, and Gloria Gaynor began her anthem as we pulled up outside Lauren's. 'Emma's playlist never lets me down,' she said, winking at Fi, as she tapped her nails on the steering wheel impatiently.

'What's all the laughter about?' asked Lauren after throwing her bag in the boot and climbing into the back seat beside me.

'Oh, just Fi being her usual dramatic self.' I grinned as I hugged her. 'Eynsford Manor here we come!' I yelled excitedly, and we whooped and high-fived, our hands meeting between the front and back seats, before singing along to one of our favourite songs of all time.

'Good God, we've got to traverse a bloody river to get to the hotel.'

'It's a tiny ford, Fi, stop being such a drama queen.' I giggled.

Lauren's phone rang as we passed Chislehurst Caves and she put it on speaker as Claire, Hayley and Emma shrieked collectively at us.

'Where are you?' shouted Lauren above the din.

'We've just got onto the A20. Where are you?'

'Close behind you. See you there.'

'Get the drinks in when you get there – mine's a large G&T. And watch out for the river.'

'What river? What's Fi on about?' asked one of them.

'It's not a river, it's Eynsford Ford, but you can drive over the bridge. Ignore Fi, she's just doing her usual thing.'

'Oh, sod that, we're taking the ford, what's life without a bit of excitement, hey, girls? Live dangerously, I say.' Jenna's laughter rattled in her throat – the sound of fun, daring, and vivacity all rolled into one.

That was Jenna all over, but that was why I loved her, why we all loved her.

Fi's directions took us off the A20 too early and we wound our way through Farningham village, looking out of the windows with interest as we muddled our way through country lanes, finally picking up Eysnford Road.

'It must be around here somewhere,' muttered Jenna. 'Have you got this, Fi?'

'Don't panic, darling, it's coming up on the right, Riverside Road. And I swear, Jen, if you get us stuck in the bloody river, I'll kill you.'

'There it is!' Lauren pointed to our right as Jenna hit the brakes, indicating and turning in one movement.

'Is that it?'

We watched as the car in front of us slowed before driving carefully across the ford, which was less than half a foot deep according to the gauge on the side of the bridge.

'Ready to get your feet wet, girls? Hold on.' She scrolled through her phone, selecting a track to play, and turned to us. 'Let's go.' She turned up the volume and opened the windows as we sang the lyrics with gusto.

Jenna's 4x4 crossed the shallow water with ease, our out-of-tune singing drowning out Wet Wet Wet, to much cheering from a bunch of middle-aged men sitting on the grass to our left, their ties loosened, holding pint glasses.

'Got room for us?' called out one of them.

'Sorry, boys, girls only.' Jenna's sexy laugh rang out as we left them behind, and I marvelled at her confidence and her effect on men.

'Turn right, turn right,' Fiona barked, and we followed the narrow lane until a sign directed us to turn left for the Eynsford Manor Country Hotel.

We tumbled out of the car, gazing at the old, ivy-clad building with delight. It was picture perfect, and I hurriedly took a photo before indicating that the other three should pose for me, taking a couple of quick shots, as Fiona sighed impatiently.

'Let's find the bar, I'm gasping.' Fi strode ahead, pulling her suitcase.

'We'll check-in first.'

When Jenna spoke, we obeyed, well, most of us did, and Lauren and I followed her to reception dutifully.

Fi turned back. 'Lauren, throw my suitcase in our room, will you? I'll find the others.'

Lauren rolled her eyes in amusement and took Fi's case.

'Looks like we're sharing a room, Jen.' I didn't mind, although sharing a room with Jenna usually meant staying up late gossiping and emptying the minibar when everyone else was probably already asleep.

'See you in the bar,' I called to Lauren as she disappeared through the door next to ours.

'Oh, it's gorgeous,' I breathed, dropping my bag on the floor and rushing to the window. 'Which bed d'you want?'

'Either one, you choose.' Jenna was busy applying more mascara, her mouth open in concentration, so that her words came out oddly, and I picked up my bag, placing it on the bed nearest the window and opening it to begin unpacking.

'Leave your bag, Abs, let's get to the bar, I'm parched.' The air filled with her perfume as she sprayed her wrists and neck liberally.

Grabbing my toiletry bag, I went into the bathroom. 'I just need a wee, give me a sec.' I repositioned the clip in my hair and adjusted my butterfly scarf. Reaching for my perfume, I sprayed my wrists and neck and walked out of the bathroom to find Jenna waiting in the corridor.

'Come on, Abs, the others have had a head start on us, we've got some catching up to do.' She walked off towards the stairs as I rushed to catch her up.

'What took you so long?' Claire swooped on us, enveloping us in a hug. 'It's a beautiful hotel. How's your room? I've got one to myself, lucky me, Em and Hayles are sharing this time.'

We all began talking at once, as Hayley passed us our drinks from the bar. 'Em started a tab, we'll sort it out later.'

'Let's sit outside, I'm dying for a smoke.'

'You only smoke when you're drunk.' Fi grinned as we followed Claire to the tables outside on the patio.

'Then you've got your answer.' Laughing, Claire pulled a packet of cigarettes from her bag and offered them to Lauren, and then Fi, who dropped her vape on the table.

'Go on then, twist my arm,' she said, taking one and picking up her G&T. 'Cheers, everyone, here's to an excellent bloody weekend.'

'To an excellent bloody weekend!' we shouted exuberantly, lifting our glasses.

4

Spice Up Your Life

The evening deteriorated from there as we drank more, talked louder, and posed for mad photos, and it was only when we headed through to the restaurant that I realised I'd forgotten to text Martin.

'I'm just going to the loo,' I said, taking my bag and going in search of the ladies.

'I need to go as well.' Hayley ran after me. 'It's down here.' She led the way across the reception area and along a thickly-carpeted corridor.

Re-appearing from the cubicle, Hayley glanced at my phone as I finished texting. 'What's Martin up to this weekend, anything exciting? Is he golfing tomorrow?'

'I'm not sure.' I popped my phone in my bag. 'He said he might have a drink with Adrian and Paul one night. What about Ross?'

Hayley shrugged, giggling. 'No idea. He mumbled something about golf, so he'll probably be playing with Martin and Craig, I suppose. Poor Craig, I think he's lonely since he and Emma split up.'

'Talking about me?' The door whooshed as Emma walked in.

We both flushed, feeling awkward.

'We were just wondering what all the men were doing this weekend,' I explained.

'Who cares?' Emma ran a hand through her hair. 'Craig's probably off chasing after one of the girls from the office, but it's not my business any more, thank God.

Queen Jenna's getting loud out there, good luck tonight, Abs. You're sharing a room with her, aren't you?'

'Yep, she'll probably keep me up half the night knowing her.'

We made our usual scene in the dining room, talking too loudly, screeching at each other's jokes, and ploughing our way through a few bottles of wine as we devoured the chef's gastronomic delights enthusiastically.

'These prawns are the best I've ever tasted,' enthused Claire, spearing one and holding it out to Hayley, her arm perilously close to her wine glass. 'Try one, Hayles.'

Jen's hand shot out, moving Claire's fork away. 'She's allergic, remember?'

'Oh God, sesame seeds, I forgot. Is it really that bad?'

Hayley nodded, swallowing her mouthful of steak and ale pie. 'Only if you want to kill me.' She giggled. 'You probably do though, sometimes.'

'Only about once a week,' joked Claire. 'You've got your pen thingy though, right?'

'I keep it in my bag. I wish I could make pies as good as this.'

'Me too,' I agreed, having had the same.

'That,' announced Fi as she dropped her knife and fork on the plate, 'was the best steak I've ever eaten. And that sauce... I've probably gained half a stone...'

'No pudding then?' Lauren joked, taking the last mouthful of her beer-battered fish and chips.

Jenna waved at the waiter. 'Another bottle of the red, please.'

Finally, we heaved ourselves from the table and returned to the bar for after dinner drinks.

I was already feeling woozy but in a nice way, warm and fuzzy, and I smiled around at my friends.

'Did you hear from Martin?' Hayley suddenly asked.

'I forgot to look.' Laughing, I fumbled for my phone, dropping it on the floor.

Jenna swooped, picking it up and opening the screen. 'Let's see what little love messages Marty's been sending his Abs, shall we?' she slurred.

'Oh, come on, Jen, give her the phone. There's nothing worse than a bitter divorcée,' drawled Fi. 'I should know.'

'Thanks,' I muttered, taking the phone from Jenna, and reading Martin's message quickly, aware of everyone's eyes on me.

'He's at a strip club,' I joked, to uproarious laughter. He wasn't, of course, he was having pizza, watching a film and then going to bed, but I knew that if I told them they'd start teasing me about my boring husband.

'Dirty bastard.' Fiona winked at me. 'Danny's probably with him, that sort of thing's right up his street, that's why I chucked him out.'

We moved back outside so that Lauren and Claire could have another smoke, and the talk slowed down as we picked up our phones to post photos and check messages.

At around eleven o'clock we started yawning, and Hayley was the first to get up.

'Bedtime for me.' She yawned. 'If I drink any more, I'll pass out and you'll have to carry me. I'll leave the light on in the bathroom for you, Em.'

Lauren was busy tapping away on her phone, oblivious to us all as she smiled at something.

Fiona waved her hand in the air. 'Sweet dreams, darling. I'm getting a nightcap. Anyone else? Where's Jenna?'

We all looked around, surprised.

'Did she go to the loo?'

'How long's she been gone?'

'I'm not sure, ages I think.'

'Shall I call her?'

'Did she take her phone?'

'And her bag. D'you think she's gone to bed?'

'I think I'll go as well.' Lauren said, standing suddenly. 'Don't wait up.' She winked at Fi, who looked non-plussed for a moment but then grinned.

'Really? Here? Go, Lauren.'

My head swivelled in confusion.

'I'll have a double whisky.' Claire pushed her chair back. 'Can you get them in, Fi? I need the loo.'

'Night, girls.' Lauren waved and blew kisses as she walked away.

'Night, babes, have fun. Abs? Em?' Fiona waited impatiently.

'Oh, why not? We can sleep in tomorrow. I'll have a brandy, thanks, Fi.'

They both looked at me.

'Um, maybe I should go up if Jen's gone to bed, I don't want to disturb her.'

'Relax, Abs, no way Jen's hit the sack yet.'

'But where is she? Alright, I'll have a whisky, thanks,' I said hurriedly as Fi gave me one of her looks.

Emma went with Fi to the bar, leaving me alone, apart from our fellow late-night drinkers at another table – a group of about five men, their ties pulled loose and shirt sleeves rolled up, who looked like they'd been here since finishing work.

'What have I missed?' A waft of perfume engulfed me, mixed with sweat... and something else... something carnal...

Arms encircled me, Jenna's face hot against mine in the cooler night air as she kissed me sloppily on the cheek. 'Where is everyone?'

'I thought you'd gone to bed!' I exclaimed. 'Where have you been?'

'Is my little Abs waiting up for me? All on her own?' Her words were slurred and she dropped into a chair beside me, running her hands through her thick mane of hair and attracting the attention of the men at the other table, as she always did.

She looked hot and vital as she lifted her hair from her neck in a sensual manner, stretching her head back. 'Phew, it's hot. You didn't answer my question.'

And she hadn't answered mine.

'Well, look at you, all messed up. Where'd the lippy go, darling?' Fiona plonked glasses down on the table as Claire arrived back from the ladies.

'On somebody else's face by the looks of her.' Emma put the other drinks down, grinning.

'Or somebody else's something else.' Claire gave a raucous laugh.

'I need a drink.' Jenna smiled, giving nothing away.

'I'll get it.' I jumped up. 'Whisky?'

'Thanks, babes.'

I hurried back with Jenna's drink, hearing their loud laughter and knowing that I was missing out on whatever the joke was.

Jenna threw half her drink back, banging the glass down and gasping. 'Christ, I needed that.'

'I bet you did...' Fiona's knowing drawl had Claire guffawing again and the penny dropped.

Could she? Had she? Here? How? I couldn't ask the questions out loud for fear of being teased, so I just smiled and nodded along as I sipped my whisky.

'One more round before we go to bed.'

Claire was in her loud mood now, and I was conscious of the men's interested stares as they assessed the drunkenness of our small group.

'Jen can tell us all her dirty secrets.'

I swear the men moved their chairs a little closer.

'Too many to tell, Claire, love.' Jenna's wink held a warning somewhere in there, I thought.

'I'm done.' I yawned. 'Jen? Ready for bed?' I picked up my bag and stood up.

'I'll catch you up, you go, darling, I've got my key card.'

'See you at breakfast,' they called as I waved and made my way back inside, feeling more than a little drunk.

I was vaguely aware of Jenna moving around our room in the darkness at some point, bumping into things and swearing as she noisily took something from the minibar – light from its opened door flashing through my closed lids for a moment – but sleep overtook me again and I sank my head into the soft pillow and oblivion.

And then I was wide awake. I sat up, trying to get my bearings as the loud banging began on our door again. 'Jen,' I whispered urgently.

I threw the duvet back and climbed out of bed, shaking Jenna's sleeping form. 'Jen, wake up.'

The banging started again and I thought I heard Fi's voice.

'Jen!' This time I shook her hard, before rushing to the door and opening it.

Fiona's face looked strange as she pushed past me, switching the lights on so that I blinked in surprise at the assault on my pupils.

'Where's Jen?' She marched to the bed where Jenna was struggling to sit up.

'Fi. What the hell? What time is it?' Jenna wiped a hand over her eyes in confusion.

'We've got a problem,' said Fiona grimly. 'I need you to come to our room, it's Lauren.'

5

Sexcrime
Come Undone

We stood in silence, gathered around the bed, our eyes fixed on Lauren's curled-up form beneath the bedclothes.

We were an eclectic bunch: me, in my safe white cotton nightdress and matching dressing gown, in direct contrast to Jenna, in her elegant black satin pyjamas; Emma, in a sleep set of camisole and shorts, her silky floral dressing gown hanging open, was quite the opposite to Hayley, whose oversized T-shirt, complete with cute teddy bear graphic, reached her knees to meet rainbow-striped slipper socks with pompoms; over her vest top, Claire's partly-buttoned shirt hung askew where she'd misaligned the buttons in her rush – her cotton pyjama trousers a clash with the purple shirt, patterned as they were with bright red roses; Fiona, at the foot of the bed, stood with her arms folded, feet spread, like a warrior woman, in a black, skin tight T-shirt and shorts, the letters BLKGRLPWR emblazoned across the taut fabric.

A soft moan came from Lauren's huddled shape, and Hayley knelt beside her, gently pulling back the bedcovers a little. Finding Lauren's hand, she held it, and we watched, transfixed, as the fingers gripped tightly onto Hayley's.

'Shhh... it's OK, Laur...' Hayley looked at me beseechingly, her eyes teary, and I moved to the other side, kneeling beside Lauren and folding the duvet back a little.

'Laur, it's Abs. You're safe now, everything's going to be alright.' I reached out and tentatively stroked her hair back from her face, gently easing a small twig from the tangled blonde strands, my hand freezing in mid-movement as she shook her head, groaning.

'I'll fucking kill him.' Jenna's words hung in the air as we all stared at our battered friend in shock.

'Not if I get to him first.' Fi spat her words out, her fury justified, as she reminded us. 'I've been there, I know what it feels like, but I'm not that person any more. I swore after my attack that if a man ever did that to me, or anyone that I knew, ever again, I'd kill him.'

Tears streamed from Lauren's right eye as she reached up to touch her left eye – swollen shut, the skin around it an angry red of broken blood vessels beneath the skin. She tried to open her mouth, making a small crying sound.

'Don't try and speak yet,' I said gently, horrified at her swollen eye, split lip, and the dried blood on her face and hands. 'I'm just going to pull the covers down a little bit more, OK, babes?' I looked at Jenna for approval.

'No....' Lauren moaned, huddling into a foetal position, her soft cries breaking my heart.

'Who did this, Lauren?' Fiona's tone was harsh with anger.

'You need to tell us everything. Where's your phone?' Jenna's voice was bossy, demanding, and I looked at her in dismay.

'She's in shock, Jen, she needs time. We must get some ice for the swelling.' I thought rapidly. 'A bucket of ice, oh, and, Claire, facecloths run under hot water so that we can wipe her face and hands. Em, can you order a brandy with the ice?'

'Well, listen to little baby Abigail, all bossy and in charge, and, Em, make it a bloody bottle, I could do with a drink myself.'

Typical Jenna, I thought, thinking of herself, but then I reprimanded myself for my disloyal thoughts – she was in shock, we all were.

'Shouldn't we call the police?' Hayley's worried face looked around at us all. 'And Paul – what about Paul?'

'No.' Lauren's words were muffled but we could understand them. 'No police. No Paul.' She tried to sit up but fell back.

Jenna pushed in next to Lauren, nudging me aside as she leant over her urgently. 'Lauren, if you're sure about that then you have to show me your phone. I need to know who he is before he blocks you, or ghosts you, or whatever they call it. Which one was it? Dare? Frisky?'

I had no idea what she was talking about and yet, at the same time, I knew it must be the dating apps we'd laughed about just a few days earlier.

'Dare.' The word came out woefully. 'Night Monster.'

I grimaced at the name. Nothing would have induced me to meet up with someone calling themselves that, especially not at night. I felt something nudging my hand and looked down to find Lauren's hand brushing mine. She pointed underneath the bed, and I lifted the over-hanging duvet, pulling out her bag.

'I'll take that.' Jenna snatched the bag from me and began rummaging through it, pulling out Lauren's phone.

Claire appeared with warm cloths as Emma gave instructions over the phone to room service.

'I'm going to gently wipe your face and hands, Laur, but once we do that, we'll be removing evidence. Are you sure?'

She nodded grimly. 'Not rape,' she managed to say through gritted teeth. 'Choice. My fault.'

'Of course it's not your fault.' Jenna's eyes flashed with anger. 'No one brings this on themselves.' She returned her attention to the phone, and I watched her fingers moving rapidly over the screen, before stilling. Her whole body seemed to tense, as if she was holding her breath, and she looked lost for a second, her eyes glazed. Blinking, she came back to life.

'Got him. Right, screenshot.' The sound of a camera shutter clicking was followed by more mumbling from Jenna. 'Abs, fetch my phone from our room, quickly.'

I felt glued to the spot, trance-like and unable to compute the horrors of the night.

'Abs, snap out of it.' Jen snapped her fingers in my face. 'Get my phone from my room.'

I jumped up automatically, my eyes still glued to the phone, the image I'd caught a glimpse of still in my mind's eye. *Lauren had… with him…* I could still picture his eyes. 'Who are you going to call?'

'Just get it, I'll explain later. Now, Abs.'

I hurried off to do her bidding, my stomach feeling queasy from the distress and shock, my mind racing, returning with her phone as the room service waiter walked away along the corridor. I tapped gently on the door and was let back in by Emma.

'Are you OK?' she whispered, noticing my white face and reaching out to give my shoulders a squeeze.

I nodded, silently handing Jenna her phone. 'I'm just upset, Em, I can't bear it, poor Lauren. I don't understand how…' I couldn't put my thoughts into words, and I floundered helplessly.

'None of us do.' Claire's face was grim as she looked over at us.

'He shouldn't get away with this.'

'Who else has he done this to?'

We all looked at Jen as if she might have the answer, but she was watching Claire slowly pull the duvet from Lauren as Hayley supported her.

Hayley let out a little gasp as she took in Lauren's torn top and bruised arms. 'Your neck.' She put her other hand over her mouth, her eyes huge as she turned to me. 'You're right, he shouldn't get away with this. We need to teach him a lesson.'

'Right, that's it. Is he staying here? What room, Laur?' Fiona paced the room agitatedly. 'He bloody tried to strangle you, the bastard. I'll show him what it's like to be strangled. Fucker.' She spat the last word out in fury.

'He's staying here?' I squeaked, imagining coming face to face with him at breakfast. 'You can't just walk into his room and strangle him, Fi. We need to think it through, at least.'

'We have to do something.' Emma's eyes blazed. 'We should lay into him and smash him around a bit, see how he likes it.'

'But he'd see us, we couldn't let him see us.'

'Typical Abigail, looking out for herself.'

Jen's snide remark stung, but she was right.

Claire nodded at me. 'Abs is right though, Jen.'

'Drink this.' Emma passed a glass of brandy to Lauren. 'The whole lot, it'll help.'

'D'you want to get out of these clothes? Have a bath, love?' Claire was good in these situations – correction, this situation, we'd never faced anything like this before – her motherly instinct kicking in.

'I'll run a bath,' I said, at Lauren's nod, running to the bathroom and turning the taps on to full-blast.

Emma walked in and stood beside me, silently handing me the brandy bottle as we watched the bath fill. I gasped as the fiery liquid burnt my throat, handing the bottle back so that I could test the bathwater, and turned the taps off.

'We'll be fine, just the two of us.' Claire nodded as she helped Lauren to the bathroom. 'Find her nightclothes, Abs.'

'Well?' Fiona stood menacingly over Jenna. 'Who is he? Where do we find him?'

6

Fuck You

'Bastard's just blocked her on the app, but don't worry, I've found him on one of mine, so he's still active. Em, are you on Dare?'

'No, sorry.' Em shook her head. 'Frisky and Freemee.'

'Hmm... neither of us are his type anyway.' Jenna looked around at us all, her eyes settling on me appraisingly.

'Me?' I squeaked. 'Why are you looking at me, I'm not on any dating apps.'

'Relax, I'm just thinking.' She picked up the brandy bottle, taking a large slug. 'We'll need a plan...'

'Damn right.' Fi nodded.

'First of all, we need to carry on as usual tomorrow, so that's all meeting for breakfast. Lauren can have breakfast in her room, Fi, you can organise that. And then we'll do the usual stuff, massages, facials, etc, followed by lunch at the pub we passed by the river.'

'The Plough,' I offered. 'But what about Lauren?'

'We'll see how she is in the morning. If she's up to it, she can come with us for lunch, it'll look more normal. She can wear sunglasses – we can sit outside – and she'll need a scarf... she can borrow your pink butterfly scarf, Abs.'

I nodded obediently.

'She'll need a top with sleeves to cover the bruises.' Emma touched the tops of her own arms.

'Like this?' I held up one of Lauren's tops that I'd found in her bag when I'd taken out her nightdress.

'Perfect.' Jenna's tone was clipped as she continued to think. 'He's probably on more than one dating app, most of us are...'

'Hardly dating,' I muttered angrily. 'I mean, how could he?' I exploded. 'How could he do that to her? D'you think they–? Did she sleep with him first, d'you think?'

'I did.'

I jumped as Lauren appeared with Claire beside her.

'Can I have some more brandy?'

We settled Lauren in bed with another full glass of brandy, gathering round as she started to haltingly tell us what had happened.

'It was just a hook up. I was a bit pissed I suppose, and I decided to just click on the location match. I've done it before, you know, when we've been away on one of our weekends. His profile came up and it said he was a couple of minutes away, so I hearted him and said I was interested, and he suggested hooking up in the carpark.'

'Which carpark? This one?' Jenna barked her questions like some kind of interrogation officer. 'Is he staying here? Do you know his real name?'

Claire laid her hand on Jenna's arm. 'Let her speak, Jen.'

Lauren shook her head, wincing in pain. 'He's not staying here, he's gone by now. He was out for dinner with... with his family...'

'Does he live around here?' I couldn't believe any of this was happening, and I hugged my stomach, feeling sick.

'Nice, real classy.' Fi scowled, ignoring me. 'So he met up with you for a little palate cleanser between courses? What did he say to his wife? Excuse me, darling, I'm just going to fuck someone in the carpark of the Eynsford Manor Hotel, back in time for pudding?'

'More like, I'm just going to beat the living daylights out of a poor defenceless woman, back in a jiffy.'

Between Jen and Fi there was enough anger for all of us.

'Was he having dinner here?' Hayley's voice cracked. 'Did we see him earlier?'

'No, the pub restaurant down the road.'

'I should have stopped you, I guessed you were hooking up with someone.' Fiona sucked on her vape like her life depended on it.

'Not your fault. Everything was fine.' Lauren glanced at Jen, as she made a snorting sound and crossed her arms in an aggravated manner, ignoring her and continuing. 'I got in his car and he drove to the end of the carpark where it's dark and... well, yeah... we did it, no problem. I was only in the car for about fifteen minutes. Then he said was I OK to walk back, he was going to have a smoke, so I got out and then he was– suddenly he was there, in front of me. I didn't even know what happened. He punched me so hard in the face, I fell over, scraping my face and arms in the gravel.'

The room was silent as we hung on Lauren's every word, our eyes fixed on her face.

'He just sort of launched himself on top of me and hit me and put his hands round my throat and squeezed. I blacked out for a second, I think, and then he got in his car and left.'

Em closed her eyes, shaking her head.

'How long did you stay there?' It was Claire's turn to ask a question.

'I don't know, ten, maybe twenty minutes... I crept round to the back of the hotel and came in by the back entrance and came up here. And then I just crawled into bed and pulled the covers over me.'

'And that's where I found you.' Fi sighed heavily. 'But only when I heard you crying in the night. Why didn't you tell me when I came in, Laur?'

'What difference would it have made? It's done, it's happened, I can't undo it, can I?'

'You need to sleep, Laur, you'll feel a bit better in the morning,' I said uselessly.

'No she won't, she won't feel better, not until we deal with him.'

We all stared at Jenna.

'Deal with him how?' Em voiced the question in all our heads.

'We need a revenge plan – I'm working on it. But Abs is right about one thing, Lauren needs to sleep.'

'I've got sleeping tablets in my room,' offered Claire. 'Will you take one, Laur?'

We settled Lauren down for what remained of the night, dimming the lights, and whispering softly until Claire returned with a strip of sleeping tablets.

'She can pop one under her tongue, it'll dissolve, there's no taste,' said Claire, as she handed me the strip and walked over to speak to Fi.

I took the strip from Claire, popping one of the tablets out and handing it to Lauren, holding her hand as she lay back in the bed. I slipped the strip of tablets into my dressing gown pocket and held Lauren's hands gently in mine.

'D'you want us to stay with you?' I asked, as my friend's eyelids drooped.

'Just Fi, you all need to sleep,' she said drowsily.

Jenna helped herself to some of the bottles from the minibar, looking at Fi's arched eyebrows defiantly. 'What? You don't like vodka.'

'Sara something...' Lauren muttered sleepily. 'Wingrove school, or Wingwood...'

'What's that? Who's that, babes? Who's Sara?' Jenna was beside the bed in a flash.

'His daughter... I don't know... gymnastics... in the car...'

'That's enough, let her sleep.' Claire had her mumsy voice on as she touched Jenna's shoulder. 'We'll come to your room.'

We softly called out our goodnights, giving Fi hugs as we left her standing sentinel at the foot of Lauren's bed.

A member of staff silently wheeled a trolley along the corridor towards us as we stood in a huddle outside Lauren and Fiona's room, his eyes barely registering the five women in their nightclothes hanging around in a hotel corridor at four o'clock in the morning as he passed by, intent as he was on collecting the next room service tray lying on the floor outside a room ahead of him.

'I'll grab some drinks from our room,' Emma said, stopping at her and Hayley's door and inserting a keycard.

'Grab some glasses too, Em,' directed Jenna.

'I'll get some as well.' Claire swooshed off to her room, disappearing through the door, and the rest of us continued into Jenna's and my room, leaving the door open.

Grimly, Jenna emptied miniatures into the glasses, passing them round, once we were all gathered. 'No ice, but we'll manage.'

'Well?' I looked at Jenna, my stomach knotted. 'What d'you mean by a revenge plan?'

7

Cloudbusting

We listened intently as Jenna outlined her plan – which was somewhat sketchy at this stage but we could see where she was going with it.

'But so what if we find out who his daughter is and which school she goes to, how does that help Lauren? What d'you want us to do, kidnap the girl? You are joking?' Emma curled her long legs up beneath her on the tub chair in the corner of the room.

'Hold her to ransom, is that what you mean? We couldn't...' Hayley looked worried as she sat on my bed cross-legged.

'No, of course not, you're not listening to me.' Jenna shook her head, impatience radiating from her.

OK, so maybe our tired brains couldn't see where she was going with her plan after all...

'Once we identify the school and the daughter, we can identify the wife, and from there we can find out where he lives.'

'So... we kidnap the wife, or...' Claire yawned. 'Throw rocks at his windows? Do you actually have a plan, Jen, because I really need some sleep.'

'Look, we're all agreed that he must pay for what he did to Lauren, yes?'

Four heads nodded slowly.

'Right, so we need to know where he lives, who he is, what his habits are, that kind of thing. At the same time, we need to find out which dating apps he's on and we need to bait him...'

At this Jenna looked at me, making me feel extremely uncomfortable.

'No.' I shook my head vehemently. 'You can't use me as bait.'

'No one's using you, Abs, but you want to help Lauren, don't you?'

'Well, we all do, but there has to be some other way...' I looked at Hayley in desperation.

'How d'you know he'd be interested in Abs, anyway? He could have all sorts of types.' She shrugged her shoulders at me.

'Exactly,' I said, relieved. 'Wouldn't it be better for you to make friends with him, Jen, or whatever it is you do on these things, seeing as you know what to do already, and then have a look at what other women he's friends with? You could warn them that he's dangerous.'

'It's not like that, love, we don't get to see his other women, and we certainly don't make friends. Men have a type, in general, and I'm just about as diametrically opposed to Lauren as you could get, so's Em, which means we need you... or Hayley, at a stretch...'

Hayley's eyes widened in alarm. 'I've got short dark hair, Lauren and Abs are blonde. They even look alike.'

I shot Hayley a look of surprise, hurt by her lack of solidarity, although it was true – Lauren and I did look remarkably similar, apart from my long hair.

'She could wear a wig? Or Abs could cut her hair?'

I stared at Emma in disbelief. 'We're sitting right here, Em. You're talking about us as if we don't have a say in the matter.'

'Well, maybe if either of you had something helpful to say for once I wouldn't have to.' Emma crossed her arms in defiance.

'Perhaps if you cared about Lauren as much as we do, you'd be more willing to do your bit.'

'Jen!' I felt hurt, so I lashed out. 'We love Laur, you know that. Why d'you always have to be so bossy, telling us all what to do? Who do you think you are? I'm fed up with it.'

'Yeah, who put you in charge, anyway? Why can't you do it? You could cut your own hair.' Hayley had my back again and I smiled at her gratefully.

'Oh for God's sake, the pair of you are behaving like babies. I thought one in the group was bad enough but now you're being just as pathetic, Hayley. Our friend was attacked, beaten, she needs our–'

'Enough!' Claire's voice cut through our tired, still-slightly-drunk, bickering, and we all shut up.

'We all need some sleep.' Claire stood up, taking charge. 'We're all friends, we all care about Lauren, and we'll come up with a plan, but not now, not at four-thirty in the morning. 'Group hug and then bed.'

Grudgingly, we gathered for a group hug and made arrangements to meet for breakfast at nine o'clock, allowing us a few hours' sleep, and Claire, Emma and Hayley left the room as I scuttled to the bathroom, still hurt from Jenna's unkind jibe about the baby in the group – a comment which I knew had been directed at me – and not quite brave enough to face her on my own immediately.

I needn't have worried, by the time I crept back into the bedroom Jenna was snoring gently, and I slid underneath my bedcovers and switched the light off, trying not to think about the events of the last few hours.

In what felt like only moments later, I squinted and yawned in the bright daylight streaming through the window where we'd forgotten to close the curtains, glancing at Jenna's bed to see if she was awake.

The bathroom door flew open, emitting a cloud of steam, and a towel-clad Jenna emerged, her hair wrapped in a second towel. 'Morning, babes,' she said brightly, picking up the remote and switching on the television.

So we were friends again, I thought, relieved, groaning and throwing back the covers, my feet feeling for my slippers beside the bed, to a smirk from Jenna.

'What?' I asked, instantly feeling miffed.

'Oh, nothing, just you and your slippers, liking everything just so, my little homely Abs.'

I was about to snap out a response when I stopped myself. There was no point in starting the day on a bad note, we had enough problems to deal with – correction, poor Lauren had enough problems to deal with. I smiled at Jen's reflection in the mirror, as she slicked on her signature red lipstick and dropped the gold tube, encrusted with sparkly stones, amidst the chaos she'd created on the dresser, watching it as it rolled silently onto the floor.

'How did you sleep?' I asked, making my way to the bathroom.

'Like a baby, and I could do it again for about ten hours, but we need to get to breakfast, we've got ten minutes. You'd better hurry up.'

You could have woken me, I thought mutinously, hurrying in to brush my teeth.

By the time I'd showered and dried myself with a hand towel, thanks to Jenna's selfishness, I was already late, and I pulled my clothes on quickly as Jenna tapped her watch.

'Don't bother with the make-up, Abs, it never makes any difference on you anyway. One day I'll show you how to look like a real woman.' She grinned, winking as she shimmied and pouted at me to take the sting out of her words, but I felt them all the same.

I watched her open our door and step outside, my foot gently nudging her fallen lipstick so that it rolled underneath the fridge.

8

We Are Family

My small rebellion made me feel empowered. 'I'm just going to check on Lauren,' I said as I left our room, turning and walking the few steps to tap softly on the door.

'How is she?' I asked a tired-looking Fi.

'Not too bad, considering, a bit tearful... Come in.'

Lauren was sitting in bed holding a cup of tea. Her eye was still swollen but at least she could open it a little. I stared at the dark purple skin in horror, wondering how she was ever going to hide it from Paul. Her lips were swollen, the split caked in dried blood, and when she spoke it was as though through gritted teeth.

Hi, Abs, how are you?'

'Worried about you.' I sat down on the bed, taking hold of one of her hands. 'How are you feeling, my love?' Tears immediately formed in her eyes and my heart ached for her.

'Like the biggest idiot in the history of idiots.'

I hugged her gently. 'Don't say that, you're not an idiot.' My stomach suddenly growled noisily and we both laughed, which lightened the atmosphere.

'You need to go and have some breakfast, Fi's ordered me room service, if I can keep it down.

'You need to eat, Laur. I'll see you later, OK?'

'Thanks for coming to see me, Abs.'

Jenna swooped in, all big hair and perfume, bending down to hug Lauren, and I moved aside, turning to speak to Fi.

'Did she sleep alright?'

'Out for the count, Claire's sleeping pill did the trick, it must have been a strong little bugger.'

'Right, let's go and join the others.' Jenna was in her bossy mode again, and we left the room, heading down the stairs towards the smell of bacon and eggs and the murmuring sounds from the breakfast room.

'Over here!' Hayley waved from a table by the open doors where she sat with Emma, and we made our way over.

'Where's Claire?' I looked around, spotting her at the counter waiting for her eggs.

The next hour was taken up with the business of breakfast, from fruit and yoghurt, accompanied by many glasses of fresh orange juice, to a full English, and finally pastries and tea and coffee. We barely spoke, avoiding each other's eyes as we guiltily shovelled food into our mouths, and we sat back, replete, not having yet broached the subject of last night but knowing that it had to be discussed. Jenna was the first to raise it, of course.

'Right, we need to continue as normal as much as we can,' she began. 'That means calls or texts to husbands, and no giving them an inkling that anything's amiss.'

That meant me, Claire, Hayley and Lauren – Jenna, Fiona and Emma were accountable to no one, of course.

'While you're doing that, I'll go and get a menu from the spa and we can book ourselves treatments.'

Claire rolled her eyes at me, giving a small salute behind Jenna's back, and I gave a little laugh, glancing at Hayley who spluttered into her coffee.

I got up and walked outside to call Martin.

'Abs, how's the weekend going?' He sounded tired and a little guarded.

'Oh fine,' I said, with forced brightness. 'Late night last night, too much to drink, the usual...'

'How's the hotel?'

'It's gorgeous,' I said flatly. 'We're about to book ourselves treatments at the spa, orders from Jenna, and then we're having lunch at the pub down the road, more orders from Jenna. Did you sleep alright? Did you miss me?'

'I slept fine.'

'Are you sure, because you sound tired?' I thought I heard him sigh.

'Just because I slept alright doesn't mean I can't sound tired, Abs. So, what are you doing today?'

'I've just told you, we're doing the spa and having lunch out. Jenna's got us all organised.' I sounded bitter, and I forced myself to give a little laugh.

'Right, so, er, how's everyone? All OK? No problems? Everything alright with Jenna?'

He was definitely being a bit odd... Did he know something? Was he picking up on my mood? 'All fine.' I gave another forced laugh. 'Why are you worried about Jenna?'

'Well, I meant everyone, but she's the bossy one, you always say, right? You sound like you're pissed off with her.'

'Everyone's fine,' I said firmly. 'I'd better go.'

I walked back to the others.

'I've booked you and me in for mud wraps, Abs.'

I looked at Jenna in surprise. 'I don't know if I want a mud wrap...'

'Of course you do, you'll enjoy it.'

I did enjoy it, as it turned out, and promptly fell asleep once I was wrapped in my blanket cocoon, waking at the therapist's gentle shake to shower and have oils massaged into my skin until I felt all warm and glowy.

'You were right,' I admitted to Jenna when we left the spa, 'it was nice.'

'I'm always right, I always know what's best for you.' Jenna was smug.

I left Jenna downstairs, where she headed in the direction of the bar, our designated meeting point for pre-lunch drinks, and went back upstairs to check on Lauren.

'Laur, it's me, Abs,' I called, when she didn't answer the door.

She'd been crying, and I hugged her gently, not wanting to hurt her. I grabbed a wad of tissues from the bathroom, handing them to her silently and waiting for her to blow her nose.

'Are you sure you want to come out for lunch, Laur? You don't have to, you know.'

'Jenna says I have to.' She sniffed. 'Everything has to look normal.'

'We don't always have to do what Jenna says, if you want to tell Paul, explain–'

'No!' Lauren's response was harsh. 'No one else can know about what happened, ever, and especially not Paul. Promise me, Abs.'

'I promise.' I looked at her purple eye and her bruised neck and arms. 'But how are you going to hide it from him?' My hand involuntarily reached out to smooth her hair behind her ear, and I noticed the deep scratch on her neck, sure that it would leave a scar.

'I don't know.' Her fingers shredded the tissue, pieces fluttering into her lap.

We started at the loud knock on the door.

'Your personal stylist is here.' Jenna pushed past me, carrying her cosmetic case and dumping it down on the bed. 'Let's have a look at you. Hmm... that's a nasty gouge on your neck, we'll need some antiseptic cream on that, but otherwise not too bad...' She walked around Lauren, studying her. 'Some concealer and foundation, a darker face powder than you usually wear, and a mocha lippy, I think... that should do it. Did you bring your summer scarf?'

Wordlessly, I held it up, as Lauren gave herself over to Jenna's expert ministrations.

'You can go, Abs, we'll be fine.' Jenna dismissed me, her concentration on the concealer she was gently dabbing around Lauren's eye.

'I can't go back home,' Lauren announced quaveringly, once we were seated with drinks at our outside table at the pub restaurant, a little while later. 'I'm going to tell Paul that I need some space.'

I dropped the menu and stared at her.

'A separation, you mean.' Fi nodded slowly.

'It would give the bruises time to fade, it makes sense.' Emma looked thoughtfully around at us all.

'Out of the blue? Won't he wonder why?' Claire sipped her wine.

'He won't even dare ask, not after all the times he's cheated on her.'

'You say that, Jen, but–' Hayley turned to Lauren. 'I suppose you're sure about his cheating?'

'Oh, I'm sure.' Lauren's voice was scornful. 'The stupid bastard left one of his apps open on his phone one day while he was in the shower. That's why I didn't feel bad about doing the same thing, the only difference is that he's started turning his hook ups into relationships – I'm pretty sure he's involved with someone right now – whereas I just had hook ups. I wish I hadn't now... I thought it was fun... exciting... a bit of payback... and all it got me was beaten up like a worthless old tart.' A tear trickled down her cheek from beneath her sunglasses and she wiped it away. 'I feel so stupid,' she whispered.

'Mind your foundation, babes.' Jenna took her hand, placing it back in her lap. 'We've got a plan, he won't get away with this. Your friends have got your back.' She looked directly at me.

'I don't know what to do. I want him to suffer.' Lauren's shoulders started to shake. 'I keep seeing his face as he hit me, feeling his hands round my neck... Sorry.' She got up, her handbag falling from her lap, and rushed away from the table.

'I'll go.' Claire followed her, and we watched them walk towards the bridge over the river.

Emma's face had turned horribly pale – we were all still feeling shocked about what had happened, I suppose.

'I'll do it,' I said, as Jenna's eyes bored into me. 'I'll be the bait. He should pay.' I didn't even know what I meant exactly, just that I couldn't bear to see my friend in so much pain.

'Good girl.' Jenna nodded at me.

'So when do we talk about the plan?'

'Not now, not with Lauren here. She should stay with either you, Em, or you, Fi.'

'Why can't she stay with me?' I asked Jenna.

'Because Martin would see the state of her and ask questions. Then he'd tell Paul, or one of the others, and they'd find out about her attack. It's too risky.'

'Maybe she won't want to stay with one of us... she might want to be on her own...'

'She can stay with me,' Fiona said firmly, giving Emma an annoyed look. 'The worst thing she could do right now is be alone.'

'That's decided then. I'll tell you one thing about the plan – once we're finished with him, that bastard will never hurt another woman like he did Lauren. Here she comes. Right, what are we going to eat? This menu looks heavenly. White wine OK for everyone?' Jenna spoke and we obeyed, our eyes dutifully dropping to peruse the menus as our minds secretly wondered what exactly Jenna had in mind.

'Feeling better, Laur?' Hayley gave our friend an encouraging smile as she and Claire re-joined us.

I stared blankly at my menu. *What had I done? Why had I said I'd be the bait?*

9

There was no further talk about Jenna's revenge plan for the rest of our weekend and we spent the time doing our best to carry on as normal, relaxing, reading, hitting the booze before dinner on Saturday night and getting so plastered that we decided to order from the bar menu rather than going formal with the restaurant's à la carte offering. Thanks to the warmth of the evening, we were able to continue sitting outside and, in the semi-darkness, Lauren was able to eat with us without attracting attention, rather than ordering room service alone. It felt almost normal, until we looked into Lauren's eyes.

We even managed a few carefully curated shots which we posted liberally on our social media accounts, taking care not to focus too closely on Lauren. Unspoken, we were following Jenna's instructions perfectly – anyone looking back at a record of our weekend would find a group of seven friends having a fantastic girls' weekend together. We were laying the groundwork flawlessly even if we still didn't quite know what for.

We'd all agreed that on the way home it would be nice to stop in the village we'd erroneously driven through, thanks to Fi's misdirection, but which had contained a riverside pub restaurant that had looked inviting.

'It will give us an opportunity to get our stories straight and for Lauren to decide how she wants to go about telling Paul that she'll be staying with Fi. We'll have a nice wander around the village and then have lunch, we never head home before lunch anyway, so it'll look like business as usual. Everyone agree?'

Of course we did. We all nodded obediently at Jenna.

'We'll meet Tuesday night at mine to discuss things,' announced Jenna as we hugged goodbye after our lunch. 'Lauren, you don't need to be there, you can stay at Fi's.'

'No, I want to be there, I want to know what you're planning.'

'You can't be involved though, you know that?' Jenna relented, granting Lauren permission with a regal nod. 'OK, we'll need details from you anyway. See you all Tuesday at eight, I'll provide the wine. Let's go.'

Lauren and I climbed into the back seat as Fi and Jen took their seats in the front and, waving goodbye to Claire, Emma and Hayley, we headed home.

Martin was a little odd with me when I got home, questioning me closely about the weekend until, finally, he came out with what must have been on his mind.

'What's going on with Lauren and Paul? He called me earlier to say she wants a separation.'

Flustered, I concentrated on my unpacking, fluttering around the bedroom as I thought quickly. I slipped Jenna's fancy tube of lipstick from my bag and pushed it to the bottom of my underwear drawer, knowing I could never wear it but liking the fact that I'd taken it from her – a small act of rebellion, if you will. Besides, she'd never notice, she had loads of them, all the same. *Did Paul know that Lauren was staying with Fi? I couldn't remember whether she'd been going to tell him or not.* I had a brainwave.

'It's not our business, Mart, it's between Laur and Paul. We have to leave them to work things out on their own.'

'Since when did you lot not know everything about each other's business? You're hiding something from me, Abs. What is it?'

I was saved from answering by a quiet ding on his phone which distracted him, and I took the opportunity to go downstairs and tidy up in the kitchen, peering into the fridge to see what I could offer him to eat later.

'What do you want tonight? I could make salad? I had a big lunch so...'

'Hmm? Salad's fine, listen, Abs, I'm popping out, bit of a pow wow with the lads, see if we can figure out what's going on with Paul. You don't mind? I'll have to take your car, mine's not back from the garage 'til tomorrow.'

Relieved to be out of the firing line, I smiled. 'Go ahead, take your time, I'll be fine.'

I poured myself a glass of wine and, feeling a little like I was doing something I shouldn't, I picked up my phone, typing in the word *dare* in the search box and clicking on the name. It wanted me to download and install the app and I hesitated, not sure if I wanted something like that on my phone. But I was curious and, remembering Jen's words, *we need to bait him*, I clicked on download. Now I had to install it... But I could always uninstall it, I told myself.

I opened the app and was faced with a sign-in screen or an option to create an account. My finger hovered over the screen as I deliberated my options – I could use my e-mail address but I wasn't keen on that idea, and I certainly couldn't use Martin's... but then I remembered Martin's old e-mail address that I'd used until I'd got my own. It was quite definitely defunct by now, neither of us having used it for years, and I couldn't even remember how to access it but that wouldn't matter. I just wanted to get into the app and have a little look, then I'd delete the whole thing. Typing it in, I tried to think of a password, looking around the lounge for inspiration, before typing in the word *armchair*.

I frowned at the screen as it told me that my password was incorrect. What was it talking about? I was trying to create an account, not log in. Suddenly I stopped. What was I doing? I uninstalled the app and put my phone down as if it would bite me, switching on the television instead.

10

We gathered at Jen's on Tuesday night a little nervously –
the general feeling seeming to be that this wasn't one of
our usual nights but more like a war summit at army
headquarters with our captain, where we would proceed
to draw up battle plans. We fussed around Lauren for a
few minutes, pleased to see that her face was beginning to
heal slowly, before falling silent and fidgeting as we looked
at Jenna.

I gulped down my wine a little too quickly, nervously
aware that I had agreed to be the bait in Jenna's plan, but
she eased us into the conversation with a little small talk.

'I trust you're all well rested after the weekend, girls,
that you all had early nights on Sunday?' She smirked and
Fi grinned.

'Which means you were up to something, Jen, I can
read that look easily. Who was it? One of your hookups?'

'Let's just say it reminded me of my youth...'

'God, don't remind me of my youth, pimply boys with
bum fluff on their chins having a grope in the back of the
car...' Claire pulled a face as we all laughed.

'Oh, he's not a pimply boy anymore... Let's just say I
reminded him of what he's been missing... OK, it's time to
make plans, ladies.' Jenna's tone changed abruptly. 'We'll
start with research.' She turned to Lauren. 'Can you
remember anything more about the name of the school
that you mentioned? You said a name... Wingrove or
Wingwood?'

Lauren shook her head. 'That's all I can remember. I was– we were– look, we were having car sex, you know what that's like?'

I didn't, but judging by the nods around the room, some of us did.

''Alright, so he had you over the seat or something…' Fi drawled, waving her hand encouragingly at Lauren. 'What did you see?'

'We reclined the front seat, and I was trying to turn to face the back seat and, well, I got my leg stuck somehow so he opened the door for a second while we kind of sorted our legs out…'

I felt mortified for Lauren and looked away, my cheeks hot.

'Too much for you, Abs?' Jenna's tone was mocking. 'Listen and learn, baby girl.'

Listen and learn? What did she mean by that?

'Carry on, Laur.'

'Right, so the interior light came on when he opened the door, and I was leaning over the seat, and there was a piece of paper on the back seat. That's where I saw the name, it was a certificate, I think, for gymnastics maybe?'

Someone sniggered.

'Sorry,' said Claire. 'It's just… gymnastics? With what you were doing?'

Even Lauren managed a smile at that.

'That's all I've got, that and the name Sara, I think, so I remember it just sort of flashed through my mind in one fleeting moment that it was his daughter's school certificate, and there we were having hot, sweaty, hook up sex in the car that his wife probably took their daughter to school in…'

'Well, it certainly sounds a lot more exciting than my sex life currently….' Fi puffed on her vape as I stared at her in disbelief.

'Fi, remember what happened to her.'

'Sorry, that was in bad taste, I wasn't thinking.'

Jenna passed over another bottle of wine and we topped up our glasses as we waited for her to speak.

'That's fine, Laur, it's more than enough to start with. Right, phones out, let's see where Wingrove or Wingwood school is.'

We were quiet for a moment as we tapped on our phone screens, Emma being the first to find it.

'Here it is – Wengrove junior school. It's in Orpington – that's only about twenty minutes away from Bromley.'

A feeling of foreboding crept through me at the thought of Lauren's attacker being so close to where we lived.

'Junior school? How old is this guy? He can only be in his thirties if he's got a kid at junior school surely?'

'Who says, Claire? He could be in his forties or, well, he could be sixty-odd. Could be a second marriage, he could be any age.'

We nodded, agreeing with Fi's thought process. But I'd caught a glimpse of his photo, so I knew.

'He looks thirty-something, wouldn't you say, Lauren?'

Lauren nodded at Jen. 'He's probably in his mid-thirties.'

'Which tells us he likes his women on the side a bit older, no offence, Laur. And, listen, I took a screenshot of his profile photo that night – can you stand to look at it? We need to know that we've got the right guy.'

Nodding uncomfortably, Lauren glanced at Jen's phone as she held it out to her. 'That's him. God, I feel sick.'

'Have some more wine.' *Jenna's answer to everything.*

We re-filled our glasses, as Jenna sent the photo to our phones, sipping our wine and staring at the face of the man who had so viciously attacked our friend.

'Night Monster,' muttered Claire, sounding angry. 'It sounds... aggressive...'

I'd caught a mere flash of his face when Jenna had found him on Lauren's phone app, and I'd been struck by his eyes, but now I could study him properly. I stared at his face, trying to control my shocked feelings. I'd wanted to be wrong. I'd wanted Lauren's attacker to be some ugly, violent-looking man with a sneer and a shaved head, wearing a tattered T-shirt. But he was... gorgeous... I thought, in surprise. His clean-shaven face stared at me from my phone, dark eyes crinkling as he smiled sensually at the camera, his dark hair cut short over the ears and long on top, combed stylishly to the side and held with gel, judging by the slight sheen. The open collar of a white shirt was just visible at the bottom of his photo, revealing a thick, twisted, leather cord holding a pendant which nestled against a patch of tanned skin...

I wanted more... to see more... to know more...

11

'Abs? Earth to Abs?'

I started, aware that someone was saying my name. 'What? Oh, Jen, sorry, I was distracted, I mean–' Flustered, I put my phone down and gulped my wine. *Was it my imagination or was she smirking at me?* 'I just didn't imagine that he'd be so...' I looked around at the others for help.

'So good-looking?' asked Lauren bitterly.

My brain searched desperately for another word, anything, aware that everyone was looking at me. 'So... normal.' I pushed the word out in relief and gulped more wine.

'It might surprise you to know, Abs, that monsters can be normal-looking.' Fi did one of her expansive arm waves.

'Or even hot.' *Jenna was definitely smirking this time.*

'I can see why you fancied him, he's totally hot.'

Lauren shot a surprised look in Emma's direction. 'Got the same taste in men now, have we?'

'No, I didn't mean that.' Emma looked uncomfortable.

Jen seemed far away for a moment, and then she looked from the photo to me, her expression unreadable.

I squirmed awkwardly under her gaze, feeling as if she was reading my mind.

She clapped her hands suddenly, as if dismissing me from her thoughts. 'Right, time to assign duties. Hayley and Emma, you can stake out Wengrove junior school – you can decide between you who does mornings and who does afternoons, and you're looking for a– what's the car, Laur?'

'The car? I don't know, you know what I'm like with cars. It was… maybe silver or… beige? But metallic, I think, and normal, not one of your big four by fours.'

'OK… anything else about it that you can remember?'

'God, Jen, I wasn't there to look at the car, was I?'

'Anything stuck in the windscreen? Or the bumper?' Jen was relentless.

'Oh, hold on… there was something on the back… it was as he drove off, but, I… A forest? Horses?'

'The New Forest.' Claire looked up triumphantly from her phone. 'It's the first thing that comes up when you search. 'Something like this, Laur?'

Lauren leant over and looked at the images on Claire's phone. 'Could be, yes, it could have been something like that.'

'Right, we're making progress. Hayles and Em, you'll be looking for a metallic silver or beige saloon car with a New Forest car sticker on it. It'll either be him or his wife on the school run, more than likely her though.'

'And what exactly do we do once we identify the car?' Emma's tone was skeptical.

'You confirm the daughter's name – Sara – and you follow them home and find out their home address.'

'That's all? Sure you don't want the wife's shoe size while we're at it?'

'Well that's up to you, you can find out her cup size for all I care.' Jenna smiled sweetly at Emma. 'OK, Claire and Fi, you'll take over once we know his address. Claire, you can do daytime surveillance, and, Fi, you can do nights as you don't have a husband to explain things to. We want to know where he works, where he drinks, what she does, where she has her nails done, that kind of thing, so that we can figure out when he has free time for his hook ups. Alright?'

'Sure, we can do that, can't we, Claire, once our super spies have identified the subject's address? Do we need to go in disguise, or can we go as us?'

'Very funny, Fi. You can be you, they'll never interact with you so it doesn't matter. The only person who must never be seen is Abs.'

'So, what's your job?'

'Mine? I'm in charge of planning everything and setting Abs up with profiles on dating apps.'

I might have let out an alarmed squeak at this point. 'How many dating apps? What if someone sees me? What are you going to make me do? Please, Jen, I don't think I can do this.' In a sudden flash of sanity, I knew that I should convince Jen to call her whole plan off.

'Typical cowardly Abigail. Relax, we just want you to look convincing, be on a few apps, look like you know what you're doing, that's all. We're just going to establish a presence for now.'

That sounded a little ominous... 'But someone could recognise me.'

'Not a chance, not once we're worked our magic on you. Right, go and smoke your ciggies if you need to, ladies, we've got work to do, Abs is about to get a smoking hot mama makeover.'

I poured myself another large glass of wine as Claire, Fi and Lauren stepped outside. Emma put some music on and disappeared upstairs with Jen, leaving me and Hayley alone.

'You don't have to do it, Abs,' Hayley said quickly, an eye on the door. 'She can't force you.'

'But how do I stop her?' I whispered. 'Can you talk to her? Please, Hayles. I know it's for Laur, but can't we think of some other plan?' *A plan that doesn't involve me baiting him into meeting with me,* my mind silently pleaded. There was a reason that someone came up with the expression to let sleeping dogs lie, after all. Maybe no plan at all would be the best plan.

'I'll talk to her.' Hayley smiled encouragingly. 'Was Martin pleased to have you home on Sunday? Ross was such a sweetie, he ordered us takeaway and we watched that film with all the weddings, you know, with Hugh Grant. It's my favourite film and I fell asleep halfway through. Can you believe it?' She jumped up as she was called to go upstairs, reappearing a few moments later laden with clothes which she dumped on the settee. Turning to me, she gave a little shake of her head and mouthed the word sorry.

We both looked round as Emma placed a pile of makeup on the dining table, followed by Jenna holding a basket filled with hairbrushes, spray, clips and an assortment of over-the-top costume jewellery.

'Getting Hayley to do your dirty work now, are you, Abs? Everyone else is playing their part, so stop being selfish and help us give this bastard some payback.'

Holding in a whimper, I moved slowly to the dining room chair that Jenna pulled out for me. 'You have to make me look different,' I pleaded. 'I can't be recognised.'

'Oh, relax, no one will know it's you by the time I'm finished with you.'

For the next hour I felt like a Girl's World styling head as my face was coated in foundation and powder, eyeshadow and mascara thickly applied, blusher blended along my cheekbones, and lipstick and gloss slicked over my lips. Jenna had worked as a hairdresser and beautician years ago and she still had that air of professionality about her, working silently, hairpins clamped between her lips as she brushed and pulled my hair into an exotic pile on top of my head and sprayed it with what felt like a can of hairspray. Standing back, she appraised me, peeling off her blue disposable gloves and dropping them into the basket, her hand reaching to pull a few strands of hair loose so that they fell either side of my face.

'More eyeshadow,' she mumbled to Fi, who obliged, coating my eyelids in yet more dark, smoky eyeshadow, as Jen fixed a scarlet flower clip into the side of my updo. 'It's got a teeny weeny chip off the tip of one of the petals, but you can't really notice it. Well, look at our little Abs,' she breathed, standing back and looking at me proudly.

'Wow.' Hayley's eyes were round in her face. 'You don't look like you at all.'

'You look amazing.' Lauren handed me my glass of wine, and I drank a large mouthful.

'Can I see?' I stood up and walked to the mirror above the mantelpiece, staring at the stranger looking back at me in relief. It wasn't me. I wasn't Abigail. For the first time in my life, I didn't look like I'd looked my whole life. I looked gorgeous, hot and sexy, and I pouted my lips, striking a pose, hand on hip as I looked round at my friends, relief making me light-headed.

We started to laugh and suddenly it all just seemed like great fun, not some kind of revenge plan of Jen's, just one of our girly nights, with me the centre of attention for once. I kind of liked it.

12

Girls Just Want To Have Fun
Vogue

Someone turned the music up and we enthusiastically joined in with Cyndi Lauper, as the clothes on the settee were held up against me to much lip-pursing and consideration from Jen – the boss – and Fi – her self-appointed second-in-command.

'So what look exactly are we going for with the clothes?' asked Claire, frowning. 'No offence, Jen, but some of your stuff is a little...'

'Tarty?' Jen grinned. 'You can say it, I don't mind, Queen of Tarts, that's me. 'They'll look different on Abs, but what we want is a wanton look, all bosom and cleavage, kind of come and get me but with a little dominance thrown in there. We want her to appeal to the younger blokes who like a woman who knows what she's doing, who looks like she can take control but can have fun while she's doing it.'

Dominance? A woman who knows what she's doing? Take control? This could not have sounded further from the Abigail they all knew, and I could tell that's what they were all thinking.

'Why so specific? How d'you know that's what he's looking for?'

Silently, Lauren held her phone out to Emma. 'She's basing it on Busty Bromley Babe – yours truly.'

We clustered around Lauren's phone, gazing at her profile pic. Jen had summed her image up perfectly.

'Abs hasn't got the boobs. You'll have to superimpose mine.' Hayley placed her hands under her boobs, bouncing them as she laughed and danced to the music. *She'd definitely had too much to drink.*

'Or mine,' Claire threw in, bouncing her own ample bosom in a parody of Hayley.

I looked down at my chest. *My boobs weren't that small...*

'Her boobs aren't that small, but they do need a little help.'

Why did I always feel as if Jenna was inside my head?

'With this.' She dramatically produced a bustier from the pile of clothing.

She was right, of course. The black bustier pushed my boobs up, appearing to double their size, and gave me a cleavage to die for. Maybe I should get one, I thought, wondering in surprise why I would even think that, and more to the point when I'd ever wear it.

'I think we've got our smoking hot mama.' Fi grinned as she looked at me. 'She should just wear the bustier on its own.'

'What? No! I have to wear a top. Jen...' I looked at her pleadingly.

Hayley rushed to the settee, sorting through the tops. 'What about this one?' She held the black top out to me and I slipped it on, giving her a smile of relief as I fastened the small buttons with fumbling fingers.

'That looks great.' Hayley beamed, pleased to have rescued me. 'Don't you think, Jen?'

Frowning, Jenna pulled the sleeves down from my shoulders, arranging the small red bows carefully. 'More boobs,' she muttered, undoing the uppermost buttons and pulling the top open a little to show the bustier. 'That's it.'

I looked nervously at the six pairs of eyes studying me, feeling like an exhibit. 'Well?' I asked finally. 'Will I do?'

'Oh, you'll do, you'll do just fine,' purred Jenna. 'Right, girls?'

'We should take some photos.' Fi looked around the room, her eyes settling on Jen's black curtains pulled across the front window. 'In front of the curtains?'

The nod was given by our captain, with an instruction to dim the lights, and I watched as furniture was shifted, picking up my wine and emptying the glass.

'Someone fill her glass. Abs, hold up your wine glass and strike a pose.'

We chuckled collectively, knowing that someone was about to change the music, and, sure enough, the recognisable beats sounded at the beginning of the song, the vocals competing against six voices all giving me directions as to how I should stand.

'Does it make any difference?' I dared to ask. ''You're only taking my top half, aren't you?'

'It's all about attitude, darling,' Fi explained, as if to a five-year-old. 'You can't stand there looking like Abigail, all diminutive and good girl. We want hot and sexy.'

'I don't know how to do that.'

'Think of what you'd like to do to Martin when you get in,' giggled Hayley.

Hardly... My mind drifted to Martin as he'd looked when I'd left earlier, slumped on the settee in his T-shirt and boxer shorts, his eyes fixed on the telly, not even glancing in my direction when I'd said I was off out.

I was beginning to feel self-conscious and my shoulders drooped as I looked around helplessly. 'I'm no good at this.'

'We need more alcohol if we're going to get this done,' sighed Jen. 'Em, grab the vodka from the freezer, there's a love. Don't bother about glasses.'

Someone turned the music up, and the vodka bottle was passed around.

'Take another swig, Abs,' encouraged Claire. 'Oh, God, that reminds me, Ade and I polished off almost three bottles of wine on Sunday after I got home, I don't know how he got up for work the next morning, I was finished, especially after our weekend. But I couldn't let him drink alone, could I? I'm such a good wife, I wonder if he knows how lucky he is. Come on, Abs, down the hatch.'

I obeyed, feeling the icy alcohol hit my bloodstream in a rush, trying to smile at Jen as she waited impatiently to take my photo, pulling my shoulders back and lifting my chin in what I hoped was a confident pose as I held up my wine glass to my mouth. *Had Hayles and Claire got their nights muddled? Martin had said he was meeting up with everyone, hadn't he?*

'Think of someone you fancy, an actor or someone. George Clooney?' Emma was doing her best to help.

I desperately tried to picture George Clooney, failing miserably.

'Brad Pitt?' called out Hayley.

'What about Idris Elba? He's hot.' Claire gave a wolf whistle.

'So that's your fantasy, is it, Claire? Who knew you liked a bit of black...' Fiona looked surprised by Claire's contribution.

'What? I can't have Idris Elba because I'm white?'

'Oh, you can have him as much as you like, babe, I'll take Robert De Niro or Al Pacino.'

'Now you're talking – we should watch Heat again one night.' Emma swigged from the bottle and passed it to me again as I looked at Fi in surprise. Danny, her ex, was a red-headed Irishman – how the hell had she married him when the men of her fantasies were so different?

'Concentrate, Abs.' Jen snapped away, taking picture after picture, as I tried valiantly to give her what she wanted.

'What about Mr Shiner who taught the kids biology? We used to say he was really cute.' Hayley was doing her best, but nothing was hitting the spot and I could feel myself tensing up.

'Jim Rockford,' Hayley yelled again as she jiggled to the music and swigged her wine, her face red as a beetroot from the booze and heat in the room.

We all stopped and stared at her.

'Who?' said Jen.

'Er, The Rockford Files?'

'James Garner's your hot fantasy man?' Fi's face was a picture.

'He was cute as Jim Rockford,' Hayley said defensively. 'He had really sparkly eyes, and a cheeky smile. My mum had the boxset, I've still got it, and I still watch it sometimes...' Her words faded out as we all continued to stare at her.

'Cute, cheeky, and sparkly is not what we're looking for, Hayles.' Jen was becoming impatient. 'Oh, for God's sake, Abs, look at my phone and think of someone you'd like to fuck.'

An image shot into my head of the photo I'd stared at earlier. Night Monster.

13

Can't Get You Out Of My Head

'Perfect, hold that look, Abs, that's what I want.'

'Who was it? Who did you think of? Whoever it is, I want a piece of him, I've never seen you with that look in your eyes before, Abs.' Claire winked at me as they all laughed.

I could feel myself flushing. 'Um, I don't know, you all got me so confused, maybe, um...'

'It was Al Pacino, am I right?' Fi gave me a knowing grin.

'Maybe it was Hayley's Mr Shiner.' Claire bellowed with laughter as Hayley looked embarrassed.

'You've got me,' I lied, grinning as my jumbled head tried to work out what had just happened. *I was a disgusting, twisted, sicko. I needed help.*

'OK, we've got some great photos here.' Jen was scrolling through the photos on her phone as we all clustered round. 'This one, I think.'

I looked at my photo, trying to see something of myself in the woman who gazed suggestively at the camera over the rim of her wine glass. 'Can you send it to my phone?'

'Sure, but don't let anyone see it, especially not Martin. You understand why, right?'

'But first we need to do a spot of editing, here, let me.' This was Fi's domain – she was the one we all went to when we had computer problems, having owned her own business in something to do with graphic art and advertising when she was younger – and although she hadn't worked for years, not since she'd sold her little company for an indecent sum of money, she still kept up with all the clever things you could do with photos these days. Her social media posts were amazing when compared to our haphazard photos thrown on unedited.

Jen handed over her phone immediately.

But Fi tsked and tutted as her fingers flew over the screen. 'Haven't you got any editing apps on here, Jen?'

Jen looked at her blankly.

'Forget it, I'll send it to my phone and work on it there.'

I watched mutely as my photo was sent to Fi's phone. 'Can I get changed now, then?'

'What? Oh, yes, we're done with you.' Jen was dismissive and I felt a little put out.

'Until you need me again.'

'What?'

'Until you need me for the next part of your plan.'

'Look, don't get your knickers in a twist, OK, Abs? Get changed, clean off the makeup and have another glass of wine. This all takes time, we have to get everything perfect.'

'We should call it a night, don't you think?' Claire yawned a short while later as a couple of us unconsciously followed suit. 'Hayles and Em need to get some sleep, one of them's on the school run in the morning.'

'I'll do it,' offered Hayley to Emma. 'I'll let you know how I get on.'

'What about my photo?'

'I'll work on it at home, add in some shadows, remove some of the colour, remove the metadata, that sort of thing.'

We looked around at each other blankly, shrugging.

'So, you'll send it to me?'

'Yep, once I'm happy with it.'

'Send it to me and I'll set up the profiles,' Jen commanded.

'Can't I set them up?' I asked, feeling overlooked the whole time.

'You don't know what you're doing, you'll probably do it all wrong. No, I'll do it and take you through it once I'm happy with it all. I'm in charge, Abs, your fate is in my hands.'

I shivered inwardly, not liking the tone of her comment.

My eyes fell on Lauren, sitting quietly in an armchair sipping her wine, and I walked over, perching on the arm. 'Are you OK?'

'I'm fine, Abs, I just can't really get into it all, you know? You should probably get changed and clean off all that makeup, unless you want to go home to Martin looking like that.'

I gasped. 'I forgot.' I hurriedly changed back into my own bra and top as taxis were ordered.

'You'll find makeup remover and cotton pads in the bathroom upstairs.'

'Five minutes, Abs,' Hayley advised me, and I rushed upstairs.

I stared at myself in the mirror. I'd never imagined I could look so different. 'Goodbye, sexy Abs,' I whispered as I wiped the cotton pad over my face and lips. My hair was a little trickier to return to the real me and I struggled to get a comb through the sprayed mass, finally giving up and tying it back in a stiff ponytail with a hair tie from Jenna's basket of hair accessories. Jenna's scarlet flower clip was lying on top of the basket where I'd dropped it, and I picked it up thoughtfully, thinking of the strange looks she'd given me and her smug bossiness. 'You're in charge, not Jenna,' I mouthed silently to my reflection, feeling better as I slipped the clip into my jeans pocket.

'Cab's here, Abs.'

I ran down the stairs, where hurried goodbyes were being said.

'Friday night meet to discuss progress. Your place OK, Fi?'

'No problem, we can order pizzas.'

'Abs, I'll call you once I've got you all set up, alright, babes?'

Hayley and I scrambled into our cab and the driver took off impatiently as I looked at her.

'Jim Rockford? Really?'

We spluttered with noisy laughter.

The house was in darkness when I got home and I guessed that Martin had gone to bed. I tiptoed up the stairs, quietly undressing and changing into my nightie, then brushed my teeth before checking the bedside tables for water. He'd forgotten, he always did, and I went back down the stairs and filled two glasses. When I walked back into the bedroom, Martin was stirring, muttering something about my phone, and I grabbed it quickly, seeing a message from Fi.

'What is it? Who's calling you in the middle of the night?' He started to push himself up and I gently nudged him back down.

'It's nothing, just spam, go back to sleep.' I leant over to kiss him goodnight.

'Your hair feels weird.' His hand reached up, touching the stiff, tangled mop.

'Go to sleep,' I whispered, wriggling down under the duvet beside him, my mind on my phone and Fi's message, as I waited for his breathing to settle into a rhythm.

After a couple of minutes, sure that he'd fallen back to sleep, I quietly sat up and picked up my phone, clicking on her message and opening the attached file. The face that wasn't my face stared back at me, and I gazed at this beautiful woman who was to be my alter ego, feeling a frisson of excitement shoot through me. Jen's photo had been good, but Fi had worked her magic, and the woman in the photo gazed at the camera with dark, mysterious eyes, her face half-cloaked in shadow, her glistening lips slightly-parted as they hovered hungrily over her glass of wine, offering a promise of... something sexual... Her breasts – I corrected myself, *my* breasts – framed with black lace, seemed to push towards the camera, inviting whoever gazed at them to reach out and touch them...

Heat rushed through me as I imagined *him* looking at my photo... Night Monster... and I closed my phone and my eyes as I lay back down, conjuring up his photo in my head, refusing to acknowledge just how wrong it was. I wriggled out of my nightie, glancing at Martin, and pushed my body up against his sleeping form as he stirred, his hand reaching for me.

His hand touched my bare bottom, his eyes glinting in the light from the streetlight shining through the crack in the curtains as they flashed open in surprise, and I wrapped my arms around him, pulling him closer.

14

Never Ever
Better The Devil You Know

Martin was already showered and dressed when I awoke the next morning, I could hear him moving around downstairs, and my eyes fell on my nightie lying in a crumpled heap on the chair where I'd thrown it the night before. About to retrieve it, I slunk back down in the bed, pulling the covers up and closing my eyes as I heard him coming up the stairs.

'Abs?' he whispered, putting a cup of tea down on my bedside table. 'Are you awake?'

'Mmm?' I opened my eyes sleepily. 'What time is it?'

'Eight o'clock. I've brought you some tea, I'm off now.' He hesitated, and from beneath my half-closed eyes I saw him glance at my nightie and then back at me.

I let my eyes close again, muttering my thanks drowsily as I heard him hovering, and lying still until I'd heard the front door close behind him before pushing the covers back, sitting up and reaching for my nightie.

Pulling my knees up to my chest, I wrapped my arms around them and forced myself to think of last night. I could feel my cheeks burning and shame engulfed me as I remembered Martin's rejection. *Why hadn't he wanted me? Was I that undesirable to him these days?*

I picked up my tea and took a comforting mouthful before picking up my phone and opening my photos, switching back and forth between my own photo and the photo of *him*. Would *he* find me desirable, I wondered? *Would other men?*

I tried to busy myself with household chores once I was showered and dressed, blasting Emma's playlist of familiar tunes as I pushed the vacuum cleaner around and cleaned the bathroom, all the time wondering when I should call Jen to find out if she'd set up my profiles. By the time I'd cleared my whole ironing pile while singing along to All Saints, and Kylie, and eaten a cheese and pickle sandwich for my lunch, I decided to call her.

'You're keen, Abs.' Her tone was its usual mix of mockery and teasing so that you never quite knew which it was. 'Got the hots for him, have you? That's a bit sick isn't it, under the circumstances?'

'Don't be silly.' I laughed, cringing at its falseness. 'I just want to get familiar with it all, you know me, I haven't got a clue about all that stuff.'

'Poor, sweet, innocent little Abs. Don't worry, by the time I give you your profiles, you'll appear like an experienced hook up chick. Tell you what, I should have things started by tomorrow night so I'll pop round and show you how it works.'

'Perfect, I'll make us a bite to eat if you like? It's Martin's pool night with Danny so he won't be in 'til late.'

'Martin won't be there? OK, I'll bring a bottle. About seven?'

Now I had to face the evening ahead with Martin, with my humiliation from last night still fresh in my mind. I prepared dinner with a sinking heart, hoping desperately that he wouldn't refer to it. Maybe he wouldn't remember, I thought hopefully, he had been half asleep after all.

He arrived home at his usual time, pulling his tie off and announcing that he was going to take a bath, reappearing just as the dinner was ready.

'Shall we eat on trays? There's a good documentary on.'

'Sure,' I said, relieved that we wouldn't have to talk. 'It's pasta so we'll only need a fork.'

I'd just taken our bowls back to the kitchen when the doorbell rang.

'I'll get it,' called Martin, and I carried on rinsing the bowls and putting them in the dishwasher, aware of low conversation at the front door.

'Who is it?' I asked, walking through to the hall. 'Oh, Jen, what are you doing here?'

'Well, that's a nice welcome for your best friend.' Jen pushed past Martin, waving a bottle of wine as her perfume pervaded the hallway. 'Come here and give me a hug.'

Martin gave me a quizzical look as I glanced at him, shaking his head and disappearing into the lounge where he turned up the volume on the television.

'Jen,' I hissed. 'What are you doing here?'

'I thought you were making us a bite to eat, look, I brought the wine as promised.'

I dragged her into the kitchen. 'That's tomorrow. We can't talk about *the thing*, not with Martin here.'

'Oh God, I got the wrong night, didn't I? What a stupid cow.'

'Of course you're not.' I felt sorry for her, imagining how awkward I'd feel in her position. 'I can make you something if you're–?'

'No, no, I'll pick something up on my way home. Shame to waste the wine though. Quick glass?'

'That'll be lovely.' I smiled. 'We can sit outside.'

Jen was already walking into the lounge. 'I'll get some glasses out,' she called over her shoulder.

I followed her into the lounge, watching her plonk the bottle down on the coffee table in front of Martin, who kept his eyes glued to the TV screen.

'Glass of wine, Mart?' Jenna asked him, with a big smile, as she moved swiftly to the sideboard and grabbed glasses with a familiarity borne from years of us being inside each other's homes.

I was still hovering awkwardly just inside the doorway, trying to catch her eye.

'No thanks, I'll make some tea.' Martin paused the documentary, getting up and walking past me.

'What's wrong with Mr Cheerful?' Jen rolled her eyes.

'He's probably just tired. Jen, let's sit outside,' I pleaded.

She gave me one of her big grins. 'Come on then. Sure I can't tempt you?' She waggled the bottle at Martin as she passed him in the kitchen, with me trailing behind.

'I'm sure you can't tempt me, Jenna, thanks.' Martin gave me a strange look and I felt myself flushing, the memories of last night flooding my head. *Was that why he was being so unfriendly?*

'We'll just have a quick glass of wine outside,' I explained unnecessarily.

'Take your time.'

'Phew, trouble in paradise? Everything alright with you two?' Jenna's eyes bored into mine once we were settled at the outside patio table with our wine.

'Everything's fine.' I shifted uncomfortably, dropping my voice to a whisper. 'It's probably me, you know, worried about Lauren, and all this app stuff...'

'You're getting yourself into your usual state, Abs, relax, there's nothing to worry about. I won't talk about it in front of Mart, and I'll show you how to hide it on your phone so he'll never see it.'

'Jen, shh, he'll hear you. We can't talk about it now.'

'Ooh, hold on.' Jen gave a sly little smile as she busied herself on her phone. 'There, that'll get him interested.'

'Who? Oh, sorry, it's none of my business,' I said, feeling embarrassed.

'Well, it is your business actually, Abs, seeing as I'm being you right now, but like you said, we can't talk about it here.'

'What? What was that? Who were you talking to? Did you send someone a message?' I looked frantically towards the lounge window.

'More like a reply, you're a very popular lady, Abs...' She had her cat that got the cream look again. 'Don't you want to know what your profile name is?'

'Well, yes, but– why are you chatting to people as me?'

'I'm getting you set up, that's all, it has to be convincing if it's going to work. I told you I'd lay the groundwork, set up a presence and stuff.'

'So you're being me?' I wasn't sure how much I liked that idea.

'Call it a joint effort. And, Abs, try to think of it as just a little bit of fun.'

'But it's not though, is it? And I still don't know exactly what we plan to do with him?'

'That is something I'm still figuring out. So, d'you want to know your name?'

I nodded.

'Tipsy Tease.'

I couldn't help but giggle as I looked at Jenna's proud expression. *Me? Tipsy Tease?*

'What d'you think? The men like it, I have to say, Abs.'

'Which men? I mean... do they look nice? Not creeps or anything? Well, it doesn't matter, I don't have to meet any of them, do I?'

'No... not at the moment, we'll see how things pan out...'

'Not at the moment? I thought this was just to reel him in, you know – Night Monster? Did he–? Has he–?'

'Has he shown any interest? No, not yet, but give him time, you're a newbie so you need to get established.'

I was about to demand that Jen tell me exactly what we were planning with Lauren's attacker, as Martin's face suddenly appeared at the back door.

'I'm hitting the sack.' He turned without another word, disappearing, and I felt Jenna's eyes studying me.

'What's going on, Abs? What's Marty's problem?'

'Nothing.' I couldn't tell her, of all people, it was too embarrassing. 'He's just tired. Another glass of wine?'

'No, I should go.' She looked at her watch and stood up.

'Are you still coming round tomorrow night then, when Martin's out? To show me how to put the stuff on my phone?'

'Shit. You know what? Tomorrow night's not good for me after all, but we can do it at Fi's on Friday.'

'OK, Friday then...' I saw Jen off and wandered back outside to collect the glasses, wondering what to do with myself. It was still early, Martin was in bed and I didn't want to disturb him and face an awkward talk about last night. I poured myself another glass and sat down, staring into space, feeling far from my alter ego, Tipsy Tease.

'Abs?'

I jumped as Martin appeared beside me.

'She's gone then?'

'I thought you'd gone to bed?'

'Changed my mind. Abs, I'd appreciate it if your friends didn't just pitch up whenever they felt like it, a bit of privacy in my own home would be nice occasionally, you know.'

'Sorry, she got the wrong night, you know what Jen's like, a bit of a scatterbrain sometimes.'

'Any wine left in that bottle?'

'Just a drop. D'you mind using Jen's glass?'

His eyes fell on the glass with its smudge of red lipstick on the rim. 'I'll grab another one.'

I waited awkwardly while he filled his glass with the last of the wine.

'Everything alright, Abs?'

'Yes, of course it is.' I could feel myself flushing. He was going to ask me about last night, I knew it. And then inspiration came. 'It was so hot last night, wasn't it? I felt like I couldn't breathe, I was tossing and turning and having such weird dreams.'

'It was a bit hot...' He glanced at me, looking relieved, before downing his wine. 'Well, reckon I'll head back up to bed. Oh, Danny can't make pool tomorrow night so we're playing on Friday. Don't stay up too late.'

'I won't, you go on ahead.' I breathed a sigh of relief, sipping my wine as I thought about what Jen had said about me. *You're a very popular lady...* But... I asked myself, would *he* be interested? And what would we do if he wasn't? *And, what would I do if he was?*

15

The Sign
No Regrets

In the end, Martin dropped me off at Fi's on Friday night on his way to play pool with her ex-husband, Danny, but I would take a cab home.

I was the last to arrive, right behind Em, and we walked in together as Jen opened the door for us, leaning out to watch Martin's car drive away.

'Martin drove you then? Why's that? He off out somewhere?'

'Nice to see you too, Jen,' I smiled. She was always so nosy, it was just a part of her that I'd got used to over the years. 'Danny changed their pool night to tonight.'

Lauren's face was slowly healing, the area around her eye now a yellowish-green, and she grimaced as we looked at her.

'Yellow and green should never be seen, right? No need to tell me how lovely I look, I can do that all by myself every time I look in the mirror.'

'You're looking much better, Laur, I promise you. How's the rest of you feeling? No aches and pains?' I tried to drag my eyes away from the small scab on her neck, sure that she would be left with a scar from where his nail had dug into her flesh.

'Nope, right as rain, Abs, a few more days and it'll be like it never happened.'

'That's the spirit, Laur.' Em gave her an encouraging smile as Jen appeared.

'No, it's not. It did happen, she can never forget it, can she? He can, it's nothing to him, but look what he's done to Lauren.'

'Oh, come on, Jen, stop going on, she'll never be able to forget it if you keep harping on about it, will she?' Claire tried to intervene on her way to collect the pizzas from the delivery man waiting at the front door.

'When do you plan on moving back home? Are you moving back or not? Paul deserves to know where he stands.'

Lauren looked at Emma. 'If Paul wants answers, he'll have to ask me, won't he? Why are you asking me? Did he ask you to talk to me, Em, because if he did, he's overstepped the mark – they can't go around talking to our friends behind our backs, that's our unwritten rule, isn't it?'

'Of course he didn't ask me,' Em placated Lauren. 'It's just me wondering, that's all. Why don't I put some music on?'

'Pizzas while they're hot, girls. Hayles, help me grab the wine will you, love?' Fi took control while Em went through her playlist, finally selecting Ace of Base to start us off, and for the next half an hour we scoffed slices of pizza, drank wine, and avoided the subject of Lauren's attacker and our reason for gathering.

Robbie was singing No Regrets, when Lauren suddenly jumped up and began to collect our plates. I got up to help her, wondering if the song's words were affecting her in some way.

'Leave them on the side, girls, I'll sort them out later. We need to get down to business.'

'Fi's right, it's time to see what Hayles and Em have found out. Top up your glasses, everyone, let's get to it.' Jen looked at Emma. 'You go first, Em. What have you got for us?'

Clearing her throat importantly, she began. 'I left my car round the corner and went for a walk past Wengrove junior school on Wednesday afternoon, just as the kids were coming out, but the car never appeared so I had no way of identifying the girl.'

Hayley was beginning to fidget-bounce in her seat – a clear sign that she was excited about something, as well as that she was getting slightly sloshed.

Em continued, 'Hayley and I conferred yesterday and it turns out that the daughter was collected by her friend's mother. We know this because–'

'Oh, let me tell...' Hayley pleaded.

'Let Emma finish.' Jen's bossy voice brooked no argument.

'Alright then, so yesterday was no good because it was the friend on lift duty again, so that just left today when we knew it would be the mother. I easily identified the car and therefore the daughter and the mother, and I followed them home. They live in a semi in Orpington, the road's called Marbeth Road, and they live at number eighteen. And, listen to this–'

We all leant forward, wondering what Emma's revelation was going to be.

16

'It's got a for sale sign up outside.'

'Shit. They're moving?' Jen jogged her crossed leg rapidly.

'That's usually what a for sale sign indicates…'

'Sarcasm, Fi…' warned Claire.

'My turn, oh, I need some more wine.'

I reached for one of the bottles, handing it to Hayles, wondering what she had to tell us that had got her so excited.

'Right, so, like Em said, I found out about the friend picking the daughter up. I was outside the school on Wednesday morning and I saw the car pull up so I pretended to be busy typing a message on my phone…' At this, Hayley looked around at us all proudly and we gave her nods of encouragement. 'And the mother called out to remind the daughter that her friend's mum was collecting her. Her friend's name is Katy, but I'm not sure that–'

'No, we don't need to know that.' Jenna sighed. 'Get on with it, we haven't got all night.'

'No, sorry.' Hayley rolled her eyes at me and I grinned in solidarity. 'So, I thought I could follow her home and find out the address, but she didn't go home, she went to have her nails done, it's got a funny name, I can't remember it now, but so… Guess what I did?'

We all shook our heads, waiting in impatient suspense.

'I went in and asked if they could fit me in, and guess what? They had a cancellation, so I had a pedicure. Look.'

She stretched her feet out and we all admired Hayley's baby blue toenails. 'That's where I–'

'Very nice, Hayles, but is there anything useful that you can tell us? Knowing where his wife has her nails done was not exactly what we needed to know.'

'But you said–' Hayley stopped, at Jenna's expression, before taking a deep breath, and saying in a rush. 'They're moving to Spain.'

'What?' Jenna's face mirrored our own. This was not what we'd been expecting. 'Are you sure? Spain? They're going on a holiday, surely?'

'Nope. They're moving abroad. I was in the chair next but one to hers and it's all she could talk about to her nail technician – how much she still had to sort out; how much packing she had to do; how the school is mainly ex-pats' children so they all speak English; how she couldn't wait to leave the miserable weather behind and have a year-round tan. But our weather's not that bad, is it? We're having gorgeous weather at the moment.'

I felt strange, a mixture of relief that I wouldn't have to go through with this foolhardy plan that could only end in disaster, and disappointment that I wouldn't get to be the woman he desired, crazy and sick as that was.

'And after you'd both had your nails done?' Claire re-filled her glass before waving the bottle around to see who wanted more wine.

'That's the thing, I was parked further on, in the car park, but she was parked in a space in the street near the salon, so I lost her. Yesterday morning I waited along the road from the school and I followed her again, but this time she went shopping. I pretended to do some shopping as well, but then Ross called and reminded me to collect his suits from the dry cleaners, and then I remembered that the window cleaner was coming and I hadn't left the side gate open, so I had to rush off.

'I told Emma about the salon and what I knew and she said I could leave it to her, that she'd get their home address today. It was much easier for Em, because they were going home, whereas in the mornings the mother was always going off somewhere...'

'Fine. Good work, Hayles. Right, so we know where he lives and we now know that he's moving to bloody Spain. When?' Jen fired out the question to Emma and Hayley, who looked at each other nonplussed. 'When. Are. They. Moving?' She enunciated each word, as if they were five-year-olds.

'Er... soon?'

'I'll find out.' Claire rescued poor Hayley from Jenna's glare. 'I'll go to the estate agent and start there. Who was it?'

We all turned our heads in Emma's direction.

'Who was–? Oh, the estate agent? Oh right, the sign... um, Propshop.'

'And I'll do a spot of night time surveillance,' added Fi. 'See if I can't get him chatting down at his local pub, although what–'

'No!' The word was sharp, stopping Fi in her tracks in surprise.

'No one talks to him, or the wife. We don't want either of them seeing any of us. Is that clear? The only one who will ever have any contact with him is Abs.'

'What's his name? Does anyone know his name yet?'

Jen gave me one of her looks. 'His name is not really the issue, Abs.'

'Isn't it time you told us what we're going to do to him?' Claire injected just the right tone of bossiness into her voice.

'Yes, I suppose so. Alright ladies, we're going to beat the living crap out of him and make him wish he'd never agreed to a hookup with Tipsy Tease. We're going to make him regret every second of hurt he caused Lauren, and we're going to give him a clear message that if he ever beats up another woman, we'll come looking for him.'

'Damn right,' said Fi, clapping.

'Who the hell is Tipsy Tease?' Lauren spoke for the first time.

'That's me.' I had the grace to blush. 'It was Jenna's idea, not mine.'

'It's good,' murmured my friends. 'Suits her profile pic.'

'Talking of my profile pic – are you going to set me up on my phone, Jen?' I was beginning to feel uncomfortable about the fact that she was being me and that I had no control over it.

She held out her hand silently, and I handed my phone over, picking up my wine and taking a large glug.

'Beat the living crap out of him how? How exactly are we going to do that?' Claire voiced what was in all our heads.

'We're going to get him on a hookup with Abs, somewhere quiet, late at night, somewhere with no one else around, with no one to hear his screams as he begs for us to stop.'

And no one to hear my screams, I thought, not sure that I liked the direction Jen was headed in.

Fi raised her eyebrows, taking a long pull on her vape as Jenna continued.

'No bloke should do that to another woman – lead her on, make her feel wanted, and then discard her for something new and shiny...'

Lauren looked puzzled.

'Jen, you're making it sound like there was more to it than there was. It was only ever a hookup, not a date, it was a hookup that went bad, not a couple break up.'

'I know that.' Jen gave a small laugh. 'But men who make a habit of treating a woman badly need to pay. He needs to pay. We just need to figure out where we'll do it.'

'And what we'll do it with...' Fi looked doubtful. 'I don't exactly drive around with a baseball bat in my boot...'

'Leave all that to me, all you need to do is find out where he likes to spend his evenings, then we can get Abs in position.'

I wasn't sure that Jen had us all convinced as we began chatting amongst ourselves and Lauren, Claire and Fi disappeared off for a smoke.

'Right, Abs, let me talk you through it.'

I joined Jen and watched and listened as she showed me how to find the apps, hidden in a folder so that Martin wouldn't discover them, taking note of my password and e-mail address for signing in – a new e-mail address created especially for me by Jen. I looked in horror at the chats she'd been having, as me, with men I'd matched with, my cheeks burning.

'How could you? This isn't me, I'd never chat with strangers like this. I'll never be able to keep this up.'

'It's not you, that's the point, it's Tipsy Tease. It's time for you to put your big girl pants on, Abs, and do your bit for Lauren. A little practice and you'll get into the swing of it – have some fun with it, you don't have to meet up with any of them, for now anyway, so go wild, say anything you like. The more active you are the more you'll get bumped up on the app so that you appear to more men, which means more chances of him seeing you and liking what he sees. And when he does, you need to be ready, hence the practice.'

'What if he doesn't find me attractive?'

'He will. But depending on our timeframe, we may have to get you to make the first move. Don't worry, I'll help you.'

It was only when I got home that I realised it had been the first evening where we hadn't really had a laugh or taken any photos. The thought made me sad and I wondered whether Jen's revenge plan was such a good idea.

The following Thursday, Martin came in from his pool night and informed me that Lauren and Paul had sorted out their differences and that she was moving back in with him at the weekend. I guessed that this mainly meant that her bruises had faded enough, rather than any major kind of reconciliation, nonetheless, I was pleased that things were returning to normal.

As if to prove just how back to normal everything was, Lauren called me after the weekend with an invitation to theirs for the coming Saturday for a barbeque – everyone was coming, including exes.

We hadn't had a get-together since the night at Fi's, and I was beginning to wonder if the whole idea of payback was dwindling. I'd dutifully accessed the apps on my phone a couple of times the first day or two after that night but had cringed at the thought of chatting with anyone. Now, though, knowing that I'd be seeing Jen, I panicked and settled myself outside with a large glass of wine, secure in the knowledge that Martin would be out for a few hours at the pub with Ross and Craig.

Taking a deep breath, I opened the app called Dare, staring in disbelief at the chat threads.

17

Beckenham2589's last message, which had a kiss response, informed me that he was doing it right now as he pictured me. *Doing what?* I scrolled up, my stomach churning in embarrassment as I read what I'd supposedly said to him. *I'd kill Jenna.*

I clicked on another chat thread, staring in shock at the photo of a close-up of a certain part of the sender's anatomy, mortified as I read my reply informing BigBoy72 that I was lying there naked thinking of him but that he was too big for me.

There were more, all along the same lines, and I dropped my phone on the table as if it might bite me. I gulped some wine, my mind racing as I considered the situation. Jenna had clearly been laying the groundwork, as she'd so innocently put it. But why? Why make me come across as such a dirty-minded woman with one thing on the brain.

Because, Abigail – I answered my own question – this is what these things are for. For some stupid reason I, in my innocent way, had somehow imagined that there would be talk of what we liked to do in our spare time, what music we liked, or whether we preferred red or white wine, or cats or dogs... no wonder Jenna had taken control. And, I thought with relief, it was all fantasy, it wasn't real. Not one of these men had suggested hooking up, they just wanted to talk dirty, to get off on a bit of sex talk...

So how did actual hookups happen then? How did Lauren and Jenna find men to meet? Why was I attracting the creeps who wanted to play with themselves while indulging in smutty chat? The answer to that was in the deleted chats, I realised, looking at my phone again. Here were men asking normal types of questions, at least as far as hooking up went.

I saw your picture, you're beautiful, said one, suggesting that we meet; another asked if I fancied meeting up to watch a film and have some fun; and yet another suggested meeting for lunch and an hour in a hotel room one day if I was ever in Lewisham. I sat up straighter. I'll be in Baxter's Wine Bar tonight, Governor informed me. Fancy hooking up at 8pm? The date was two nights earlier and his next message was a cancellation, with the words *maybe another time.*

I guessed that meant that he'd approached a few women and someone else had taken him up on his offer. I clicked on his profile and found myself looking at a middle-aged man with short, mid-brown hair greying at the temples, brown eyes, his mouth turned up in a slight smile as he looked at the camera. He was handsome, I thought in surprise. He reminded me of Martin...

My phone made a strange little whooping noise and I froze as a new chat message appeared. *What are you doing right now?* Terrified, I held my breath, looking around frantically as if the rose bushes could help me. Calm down, I instructed myself, he can't see you, think rationally. Carefully, I clicked on his name, bringing up his profile, nodding as I saw that we'd hearted each other. Jenna's work again, of course, she'd been busy.

He was nice-looking and much younger than me, blonde-haired, with the glint of an earring in his left earlobe. Harmless. I'd show Jenna that I could do this, that I didn't need her help, I thought defiantly. Clicking on the message, I paused, considering my reply... Why not the truth? *Sitting in my garden drinking a glass of wine.* About to send it, I added a kiss to make it look authentic. And then I waited.

Send me your address, I'll come round.

Oh shit, that wasn't what I'd expected. I began to type. *No good, my husband will be coming home–* no, I deleted that, no personal information, Jenna had been explicit about that. *Sorry, I'm already booked–* no, that made me sound like a prostitute. *Sorry, I have plans.* That was better, I nodded, hitting send before sitting back and taking a deep breath. My hand trembled as I picked up my wine, draining my glass and getting up to fetch the bottle from the kitchen.

Feeling braver now, I opened up the other two apps, finding similar chat threads to the first app. Curiosity getting the better of me, I began to scroll through the profiles, staring in amazement at the faces looking back at me. There were all sorts: young, middle-aged, even elderly; every race and mix of races under the sun; men with short hair, long hair, lots of hair, little to no hair; men who looked like boring businessmen, or film stars; was this one even shaving yet? There were men who looked like they should be charging by the hour, and men who looked like potential serial killers...

The chilling thought stopped me in my tracks. There would be predators on these things, of course there would be. Of course there *was... he* was a predator... *Night Monster.* Just thinking of his profile name sent a frisson through me. I knew he was dangerous, for so many reasons, I knew what he'd done to Lauren and I hated him for it, but... he was just so handsome... and he hadn't shown any interest in me... which was good, if I was honest, because I was terrified at the prospect of meeting him face to face. But I fancied him. I was sick and twisted. I was a psycho.

I clicked on my profile, gazing at it, knowing that I looked hot and inviting. Maybe he'd hearted me and I just didn't know, I thought, clicking on the heart icon and skimming down the list of profile names. He hadn't. I tried all three apps to no avail. Was he even still on any of these apps? There was only one way to find out...

I was halfway through a second bottle of wine when I found him on the app called Frisky. I sat staring at his photo, trying to imagine him as the kind of man who could do to Lauren what she'd said he'd done, feeling guilty that my sub-conscious could even suggest that I doubted her story – I'd seen the evidence of his attack with my own eyes after all. He looked thoroughly decent, the kind of man you'd let buy you a drink in a bar without worry. Maybe she'd identified the wrong man. Of course! Why hadn't any of us considered that?

But she'd hooked up with him via the app, he wasn't a stranger she'd bumped into in the carpark, although she had been terribly drunk, we all had... so was it possible that the man she'd had car sex with had been someone else? Another profile that she'd muddled with his, when Jenna had begun interrogating her?

The more I thought about it, the more certain I was that I was right. I could prove it. I could meet up with him and have a harmless drink, put my own mind at ease, and I could tell the others that they'd got the wrong man. I hesitated for a second before clicking on the heart, sitting back and drinking my wine as I stared at my phone willing it to tell me that he'd hearted me back.

Is it him, or isn't it him? My mind played tricks with me as I sat there. *You could be playing a dangerous game,* the voice in my head nagged. *If it is him and you meet him, what then? How far are you prepared to go? But what if it isn't him? What would be the harm then? But how could you ever really be sure? And again, how far are you prepared to go?*

I hated the side of me that was coming out, I wanted to bury it, to lock it up and throw away the key, but I knew that I couldn't do that. We'd started the ball rolling and I was powerless to stop what was coming. I'd have to see it through now, to the bitter end, whatever that turned out to be.

I was still sitting there when I heard Martin's key in the front door and I frantically closed all the apps, getting up quickly and wobbling slightly from my over-indulgence.

'Nice time with Ross and Craig?' I leant against the kitchen doorframe smiling brightly as Martin turned from locking the front door.

'Yeah, fine.' His eyes strayed to the open kitchen door and then to the empty bottle of wine on the counter. 'Is someone here?' His expression turned guarded.

'No, just me. I've got some wine outside, fancy a glass?'

He checked his watch, hesitated, then said, 'I think I'll hit the sack.'

'Just one glass? We can tell each other about our day.' *Like we used to. When you still loved me.* 'Please?' I tilted my head and gave him my cute smile, the one that always got me what I wanted.

'I'm tired, it's late, I already told you I'm going to bed, and you look like you've had more than enough wine for both of us.' His eyes met mine for a second before he turned and climbed the stairs.

Rejected again, I defiantly sat myself outside and filled my glass to the brim, going through the messages on the dating apps and drunkenly tapping away on my phone's keyboard. I had a comfortable rhythm going – gulp wine, click on a message thread, type a reply, look at Night Monster's photo, and repeat.

18

I spent the next day checking the apps on my phone every few minutes like some kind of obsessed madwoman, with absolutely no idea what I would do if he hearted me back and suggested hooking up. I never went out in the evenings on my own, only for nights with the girls, so Martin would wonder what the hell I was up to anyway. 'Would he actually notice though?' a little voice chirped in my head. Not that any of that mattered – Night Monster showed no interest in me.

Others, of course, showed plenty of interest in me, and no wonder, my drunken fingers had sent some pretty interesting messages the night before. I cringed as I read some of them, blaming Martin for what he'd made me do.

I lay in bed that Thursday night with rambling thoughts as the now familiar image slid into my head – even if he wanted to meet me, he'd be expecting Tipsy Tease, not Abigail, boring housewife – which took me down a rabbit hole of self-doubt and the whole Martin thing.

I had nothing in my wardrobe remotely like the kind of clothes someone like my alter ego would wear. But there was something I could do about that, I thought happily the next morning as I allowed myself to play into my fruitless fantasy, all the time knowing that I could never really meet him face to face, not unless I was sure it wasn't him, it would be too risky. It would be reckless and dangerous...

And then I had another thought... I knew his address... and I knew the agent they were selling their house with...

An overwhelming urge took hold of me as I jumped out of bed.

'Abs?' Martin's surprised face peered round the bathroom door as I towelled myself dry. 'You're up early, what's going on?'

'I thought I'd do some shopping, get something new to wear to the barbeque tomorrow. You could do with a couple of new shirts as well, so I'm off for some retail therapy.'

'Who are you going with?' Martin turned the shower on, stepping in without waiting for my reply.

Now that I'd decided on my mission I could hardly contain my impatience, and I laid out some breakfast for Martin to hurry him along. 'Mart,' I called up the stairs. 'I've made you some tea and toast, it's going cold.'

I all but shooed him out of the front door before hurrying upstairs to dress, taking care to choose an outfit that was the opposite of what my alter ego would wear. Keeping my hair down, I appraised myself in the mirror, nodding in satisfaction – beige trousers and shoes, a cream top, and large sunglasses to hide my face as much as possible – it was perfect.

Butterflies swarmed in my stomach as I drove to Orpington, following the directions on the car's GPS so that I pulled up right outside Propshop. I walked to the window and studied the pictures of properties for sale, looking for semi-detached houses and finding several. Taking a deep breath, I pushed open the door.

'Morning, what can I do for you? Buying or selling?' The agent's smiling face looked up from behind her computer.

'Er, buying, well, looking really... but hoping to buy. You've got some nice-looking semis in the window, I was wondering which roads they're in?'

'How many bedrooms are you looking for? Bathrooms? Off-road parking? And price, of course – what's your range?' She tapped importantly on her computer as I realised I should have thought this out a bit more carefully.

'Um... price isn't really the issue, we're flexible, maybe two or three bedrooms?'

'Just the two of you, is it? Or a family? You mentioned semis but we've got a couple of lovely detacheds just come onto our books.' The printer whirred and she sprang up from her chair, grabbing the papers and holding them out to me. 'Have a look at these, hot off the press, I haven't got them on the system yet so you're the first to see them. It's your lucky day.'

No, it wasn't, I thought, wondering how to turn her attention to the semis. I made a show of studying the papers, frowning thoughtfully. 'I'd really prefer to know where in Orpington the properties are, could you show me on the map?' Pleased with my brainwave, I joined her in front of the large wall map as she pointed out the location of the two detached houses, my eyes scanning desperately for Marbeth Road.

'Are some areas better than others?' I stalled for time, nodding and murmuring as she circled different parts of the map with her finger and explained about schools and supermarkets, all the time searching for Marbeth without success. *It had to be on there somewhere...*

'Where are you currently living?' Her question caught me completely off guard and my brain stalled.

And then I got it started again. 'We've just moved back from Spain, my husband had work out there.' *Clever, Abigail... but she's going to ask you where in Spain. Think.*

'Oh, whereabouts? God, if I lived in Spain I'd never leave, who'd want to move back here to our miserable weather?' She laughed, catching herself as she realised she was in the business of selling houses here, miserable weather and all. 'But of course, it's home isn't it? I expect you missed it? Home sweet home. The country of our birth. Dear Old Blighty, there's really nothing like it is there? White cliffs of Dover and all that.'

Stop while you're ahead, lady, you're heading for overkill.

'You're not very tanned.'

I stared at her blankly.

'For Spain, I mean. Not a sun person?'

'Oh, I, er–'

'I expect you're like me. I'm a disaster. You should see me after I so much as look at the sun – lobster red, just like that.' She snapped her fingers as she chuckled. 'And don't mention the blisters the next day.'

I was beginning to realise that I wasn't expected to answer her questions most of the time.

'Right, let's see what we can find for you, I'm sure we've got the perfect house for you to settle down in, although it will be a bit different to Spain, I'm sure. Where did you say you were staying out there? Orpington's really got an awful lot to offer, it's very convenient for–'

I was saved by the ringing of the office phone and she excused herself regretfully. As soon as she sat down, I took out my phone, typing in Madrid and reading rapidly. *Preparation was key after all, it's just a pity I hadn't thought of that earlier...*

'Sorry about that, now, where were we? So, Spain, you said, and that was where exactly...?'

'Madrid, just for a year, we had a rented apartment.'

'It sounds so sophisticated. Lots of art galleries and things there, aren't there? What does your husband do? I bet they've got some lovely shops. Oh, I'm so sorry, I don't know what's the matter with me today, I haven't even introduced myself, I'm Becca.'

'Victoria, Victoria...'

Becca smiled and nodded encouragingly as we looked at each other, the sudden silence filled with nothing but the sound of the wall clock as it ticked off each passing second.

19

Think of a name. Any name. Say something. 'Beckingham.' I held out my hand.

'I thought you were going to say Beckham for a minute.' Becca laughed at her own humour, not realising how close she'd come to my hopeless attempts at ad-libbing.

'I wish.' We laughed, all girls together, as Becca handed me the prize I'd been hoping for.

'We've got clients moving to Spain, how much of a coincidence is that? They leave in three weeks. Wouldn't it be funny if they moved into your apartment? And imagine if you bought their house? That would be so weird, wouldn't it?'

Three weeks? He was leaving the country in three short weeks?

'Really? That is a coincidence.' We shared another little chuckle. 'Which is their house?' *Nice segue, Abigail.*

Moving back to her computer, Becca tapped rapidly and whipped a sheet of paper from the printer. 'It's a lovely house, three bedrooms, upstairs bathroom and downstairs loo, nice garden.' Sprinting to the map on the wall as she sensed my interest, she jabbed a finger at the top. 'Here we are, nice area, right next to Petts Wood, it virtually is Petts Wood really.'

'It sounds great.' I took the sheet of paper from her, disappointed to only see an image of the house itself. 'No other photos?'

'On the computer, here, come and have a look. No, you know what?' Her head tilted to the side as she regarded me with twinkling eyes. 'We can do better than that, Victoria. Why don't I take you to see it? Let me give Mrs Parker a quick call, she'll be thrilled.'

I smiled politely, swallowing as bile rose in my throat. It was becoming too real. *Parker...* It was a common name. My best friend, Natalie, had been a Parker, as were the people two doors down from us, and I was pretty sure that one of the girls' maiden name had been Parker.

It's not too late to back out, you don't need to do this. What do you even think you're going to prove by going to his house? What if it is him? How could you find him attractive? You're sick. The quarrel in my head continued, but my morbid fascination with him got the better of me, and five minutes later I was sitting in the passenger seat of Becca's car as she zoomed in and out of the traffic.

'What a bit of luck, half an hour later and we'd have missed her. I've got a really good feeling about you and this house, Victoria.'

I made a show of studying the house's exterior before walking up the path and being introduced to a tall, slender woman with a sleek bob and an impatient air. My eyes took in her heavy make-up, as well as the slight bruise beneath her right eye. *An accident with a cupboard door? Or him?*

'I'll leave you to it, Becca, if you don't mind, but please hurry it along, I've got a ton of things to do.' Her tone was impatient and just a little superior.

'No problem, we'll be fine. Let's start upstairs, shall we?'

She chatted nonstop, pointing out the positives, as my eyes raked each room with interest.

'And this...' Becca waved an arm as we entered the last upstairs room, 'is the master bedroom. Plenty of wardrobe space, and a nice view onto the garden.'

My eyes strayed to the neatly-made bed, taking in the book on one of the bedside tables. Unless he read romance novels, then he slept on the left-hand side... Yes, men's navy slippers beside the bed... 'D'you mind if I just take another walk around up here, to get the feel for it all?'

'No problem, we've got a bit of time, I'll pop back downstairs, see you in a jiff.'

With one ear on her footsteps descending the stairs, I quietly slid open the wardrobe doors on his side of the room, trailing my fingers across the line of shirts hanging inside and leaning in to breathe in their scent. I walked over to the dressing table, picking up a bottle of men's Eau de Cologne and removing the lid to sniff it. Footsteps sounded and I hurriedly replaced the lid, putting the bottle down as his wife appeared in the doorway.

'You've got a lovely house.'

'Thanks.' Her eyes glanced around the room, landing on the open wardrobe door as my stomach lurched. Tutting to herself, she crossed the room and closed it in a swift movement. 'Seen enough?' Her smile was a little tight. 'Only I'm in a bit of a rush.'

'Sorry, yes of course.' I moved past her and down the stairs to a waiting Becca.

'We've only got a few minutes, come and see the lounge first, it's really very spacious.' She rushed ahead of me and I dutifully followed, my eyes drawn to the array of framed photos on the sideboard, and what looked like old photo albums on the shelf. I wanted to study them but Becca was moving me along too fast. 'And then it's open to the kitchen, a lovely counter, don't you think? And you could add a conservatory, there's plenty of room, you could make it your dining room if you wanted to.' Becca twittered on happily. 'Plenty of cupboard space in the kitchen, nice big gas oven, room for a double fridge if you wanted. D'you like to cook, Victoria?'

It took me a moment to remember that I was Victoria and I flushed. 'Er, yes, I do. It's all very nice.' I was distracted by a small photo on the fridge, hidden amidst reminders and funny fridge magnets and a calendar.

'I'll let you take it in for a bit while I speak to Mrs Parker. She wants to ask me something about the garden shed.'

My hand reached out, snatching the photo and shoving it into my pocket. *What had I just done?* I glanced out of the window, seeing Becca and Mrs Parker head round the back of the shed at the far end of the garden, deep in conversation, and crept back into the lounge.

Taking another look out of the French doors, I pulled one of the old albums from the shelf, not quite sure what I hoped to find, but unable to stop myself. I hurriedly flipped the stiff pages over, smoothing the yellowing film covering the family photos. *His family photos*.

Mesmerised, I pored over photo after photo – my ears attuned for sounds of Becca returning. This was the man who had so cruelly attacked Lauren – as a sweet young boy, slouched on the settee with his older sister, with his parents, grinning on a beach holiday...

Becca's chatty voice was getting closer as I flipped through photos of him and his wife on their wedding day and on various holidays, and I slipped the close-up photo of him, grinning into the camera as he clung to the side of a swimming pool, from its sticky film, sliding it into my pocket as I heard the kitchen door open. I think I had seriously become deranged at that moment. I shoved the album back onto the shelf and stepped away, pretending to be studying the ceiling light. My morbid fascination with this man was spinning out of control.

We said our goodbyes, and I walked beside Becca to her car, keen to get back to her office and retrieve my own car.

'Right, come on, Victoria, I'm all yours for the next couple of hours, let's have some fun.'

I looked at Becca in confusion as we got into her car.

'We'll start with a house just a few roads from here, it's another semi, might need a little freshening up but that's reflected in the price, and if you like gardening then wait until you see the size of the garden.'

My heart sank as Becca flashed me an enthusiastic smile, and I forced myself to return it. 'Sounds great,' I said, my thoughts on the photos burning a hole in my pocket.

Five houses, and three hours later, Becca deposited me back at Propshop, stopping me as I was about to unlock my car.

'Pop inside with me, Victoria, I just need a few details from you. Come in, come in. Fancy a cuppa? I'm parched.'

Anxiously checking the time, I followed her inside. *Details? What details? My contact details, of course.*

'Right, I'll get the kettle on and then get your details. Tea or coffee?'

'Er, nothing for me, thanks, I really have to go...'

'No problem, give me a sec. Right, Victoria Beckingham...' She typed my stupid made-up name into her computer and looked at me expectantly. 'Phone number?'

'Er...' I had a brainwave, giving her my number but swapping the last couple of digits round.

'Perfect, and have you got an address for me?'

'No, not really, we're staying with friends. But the number is fine, you can get me any time.'

'Great, not a problem. Now, let me print the details of the houses I showed you so that you can show your husband. He'll be impressed, I reckon I'll be seeing you both very soon. I'd put money on it that we found your new house today, you see if I'm right. And here's my card.'

I escaped finally, feeling exhausted from keeping up the act of interested house-viewer, and drove back to Bromley, hitting The Glades with rather less energy and enthusiasm than I'd started the day with. I needed a drink desperately and marched straight to Costa Coffee, ordering a sandwich and a tea before sinking gratefully into a seat. Looking around first, I took the photos from my pocket, laying them on the table and staring at them as I ate my sandwich.

20

He was a few years younger in the pool photo, his hair was shorter, and his smooth chest was tanned. He looked... happy... sexy... and desirable... and I could feel heat rising in me as I shifted in my seat, looking around guiltily, as if the other customers knew what I'd done. *I'd falsely represented myself, I'd been inside his house, sniffed his shirts, and stolen his photos... What the hell was I thinking?*

I was thinking that I wanted Lauren to be wrong about him, that I wanted to be wrong about him. But why? So that I wouldn't have to face him, or so that I could? I peered closer at one of the photos, as if it could tell me more about him, noticing a mark on his neck – a single blemish on an otherwise perfect male specimen. It hadn't been visible in his profile photo because he'd been wearing some kind of pendant on a leather thong. For a moment, I confused myself, thinking that it was a scratch mark from Lauren, but then I realised it couldn't be – this was an old photo, and the tiny scar obviously much older. *Stop obsessing*, the voice whispered in my head.

Was this the face of the man who hooked up with women and then beat them black and blue? A chill passed through me as I stared at his face. *Was it true? Could it be?* He'd been a young innocent boy once. *What had made him become a man who beat up women? An incident in his youth?* I felt confused and conflicted – not wanting it to be him. If Lauren could just admit she'd made a mistake, we could call the whole thing off and I would never have to meet him as bait in Jen's stupid plan, because I couldn't, I simply couldn't do it. I looked regretfully at the photo I'd snatched from the fridge, running my finger over his naked chest above the bed sheets. In three weeks, he'd be gone and we could go on with our lives and forget about it all. Except for poor Lauren...

But I was living in fantasy land if I thought I could extricate myself from the situation, there was no way that Jenna would let me wriggle out of it.

I now had about three hours of shopping time left before I had to beat the traffic to get home before Martin, I realised as I left the coffee shop. I made a beeline for Marks and Sparks, heading straight for the men's clothing and grabbing a couple of shirts for Martin, throwing in some socks and underpants for good measure, before moving on to the ladies' underwear section.

I picked myself out some underwear, black, lacy stuff, feeling all sophisticated and worldly-wise as I dropped it nonchalantly into the trolley. Next up – some new clothes for the new Abigail... Nothing really took my fancy and I could feel panic building as I realised that I had no idea where to look for a couple of sexy but tasteful dresses. Where did Jenna shop, I wondered? No, I wasn't looking for Jenna's mutton dressed as lamb style, I reminded myself, I wanted something that Tipsy Tease would wear... and my go-to M&S wasn't going to swing it this time.

I was tempted to pop into Ann Summers as I passed the window filled with lingerie, but knew that Martin would have questions if I produced underwear so overtly sexy. I stopped, apologising to the lady who bumped into me. Maybe that was the problem... maybe if I spiced things up a bit, Martin would show renewed interest in me in bed... but I couldn't face another humiliation, I thought miserably, walking past to make my way to Monsoon and

River Island – shops I'd bought many clothes from in my younger years.

I wished I had Hayley with me, shopping with her was always so much fun, and even though neither of us had figures that we were exactly happy about, we always had a laugh trying on clothes. Nonetheless, once I'd picked out a few dresses to try on in Monsoon, I began to enjoy myself, and by the time I'd been to River Island and H&M, I was carrying three bags containing, respectively, a black silk embroidered Kaftan dress, a puff sleeve wrap midi in an animal print, and a gorgeous black satin halterneck. Mission accomplished, I thought happily as I made my way to the car, deciding that I'd wear the black halterneck to Lauren and Paul's barbeque the following day. Maybe my husband would be driven crazy with desire at how gorgeous I looked.

21

The girls were full of compliments about my dress as I twirled for them while the men gathered around the barbeque offering Paul advice on how to cook the chicken kebabs.

'What's brought this on, Abs?' Jen gave me one of her knowing looks that made me feel she was inside my head.

'Nothing, I just thought my wardrobe needed a bit of a facelift.'

'You should have called me, I'd have come with you,' said Hayles.

'And me, I could do with some new clothes.' Claire tugged at her tiered skirt, pulling a face.

'It was a spur of the moment thing.' I pushed a tendril of hair behind my ear, hoping my attempt at an updo would last – it should do, I'd used about half a can of hairspray.

Jenna's eyes skimmed over me, and I thought I detected a slight jealousy in them.

I stood up a little straighter, feeling confident as I covertly studied her own outfit. A garish, to my mind, silver top, in some kind of satin fabric, clung to her large breasts, showing the bumpy lace of her bra beneath it, her black skirt was short, and her heels high.

A burst of laugher from the men distracted me and I watched Jenna's scarlet, grinning mouth, as she turned to look at them. Following her gaze, my eyes rested on Martin for a moment, as his friends clapped him on the back and laughed at something he was saying.

He always seemed to come alive at our get-togethers – like the Martin I'd first known. I suppose I'd changed him over the years.

About to smile back at him, I realised that he was looking at Jenna, and his unguarded expression wrenched my insides painfully. Now I was the jealous one.

As if sensing my gaze, Martin's eyes flicked towards me, and he gave me an uncertain smile, before turning his attention back to the cluster of men around the barbeque.

I'd seen that wistful look in his eyes before, but he'd catch me looking at him and he'd give me a little smile and squeeze my hand. 'It's alright,' he was telling me silently, 'I'm glad I chose you...' And I knew that he was, after all, he could never regret not ending up with someone like tarty, loud, Jen, could he...

'Right, while the menfolk are occupied, we have plans to make.' Jen pulled us into a huddle. 'Important information has come to our attention courtesy of Fi's and Claire's surveillance of our subject.'

'We can't talk about it here.' Em looked around awkwardly. 'Can't we meet in the week?'

'No time. We're having a weekend away next weekend – not optional.'

'Why? What's happened?' Lauren looked worried as she glanced in Paul's direction.

'They're moving to Spain in three weeks.'

Claire's statement dropped like a bombshell and we stood there silently absorbing its impact. Correction – everyone else stood there absorbing its impact, I just stood there, already au fait with the news. I should have guessed she'd find out about it – all it took was to walk into Propshop, and chatty little Becca would have started talking.

'So what's this weekend got to do with it?' Emma asked the question for us all.

'They're going down to visit her parents in the New Forest for the weekend,' Fi informed us. 'He's not looking forward to it, is dreading it, in fact. Apparently, they live in the middle of nowhere with only one pub for him to escape to.'

I stared from Fi to Claire. 'How on earth did you find all that out?' *Would I have to face him? Was this it? Was Jen sending me to him as bait this coming weekend?*

'I went into Propshop and literally couldn't stop the girl talking – if I'd stayed there any longer, she'd have told me the titles of their favourite films and what the daughter's favourite cuddly toy was. She was totally caught up in the excitement of their big move and how they were going even though they hadn't sold the house yet.'

I expressed admiration, along with everyone else, while a little monologue played out in my head. *Becca, she's talking about Becca, and you know what some of their favourite films are, don't you, Abigail? You saw them on the shelf in their lounge while you were pretending to be somebody else. And the daughter's favourite cuddly toy? Probably that cute little teddy bear sitting on her bed. Why don't you tell them what cereal they like to have for breakfast? Or what colour his slippers are? Don't forget the romance book she was reading – tell them about that.*

'And I followed him to his local drinking hole and shamelessly eavesdropped – not difficult, he's got a huge gob on him.'

A feeling something like jealousy infused me for a moment – there'd been me waiting for him to notice me on a dating app and Fi had just followed him to a pub and sat right next to him. *But you sniffed his shirts, Abs... in his bedroom...* The thought suddenly made me feel ill.

'How do we know it's him?' I asked the question without thinking, surprised by the looks I received. *And you stole his photos and hid them in your underwear drawer...*

'What are you talking about, Abs?'

'I just– I mean– could you have got it wrong, Laur? It's just that, well, we were all pretty drunk that night and I thought that maybe, you know, maybe it was someone else? Someone else that did that to you and you muddled up the faces on the app?' I could feel my cheeks burning as they all stared at me.

I willed Lauren to nod, to say that, yes, maybe she'd made a mistake. I would be off the hook and we could stop all this nonsense. I started to panic – I couldn't do it – I couldn't be the femme fatale hooking up with him, not if she'd got the right man. But how could I tell them that without looking like a coward?

'I didn't get it wrong, I didn't muddle him up with anyone.' Lauren was angry with me, I could tell. 'You want to me to prove it?' she hissed.

'Not now, babes.' Jenna's voice suddenly changed to bright and cheery. 'Abs, you look fabulous in that dress. Don't you think so, Adrian? Doesn't she look ravishing?'

Adrian looked embarrassed as he joined us. 'Er, yes, lovely. Claire, what was the name of that villa we stayed at in France last year? I was telling Craig about it.'

'Why does Craig want to know about a villa in France?' Emma shot a glare towards Craig, throwing the rest of her wine back, as Adrian shrugged helplessly at Claire.

'I'm going to check on the barbeque.' Lauren gave me a sniffy look and flounced off, there was no other word for it.

'I could do with another glass of wine, darling.' Claire held out her glass to her husband, who was looking after Lauren in a slightly bewildered manner, whispering, 'Villa Du Vin, I think.'

Adrian scuttled off, relieved to escape the complicated world of women.

'I bet he's got some chick he wants to take away.'

'Who? Adrian?' Claire doubled over at her own humour.

'You are separated, Em, you can't have it both ways,' said Fi, reasonably.

'You think I want him?' Em said bitterly. 'Men are all the same, aren't they? Fickle bastards.'

'Right, forget all that, listen carefully, we need to announce that we're having a girls' weekend away this weekend. We can use Fi's birthday as the reason.'

'Christ, Jen, I'm not forty-eight for another six weeks, don't speed it up, I feel old enough as it is.'

'It's the best reason we've got, otherwise those of you with husbands will have them wondering why we're going away so soon after our last weekend away. It's not up for debate, ladies, we're doing it. This is it, this is our revenge plan and it's happening in one week, so you'd better start mentioning it today to get the ball rolling, and if you had any plans, cancel them.' She turned to look directly at me. 'And, Abs, whatever's going on in your empty little head, ideas about it not being him, you can forget it. It is him, and you're doing it, no argument.'

I flushed. 'But—'

22

Girls & Boys
(I Can't Help) Falling In Love With You

'Sausages are ready, chicken's getting cold.' Paul's shout got us moving and we headed for the table where Lauren had laid out plates and cutlery, together with bowls of salad, foil-wrapped jacket potatoes, roasted peppers, and baskets of bread rolls.

'Here's to Paul and Lauren,' a slightly drunk Emma toasted after we'd eaten, lifting up her glass. 'Lauren's a lucky girl. A great barbeque, thanks to Paul's expertise.'

'And my guidance, otherwise the sausages would have been burnt offerings.' Danny nudged Paul's arm.

'It was a delicious pasta salad, Laur,' I proffered, giving her an anxious look. I couldn't bear for her to be angry with me. 'And those roasted peppers were delicious.' I was rewarded with a lukewarm smile.

'So... did anyone mention my birthday weekend away?' Fi had obviously decided to get the ball rolling.

'Your birthday's not for ages.'

'Since when did you ever remember my birthday, Danny dear? Certainly not while we were married.'

'God, we're all getting older, beats me why you want to acknowledge it with a weekend away. You didn't mention it, Abs, when did you girls decide this?'

I looked at Jen anxiously, and then back at Martin. 'Spur of the moment decision, Jen thought of it.'

Everyone looked at Jen as she took a slow drink from her glass, her neck stretched back alluringly. I looked around the table. How did she do it? All the men were mesmerised. *Including my husband.* The women too.

'Fi's always wanted to see the New Forest ponies, so we thought we'd indulge her.' She put her glass down as I admired her sangfroid.

'Where are you staying?' Adrian leant forward interestedly. 'Claire and I spent our first weekend together in Lymington. Remember that? We rented a cottage down by the quay, had those marvellous mussels in that little restaurant. I was your rebound fellow after you were dumped and I was determined to impress you.'

'I was not dumped, Adrian, I don't know why you persist in saying that. I dumped him.' Claire's face was red as she gulped her wine.

'Good for you.' Jenna applauded, clapping noisily. 'Was he the one who got obsessed with you and stalked you for a bit? D'you reckon he's still after you?'

'If he is, he'd never recognise me these days, I'm double the size I was all those years ago, twice as old, and he wouldn't know my married name, so I think I'm safe.' Claire laughed, sounding a little unsure, and I wondered what exactly had happened that she didn't talk about.

'He was too young for you, he couldn't handle you. You needed a real man.' Adrian nodded complacently. 'And I still say he dumped you.' He ducked as Claire's hand shot out, missing him completely.

Shane laughed. 'Join the club, mate. I was Jen's rebound when she was dumped because someone told porky pies about her, or so she says. No social media in those days, just the good old rumour mill. Still, it did me a favour — I got the hot chick, didn't I? And all I had to do was buy her a cheap glass of wine to make her mine, if you get my drift.' He sniggered dirtily as he winked at Jen.

In the awkward silence, we all searched for something to say.

A look of hurt flashed across Jen's face and then she grinned. 'Well, I thought, if someone's going to spread lies about me, I might as well live up to them.'

I glanced at Martin as he shifted in his chair and cleared his throat to speak, avoiding my eyes.

'So, er, where are you all staying?'

Hayley smiled at him in relief and nodded as she looked at Jen for guidance.

'It's a surprise, we can't talk about it in front of Fi.'

'I do love a surprise.' Fi picked up her vape as Lauren took out her cigarettes.

'Since when did you love ponies?' Danny was still looking at his ex-wife in surprise.

'There's a lot you don't know about me, Dan. I always wanted a pony when I was growing up.'

'You lived in a flat in Streatham, where the hell did you think you were going to keep a pony – on the balcony?'

'A girl can dream.' Fi was calm and I was impressed by her ability to make up a story on the hop.

'That was when that girl died, wasn't it, when we got together?' Shane looked a little hazily over at Jenna. 'She fell off a balcony, didn't she? Wasn't she some long lost relative, or something?'

'On the estate,' Martin added, nodding. 'She went to my school. She was Abigail's friend.'

All eyes turned to me, expecting me to contribute.

'She was my best friend,' I said softly. 'But I don't like to talk about it.'

'No wonder. Abs was there at the time. Quite the hero, weren't you?'

'Didn't you save her little brother?' Claire lit a cigarette, ignoring Adrian's disapproving glance.

'They should tear that block down, there was another accident a couple of years after that, a little boy, I think. And a woman jumped from one of the balconies just after that.' Adrian gave Claire another look, which she ignored.

'From one of the top floor balconies, wasn't it? Wouldn't fancy living somewhere so high up myself.'

'That's why Abs was so brave. She's terrified of heights, nothing would have got her out on that balcony, normally, would it?' Martin patted my shoulder – the first sign of affection he'd shown me all day.

'She was called something foreign-sounding...' Adrian murmured to no one in particular, his eyes still on Claire.

'What was his name? Little Matty, I think they called him in the newspaper.' Claire turned her back on her husband, downing her wine and holding her glass out for a refill.

'Claudia... Claudia Bandini? Bondini? No, Baraldi, that was it.' Adrian sat back, pleased at his recall.

'She'd been going to meet me to tell me something important.'

Fi nodded at Jenna disinterestedly. 'Can I pinch a ciggie, Claire?'

'Of course you can, here.' Claire passed her packet of cigarettes across to Fi, blowing smoke in Adrian's direction, causing him to frown.

'They said she gave her kids their tea, walked out to the balcony and jumped right off.'

'This wine's delicious, did you get it from your local offie?'

That's awful.'

'What, the wine?'

'Cut it out, Craig.'

'I suppose I'll never know what it was...' Jen's glass had tilted, and her wine was dripping onto the table. 'I always wondered...'

Lauren took Jen's glass from her. 'Careful, babe.'

'Yeah, don't waste it, it cost me a fortune.' Danny laughed loudly, as Fi shot him an irritated look.

'For God's sake, Danny, we all know you only go in there because you fancy the girl who works there.'

'Natalie? My cousin was in her class, she called her Nats, I think.'

'Wasn't he called Robin? Or Robbie?'

'The little boy who died?'

'Robbie Trenton, I knew his brother, he never got over it.'

'Didn't they have to put him in hospital for a while? He kept saying it wasn't an accident, or something? Then they moved abroad. That's what I heard anyway.'

'Lauren does love her gossip.' Paul put his arm around Lauren, laughing. 'She believes everything she reads in the paper, don't you, love? You women are so gullible.'

'Is that what we are? Gullible? Good to know.' Emma threw back the rest of her wine.

'Now you've asked for it.' Adrian laughed loudly. 'Never tell women they're gullible, take it from me, Paul.'

'You're taking your life in your hands. Don't go there, mate.' Danny grinned at Paul.

'Didn't you have the same last name? How did that work then?' Shane glanced in Jenna's direction, as she shrugged, draining her glass.

'How did you save him?'

I realised that Adrian was addressing me and I gulped my wine in embarrassment. 'I just grabbed him, that's all.'

'You're being modest, Abs.' Hayley patted my arm. 'She grabbed him by the neck just before he went over the side. I remember my mum telling me. You wouldn't let go, his mum had to prise your hands off where you were holding onto him so tightly.'

'Cheers to Abs.' Danny sloppily topped up our glasses.

'But where was the mother?' Paul asked, looking confused as he tried to keep up.

'She'd left him there on his own, they said she was a— you know...' Martin looked around, nodding knowingly.

'That was just a terrible rumour,' Emma said.

'Not a rumour, she was out on the job, that's what I heard. Is there any more wine?' Jen held out her glass to Martin, who picked up a bottle. 'But she had you there to comfort her, didn't she, Marty? So sweet.' Jen blew a drunken kiss at me, or it might have been at Martin.

'Who? The prostitute?' Ross looked at Martin in astonishment.

'You dirty old goat, you can only have been a teenager.' Danny slapped Martin on the back, making him spill the wine as he topped up Jenna's glass.

'Not her, lovely little Abigail.' Jen was slurring her words. 'Poor little Abigail lost her best friend and kind Marty rushed to her comfort, didn't he, Abs?' She blew another kiss in my direction, her eyes hooded. 'My lucky little Abigail.'

'My gain, cheers Marty.' Shane cackled.

'Abs was so cut up, her parents were going to sell up and move away, weren't they, Abs?'

I nodded at Martin, willing him not to dredge up further pain from the past.

'Until her mum died, and her dad decided a move to a new area was too much for her to cope with.'

'Please, Martin,' I whispered.

'Oh God, that's awful, Abs, I never realised.' Claire gave me a look of gut-wrenching sympathy. 'What happened?'

'She was up a ladder, cleaning out the gutters–'

'I can't talk about it,' I said to no one in particular.

'Wasn't there a sister?' Claire rushed to my aid, and I flashed her a grateful smile.

'Half-sister, I believe.'

'She lived with her mum. Her dad left them for his new family.'

'Those poor children, they got taken into care. There was no dad.'

'That's so sad.'

'They moved away, didn't they? The family?'

My mind had wandered, memories of my best friend flooding my head. I'd been devastated to lose her in such a way. I could still picture her perched on the top of the balcony wall, talking to me in her earnest manner. And then she was gone, her little brother screaming as he leant precariously over the edge, my hands reaching for him, their mum running out and shouting. I shuddered, pulling myself back to the present, and looked around. I was lucky, I reminded myself, thinking in surprise how apt Jenna's nickname of lucky Abigail was. I'd lost my childhood friend, but had gained so many wonderful new ones. And Martin's mum had turned out to be a wonderful mother-in-law, not quite a replacement for my own mum, but good enough, until she'd sadly passed away two years earlier.

Someone turned up the music, Shane produced a bottle of tequila, and the mood lifted as we proceeded to down shots, drunkenly singing along to Blur and laughing at Shane's impression of Damon Albarn, the late afternoon soon becoming evening. Lauren switched on the fairy lights strung up around the patio, and Hayley and I ferried the dirty plates and leftovers to the kitchen.

I looked out of the window as Paul took Lauren's hand, pulling her close and dancing with her to UB40.

'They look like the perfect couple,' breathed Hayley, joining me at the window.

We left the kitchen, and I walked over to Martin, standing close to him as we watched Adrian and Claire join them. Paul and Lauren looked so happy and I tried to equate that with their extra-marital activities. I felt like all the unspoken rules were being turned on their head – be faithful to each other, don't cheat, don't keep secrets...

23

She's The One
Saturday Night

'Come on, Marty, dance with your beautiful wife,' called out a pissed Ross as he pulled Hayley into his arms.

'Yes, go on, Marty, she looks so delectable, doesn't she? Good enough to eat.' Jen's teasing voice made Martin bristle. I could feel him stiffening beside me.

'We don't have to,' I murmured hurriedly.

'I need to pee.' He headed off to the house and I was left standing awkwardly, pasting a smile on my face.

'Come on, Abs, I fancy a dance.' Paul grabbed my arm as Lauren began slow-dancing with Danny, much to Fi's amusement – she'd always said he had two left feet and she wasn't wrong – his apology as he stepped on Lauren's foot making us all grin.

Paul pulled me closer, and not sure what to do with my arms, I reached up and held his upper arms a little awkwardly, grateful that he'd asked me to dance to spare my embarrassment at Martin's behaviour.

'Relax, Abs, I don't bite.' His breath was hot on my face and I turned away slightly, catching sight of Jenna walking into the house. I always felt sorry for her in these situations, sure that she put on a brave front, and I thought I should go and find her.

'I need to go.'

'Not yet, the song's only halfway through.' Paul's grip on me tightened, his mouth close to my neck as he moved me away from the lights, his hands sliding down to casually rest on my bottom.

I froze, not sure what to do. Maybe it was unintentional, I reassured myself, glancing over at the kitchen window to see Martin and Jenna deep in conversation.

'I've always fancied you, did you know that?' His fingers squeezed the flesh of my buttocks. *OK, not unintentional then...*

Robbie finished singing She's The One and I extricated myself with relief, laughing loudly so that the others looked in our direction. 'That's enough dancing for me, thanks, Paul, I think I need some wine.'

'And you can get your hands off my wife, Paul, you old dog.' Martin laughed to show that he was joking, seeming to swoop from the house and towards me in one second, his hands pulling me into the lighted patio area. 'Come on, Abs, let's show them how it's done.'

Surprised, I let him twirl me around, my eyes catching sight of Jenna watching unsmilingly from the kitchen window. 'I need to go and see if Jen's alright.'

'She's fine, we're dancing, don't spoil it.'

I rolled my eyes at Emma, expecting her to grin, but her face was stony and I felt confusion crowding in, as if I'd missed something. *Of course, Paul... me dancing with Paul...* After everything that had happened between him and Lauren, I should never have let him dance with me, it was insensitive. I always seemed to get it all wrong, I thought miserably, as Martin suddenly released his grip on me.

'Hayley, come and dance with me.' Martin's exuberance surprised me, but Hayley acquiesced happily as Whigfield began to blast from the speakers, and as some of the others joined them, I took the opportunity to go and find Jenna.

'Are you OK, Jen?' She was still standing at the kitchen window, watching everyone.

'Me? I'm fine, always am. Did I tell you I went to Baxter's Monday night? He kind of reminded me of Marty, didn't you think? I think I'll go and dance with one of those handsome men out there now. But not your Martin, he looks like he's got his hands full. Has Hayley put on more weight, d'you think?' She left, not waiting for my reply.

Hayley looked the same as she always did to me, I decided. No, that was just Jenna being mean, lashing out because she felt left out of the whole couple thing. I wished she'd meet a decent man... maybe whoever she had a drink with on Monday night would turn into something... The man she'd had a drink with at Baxter's... who had reminded her of Martin... of course... I'd thought the same thing when I'd looked at his photo. What had he called himself? Governor? The Governor? I was certain, suddenly, that Jenna had been letting me know that she knew I'd been into the apps, which meant... Oh God, which meant she knew I'd hearted Night Monster... and worse than that, I'd suggested that he hadn't been Lauren's attacker... and judging by Jenna's uncanny ability to get inside my head, she probably guessed that he held some kind of fascination for me...

24

'You made quite a spectacle of yourself this evening.' Martin said as we sat in the back of the cab on our way home.

'What? No, I– Do you mean Paul? He was drunk,' I said, hurt at his comment as I dragged my mind from my musings about Jenna's interference in the dating apps.

'You get dressed up like the dog's dinner, what do you expect?'

'A dog's dinner,' I said, without thinking, feeling hurt.

'The dog's dinner, a dog's dinner. What's the bloody difference? Do you always have to be so pedantic? Anal Abs, that's what they call you, isn't it?'

'Who? Who calls me that, Martin?'

'Look, all I'm saying is, you know what he's like. I thought you'd have been a bit more sensitive for Lauren's sake, not encouraging him to paw all over you.'

'I wasn't– I just wanted to look nice,' I said miserably, feeling as if my whole life was beginning to tilt horribly off-balance.

'It just doesn't suit you, getting all tarted up.

'Well what about Jenna? What about the way she was dressed?' Even as I spoke, I wondered about the wisdom of my words.

'That's Jenna, that's just how she is. It's how she's always been.'

'And you should know, shouldn't you?' The booze was making me dangerously combative, and I panicked, trying to soothe things. 'Please don't let's argue.'

'You're the one who's arguing, Abs. At least Jenna wasn't all over Paul. And talking of Jenna, all that stuff about her, the stories about her...'

'Marty, please...' I touched his arm. 'Let's not fight.'

He sighed. 'No, let's not. This is us, mate.'

It took me a moment to realise that he was speaking to the cab driver, who glanced sympathetically at me in his rearview mirror as he pulled up outside our house.

I walked to the front door and fumbled for my key as Martin paid the driver, my mind half on his cruel comments and half on what to do about Jenna's access to my profiles in the apps.

'Sorry for bringing that up about your mum's accident, I got caught up in all the talk, it was wrong of me.'

'It's fine,' I said, realising that Martin was trying to make amends in his own way. 'I just prefer not to rake up painful memories, that's all.'

'I know, I'm sorry. I'm tired, I think I'll head straight up.' Martin yawned loudly as he locked the front door behind us. 'You coming?'

'In a minute, I'll catch you up. I just need to get some bits out of the freezer for tomorrow,' I improvised hurriedly at his questioning look. All I had to do was stop her accessing the apps. Why hadn't I thought of that?

'Have we got people coming for lunch then?'

'No, I just thought I'd do us a roast.'

'Sounds good.'

I could simply change the passwords and Jenna wouldn't be able to access them as me anymore. It was a small act of rebellion, but at least I'd be able to control my own narrative. The thought gave me anxiety, a suspicion that Jenna would find my act annoying, but she had told me that I needed to get familiar with them so that I looked like I knew what I was doing. Why shouldn't I just take control? She couldn't stop me, could she?

I rummaged in the freezer, hoping I'd got a joint of something in there, groaning inwardly at the idea of having to do a whole roast dinner for the two of us thanks to my feeble excuse. Pulling out a joint of beef triumphantly, I put it in a dish and into the fridge, checking that I had potatoes and vegetables. I tiptoed up the stairs, changed into my nightie and, after checking that Martin was asleep, quietly went back downstairs. Pouring two glasses of water for us, I stood them on the counter and quickly accessed the first app.

I found the change password section and clicked on it, typing in a new password twice and hitting enter. Easy peasy. About to close the app and open the next one, I frowned, reading the message instructing me to click on the link in the e-mail that had been sent to me. E-mail? To where? Oh no, my shoulders sank – to the e-mail address Jenna had set up for me, which she had conveniently omitted to give me the password for.

She'd done it deliberately, I was sure of it, to keep control over me and of what was said in the apps. And now she'd know I'd tried to change the password... Well, I squared my shoulders defiantly, I'd just ask her for the e-mail password on Monday evening when we all got together at Emma's to plan our weekend in the New Forest. She could hardly say no, she didn't own me, did she? I was Tipsy Tease, not Jenna, and I was perfectly capable of handling myself on dating apps.

I was about to exit the app when it made a little whooping noise. *Are you in bed yet? I'm thinking about you. When can we hook up?*

It was the same person from Wednesday night – Gavin72.

I know you're there. I can't stop thinking about you.

My fear mingled with a teeny bit of pride – pride that a strange man couldn't stop thinking about me – and I replied with a recklessness formed from an afternoon and evening's drinking and a need to salve my wounds from Martin's comments.

I can't stop thinking about you either. Shocked at what I'd just sent, I closed the app in a panic, breathing heavily. Stepping to the bottom of the stairs, I listened for any sounds of movement but all was quiet. I tiptoed back into the kitchen and opened up Frisky – just a quick check to see if he'd hearted me back, and then I'd go to bed.

He'd hearted me. I double-checked that it was him – it was. Night Monster liked me, he found me attractive. And he'd sent me a message... I reached a hand out to the counter to steady myself as I read it again.

Hi, I'm tempted badly... Want to meet you in the flesh. When?

It was exactly what Jen had wanted to happen, but it was sick. What was wrong with me? I reminded myself of how adamant Lauren had been earlier. He was her attacker. How could I be drawn to him even though I knew I should have nothing to do with this man, ever?

The toilet flushed upstairs and I closed the app in a fluster, switching off the light and grabbing the glasses of water.

'Abs? Are you down there?' Martin's voice was half asleep.

'Coming, I forgot our water.' I rushed up the stairs, my heart hammering in my chest, to find Martin curled up under the duvet and already well on his way back to dreamland. I slipped in beside him, pulling the duvet up and lying rigidly, flat on my back, my eyes staring up at the ceiling in the dark room, seeing not the vague shape of the lightshade but *his* face...

He wanted to meet me in the flesh... Why, oh, why, did I have to find him so attractive? My life was safe, and free from risks, I'd be crazy to upset things.

I shouldn't have hearted him, all I'd done was complicate things, and unless Lauren could be convinced that she'd got the wrong man – which was becoming more and more unlikely – I was to be paraded in front of him to lure him into some kind of trap. I wanted desperately to be able to put the clock back to before we'd gone to Eynsford, when life had been fine and uncomplicated.

25

Fastlove, Pt. 1

There was a feeling of expectancy on Monday evening when we gathered at Emma's, as if we were finally taking some solid action after all the talk of revenge. I felt conflicted, I wanted Lauren to find some closure, of course I did, and I was happy for the monster who'd hurt her to suffer, but I still harboured doubts, and I was trying to muster up the courage to say something, all the time aware of how I'd upset Lauren on Saturday when I'd questioned her certainty, when Jen put me on the spot.

'Abs has some news for us, don't you, Abs?'

'What?'

'Abs has made contact with Night Monster and he's taken the bait. Tell us all about it, Abs, don't be shy.'

'Nice one, Abs. What did you say to him?'

'Nothing, I just hearted him.' My whole face felt like it was on fire as they all looked at me waiting for me to give them the details.

'And?' Claire made a rolling motion with her hand. 'There must be more to it than that.'

'He hearted me back.' I could see that Jenna was becoming impatient, but the whole thing felt embarrassing... *and what if it wasn't him?*

'Get on with it, Abs, we've got a lot to cover tonight. Oh, I'll do it.' Jenna whipped out her phone and tapped on it. 'Here we go... *Hi, I'm tempted badly... Want to meet you in the flesh. When?*'

'Abigail...' Fi looked at me with a mix of pride and surprise. 'I never knew you had it in you.'

'What? No, that wasn't me, that was him.'

'Well don't look so upset about it, this is perfect, it's exactly what we wanted isn't it?'

'Emma's right, you've got him interested, now we just have to reel him in. And well done for taking the initiative, Abs.'

I looked at Jenna awkwardly, knowing she'd been watching my every move anyway. 'I thought it was time,' I said softly, 'but it still feels a bit...'

'A bit what?' Lauren gave me a funny look. 'Listen, Abs, if you're still harbouring any thoughts about me getting it wrong, think again. I wouldn't have been able to prove it myself, but thanks to Jen's quick thinking on the night we have proof.'

Jen cleared her throat. 'You need to see this. I didn't just screenshot his mugshot that night, I also saved images of the chat Lauren had with him.' She held her phone out to me and I took it, staring at the words on the screen, at his photo and profile name and, in that instant, I knew that there was no doubt and no backing out. I looked at Lauren miserably.

'I'm sorry for doubting you, Laur.' I could feel my eyes welling up.

'Hey, it's alright, come here.' Lauren perched on the arm of my chair and hugged me. 'You just didn't want us to make a mistake, but now you know.'

'It's just the way you are, Abs, you're a big softie, we all know that. And you were right to be concerned and to want us to be sure. Wasn't she, everyone?' Hayley gave me a reassuring smile, as everyone murmured agreement.

'Right, now that we've cleared that up let's get refills and finalise plans. And, Em, much as I love George, I think we need to turn the music off and concentrate.' Jen clapped her hands like a teacher and we all got up to do her bidding as she pulled me aside, whispering, 'Don't try and change the passwords, Abs, there's a good girl.'

I blushed, embarrassed, as I also felt a fury inside myself, anger at my stupidity and my naivety, at my easy betrayal of one of my dearest friends, but most of all at him... I'd wanted to believe him innocent of the horrific attack on Lauren because... Because I'd been attracted to him? Because I didn't want him to be the man I would bait into an encounter which would end badly? Now, instead of fury it was bile rising in me and I rushed up the stairs to the bathroom.

I stared at my mottled reflection in disgust, splashing some water on my face to calm my angry cheeks, and transferred all my anger onto him. I would do whatever Jenna wanted me to do, no matter how risky it was. I would find a way to deal with it. 'You, Abigail Hawthorn, can do whatever needs to be done. You're strong, determined, and you can take control, you'll be fine, you always are. You're lucky Abigail.' Smiling grimly at Jenna's nickname for me, and feeling better after my pep talk, I returned downstairs.

'Sorry, I needed the loo.' I took the remaining seat at the dining table. 'What's our next move?' I looked directly at Jen, receiving an approving nod.

'You're going to reply to his message, saying that you'd love to have hooked up this weekend but you'll be away in the New Forest. Actually, make it even more irresistible for him... type this: I'm tempted more than you know... Meeting in the flesh sounds perfect. Wish it could be this weekend but I'm away in the New Forest on my own with no one to enjoy it with...'

I typed the message and sent it, wondering if it would do the trick. 'What next?'

'Next we decide where to stay,' said Claire.

'We know that he's staying at the in-laws' farmhouse just outside a village called Frogham, thanks to Fi's eavesdropping.'

Fi preened. 'Oh God, I forgot about this. We know his name, don't we, Claire? It's Matthew, I picked it up at the pub.'

'Matthew, the sick bastard who enjoys beating up women after he's had his way with them,' added Claire, viciously. 'I should go round to his house right now and smash his head in.'

I shifted uncomfortably as Jen's shoulders stiffened imperceptibly, and she shot me a quizzical look. *Did she know what I'd done? Did she know that I'd been to his house?*

'Good to know, ladies, well done. And, Claire, hold onto that anger, we'll find a use for it soon enough, don't you worry. Now, we have a few options but I think we should stay here, in fact, I've taken the liberty of putting a hold on it.' Jenna picked up her phone, sending us all the link, and we studied the cottage, situated in somewhere called Blissford, five minutes' drive away from Frogham.

'Good location.'

'I love the name of the village.'

'It's quite big, four bedrooms, that's perfect, oh wait, one of them's got bunk beds though.'

'Oh my God, it's got a hot tub on the deck.'

'We're not there for fun, ladies, remember.'

'So what's the plan?'

'Abs arranges to meet him at the pub with the promise of a hookup. He'll probably try to follow his usual routine – flip her over the car seat, fuck her senseless and then beat the living daylights out of her when he's done.'

We all stared at Jenna, aghast at her coarse words.

'Jen, what kind of talk is that?' Claire remonstrated. 'Think of Lauren's feelings, won't you?'

And mine, I wanted to cry out.

'She's right, though,' Lauren spoke up. 'That's probably his modus operandi, I should know after all.'

'But how do we know he'll even agree to meet me? How do we know he'll go to the pub? And even if he does both of those things, what then?' I looked at Jenna in horror. 'You're not suggesting that I actually have sex with him in his car?' He wouldn't want that, not once he saw me, I knew. I couldn't kid myself. But it was the last thing I wanted with him either, not now.

The room fell quiet as we all looked at Jenna.

'Absolutely not.' Claire was firm. 'That is not happening, Jenna. Using Abs as bait is one thing, but she is not being forced to have sex with a stranger in his car, especially not when the monster would beat her up afterwards.'

'Relax, I wasn't suggesting that for a moment.' Jenna looked at me strangely and gave me a smile which I supposed was meant to be reassuring but which looked a little cruel to my mind.

If I didn't know better, I'd think she was enjoying herself.

'Well?'

'What then?'

'Abs meets him at the pub, and then?'

'The hot tub.' Jenna grinned. 'The bloody hot tub, ladies.'

We all exchanged confused looks.

'What man could resist a woman hooking up with him and suggesting they go to her cottage, which has a hot tub?'

It was brilliant, we all agreed.

'But, so... assuming I can get him to agree to a drink in the pub and all that, that's if he even sends me any more messages, then... what? I drive him to the cottage? He drives me? What if he stops on the way? I don't know, Jen, there are so many ifs and buts...' *It would never work, he'd take one look at me and our plan would fail.* 'It's my photo that he likes, he'd never want me, not the real me.

I'm not like you, Jen.' I appealed to her ego. 'Men don't fancy me, they don't even notice me.'

'Well, that's not true, Martin fancied you, didn't he?'

Was it my imagination or had Jen used the past tense deliberately?

'Paul seemed to be quite taken with you on Saturday.' Fi's eyes widened as she realised her faux pas.

'He was drunk.' Em frowned at Fi as Lauren shot me an unfriendly look.

Mortified, I looked pleadingly at Jen.

'Relax, Abs, and trust me, alright? There are loads of ways to make this work – we have a few days for you to chat to him some more, and even if he hasn't taken the bait by the time we reach the weekend, then we do the whole location match thing, like Lauren did. You'll just send out an alert that you're looking for a hookup in the area. I mean, honestly, what are the odds that there are any blokes in deepest darkest Frogham and Blissford, other than him, who are looking to hook up at that moment? It's foolproof. We've got him.'

She looked directly at me. 'We have to get him, Abs, for Lauren's sake, and it's all on you. Don't let us down. Which reminds me, I'm waiting for my new bank cards. Have you got your credit card handy? I need to finalise the booking, if we're all agreed?' She held her hand out towards me expectantly.

Feeling awkward under everyone's gaze, I pulled my purse from my bag and handed Jenna my card.

'And what do we do to him once we've got him? It's time to be specific, Jen. He'll have seen Abs – what about the rest of us? Will he see us?'

'We'll wear masks. Here's what I've got so far...'

We listened intently as Jenna outlined her plan, throwing in a few questions but overall liking the sound of it. As a revenge plan it was pretty good – and the mask idea was great, everyone agreed, he wouldn't see anyone's faces.

Apart from mine... he'd see my face in close-up the moment I walked into the pub...

26

I checked the Frisky app with apprehension the next night, once Martin was asleep, but there was no reply from *him* and I began to panic. Jenna had been pretty clear about what had to happen, and we only had a few more days to reel him in.

'Jen,' I said into the phone the next morning. 'He hasn't replied. What should I do?'

'We'll give it today, no need to sound too keen. Men like him like to do the chasing, trust me.'

'And if he doesn't?'

'I'll handle it.'

'But I can—'

'I said I'll handle it, Abs. From now on I'll deal with him, not you. You don't always just get to click your fingers and give a man that cute little Abigail smile and have him come running, you know. That might have worked with Martin but that was a one off.' She rang off, dismissing me abruptly.

I sighed heavily. Martin? Really? Sometimes Jenna could be quite ridiculous – that had been years ago, long before we'd met and become friends. She and Martin had supposedly had a 'thing' before he and I started going out together. And anyway, she'd got together with Shane the minute Martin had broken up with her, and, aside from being good-looking, Shane had the added attraction of a bad boy reputation, which he'd retained for quite a few years into their marriage. In a moment of drunken confidence, when we'd cemented our adult friendship, Jen had told us that both she and Shane had been in trouble with the police thanks to his shady dealings. She hadn't gone into details but had made it clear that she had a long-standing fear of the police. That revelation had just made me feel more in awe of her.

My mind drifted back to the first, and only, time I saw Jenna before we met in our twenties, certain that she had no recollection of it. My friend Natalie had taken me with her to her school disco, where I'd lurked in the corner with the other wallflowers, watching the couples jealously as they laughed and danced together. I was mesmerised by her – she was the centre of attention, she was sexy, she was a good dancer, and she was with a boy who took my breath away... I wanted to be like her. I wanted to *be* her...

The boy was Martin, of course, and I felt myself smiling as I remembered him bumping into me, sweaty from the dancefloor – my drink spilling down my dress – and his embarrassed apology. Natalie had introduced me proudly, 'This is Abigail, my best friend.'

Shy and tongue-tied, I was sure he'd forgotten all about me the minute he'd returned to the dancefloor and Jenna, but after Natalie's death, and all the nasty gossip, he'd turned up with flowers...

He had been, along with gorgeous-looking, steady and kind, sweet and fun and, as it turned out, extremely good in bed, certainly by my inexperienced standards. He was way out of my league, I'd always known that. I'd see the surprise on people's faces sometimes when he'd say, 'This is my wife,' as if they'd expected better...

I could still picture the shock on Martin's face when he'd met 'my friend Jenna' all those years later, at our first barbeque – it had given us all such a laugh and there'd been quite a lot of teasing all round. I smiled at the memory as I pegged the washing on the line, admitting to myself that I'd secretly felt quite thrilled that Martin had chosen me over sexy Jenna...

That brought my thoughts back to our current situation and Jenna's hijacking of my profile on the dating app. Did I mind really? No. To be honest, I was happy to leave the reeling in to her, the whole thing was leaving a bad taste in my mouth, especially now that I knew it was all true about *him*... I'd gone over and over Jen's revenge plan in my head – *our* revenge plan – and had begun to believe that I could actually carry it off.

Now that there was no way to avoid it, I was fully prepared to take the action required.

27

Mambo No. 5

Jenna had asked me to drive us down to our cottage on Friday afternoon, and we'd picked up Hayley and Claire, leaving Emma to bring Fiona and Lauren. We'd brought food and drinks with us in case we didn't venture out as much as we usually did, this being somewhat of a departure from our usual girls' weekend away.

I'd decided not to even look at the Frisky app in the interim, trusting Jenna to deal with everything and make the plan work – a plan that I felt I now knew backwards. *Could I do what needed doing? Could I really see it through?* Deep down, I still harboured doubts that I would have to do anything, not quite believing that he would fall for the whole idea. I was, therefore, completely caught off guard when she announced, as we emerged at the end of the long leafy driveway and arrived at the cottage, that he'd suggested hooking up the following night.

'I, well *you*, sent him a little message saying that staying in a lonely cottage in Blissford would have been so much more blissful if he'd been able to join you for some fun,' she said, giving us all her huge grin.

'Well, it's certainly lonely,' said Claire, looking around as Hayley exclaimed in excitement about the cottage.

Emma pulled in behind us as Jenna went in search of the key box and we unloaded both cars, our reason for being there forgotten about for now as we explored the cottage.

'Abs and Hayley should have the bunkbeds.' Fi emerged from what was clearly a children's bedroom. 'Em and I will take the twins – they look long enough for us, so that leaves one room with a double bed and one with a single. That had better be you, Laur, the bed's a kid's bed and you've got short legs.'

'Looks like we're top and tailing then.' Claire rolled her eyes at Jen, laughing.

'Oh my God!' Hayley's shriek reached us from the deck outside the lounge doors and we rushed out to see what she was so excited about, piling into each other as we stopped and stared at the hot tub in delight. 'It's big enough for all of us. Oh, I love it. Look at the gorgeous mermaid statue.'

Jenna smiled indulgently as she surveyed the scene. 'It's absolutely perfect,' she murmured. 'Right, let's get some drinks, ladies.'

Hayley fluttered around, finding a cloth to wipe the outside chairs and table with, while Claire rinsed the glasses from the cupboard and dried them. Lauren produced some crisps and peanuts and tipped them into bowls, as Emma put some music on, and all of a sudden we were seven best friends away on a fantastic girls' weekend in the most heavenly place imaginable.

'I could live here,' expressed Hayley dreamily.

'Cheers, everyone, here's to a successful weekend.' Fi held up her glass as we all followed.

'To the revenge plan.' Jenna clinked each of our glasses in turn as we repeated her words.

'So, he's taken the bait so far, we just have to play our trump card.'

We all fell silent as Jenna updated us.

'He says it's a sign that we, as in he and Abs, should definitely hook up, both being within five minutes of each other, but he mentioned the pub in Frogham. This means that we either have to send Abs to the pub and hope that she can get him back here by suggesting the hot tub, or we have to get him to come here of his own accord. Whichever way, we have to get him here and in the hot tub.'

'Can't I just tempt him about the hot tub from here?' I pleaded, looking around for support. 'I don't know, tell him I've got a hot tub, or something?'

It was Hayley who had the brainwave. 'How about a photo of Abs in the hot tub with a glass of wine?'

'To send to him, you mean?' Jenna tilted her head, her eyes thoughtful. 'Yes... to tempt him... that would work, Hayles, clever girl. We'll take a photo later, so that the light's right, and send it tomorrow evening. He'll already be anticipating his hookup and won't be able to resist the lure of the hot tub. But the focus must be on sex, a quick screw before he gets to his favourite part – and we all know what that is – not cosy romantic chats in the tub. You must remember that, Abs.'

'I know what it's all about,' I said quietly. 'Romantic chats are the last thing I want with him. What about time? How will we know when he wants to hook up? What if he can't get away from his wife? She's a bit on the bossy side.'

'Don't worry about him, he's obviously highly adept at sneaking off for his extracurricular activities. He's probably done it more times than we can imagine.'

'What makes you think his wife's bossy?'

I stared at Fi wide-eyed. 'Er.' My brain went into panic mode. 'You said, didn't you? When you saw her outside the school?'

'No... I was at the pub watching him, not his bloody wife.'

'It must have been Hayles.' My mind flailed helplessly, unable to recall who'd seen his wife where. *Had it been Hayley? Or maybe Emma?*

'It was probably me,' offered Hayley. 'She did seem rather the bossy type when I followed her to the nail salon.'

'That must have been it.' I willed my cheeks to cool down.

'We need more wine.' Claire bustled off to grab a couple of bottles and we topped our glasses up, falling quiet as we enjoyed the setting for a moment. The sun was going down and Lauren went in search of a switch for the outside lights. Soft lights appeared, set in the deck at intervals, and pretty fairy lights began to twinkle above the hot tub.

'We should check how the hot tub works.' Emma went to fiddle with the control switches.

'We can give it a test run.' Hayley clapped her hands in delight.

'It's got water in it already,' called Emma, pulling off the cover. 'I think this is the power button.'

The water began to move gently as a soft whirring sound came from the motor.

We refilled our glasses as Jenna produced a bottle of Tequila, thumping it down on the table. 'Did anyone see if there were shot glasses in the kitchen?'

'I'll check.' Claire went back into the kitchen, reappearing a moment later with a stack of glasses.

'Shooter time, ladies.'

Two shots each, later, and we were beginning to feel nicely fired up.

'Wait until you see the masks.' Fi suddenly grinned, pushing her chair back. 'They're fantastic.'

She returned a couple of minutes later, dropping a large carrier bag on the floor, and reached into it to pull out a mask.

We all stared at the Latex horse's head in Fi's hand, spontaneously erupting into shrieks of laughter.

'We had such a laugh choosing them.' Em wiped her eyes. 'The horse is mine, I'm claiming it.'

'Here you go.' Fi threw the horse's head at Emma, who caught it, pulling it on over her head.

'What d'you think?' Her hand reached up to flick the black faux fur mane.

It took a moment for us to stop laughing.

'What else have you got?' Hayley eyed the bag impatiently.

A penguin head appeared in Fi's hand, to much screeching.

'Me, me, me.' Claire reached for the Penguin, pulling it on as we collapsed in giggles.

'Does it suit me?' The penguin's head bobbed around at us, its open beak giving the uncanny impression of speech.

'Oh my God... this is too much.' Tears ran down Lauren's face. 'Come on, what else have you got? The next one out of the bag's mine.'

'Here you go.' Fi flung what looked like a bundle of brown faux fur at Lauren.

'It's a chimp.' The penguin head seemed to bob around crazily as Claire's laughter spluttered from it.

We watched Lauren pull the chimp mask on, and had another fit of laughter.

'Right, next up is...'

'It's a rabbit. I want it. Can I have it? Please? Oh, it's so cute.' Hayley reached for the rabbit mask, pulling it on and looking around at us.

It did look kind of cute, we agreed, as Hayley did little rabbit movements with her hands, but also hilarious. We were slightly hysterical by now.

'Sorry, Jen, but this one's for you.' Fi threw a pink bundle of rubber at Jenna. 'I'm taking the panda.'

'That is the scariest pig I've ever seen.' The rabbit stopped its frantic hand motions as we all considered Jenna's transformation into horror pig.

'Grrr.' Jenna lunged around the table at us, to much collective squealing, her pig's face grinning manically and terrifyingly.

'Pigs oink, they don't growl,' said Fi's panda head, its red eyes burning menacingly as it looked at Jenna the horror pig.

'Poor Abs, she's the only one without a mask,' said Hayley, her rabbit ears wiggling.

'Well...' Fi drawled as she reached into the carrier bag again. 'We can't have that can we?' She threw a flimsy piece of black lace at me as the six animals' heads turned in my direction.

'What is it? Show us, Abs.'

'Oh, it's gorgeous,' I breathed, holding up the lace Masquerade mask and fastening the silky ribbons behind my head. 'Thanks, Fi.' The relief was intense. I would be, like the girls, unrecognisable, or partially at least. I would be safe, my face obscured. I would be Tipsy Tease, not Abigail Hawthorn.

'Now you're one of us,' said the rabbit head happily.

'Er, not quite, Hayles, we look like a bunch of crazed comical creatures while Abs looks all sultry and sophisticated.'

'I don't know about that.' I laughed, feeling quite giddy. 'But I am so relieved that I'll be able to hide my face a bit, although I'd prefer a mask like you all have, you'll all be completely unidentifiable.'

Claire pulled off her penguin head. 'I'd suggest that we swap, but I don't think he'd be quite so keen to hook up with you if you were wearing this – he'd probably run a mile, thinking it was some kind of weird sex kink.'

'It might make him want her more.' Fi's panda head looked around at us all as we collapsed with laughter, and Claire snorted her drink, clutching her sides.

'I need a ciggie and another drink before I die of laughter.' She straightened up, looking around her.

'Now you're talking.' Lauren's chimp head came off as she reached for her cigarettes, passing one to both Claire and Fi, and we resumed our normal appearances, laughing at Jen as she struggled with the pig mask, swearing as she wrestled it off minus a substantial amount of her hair.

Throwing back more shots of Tequila, we tried to stop ourselves from further attacks of the giggles.

'The water's quite warm now,' Hayley reported a while later, shouting over the music which Emma had notched up at some point. 'We could get in.'

'Time to strip off, ladies. More wine, I think. Abs, be a darling and fetch a couple more bottles out.'

I left the girls stripping down to their underwear, and grabbed some bottles, stopping to look out at them from the kitchen window as I heard them squealing with laughter. My phone was lying on the counter and I picked it up, zooming in on Jenna as she sat resplendently alone in the hot tub with her pig mask back on, her arms stretched along the sides, her ample bosom, encased in a purple bra, seeming to float on the surface of the gently steaming water. I took a quick photo and put my phone down as they all jumped in.

'Come on, Abs, get 'em off,' yelled Claire as I reappeared.

'Oh my God, if you could see yourselves,' I spluttered as I giggled at the girls all wearing their animal masks and sitting in the hot tub in their underwear, bopping and singing to Mambo No. 5.

'Don't forget I can't swim,' Lauren's chimp head spun back and forth to look at the others.

'It's not a swimming pool, Laur.'

The penguin's comment had everyone shrieking with laughter as they splashed crazily at Lauren.

'Take a photo, please...' begged Hayley. 'My phone's on the table. We have to capture this moment.'

'No!' Jen's voice beneath her pig mask was sharp. 'No photos at the cottage, ladies. Sorry, Hayles, but fun as this is, we don't want any record of the masks or the hot tub.'

I thought awkwardly of the photo I'd just taken. 'But, Jen, we're here for Fi's birthday supposedly, won't it be weird if we don't have any photos?'

Five masked heads turned to await the pig's comment, while I pulled off my skirt and top and slipped into the warm water.

I rested my head back on the edge of the tub and looked up at the fairy lights, as Jen answered, tugging off her mask and throwing it on the deck. Soft thuds followed as the others did the same.

'We'll take some photos somewhere else. It's just best that we don't draw attention to our stay here in this cottage.'

'So that he can't prove anything?' Emma nodded. 'Makes sense.'

'Not that he'll want to even try.' Fi picked up her wine glass and took a huge gulp. 'Like he'll ever own up to seven women teaching him a lesson for what he did to Lauren.'

'Exactly, and think about it, who's going to believe him about the animal head masks? It sounds mad.'

'We are bloody mad.' Claire started laughing again and I thought what a good job it was that we were in the middle of nowhere – if anyone had heard us, we sounded like a pack of wild hyaenas.

'We do need one photo though... Abs, I need to fix your hair up. Let's do this before we get too pissed.'

'Too late for that, darling,' drawled Fi, as Jen and I got out of the hot tub.

'Can you bring some towels?' called Emma as we went inside.

A few minutes later I was alone in the hot tub, my masquerade mask in place, glass of wine in hand, and lips slicked in a hurriedly applied coat of deep red lipstick courtesy of Jenna.

'Lose the bra straps, babes,' directed Jenna as she appraised my attempt at a provocative pose. 'That's better. Who's got a phone handy?'

'I'll take the photo.' Fi began to crouch and snap pictures as I tried to look sexy and inviting.

It wasn't difficult as it turned out, the mask did the work for me, and I leant my head back, moving aside slightly to avoid the ferny leaves protruding lushly from the pot on the edge of the tub. I stepped out, wrapping a towel around my wet body as we clustered around Fi's phone to see the photos.

'That one.' Jen jabbed a finger at one of the images. 'It's perfect. Send it to Abs' phone and then delete them all, leave no trace behind.'

To listen to Jen, you'd have thought we were planning a bank heist, not just getting revenge on some man who deserved it anyway, and I could tell that Fi was on my wavelength by the odd look she gave Jenna.

'I'm starving, what are we eating tonight?' Hayley was pulling her clothes back on, and we finished off our evening a while later with a huge lasagne and buttery garlic bread smothered in mozzarella, accompanied by a couple more bottles of red wine, before crashing into our beds for the night – seven girlfriends happily falling asleep on the first night of a great girls' weekend away together.

I felt so relaxed, I completely forgot about what I had to do for a few blissful hours.

28

'Wakey, wakey, ladies.' Jenna's voice boomed through the cottage as she banged on doors and yelled at us to wake up. 'We're going out for breakfast – leaving in half an hour.'

This was typical Jenna, I thought mutinously, finding her showered and dressed when I stepped gingerly into the kitchen to see if anyone had made any tea.

'Sore head, Abs?' She handed me a mug of tea, smiling sympathetically. 'Big day today.'

Thanks for reminding me. My stomach quailed at the thought as I groaned. 'Thanks, Jen, I need this. How come you're so chirpy this morning?'

'Oh, I don't know, it just feels like a good day. Here we all are, the sun's shining, and our revenge plan is finally happening – what more could we ask for?'

'A huge plate of fried eggs and bacon with a ton of buttered toast please.' Fi appeared wearing a black silk kaftan, patterned with huge white butterflies. 'Shower's free, Abs.'

'I brought bacon and eggs with me.' Claire bustled into the kitchen, opening the fridge as if to prove her point. 'Why don't I just cook us up some brekkie here? I've got some porkers as well.'

My stomach rumbled as we looked at Jenna – awaiting her decision, *of course.*

'No, you can do that tomorrow, today's my treat. Breakfast on me. GET A MOVE ON, GIRLS!' Her sudden roar thundered around the cottage as sounds of doors opening and closing followed rapidly.

'Where are we going for breakfast, then?' I asked as I drove along the driveway with Emma following, a little later.

'Somewhere with rave reviews.' Jenna settled her head back in the passenger seat.

Trees, fields, vast forested areas and pretty little villages all occupied our attention as we passed them by, enjoying the beautiful drive with its promise of breakfast at the end.

'Oh look, horses!' Hayley clapped her hands in delight from the back seat.

'Technically they're ponies, but yes, gorgeous, aren't they?' Jenna smiled contentedly, her eyes hidden behind her sunglasses. 'We're almost there, turn here...'

Ahead of us, water ran across the road as ponies stood drinking from it and we pretty much collectively gasped at the perfect scene. I pulled over and waited for the ponies to move, feeling happy and relaxed and wondering if I should suggest a weekend around here with Martin in the future – it might do us good. I think, at this moment, we had all completely forgotten the reason for our sudden weekend away.

'Just up ahead you can take a left and park in the car park. Then I'll take you all for a fabulous breakfast. You're going to love it. Tell you what, let's walk back and take some photos of the ponies first, yeah?'

'Wow.' Fi grinned as she got out of Emma's car beside us. How pretty is everything? I'm beginning to think I really did want a pony when I was a little girl. It's all so... picture perfect, it's like...'

'Like living in a wonderful dream.' Hayley hugged Fi, unable to contain her childlike delight at everything – one of the many reasons we all adored her.

'Where nothing bad ever happens to anyone.'

Lauren's voice was harsh and I looked at her in surprise before realising what must be going through her head. Here we all were, having this great time, laughing and joking, and all the time we were overlooking the reason for it all – to get revenge for what had happened to her...

'It's the way life should be, Laur.' I tried to make her feel better.

'Yeah, right.'

I ignored Jen's snorted comment, continuing to attempt to reassure my friend, whose outward signs of hurt might have faded but whose inner pain clearly still racked her.

'It'll get better, Laur, everything will, life, you, your feelings, you'll see – you'll be back to your old self in no time, our fun-loving Lauren who makes us laugh all the time. Won't she?' I looked around for support and the girls rallied, agreeing firmly. Even Jen managed a nod and an assenting mumble.

After taking some photos of us all with the ponies at the watersplash, Jen marched us off along the main street, by which time I'd have eaten anything I was so starving. I wasn't the only one.

'For God's sake, Jen, does it matter which place we eat breakfast at? Here, what's wrong with this place? I'm going to gnaw off my own hand in a minute.'

'Stop with the drama, Fi, we're here, this is it, it gets great reviews, that's why I brought you all here. It's the kind of place we'd have sought out on one of our girls' weekends away, so, to keep things convincing, here we are...'

The breakfasts were enormous – maybe that's what the reviews had raved about, I thought, gazing at plates loaded with fried eggs, bacon, pork bangers, tomato, baked beans, mushroom, hash browns, and toast.

'Wow.' Claire picked up her knife and fork with relish.

'Hold on – photos.' Jen whipped out her phone. 'Smile.' She clicked away, encouraging us to do likewise, something she proceeded to do repeatedly – as we walked around Brockenhurst village after our breakfast, passing yet more ponies, and on our arrival in Lymington.

By the time we'd walked around and shopped up a storm in Lymington, stopping for photo opportunities every time one of us held a new carrier bag, we'd worked up an appetite again, but first we had to walk down to the quay to see the boats, Jenna informed us. It took us a while to make our way down along the little cobbled street with its boutiques and gift shops, but eventually we emerged at the quay to gently bobbing yachts and motorboats moored on the sparkling water.

It was hard to equate the scene with the evening ahead and I forced myself to remain calm as my nerves began to act up.

'Group shot!' Jenna requisitioned a passing man to take our photo, turning on the Jenna charm so that he was helpless to resist.

'Where are we lunching?' Hayley asked our self-appointed tour guide.

'It's just along here. Who's in the mood for fish and chips?'

We all were, and once the staff had rushed to shift two tables together on the waterside terrace, we sank down into our chairs and gazed out at the boats lined up on the river.

'I feel like I'm on holiday.' Claire leant back, closing her eyes. 'I think Adrian and I ate here when we stayed in Lymington. In fact–' She craned her neck round. 'I think the cottage we stayed in was just up the road from here.'

By mutual consent, we gave the wine a miss, doing the unthinkable and ordering bottles of water to accompany our meal, which was delicious – the cod encased in a batter as light as air, the chips golden with just the right amount of crunch, and the pea purée a perfect creamy sweetness.

I placed my knife and fork together regretfully after only a few mouthfuls, my mind beginning to picture what lay ahead, my stomach telling me, in no uncertain terms, that if I ate any more it would not stay down for long.

'Where's that Abigail appetite gone? Not like you to leave food on your plate.'

I glanced at Jen, not sure if she was being sarcastic or not. 'I'm not feeling so good,' I muttered. 'I'm a bag of nerves about tonight.'

'Oh, come on, what have you got to feel nervous about? You can't let us down now, Abs. Claire, move your chair closer to Hayley, and Em, lean in, that's it, smile, ladies.'

I'd been dismissed, as usual, my central role in the revenge plan clearly not deemed worthy of even a smidgen of anxiety.

'No more photos, Jen, please...' Fi groaned when our plates had been cleared. 'We've got about fifty pictures of the fish and chips alone, which was, by the way, probably the best fish and chips I've ever eaten.'

'I'll second that.' Lauren patted her stomach. 'I'm stuffed. Is anyone having pudding?'

'No time I'm afraid, lovies, we need to head back and begin preparations for this evening.'

A shadow passed over Lauren's face and I felt it in the pit of my stomach.

29

We were back at the cottage in just under an hour and Jenna swung into action, dispatching Emma to move her car round to the back of the cottage, and barking instructions at the rest of us, so that we ran around like headless chickens.

Needing a moment alone, I unloaded the dishwasher, stacking the plates, and piling the cutlery on the counter to sort it, my mind on what was to come, my hands moving the knives and forks around in a disembodied manner. I jumped nervously as Jen appeared, my insides feeling like jelly.

'Really, Abs? Now? Leave it, I need to do your hair and make-up.' She tried to grab the handful of cutlery from me. 'Go and sit at the dinner table, I'll be right with you.'

My fingers loosened before she'd had a chance to take hold of everything properly, and I flinched as the cutlery crashed onto the floor, and Jen cursed loudly.

'Go.' Jen pushed me towards the door as she bent down to pick up the knives and forks.

'I'll pick those up, Jen, you go and sort Abs out,' Claire said, as she bustled past me into the kitchen.

I walked out of the lounge onto the deck, bending down by the hot tub, my hand feeling for the potted fern, steadying myself as I wobbled and my heart pounded in my chest. I stared at the water, willing the night to be over.

'Hayley's looking for you, Claire.' Lauren's voice became louder as she walked out onto the deck, looking over at me as I crouched beside the hot tub, our eyes

meeting for a split second before she walked round and through the open kitchen door. 'Oh, where did she go? Anyone seen Claire?' Her words were lost beneath the sound of kitchen drawers opening and closing.

I jumped as Claire's hand patted my shoulder, my hand catching against the fern fronds as I stood up, soil particles falling into the tub. My nerves were so shot, I hadn't even realised she'd been behind me. I seriously needed to get my act together.

'You'll be fine,' she said. 'You'd better go in. And clean your nails, you've got dirt under them, love.'

'Abs? Get in here.'

Jen's bellow got me moving and I hurried back into the lounge, picking at my nails nervously.

'I'm here, I went out the back way to check that the hot tub was ready.' Claire appeared at the sliding doors from the deck, her cheeks flushed.

'Fi? Why are you holding a knife?' Emma's voice sounded strained and we all looked towards the kitchen, where a whispered exchange could be heard taking place, followed by a scuffling noise.

'What the hell is going on?' Jen marched to the kitchen.

'I couldn't get the damn lid open, it was stuck.'

'I told her she shouldn't drink now, not before we do it.'

'Your hand's bleeding.'

'Oh, sod this.' A door slammed and the thump of footsteps could be heard crossing the deck.

'Clean that blood up will you, Hayles?' Jen took control. 'Claire, find a plaster and have a look at Fi's hand.'

'Where did the knife go?'

'Who cares at this moment, Hayley?' Jen was beginning to sound exasperated. 'I have to get Abs ready and we're running out of time. Someone calm Fi down, she's got the jitters, which isn't like her. Give her a shot of that vodka, in fact, everyone have one, it looks like we all need it.'

'But Emma, you had it, I saw you.'

'Claire was holding a bunch of knives earlier.'

'Abs dropped them, that's why.'

'That wasn't me,' I defended myself. 'That was Jen.'

'Who cares? Who bloody cares?' Jan slammed her fist on the table. 'Shut up, and have a shot of vodka, for Christ's sake.'

Fi downed her shot, filling her glass again, and holding it up. 'We should use a bloody knife on the bastard, cut him up a bit. Who's with me?' She looked around challengingly.

Emma gasped. 'You weren't using that knife to open the vodka, you were going to take it and use it.'

'Fi's all talk, aren't you, Fi?' Hayley gave a nervous giggle. 'Who's to say we didn't all think of it at some point? I was in the kitchen a minute ago, maybe I was tempted. Or Lauren, you were rummaging through the drawers, you could have–'

I forced a laugh, distracting Hayley, not wanting to hear any more talk of knives. 'Hayles, as if any of us could believe that you were tempted to take a knife and cut up some bloke.'

'Can you imagine it? Sweet little Hayley? Oh, I'm sorry, I hope this doesn't hurt you, do you mind? I'll just make a tiny cut. Oh, let me get you a plaster.'

We all laughed at Jen's impersonation of Hayley, the tension easing a little.

Finally, with everyone calmed down, I was primped and preened in readiness for my assignation. I marvelled at Jenna's composure and kept my doubts about the evening ahead to myself – I still couldn't believe that she'd convince him to come to the cottage, no matter how alluring I supposedly looked sitting in the hot tub. But if he came, there was no reason that the rest of the plan shouldn't work, I tried to reassure myself.

'When do we send him the photo?' I looked anxiously at Jenna as we gathered around the outside table with glasses of wine that our leader had graciously permitted. 'Oh bugger it, the more booze the better,' had been her exact words.

'It's not dark enough yet, babes. Don't worry, I've sent him a little message to whet his appetite, believe me, he's champing at the bit to escape his in-laws and get his mitts on your sweet little bod.'

Blushing furiously, I gulped some wine, choking as it went down the wrong pipe.

'Take it easy, Abs, it's going to go exactly as I've planned it. What are you in such a stew about?' Her eyes bored into mine for a moment, as if she could extract my thoughts by telepathy, until I looked away.

Where d'you want me to begin, Jenna?

'Someone pour Abs another glass of wine, in fact, everyone have another. Right, let's just run through everything again.'

When she'd finished and was satisfied that we all knew what to do, she relaxed a bit, topping my glass up again and emptying her own before heading to the kitchen to fetch another bottle.

'I don't know,' Lauren whispered suddenly. 'This is madness, isn't it? What are we doing even getting this far?'

Relief flooded my body and I looked around hopefully at the others. Maybe it wasn't too late to just forget the whole thing. 'I could just send him a message saying I'm not meeting him after all?'

Hayley and Claire looked like they agreed with us, and even Fi looked uncertain.

'Not on your nelly.' Jenna swooped back and in one movement took my phone from where it lay on the table. 'I'll take control of this. We've come this far, why stop now? If we don't teach him a lesson, who will? Who's he going to beat up next? Think about it. Why do blokes

always think they can trample all over us, treat us like shit, make us think they like us and then break us into a thousand pieces, leaving us feeling worthless? This is for Lauren, this is what we do, we look out for each other.'

It was hard to argue with that, even if Jenna had made it sound like her own personal battle.

'What if something goes wrong?' Fi's voice quavered slightly.

'What could possibly go wrong?' Jen's confident smile brooked no further argument.

30

Stars
Firework

I looked at the assorted items lying on the deck – Jenna's 'weapons' with which we were going to teach him the aforementioned lesson: a beard clipper, scissors, permanent marker pens, a large lady's dress in a floral pattern, a bottle of strong ladies' perfume, and, rather more ominous-looking, a baseball bat, a heavy frying pan, a shovel, and a packet of large cable ties.

It was all pretty harmless stuff really – it also looked totally absurd, if I was honest – and if the plan went the way Jenna had planned it, he'd probably leave with a couple of bruises and his ego hurt more than anything else, I told myself. After all, how much damage could a bunch of women really do to him?

The sun began to dip in the sky and things became real quite quickly. The 'weapons' were hidden behind an armchair just inside the lounge door, and Jenna dispatched the girls into one of the bedrooms, checking my phone and informing me that it was time to get into the hot tub.

'He's on his way, I told you he'd be helpless to resist. All you've got to do is get him to undress and join you, Abs, and leave the rest to us, OK? Now, drink this down and I'll refill your glass, a little Dutch courage won't do you any harm.'

She disappeared and the next moment the soft sound of Simply Red reached my ears as I sat alone in the hot water, in the same place I'd sat the night before, when it had all seemed like such fun, feeling more than a little woozy from all the wine Jen had pushed on me. I shouldn't have drunk so much, I reprimanded myself angrily, I desperately needed a clear head if I was going to see this through. I looked around anxiously at the dark shapes below the deck.

I self-indulged for a moment, allowing myself a moment of self-pity. *It was all Jenna's fault, she was making me do this. It wasn't the first time she'd made me do something. I was sweet, little Abigail. Why was she making me behave so badly?* I was surprised at the anger I felt at her at that moment. Patting the plant pot on the side of the hot tub for reassurance, I muttered to myself, 'You can do this, you can see it through.'

My ears picked up the sound of a car engine coming closer, and headlights made their way along the drive to the cottage. I strained my ears, listening to the sound of a car door closing, footsteps crunching on the gravel, a man's voice calling out... I swallowed nervously.

His steps sounded loud as they made their way out onto the deck and I looked up at him as he appeared, forcing myself to smile in what I hoped was a seductive manner, grateful for the masquerade mask.

'You made it,' I murmured, hoping I wasn't slurring my words. I felt terrified.

'Nothing was going to keep me away.' He grinned, but it didn't look friendly, and my stomach churned.

'I hope you're naked in there.'

'Join me and find out, I've poured you a glass of wine.' *Had I really just said that? I deserved an award for my performance – which wasn't over yet...*

His eyes strayed over the bottle and two glasses before returning to rest on me, a glazed expression in them. 'It's really you, isn't it? So many photos are fake, you never know what you're going to find. But you, you're the real deal... you look like you... As soon as I saw your photo, I knew what I wanted to do to you. I couldn't believe my luck when you hearted me on Frisky.'

I tried to control the squirming feeling in my stomach, finding him both attractive but terrifying at the same time. I glanced covertly at him, taking in his firm body beneath his coolly faded Ibiza T-shirt, knowing that I needed to get this over with, and fast. 'You'll have to get out of those clothes, we won't have much fun if you're fully clothed...' I was done, I didn't feel that I could say another thing without breaking down in a mass of nerves.

'You think I'm here for fun?' He kicked off his shoes, pulled off his T-shirt, and dropped his jeans seemingly all in one movement, leaving me gasping as I took in his firm body – naked apart from his boxer shorts – which he dropped as I stared at him, revealing his enthusiastic partner in crime.

His eyes narrowed for a second as he stared at me, his hand touching his neck, as something fell to the deck and slipped through one of the gaps. 'Bloody gnats,' he said angrily, rubbing at his neck. 'I've been looking forward to this, you bitch, you have no idea how much.'

I felt my skin crawl in terror, *he'd revealed himself*, and I inadvertently rubbed at my arms, keeping my hands in place protectively as I saw the horror pig's head silently draw closer behind him, the chimp's head beside it, like a scene from a scary film.

He stepped to the edge of the hot tub. 'You deserve everything you're going to–'

He didn't get to finish. The horror pig's head rose up behind him, its red eyes gleaming manically in the sparkle from the fairy lights, the baseball bat swinging and meeting his head with a resounding crunch. His eyes seemed to widen in confusion momentarily as he looked around in bewilderment at the sound of a group of howling banshees advancing on him.

He opened his mouth as if to speak, his eyes virtually popping out of his head as the rest of the wild menagerie joined the fray, his body falling against me as the frying pan made contact with his shoulder and the shovel smashed down on his head, causing him to drop beneath the now swirling water.

My hand grabbed at the plant pot, toppling it over in my panic, and screams and howls of rage filled the air as bodies splashed into the hot tub, hands and fists flying. Flashes of the various animals' heads appeared in front of me as I was pushed beneath the water, my hands desperately clawing for something to pull myself back up with.

'Hit him, smash him!'

'Take that, you bastard!'

'Woman beater!'

'Punch him, hurt him!'

'This is payback!'

'Hit him harder!'

The cries filled my head, the hateful energy filling me with vengeful power, and I lashed out at him, smashing my hand into him again and again as shouts encouraged me, our hands and fists smashing against each other, my eyes seeing red as I gasped, desperately reaching for anything to hold onto as I fell beneath the water again and all sound seemed to die away.

I pushed him aside, desperately fighting for air as I choked on a mouthful of water, spluttering and groping for the side of the hot tub as the six animals' faces seemed to loom over me.

'What?' I pushed the eye mask up and looked around in confusion in the sudden calm, the only sound the soft music coming from the lounge.

'What did you do, Abs?'

'I– what happened? The water...' In shock, my sub-conscious registered incongruous points – the penguin head morphing into Claire's shocked face; the horrific pig's head not moving as it loomed over me – one side of it smudged with claw-like fingerprints the same colour as its eyes; Hayley's body crumpled on the deck, her hands held to the rabbit mask as if she were covering her own eyes; Jenna's hands blue with cold as the pig's head became her face; the panda launching itself at me; a flash of pink as Lauren howled, throwing her arms in the air; Jenna's look of incomprehension; and the water... oh God, the water... turning a deeper shade of red with every passing second...

31

It's The End Of The World As We Know It

I let out a cry as his body bumped against me and I scrambled to the side of the hot tub, trying to get away from him as I looked at my clenched hand in puzzlement.

A hand grasped my wrist and I looked up at the panda head as Fi's voice said, 'Drop it, Abs.'

Animals' head masks thumped onto the deck as they were removed, rolling and crumpling grotesquely, the horse's head landing upright beside the knife and staring into my eyes accusingly as it pooled pink water onto the deck.

'Is he dead?' Lauren's hysterical cry seemed to echo around us, and I stared back at his floating body, screaming as his hand brushed my thigh.

'Get me out! Get me out!' I screeched, as I tried to climb out, falling back against him as hands reached for me and pulled me onto the deck. I lay there, panting and shivering as someone threw a towel around me and hands rubbed my shoulders.

The music was still playing and my eyes flickered about manically, taking in the tableau of motionless figures – motionless except one, the gently bobbing body floating face down in the red water of the hot tub.

'For fuck's sake will someone turn off that infernal music?' Jenna's voice was tight as we all turned to look at her, waiting for her direction.

Claire walked silently into the lounge and the music stopped, bringing silence.

Jenna picked up the shovel, prodding his body with it so that it bumped and rolled, hitting the side of the hot tub and turning over as we watched in horror. His eyes stared up at the night sky unseeingly as his body continued to float gently around the tub, bouncing slowly from one side to another like a bumper car at a fairground. Jenna's gaze rested on his face for a moment before she turned and looked at me with an odd expression in her eyes, her lips curling upwards in a weird version of a smile.

'Get her a blanket, she's still shivering.'

'But it's so bloody hot.'

'She had a knife.'

'She's in shock.'

'Aren't we all?'

Someone placed a soft blanket around my shoulders and I huddled beneath it, keeping my eyes averted from the hot tub, watching Jenna inexplicably picking up his clothes and folding them, wondering why one of the comments had jarred my senses.

'Where did you get the knife, Abs?'

'What have you done?'

'What do we do now?'

'Is that his wallet?'

'She looks as white as a ghost.'

'Where did the knife come from?'

'We need to call an ambulance.'

'It's too late for that.'

'We need to call the police.'

'No.'

'I think I'm going to be sick.' I shoved the blanket aside, scrambling to my feet and rushing to the side of the deck where I vomited furiously. Claire appeared beside me, silently handing me a cloth to wipe my face with as she gently rubbed my back.

'I don't know what happened.' I stared at Claire. 'Did I—? Are you sure he's dead? The knife – I didn't know I was holding it. Where did it come from? Oh, Claire, you've got to help me.' I began to cry and she led me to a chair, pressing on my shoulders gently so that I sat down.

Fi was shouting at Jenna but my brain didn't seem able to unscramble her words. Jenna paced the deck, shaking her head as she shouted something back at Fi, before storming through the open lounge doors. I watched Lauren as she knelt beside the hot tub, her hands reaching for something, Emma's arms stretching over her to pull her away, Lauren's mouth opening in a hideous shape. Her scream snapped me from my stupor and my brain began to function again.

I was a murderer. I'd just killed a man. What now? 'Jen?' My voice was little more than a croak. 'Where's Jen?'

'Jen doesn't have all the bloody answers, Abs, when are you going to get that into your head?' Fi's hands clawed at her head as she shouted at me.

I flinched, as everyone began arguing again. 'Please, stop,' I whispered. 'STOP!'

They fell silent as a door banged and Jen re-appeared.

'OK, we all need to calm down so that I can think. Emma, get me some dustbin bags from the kitchen. Hayley, switch off the hot tub pump. Lauren, there's a bottle of whisky in the kitchen, bring that out, and, Fi, fetch glasses.'

Relief passed over faces as Jen took control and issued instructions.

We sat around the table holding our whiskies as Jen placed the knife in one of the dustbin bags, wrapping it up and placing it on the floor beside her chair, while Emma silently picked up the animals' head masks, putting them all in another bag.

I flinched as Emma tied up the bag and dropped it on the deck, her look of disappointment and anger as she glared at me making it clear that she blamed me for everything.

'Where's the mask Abs was wearing?' Hayley's eyes strayed from me to the hot tub as my hand involuntarily reached up to touch my face.

I stood up and walked stiffly to the hot tub, gazing into the bloodied water, ignoring his body, and looked around for something to retrieve the whisp of black lace with from the bottom of the tub. Picking up the shovel, I lowered it into the water and managed to nudge the masquerade mask so that it floated up to the surface. Grabbing it, I dropped the shovel with a clutter and handed the mask to Jenna.

Our eyes met as she took the mask, her expression unreadable, a small, incongruous smile playing on her lips.

'First of all, we'll have no more talk about the knife and where it came from or how it ended up in Abigail's hand, alright? It doesn't matter now. No one knows he was here, right? We have to get his body out of the hot tub and as far away from here as possible.'

'What about his car?' Claire reached for the whisky bottle, pouring herself another generous measure, and passed the bottle round. 'I have to go the loo, my stomach's churning.'

'Someone will have to drive it.'

'What about the dress and the shaver and stuff?'

Jen gave a bitter laugh. 'It's a bit late for that, we've kind of passed the point of humiliating him, don't you think? No, we have to forget all about that and concentrate on disposing of his body and car.'

'At least he's clean.'

We all stared at Hayley in surprise.

'I mean, there's no evidence on him, you know, like in the detective stories where they find fibres and DNA and stuff.' She shrugged awkwardly. 'He's naked in the water, it's all washed away, at least I think it is, and his car's not been touched by any of us...'

'Except, Hayley dear, we have to get him out of the tub and into his car and one of us has to drive the damn thing away from here.' Fi's words dripped with sarcasm, and she pushed her chair back. 'I need a moment.'

We watched her walk off into the lounge, as Lauren spoke.

'What about the stab wounds? Won't they match them to the knife?'

'Not if they can't find the knife.'

'It must have got put with the other things by mistake,' I whispered, my eyes wide as I looked pleadingly at my friends, my bottom lip trembling at my effort to hold back my tears. I could hear Fi's voice speaking, but I couldn't see her. 'Where's Fi?' I looked around in a panic.

'This is all your bloody fault, Jen.' Lauren rocked back and forth, her arms wrapped around herself. 'We should never have let you talk us into this.'

'My fault?' screeched Jenna. 'You started all this when you went on one of your reckless hook ups and got yourself beaten black and blue.'

'Like you've never done it, Jen. You can't lay this on me.' Lauren stormed off, disappearing down the steps from the deck and into the darkness of the garden below.

Jenna visibly pulled her mind back to the matter in hand. 'Right, we need to do this in the next few hours, before daylight. We have to get him out of the tub, get him and his car far away, drain and clean the hot tub and refill it, re-pot that bloody fern thing and clean up the mess, wash down the deck, dispose of the masks and the knife, wash and dry anything that might have his blood on it – like the blanket Abs had round her shoulders... Have I missed anything?'

Our blank faces stared back at Jenna, all totally clueless as to whether she had adequately covered the steps required to cover up a murder.

32

'It's a start.' Claire stood up, breaking the momentary silence. 'We can figure it out as we go. How do we get him out?'

'A blanket under his body, then we can pull him out onto the deck.'

Emma's suggestion was met with a nod from Jen which galvanized us into action. Someone called Lauren back from the darkness beyond the deck, and, using the blanket I'd had around my shoulders earlier, we dropped one side of it into the water and used the shovel to push it beneath his body where Emma, Fi and Claire leant over and grabbed hold of it. Jenna, Hayley, Lauren and I held firmly to the other side and we heaved upwards, gasping as the water pulled at the blanket, resisting our efforts.

'It's no good, two of us need to get in and push him up as the rest of you pull.' Jen kicked off her sandals, stepping over the side of the hot tub and into the water. 'Claire, sorry darling, in you get.'

With Jenna and Claire pushing as the rest of us pulled, we finally got him out and onto the deck, dropping his body with a squelching thud as we all caught our breath.

'We need to hurry, there's rigor mortis to think about. Anyone know how quickly it sets in?'

Emma reached out a foot and nudged his arm. 'He's still soft.'

'Do we put his clothes back on before he goes stiff?'

'No, if we do that, they'll know he was naked when he was stabbed, and then dressed again.'

'That's if they find his body.'

'Leave him naked, the less touching of anything the better. We'll wrap him in dustbin bags and seal them up for now. Then we'll get him into the boot of his car. Hayley, go and see what you can find to tie round him.'

Hayley scuttled off, relieved to be away from the naked corpse on the deck.

'Does anyone know how to drain this thing?' Fi's hand rested on the mermaid statue as she bent down, peering around the base of the hot tub.

'I think I saw a leaflet in the kitchen drawer, I'll get it.' Claire hurried off, returning with the instructions. 'I need my glasses, they must be inside.'

'Give me the leaflet, I'll read the instructions.' Fi stretched out her hand.

'Abs, I need you to look something up on your phone, alright?'

I nodded mutely at Jenna.

'Good, search for cliffs, dangerous spots, anywhere on the coast within an hour or so's drive, but we need to be able to get the car as close as possible.

'Lauren, can you get a plastic bag for his clothes? Then put it with the other bags until we can figure out what to do with everything.' As Lauren disappeared, Jen bent down, piling his folded clothes, and placing his deck shoes neatly on top of them. 'Claire, go and see if Hayley's found anything to tie the dustbin bags around his body with.' Pacing the deck, Jenna muttered to herself.

My fingers fumbled on my phone screen as I tried to find somewhere to dispose of the body of the man I'd just killed. My brain frantically registered names like Peveril Point, Dancing Ledge, Guillemot Ledge, Studland Naturist Beach, Anvil Point, and I stuttered out information to Jenna as she oversaw the activities on the deck, giving her approximate driving times.

'The naturist beach – only an hour to get there? That could work...'

'Yes, but it's about half an hour's walk to the beach from the parking. There's a lighthouse which we can drive right up to, but there might be people staying in the cottages... From there we can get to the edge of the cliff on foot in maybe five or ten minutes? It looks like it's about forty miles away so it would take us about an hour and a half at the most.'

'Right.' Jenna stopped her pacing. 'So we've got the choice of leaving him on a nudey beach or throwing him off a cliff and hoping he washes out to sea...'

'Got it.' Fi lifted the hosepipe over the side of the deck and lowered it into the garden below. 'Here we go.' A soft hissing noise heralded the start of the draining process, and Fi disappeared off below, stretching the pipe so that the water ran down a bank.

'How long does it take to drain?' Jenna checked her watch as she spoke.

'An hour or two. Then we need two or three hours to fill it again. Should be done before the sun's up, if we're lucky.'

'He's ready to go,' said Emma, indicating the black plastic-wrapped corpse tied with garden string and bound with some packing tape, courtesy of Hayley and Claire.

'We need to hurry, his wife may have reported him missing, although it's doubtful, she has to have some kind of idea about his extracurricular activities so hopefully she won't raise the alarm until morning. OK, everyone, gather round, one of our options requires carrying him for half an hour, but both will take about the same time overall. So – we have a toss-up between leaving him starkers on a nudist beach so that it looks like he was out there at night doing who knows what and got attacked and killed, or we chuck him off the cliff and his body might not be found for days, maybe even forever...'

'Won't they know? The cops, I mean? If they find his body lying dead on the beach, they'll immediately be looking for his killer and they'll have all the evidence of the stab wounds and stuff.'

'Yes, yes, we get it Hayley, thank you.' Jenna tutted impatiently but Hayley bravely ignored her.

'They'll be able to tell that he was taken there after he was killed, they'll know he was wrapped in plastic, he'll probably be in full rigor mortis so his position will look unnatural, they'll be able to tell time of death...'

It seemed that Hayley's love of crime fiction was proving useful as she continued, clearly on a roll.

'But if we throw him off the cliff into the sea then evidence will be washed away, his limbs will probably break as he crashes against the cliffside on his way down, and the cold water means he should stay under water for longer, bits of him might even be eaten... by fish and things...' Here she appeared to stumble, not quite sure where to go, and she shrugged. 'It's just from stuff I've read, I'm not totally sure...'

'We'd rather not have to carry him for half an hour.' Claire's exhausted face and sentiment was felt by us all and we nodded in agreement. 'And it's got to be a better bet to try and get rid of him permanently than to just leave him lying on a beach to be found in the morning, surely?'

'And someone might find him before then, anyone could be walking on a beach at night...' Fi helped herself to one of Lauren's cigarettes, lighting it and inhaling gratefully.

'There won't be much night left if we don't get going. OK, we'll go with the cliff edge at the lighthouse. Let's get him into his car. Abs, you'll drive your car, Hayley can go with you. I'll drive his car and take Fi, Lauren and Emma with me.'

'What about me?' Claire held out her hands. 'What do I do?'

'You stay here, clean the hot tub once it's drained and refill it, sort out the pot plant thing, then wash down the deck with the hosepipe, clean all the furniture, anything we've touched that might have blood on it, wash up everything in the kitchen and put it away. Oh, and then pack everyone's bags so that we're ready to leave when we get back, and pack the food up as well – we don't want to alert the owners to the fact that we left earlier than planned. Just make sure we leave nothing incriminating – nothing at all, Claire.'

'She'll never manage all that, not on her own.' Fi lit a second cigarette, forgetting about the one burning in the ashtray.'

'I'll help her.' Lauren turned to Jenna for approval.

'That'll mean only five of us to carry him when we get there.' Jenna tapped her foot, her lips pursed in thought.

'We can manage,' I said, relief at the plan making me confident. 'It's not far.'

'Won't we need to use a blanket to carry him on? What about washing that?'

'What about his car? Won't we leave evidence in it, hairs and stuff?'

'What about the knife and the masks?'

'We could soak the knife in bleach and then wash it and put it back? No one will ever know, will they?'

For a moment, we all silently considered future holidaymakers preparing their meals with a knife that had stabbed a man to death.

'Yes to the knife – I'll do that. I hadn't thought about the blanket – is there anything in his car that we can use? Someone go and check, it's unlocked.' Jen stood up and picked up the plastic-wrapped knife, adding, 'I didn't hear him lock it when he arrived.'

Emma knelt and felt for his keys in his jeans pockets. 'It must be unlocked, there are no keys here. I'll go and check his car. What did you do with his wallet?' She looked up at Jen.

'It's safe, I'll dispose of it.'

'I'll wash the knife.' I stood up, taking the bag from Jen and holding it at arm's length as if it might bite me. I walked into the kitchen with trembling legs and tipped the knife into the sink, running the hot tap until steam filled my eyes. Squirting washing-up liquid over it, I scrubbed it with the scourer until my hands felt raw, then filled the sink with cold water and poured bleach into it, leaving it to soak for a while. They were my fingerprints on it, I wasn't going to take any chances

'This is crazy, we're never going to get away with it.' Lauren sank into a chair as I rejoined them after passing Jen as she disappeared inside. 'What are we doing? We should just call the police and tell them everything.'

We fell silent, our eyes flicking to one another as we tried to gauge each other's mindset.

She picked up her phone from the table, waiting for us to agree.

33

Jenna stormed back, snatching Lauren's phone from her hand. 'Yeah? Tell them what? That we planned to entice him here and then he just got killed by accident? You think they'll believe us?' Jenna snorted in derision.

'It *was* an accident,' I whispered.

'What was that, Abs? Care to share?'

'I said it *was* an accident, Jen. I don't even know where the knife came from, it was just... there... We were just going to teach him a lesson, shave his hair and eyebrows off, write stuff on him and make him wear a dress... Maybe if we explain it all, if we tell the truth, they'll believe us...' At that moment, I think I honestly wanted to believe my own words.

Claire looked from me to Lauren, then at Jen. 'We could try, after all, look what he did to Lauren.'

'That's exactly the point, Claire,' Jen spat. 'And do I need to remind everyone that Lauren did not want the police involved at the time?'

'But we didn't mean to kill him,' I cried. 'We all know it was an accident, we could–'

'No, it's too late, they'll never believe us now, not now that he's dead.'

Jenna meant me... no police officer would believe me... She was right, of course...

She sighed. 'Sweet little Abigail, living in her little world where everything always works out perfectly. Well, you're not lucky Abigail this time. I've got news for you, sugarplum, you don't get to snap your little fingers and have everything go your way – not this time, not when it's your fault we're in this mess.' Jenna's face was ugly as she leant in close to me and spat out her cruel words.

Hurt, I wiped a drop of her spittle from my face.

'That's not fair, you can't pin this all on Abs.'

I gave Hayley a grateful smile.

'No? Well she's the one who killed him, isn't she? And aren't we all trying to get her out of this mess so that she doesn't spend the rest of her life in prison?'

'Jen, ease up, OK?' Fi's hand grasped Jenna's arm. 'We're here because of what happened to Lauren, and it was your idea that we take revenge on him, in case you've forgotten.'

'I didn't hear any of you objecting at the time, not when Lauren was black and blue and crying in her bed in the middle of the night.' Jen shook Fi's hand off, her eyes flashing dangerously.

'That's because you'd made your mind up,' cried Lauren.

'You didn't give us a choice, typical bossy Jenna, always telling us what to do.'

'We didn't get a say in the matter.'

'You set things in motion before we had a chance to think straight.'

'I wanted to call the police.'

'Everybody shut up!' Claire's command brought sudden silence. 'We're friends, or have we forgotten that? Turning on each other will get us nowhere, it is what it is and we have to go from here.'

'Thank you, Claire.' Jenna's smile had a hint of the triumphant about it. 'We stick with the plan. We've come too far to backtrack, we're almost there and the hard work is done, it's just the final clean-up. And in case anyone's forgotten, I'm on a bloody police database somewhere, thanks to Shane. The last thing I need is them sniffing around this and finding out about my past. No more discussion, let's move.'

Emma turned silently and disappeared.

'We should get him to his car.'

The next few minutes passed with heaving and grunting as we carried the body through the cottage and out to his car, where Emma stood beside it.

'There's a blanket on the back seat.'

'Great, Lauren, take this blanket back and make sure it gets washed and dried. Lucky it's an estate car, that makes things easier. Let's get him in the back.'

'Wait.'

We all turned to Hayley.

'If we use his blanket we might leave fingerprints on it, I'm not sure, but... Couldn't we try to just carry him in the plastic at the other end?'

'We could... saves us worrying about the blanket...'

'We can just tear open the plastic when we throw him off the cliff, then ditch the plastic in a rubbish bin somewhere.'

Jenna gave a nod of approval.

'What are we going to do about his car?' asked Emma, as we stood poised around his body lying on the ground in its plastic shroud.

'I haven't a frigging clue.'

'We need to torch it.'

'And how exactly does one do that, oh wise one?' Jenna arched an eyebrow at Fi.

'Don't ask me, I've just seen it on the telly. Stick a lighted cigarette in the petrol tank, maybe?'

For some reason we all turned to Hayley.

'I don't know, I'm not a criminal expert you know. It's not something any of my detective books ever went into details about.'

'What if we left it back at the pub he was at? There won't be anyone there in the early hours of the morning. We could wipe it down.'

'Wipe it down? With what, Fi? A tissue? How about, we forget the telly talk from crime shows? We'll never leave it clean enough after being in it anyway, and the police would go over it with a fine-tooth comb presumably.'

'What if you're the only one who goes in it? You could wear the washing up gloves and cover your hair, we haven't touched anything yet, apart from Em opening the doors, so there wouldn't be anything for the cops to find.'

'Why are we moving him in his car? Why not Abigail's? Why would we drive his car to the coast and back? We can all fit in Abs' car, can't we?'

Jenna nodded slowly. 'True... you know what? It makes sense. We'll get him into Abs' boot and I'll drive his car to the pub and leave it there, then we'll all go to this lighthouse place and get rid of him. Let's do this. Abs, where are your car keys?'

I scurried back into the cottage to retrieve my keys, the sound of the washing machine a loud whir in the silence of the night.

'He's starting to get stiff, I think.' Emma's foot nudged the body as I re-joined them. 'We need to hurry.'

I unlocked my car and we grunted and gasped, forcing his body into the boot of my car, uncomfortably aware that Emma was right – he was definitely stiffening up.

Out of nowhere, I had an idea. 'You could wear his clothes to drive his car, then you wouldn't leave any evidence.'

I felt quite proud of myself as everyone nodded in admiration. But Jenna rained on my parade immediately and, to be fair, she had a point.

'His clothes won't fit me, he's quite slim, in case you hadn't noticed, there's not a chance in hell that my arse will fit in his jeans.'

Our eyes darted around as we assessed each other, finally landing on Emma.

'Me? But then what do we do with his clothes? Which will have me all over them, by the way.'

'Don't worry about that, we can drop them off at charity shops next week, mix them with old clothes of our husbands. No one would ever guess in a million years. Who'd be looking for him in Bromley when he went missing in the New Forest?'

'Another insight into the criminal mind from our crime-reading friend, Hayley.' Fi's joking comment made us all smile, lessening the tension for a second.

'Right, I'll go and cover my hair, grab the gloves, and get into his clothes.' Emma pulled off her shirt, wriggled out of her cropped jeans, and kicked off her flip flops. 'Put these in your car, Abs, I'm not getting rid of a body in my bra and knickers. Whose mask was easy to see out of?'

'Er, I could see pretty clearly from the eyeholes in the panda head.' Fi looked as puzzled as the rest of us, as she shrugged and rolled her eyes.

'I couldn't see that much from the bunny mask.'

'The pig's eyeholes were alright, I suppose.'

'I'll use the panda, all I could see in the horse's head was his muzzle.'

Now we got it.

A couple of minutes later, I drove out of the driveway, following Jenna's directions to the pub in Frogham five minutes away, as what appeared to be a panda bear followed us in his car. I pulled up on the side of the road, and we watched silently as Emma drove to the furthest end of the parking area and parked the car under a tree, exited it and locked it, and walked over to us – a panda wearing an Ibiza T-shirt, men's jeans, and pink rubber gloves, her feet making thwacking sounds on the tarmac with every clumsy step from his oversized deck shoes. Someone sniggered.

34

The Passenger

It was too much. The tension and strain needed a release and we burst into fits of hysterical laughter as Emma squeezed into the back of the car, next to Hayley and Fi, and pulled off the panda head.

'What's so funny?' she asked.

No one could answer for a few seconds, we'd temporarily lost control and it felt so good.

I pulled away and we began our drive to the coast in silence, peppered with the odd small explosion of snorting giggles as one of us pictured Emma walking towards us all over again.

'I wish we'd taken a photo,' wailed Hayley suddenly, tears trickling down her cheeks.

'Alright, alright, the laugh's over, I get it, I looked like some kind of kinky psycho killer on the loose, very funny and all that, but right now I need a bit of space to get these clothes off. Please...'

My eyes caught Emma's in the rearview mirror and I realised what she must be feeling – *she was wearing a dead man's clothes.*

As Emma performed awkward manoeuvres in the back to remove his clothes and put her own back on, my mind registered the names of the villages as we wound our way through the night towards our destination. I thought enviously of the people tucked up in their beds fast asleep all around us as we passed them by, village after village, names associated with holidays and happy times... Mockbeggar, Ringwood, Little Canford, Upton, Lytchett

Minster, Wareham, Corfe Castle, Harman's Cross, Swanage, Durlston Castle and, finally, a sign for Anvil Point Lighthouse.

'Shit, there's a gate. Is it locked?' Jenna stared out at the closed gate ahead of us. 'It'd better bloody not be, Abigail.'

Like it was my fault. 'I didn't know anything about a gate.'

'I'll check, give me a chance to get some blood back in my legs.'

We watched Fi inspect the gate and, with relief, saw it swing open as she beckoned us through, closing it again behind us.

I crawled up the last stretch of narrow road, keeping my lights on low and peering ahead anxiously.

'We'll have to stop here.' I switched off the engine and we sat silently for a moment, staring out at the light as it flashed intermittently from the lighthouse.

'Can't we get any closer?' whispered Hayley.

'No, see those gates on our left? There might be people in there.'

'I don't think they have lighthouse keepers anymore,' said Emma, trying to be helpful.

'No, they're holiday cottages – there are two, I think.'

'I'll go and have a look through the gates.' Jenna eased her door open and stepped out, returning almost immediately. 'There's no one there, no cars, no lights.'

'We should still leave the car here, there's no more road anyway.'

'Well then, let's do this. A few minutes and we'll be headed back.'

I opened the boot and we reached for the body. Which was stuck.

'We'll never get him out.' Emma wrapped her arms around her body, turning in rapid circles. 'It's rigor mortis, we're fucked.' Her words became a horrifying wail. 'He's stuck in the bloody boot and we're fucked.'

'There's a car coming.' Fi's voice, usually so calm, was filled with panic.

'Abs, you need to hide the car, everyone else up past the end of the wall, quick.'

'Hide the car where?' My heart started hammering in my chest as the headlights drew closer. 'Where do I hide the car?' I called to the retreating bodies of my friends.

'Follow us, you can park behind the wall, just drive on the grass. Hurry up, Abs.'

I looked back at the headlights, falling awkwardly into the driver's seat and fumbling with my keys. My sweaty hand slipped on the lever, shooting the car backwards by mistake, and I pulled up the handbrake, the car jerking as I forced myself to remain calm. I put the car into drive and shot up past the gates and onto the uneven ground ahead, the open door of the boot bouncing up and down affording me glimpses of the approaching car's headlights in my rearview mirror. I hit the brakes as I reached the end of the wall and swung the car to the left, hoping desperately that I wasn't about to go flying off the edge of the cliff.

'Turn off the engine and lights,' hissed Jen, yanking my door open as I gasped raggedly for air.

'The boot's still open.' I was shaking all over, and Jen reached in, switching off the engine and turning the lights off just as we heard music playing from the open window of the car as it pulled up at the gates to the cottages.

'Shh, everybody quiet.'

We heard the gate being opened, the car moving again, voices, a door slamming, and then silence. Lights appeared from the windows of one of the cottages as we held our breath. The lights dimmed as curtains were pulled, and the muffled sound of music reached our ears.

Jenna touched my shoulder, indicating that I should get out, and I climbed out, my legs feeling like jelly.

'I didn't close the boot. Is he–? Is he still there?'

We gathered silently around the boot, reassuring ourselves that I hadn't lost our corpse in my erratic drive across the rough ground.

Jenna reached in and pulled at him with both hands. 'The bouncing's shifted him around, I think we can get him out.'

We spoke in low voices, instructing each other as to where to hold him, our clammy hands slipping on his plastic shroud as we pulled him free from the boot of my car, so that he tumbled onto the ground. The plastic was beginning to tear as we picked him up again, his stiffness making it easier to carry him than his earlier limp form had, and we began a slow, crab-like procession towards the cliff edge, stopping to catch our breath every now and then as the sound of the crashing waves below grew louder.

'Put him down,' grunted Jenna, as we reached the edge, and we dropped him gratefully, the plastic now shredded in places, exposing his nakedness. 'Here, we'll throw him off here.'

'We're not really at the edge, I don't think.' Hayley peered through the darkness, taking cautious steps closer before backing away. 'It slopes, and we can't get any closer, it's too dangerous.'

'Then we'll have to swing him from here.'

We picked him up again, ready to swing him over the edge.

'Wait, we need to keep a grip on the plastic so that only his body goes over. Tear that bit at the end open, Fi.'

'Hurry up, I'm going to drop him.'

'What about the cottages? Shouldn't we move further away?'

'You're joking.'

'My hand's slipping.'

'But what about people who stay here?'

'What about them? They'll be offended? They'll never know.'

'I can't hold him much longer.'

'Won't he be taken out to sea anyway?'

'We could move along a bit further.'

'Seriously? You're kidding, right?'

'Too late.'

The weight we were holding was gone, our hands left holding only the torn, shredded black dustbin bags.

35

Way Down We Go

'Where'd he go?'

'Did he go over the edge?'

'He must have.'

We stared at the empty ground around us as the light from the lighthouse flashed, illuminating the area for a moment.

'How do we know if he fell into the water or not? What if he got caught on something?'

'And if he did?' Fi's tone was mocking. 'Which one of us is going to abseil down there and untangle him?'

'Let's get out of here.' Jenna didn't have to say it twice.

'The keys. My keys. They're not here. What did I do with them?' I stared around at the others in alarm.

'Please tell me you didn't drop the keys, Abs? Could you try any harder to destroy my life? All our lives?'

Emma's tense tone increased my stress as I bent down to peer beneath the car, in the footwell, back at the path we'd trodden to the cliff edge... I patted at non-existent pockets, my hands shaking, feeling my lips begin to tremble. *Had they been in my hand when I was carrying him? Had they gone over the edge with his body?*

'I've lost them. They're gone. No, no, no...' Hunching over, I wrapped my arms around myself. 'I'm sorry,' I wailed. 'I'm sorry.'

'What do we do?' Hayley started pulling at Emma's arm. 'Em?'

Emma grabbed Hayley's hand. 'Stop crying, calm down.'

'Calm down? Fi confronted Emma. 'Calm down, when we've just chucked a dead body over the cliff and we've lost the car keys?'

'Don't shout at me, Fi, I didn't lose them.'

'Oh my God, this is a nightmare.' Hayley grabbed my arm and we held onto each other, our eyes wild.

I wailed louder, my whole body shaking in panic.

'Here they are, you must have dropped them on the seat.' Jen held up my car keys. 'Someone shut her up before she gets hysterical. Everyone else, calm down.' Her hand whipped across my face, the shock of my stinging cheek silencing me. She looked at me for a moment. 'I'll drive. Fi, you're in the front with me.'

Hayley shushed and cosseted me as Jenna drove us back, whispering little things to try to calm me, and eventually my breathing settled as my heart stopped hammering out of my chest.

'You had a panic attack, Abs, and no wonder.' Hayley squeezed my hand as she whispered, 'We all did. You're alright now.'

My head jerked in what seemed like only a moment later, and I looked up to see our cottage in front of us, an anxious-looking Claire and Lauren standing outside.

'Did you do it?' Lauren's whole face looked grey, her eyes dark, the skin around them puffy and shadowy. 'Is he gone?'

'He's gone, the car's dropped off, we're in the clear. Is everything done? Are we ready to go?'

'Are we really leaving now? It's four thirty in the bloody morning and we're all knackered.'

'We can't go yet, the blanket's still in the tumble dryer, we need another half an hour.'

'Alright, we'll wait, I'll just check through the cottage. Em, you should bring your car back round.' Jenna marched off, leaving us standing in a huddle by the car.

'Let's go in, I'll make some tea, you look like you all need it.'

We nodded gratefully, following Claire inside, past our packed bags lined up by the door.

We perched on the edges of the settee and armchairs, nursing our mugs of hot tea in silence, a short while later.

'Well?' Lauren could stand it no longer. 'Are you going to tell us how it all went?'

We all chipped in with garbled details, as Claire and Lauren hung on our every word.

'So we can all relax, everything's going to be fine?'

'Everything's going to be fine. Just one thing, we never mention the name of this cottage, alright? Forget it ever existed. If anyone asks, we stayed in Beaulieu. Be vague, it's no biggie, we had a great weekend, we drank too much, ate too much, and Fi got to see her ponies. Hell, we've even got photos of them.'

'I'll go and check if the blanket's dry.' Claire heaved herself from the chair, yawning.

'Great, then I'm going for a smoke. Where are your fags, Laur?'

'No, we can't make any more mess.'

'Sod that, I need a cigarette.' Fi pulled the lounge door open and stood on the deck, as Lauren joined her.

'OK, all done.' Claire looked exhausted as she slumped back into her chair.

'Are you alright to drive now, Abs?'

I nodded, yawning, the guilt of the trouble I'd caused weighing heavily inside. I needed to think about the knife, to try and come up with an explanation for how I'd come to have it in my hand, but my tired brain provided only blankness, and I turned to my friends for help.

'Are you sure none of you remember picking up the knife when you grabbed all the other things?' I looked around at the tired faces, willing someone to recall something. 'Maybe it got caught on something somehow?'

My eyes met with Hayley's, hers earnest in her nodding face as they met mine. 'Or fell on the floor, or something, and then ended up there by mistake?'

Hayley nodded slowly. 'What about when the cutlery fell on the floor in the kitchen?'

'Fi had a knife.' Emma cast a suspicious glance out through the door, towards Fi.

'I was trying to open the blasted vodka. What? D'you think I put the knife there deliberately?' Storming back in, Fi stood with her hands on her hips in front of Emma. 'And why in God's name would I do that, Emma?'

'No one did anything deliberately.' Jen looked slowly at each of us in turn. 'We'll hit the road and find somewhere for breakfast, we need to get away from here, and kill some time.'

I think we all flinched at her choice of word.

We loaded up the cars in silence and waited for Jenna to lock the door and replace the keys in the key box, then we made our winding way to the motorway, breathing a little easier with each passing mile.

'Pull in here.'

Jenna's words, the first that had been spoken since we'd left Blissford about an hour and a half earlier, roused us from our collective stupor, and I indicated, checking that Emma followed suit behind me, pulling into the services area as I realised, with surprise, that I was hungry.

I wasn't the only one, it turned out, once we'd all climbed out of the cars and stretched our arms and legs amidst much yawning.

'I'm starving, I guess getting rid of dead bodies gives one an appetite.'

'Fi, shut the fuck up. I'm not joking.' Jen glared at Fi, who had the grace to look abashed.

'We all need to eat and drink something, we need some energy, we've been on the go for twenty-four hours straight with no sleep.'

'Claire's right.' Jen nodded. 'We need sustenance, and we need to waste a bit of time, so let's get inside and see what's on the menu.'

As it turned out, there were various outlets offering food, and it took us a while to decide who wanted what and from where. We finally convened at a cluster of tables on the outside deck, away from anyone else, the early morning chill already surrendering to the warmth of the sun.

Having had our fill of coffee, we'd moved on to tea, accompanied by a box of doughnuts that Lauren had appeared with, when Hayley suddenly piped up out of nowhere.

'What about the masks?'

It took me a moment to work out what Hayley was talking about, almost as if my mind was already blocking memories of our deadly weekend. My teeth crunched through the sweet pink icing, sinking into the softness of the doughnut, before reaching the creamy strawberry filling, and I had to stop myself from groaning out loud in pleasure.

'Shit, I forgot about them. Any suggestions? Anyone?'

'I always had this idea...'

We all looked at Hayley, wondering what she was going to say.

'You know, like, when the killer has to get rid of the gloves or the knife...'

I fought to keep down the bile rising in my throat as Hayley continued, the enjoyment in my doughnut ruined at her mention of a knife.

'Why doesn't he just put bits in carrier bags, tie them up and drop them in public rubbish bins in high streets of different towns? Who would ever find them or make sense of them? The bins are just tipped into rubbish trucks or whatever, and the whole lot goes to the dump, doesn't it?'

'Someone missed their vocation,' said Fi, dryly.

'It's a good idea, Hayles.' Claire looked at Jenna. 'Don't you think, Jen?'

'Fine, why not? Can you do it, Hayles? Can we leave them with you?'

'Sure, I'll get rid of them in the week. Oh, and don't forget, everyone, we'll need some men's clothes to make up charity shop bags. We only have four items of his to mix in, so that's me, Claire, Lauren and Abs.'

'Great, it'll give me a good excuse to get rid of some of Adrian's awful shirts.' Claire's forced laugh didn't reach her eyes.

'What size are his shoes?'

Realising that his clothes were still squashed in the rear footwell of my car, I said I'd go and check, returning to announce that they were a size ten.

'I'll take the shoes and chuck in some old ones of Paul's, he's a ten,' Lauren offered.

'I'll do the jeans.' That was Hayley.

That left the T-shirt and his boxer shorts, my mind informed me in a detached manner.

'Oh God, not the boxer shorts, please. I'll take the T-shirt.' That was Claire.

Which left me with a pair of boxer shorts worn by the man I'd stabbed to death... *Had it really only been the night before?* 'I'll do the boxers, then,' I mumbled, pushing my chair back and rushing to the ladies' toilets to throw up my breakfast.

Under Pressure

'You're home early. Rough time? You look terrible.'

Martin certainly knew how to make a murderer feel good about herself. I forced myself to smile at him as I dropped my bags on the hall floor. 'Great, knackering, you know how it is.'

'Not really.' He studied me quizzically. 'No messages from you? No calls? I was beginning to wonder if something had happened.'

I froze for a second, my mind whirring frantically. I always called him when we went away on a girls' weekend, without fail. *But he could have called you*, a voice in my head said. 'The signal was bad.'

He shrugged, accepting my poor explanation. 'Want some tea? Did you want some lunch? I just had a sandwich, there's some cold chicken left in the fridge, I could make you a sandwich if you want?'

I wanted to fall into my bed and pass out into oblivion, but I pasted another smile on my face in an effort to appear as if nothing was wrong. 'That would be great, thanks.'

'Come and tell me about the weekend.'

I followed him into the kitchen, watching him take the bread out of the bread bin and place two slices on the bread board.

'So, where did you stay in the end? It was a big secret from Fi, if I remember rightly.' He took the butter from the fridge and buttered the bread, looking up as I remained silent. 'Abs?'

I stared at the hard bits of butter on the torn bread, usually a pet peeve of mine, my mind blank. I couldn't remember the name that Jen had said, and I felt my face flush with heat as panic rose inside me. *Not Blissford, don't say Blissford. But it began with a B...*

'Earth to Abs? Where did you stay?' He replaced the lid on the butter and took the chicken from the fridge, placing it on a chopping board and reaching for a knife.

'Beaulieu.' The name exploded from my mouth in relief. 'We stayed in Beaulieu.'

'OK... Got some big motor place there, haven't they? Old cars, or something?' He took the large knife from the block, stabbing it into the chicken's corpse. 'Not that old cars are exactly the kind of thing you lot would be interested in. Abs?'

I stumbled up the stairs and into the bathroom, throwing the lid of the toilet up and heaving, hearing Martin's steps on the stairs.

'Abs? You alright?' His hand patted my back as I straightened.

'Sorry, I think I need to lie down for a while.'

'Must have been a pretty wild time, haven't seen you looking this rough after a weekend with the girls. Get yourself into bed and I'll bring you your sandwich.'

'No. No, thanks, I don't think I can eat right now.'

'Some tea then.'

I nodded feebly. 'Thanks.'

When I opened my eyes, it was getting dark outside and I forced myself to wake up, knowing that I needed to present some semblance of normality. I took a quick shower and pulled on a T-shirt and some loose cotton trousers, turning round as Martin came into the bedroom.

'Thought I heard movements, you've been out for hours. Feeling a bit better?'

My eyes fell on my empty bag lying on the chair.

Seeing my glance, Martin explained, clearly feeling pleased with himself. 'I unpacked your bags and did the washing and, for extra brownie points, I cleaned your car inside and out.' He paused, a strange look flickering across his eyes for a second. 'D'you feel like that sandwich now, or shall I order a pizza?'

'Pizza sounds good, thanks, and thanks for doing everything, you didn't have to.'

I came downstairs to find a glass of wine waiting for me, and I curled up in an armchair, sipping my wine, knowing that I had to say something about the weekend.

'Let's see the photos then, see what you got up to.' Martin reached for my phone before I could grab it.

'Is that a guilty look, Abs? What are you hiding? Had a secret rendezvous with a bloke, did you?' He laughed at his own joke as the doorbell rang.

I swiped my phone from where he'd dropped it on the coffee table, frantically opening my gallery and searching for the photo of Jen in the hot tub. Keeping one ear on Martin's voice as he chatted to the pizza delivery man, I deleted the photo and put my phone back down on the coffee table as I heard him close the front door. *Saved by pizza.*

'Pizza's here,' Martin informed me somewhat unnecessarily, poking his head round the door on his way to the kitchen. 'Fingers or cutlery?'

'Fingers are fine.'

Martin was being overly nice to me, even insisting that I choose which film to watch, and not complaining when I opted for one of my favourite chick flicks. He chuckled at the familiar dialogue between Harry and Sally, laughing out loud at the famous scene in the diner, even though we'd seen it numerous times before, appearing not to notice that I failed to raise a smile. I forced my brain to focus on the film and not the events of the last forty-eight hours, breaking up a slice of pizza and nibbling tiny pieces, while Martin ate the rest, oblivious to my lack of appetite, and headed gratefully upstairs to bed – sleep coming instantly the moment my head touched the pillow.

I sat up in bed, my heart racing in the darkness. *He'd cleaned out my car inside.* The clothes... the T-shirt, jeans, boxer shorts, and shoes... all dropped on the floor in the back of the car when Emma had changed out of them... Except she hadn't worn the boxer shorts, of course... Had the rest of the clothes still been there? And what had happened to the boxer shorts? Moaning softly, I rocked back and forth, trying to think. Maybe Hayley had taken the clothes? Or distributed them to the others for making up charity shop bags? Yes, she'd have done that, she must have... But the boxers? Had she left them in my car? I had to know.

My rational brain told me that if Martin had found a pair of men's boxer shorts in the back of my car, he'd have wanted to know what the hell was going on, but my stupid brain said I had to go and look anyway, after all, he could have missed them if they were pushed under the front seat...

Martin was out for the count, and I tiptoed down the stairs, slipping out of the front door and unlocking my car, flinching at the soft beep amplified in the silence of the night. Climbing into the back seat, I reached under the driver's seat and felt around, doing the same beneath the passenger seat, but finding nothing. I checked the pockets in the backs of the seats, flipped down the armrest and checked the cavity, climbed into the front and checked the footwells and the glove compartment, my panic rising. Where were they? Finally, I checked the boot, but everything was empty and extremely clean – Martin had done a good job.

I locked my car and stood in the driveway in my nightie and slippers, considering the unthinkable – that we'd somehow managed to leave the boxer shorts folded up on the deck at the cottage... After all our efforts, had we left a piece of damning evidence lying there, just waiting to be discovered? I wanted to laugh and knew that I was in danger of cracking up.

'Abs?'

I turned to find Martin standing at the front door, his hair tousled from sleep, his expression unreadable.

'What's going on? What are you doing? Come inside.'

I walked slowly back indoors and up the stairs, unable to think of a single plausible thing to say to explain my actions. I climbed into bed and lay down, pulling the duvet up and closing my eyes.

The mattress shifted as Martin climbed back into bed beside me, and I held my breath as I felt him lie down.

'Abs.' His hand uncurled my own and took the car keys from its grasp. 'Is there something you want to say? To ask me? Did you–? Did something happen while you were away? Was it Jenna? Did she say something? You're upset, we can talk about it, just... say something... don't give me the silent treatment...'

Oh, the relief. He thought Jenna and I had fallen out and that I was upset. He cared, I thought with surprise, he actually cared about my relationships with my friends.

'No, Jenna and I are fine,' I whispered. 'Nothing happened, everything's fine.'

I felt his body relax beside mine, but could sense his indecision about whether to question me further about my strange behaviour. 'I just thought Hayley had left some chocolate in the back seat pocket.' I apologised silently to Hayley.

Martin gave a small chuckle. 'Poor old Hayley, she should really lay off the chocolate, she's getting a bit tubby. Mind you, so are you. Too many weekends away with the girls and lunches out. Nope, there was no chocolate in the car, I cleaned it out, remember?'

'Oh yes...' I feigned sleepiness, turning over and snuggling into my pillow, his unkind words barely registering, as my brain screamed the question at me over and over again. *Where are the boxer shorts?*

The next morning, I called Hayley as soon as Martin had left for work, leaving her a message to call me, and threw myself into the housework, changing the bed and washing the bedlinen and towels, before setting up the ironing board to plough through the huge ironing pile on the spare bed. I sorted through the untidy mass of clean washing, folding the things that didn't need ironing and putting them on our bed to put away later, my hands working on autopilot, my eyes staring at nothing, my mind a black hole of emptiness. I set to, ironing Martin's work shirts first and hanging them neatly in the wardrobe, before moving onto the easier bits, finishing with the pillowcases.

I was headfirst in the airing cupboard, squeezing the ironed pillowcases onto their small pile on the top shelf, when I heard my phone ringing from the bedroom.

'Hayles?' I caught her just before she rang off, putting her on speaker and placing my phone on the bed.

'Abs, hi. How are you? Are you OK? I feel... I don't know... a bit odd... like I'm sleep walking or something. I can't seem to clear my head properly, and I feel nervous and sick. I'm sure Ross was suspicious when I got home.'

I knew exactly what she meant. 'Same, Hayles.' It felt good just to hear her voice, but to know that she felt like I did was a comfort.

'I don't know what to do with the weekend in my head. D'you know what I mean?'

'I do, it's like we want to forget it but we have to make up all these stories about a weekend that didn't happen, and every time we do that, we actually re-live the real weekend...'

'Have you done anything about the photos yet? Jenna said we had to post them as proof of where we were and what we did.'

'Not yet, I think I've been trying to avoid thinking about it all, and the thought of having to write stupid little captions just makes me feel like throwing up.' I started to put some of the clean, folded, clothes away as we chatted, moving back and forth between the bed and the cupboards and drawers.

'I looked up the news online this morning.' Hayley's voice was a whisper, and I strained to hear her. 'You know, for that area. There's a man reported missing. It's out there, Abs, *he's* out there – they're going to start looking for him.'

Icy tentacles crawled around my head and neck, creeping down my back and shoulders to wrap themselves around my arms, turning my fingers numb so that I dropped the pile of Martin's underwear I'd been about to put into his drawer. Frozen to the spot, I made myself breathe.

'Abs? Are you still there?'

'I'm still here,' I called out, taking stiff steps to the bed and sitting down. 'Oh God. I don't think I can take this. I can't do it, I can't carry on as normal, not after what I did. I killed him, Hayles, I killed a man.'

'We were all involved, Abs, it wasn't just you.'

'But I'm the one who stabbed him.' My voice sounded high and strained and I knew that I probably sounded unstable. Hell, I *was* unstable.

'I still don't understand it – the knife – where did it even come from?'

'I don't know,' I wailed. 'It was just in my hand. Everything's such a blur, I'd drunk too much wine, Jenna kept filling my glass to give me courage, and then there was so much rage, everybody screaming and hitting him, and I was hitting him as well, except I wasn't just hitting him, I must have been stabbing him... I'm sorry I've involved you in all this, Hayles, I'm sorry about it all, I can't even bear to think about his wife and daughter...'

'Don't– don't go there, it'll destroy you. We must remember what he did to Lauren. We have to keep moving forward, Jenna's expecting us to get rid of the last pieces of evidence, and once we've done that no one will ever be able to connect us to it. It will all be in the past.'

'But not in our heads,' I said bitterly, suddenly remembering my reason for wanting to speak to Hayley in the first place. 'You've just reminded me... the clothes... did you give them to Lauren and Claire? Did you take the, um, what were you going to take?'

'The jeans, yes, I took them, and I gave them the other bits. Oh, I put the boxer shorts in the back seat pocket of your car. I can't believe I forgot to tell you. It's OK though, I pushed them right down to the bottom so no one would find them unless they were looking for them, which they're not. Have you sorted out some old clothes of Martin's yet?'

'No...' I felt strange, like something ominous was happening. 'I'll do that now, thanks, Hayley. I have to go.' I walked slowly out of the bedroom and down the stairs, picking up my car keys and walking out of the front door in a repeat of the night before. *I checked the seat pockets... I couldn't have missed them...*

Because they weren't there... I backed out of my car, a strange crashing sound filling my head. *They weren't there... Hayley had put them in the pocket and now they were gone...*

Martin.

'No...' I moaned, clambering back into my car and feverishly scrabbling about like some kind of crazed drug addict searching for their last remaining fix.

38

Martin knew. Martin knew what? My rational inner voice reasoned with my unhinged one. So what if he found the boxer shorts? He doesn't know they belonged to a dead man. No, he'll just think I've been having an affair. Well that's just perfect. But why hasn't he said anything?

I'm not sure how long I sat on the stairs trying to decide what to do. Part of me wanted to tell Martin everything, but part of me knew that would be a terrible move – I'd be betraying the girls, my six friends who'd rallied round and gone to such extremes to help cover up my murderous act. Martin would insist that we go to the police and tell them everything... we'd all go to prison... my friends would hate me, I'd lose Martin, and Jenna would kill me...

Jenna – maybe I should call her and ask her what to do? But I just couldn't face her anger, especially after everything we'd gone through. I could imagine her scathing voice mocking me at my absolute ineptitude at spectacularly managing to leave my murder victim's underpants in my car for my husband to find.

So I did nothing. I shoved it to the back of my mind and got up, went back up the stairs, stepped over Martin's underwear dropped all over the floor, and carried on putting the rest of the washing away. I even hummed a tune to myself, deliberately keeping my mind blank.

Stooping, I picked up the scattered underwear and dropped everything on the bed, folding the pants and shorts again one by one, my hand stilling as it picked up a pair of red gingham check boxers. Frowning, I checked through the pile, trying to remember how many pairs of that particular design Martin had.

Three – he had three pairs in varying designs and shades of red, I was sure of it – bought by me in a pack about a year ago. I turned to his underwear drawer, rummaging through and pulling out two pairs – which, with the two pairs I'd just folded made four... My fingers fumbled with the waistbands, turning them over to check the labels – three from Marks and Spencer... and one from Next...

I slid down to the floor with my back against the bed and sobbed, clutching the pair of boxers from Next to my breast. I'd found them. I was so relieved, it didn't even cross my mind to wonder how they'd made it from the back seat pocket of my car into the laundry.

My relief was euphoric, and I fetched a black dustbin bag from the kitchen drawer, rolled it open, and began to search through Martin's clothing for items that could go to the charity shop, throwing in shirts, a pair of old jeans, a couple of jumpers, some of his older boxer shorts – to which I added *the* pair – and a pair of shoes that he hadn't worn claiming that they hurt his feet. I tied up the bag, taking it downstairs and out to the boot of my car. Mission accomplished.

Well, almost... I still had to drop the bag off somewhere... somewhere away from here, away from me...

With no particular place in mind, I left Bromley, unconsciously following the route we'd taken on that fated weekend when it had all started, finding myself on the M25 as a sign for the Dartford tunnel appeared ahead of me. I drove into Dartford and parked at the Priory Centre, dropped off the bag of clothing at the first charity shop that I came across, and returned to my car, driving on to Bluewater Shopping Centre and sitting down with a pistachio latte and a sausage roll at Caffè Nero. It was done. Surprised at how hungry I was, I took huge bites of the sausage roll, savouring the pork and pancetta encased in its flaky pastry.

I felt quite light-hearted as I squandered money left, right and centre, buying things we didn't need, including a new teapot and a blender, and returned home with a boot full of shopping bags and groceries, busying myself in the kitchen preparing a dinner of roast beef, roast potatoes and roasted Mediterranean vegetables. Everything was going to be alright... as long as I didn't think about what I'd done ever again.

Jenna's text came in as I was putting the plates in the dishwasher that evening. *Girls' night at Emma's Friday. Where are your photos? You're last as usual.* She'd added a silly face to take the sting out of her insult, and I smiled, feeling suddenly that we'd got through the worst of it. It was over.

While Martin watched the news after dinner, I sat at the dining room table and went through my photos from our weekend, posting them in random photo dumps and adding short captions, albeit lacking in any kind of humour, and tagging my friends. I scrolled through everything once I was done, nodding at how busy our weekend looked, and felt almost convinced that we'd had a fun weekend away.

'Bloke's gone missing down in the New Forest.' Martin's voice pierced my consciousness and I looked over at him.

'What?' Unable to move, I listened to the newsreader informing us about a missing Matthew Parker, of Orpington, Kent, last seen at a local pub near the village of Frogham on Saturday evening. I risked a glance at the television screen, flinching at the photo of his face.

'Bit of a mystery, that.' Martin glanced over at me. 'Bloke has a few pints at the pub, leaves his car in the car park and completely disappears. No signs of a struggle, his wife and kid waiting for him back at her parents who live nearby... and he's from Orpington, not far from us. Small world. And listen to this, they were supposed to be moving to Spain in a few weeks.'

I shot an irritated look at an oblivious Martin as he continued to speak over the newsreader, meaning that I was hearing everything twice in a jumble of overlapping voices.

'There's his wife, poor thing, and his poor little girl, she must be so upset having her daddy go missing, ah – they're organising search parties starting tomorrow. Wonder what happened to him? Someone bumped him off maybe? Not the sort of area you expect violence though, is it? Frogham... Is that close to where you girls stayed? Hmm?' Martin turned to me expectantly.

'Er, Frogham? Never heard of it. We were in Beaulieu, I told you, so...' My insides twisted and tore at themselves as I thought about his little girl... *I'd killed her daddy... I was a monster...*

'Maybe he just wanted out, you know, of his life, and just started walking. He'll probably be spotted in some town up north in six months, living under a new identity. Maybe he has another family, wouldn't be the first time that's happened. Oh, you've put your photos on.' Martin was now looking at his phone, scrolling through my posts. 'And here's some photos from Fi, and Emma... wow, looks like you all enjoyed some good meals... Wait a minute? Are those bottles of water on the table? That's not like you lot. Ah, New Forest ponies... looks like a busy weekend... wait a minute... Where's that, then? Brockenhurst... that looks nice, so that's... hold on while I look at a map... you were only half an hour from that pub where that fellow went missing. You could have seen him and his family while you were out and about. Imagine that, if you had some vital clue that you could tell the cops and help them find him – Abigail Hawthorn, super sleuth, solves the mystery.'

I forced my mouth into a tortured grin, as Martin looked over at me.

39

I spent a restless night dreaming of him... sick feelings of desire for him, the look of cruel hunger in his eyes as he'd looked at me in the hot tub, swiftly followed by violent scenes of his body falling into the tub as figures with animals' heads shrieked and attacked him, and then my own hand clenched into a fist...

I woke up in the morning feeling dreadful, my mind still picturing the last image of my nightmares – his little girl screaming at me as she asked me why I'd killed Daddy. My nightie was damp, my mind a swamp of anxiety, and I was overtaken by the jitters, my hands shaking so badly that I spilt tea all over the kitchen counter.

Hayley's voice, when she phoned me, was wretched, and I felt bad for the way I'd ended our call the day before.

'Hayles, I'm sorry about the way I was yesterday, I was just a bit out of sorts, you know, after everything...'

'Can I come round? I need to talk to you. I think we might have made a really bad mistake.'

My mind ran through about a million types of really bad mistakes that we could have made, starting with me stabbing a man to death... 'Of course you can, I'll put the kettle on.'

I opened the front door a short while later to a white-faced Hayley, and wrapped my arms around her as she threw herself at me. 'Come in, I've made a pot of tea. What is it? What's happened?'

Haltingly, Hayley explained how she'd put the masks in plastic bags, tied them up, and dropped them into public litter bins in different places.

'I drove to Woolwich and dropped two in two different bins, then I drove to Welling and got rid of one there, then Bexleyheath, where I got rid of two more, as well as my bag of Ross's old clothes and the jeans, then Sidcup, then I made my way home, stopping in Eltham to get rid of the last one, and that's when– Promise me you won't say anything to Jenna? You know what she's like when she gets angry.'

'I promise, but, Hayles, what happened?' Images of Hayley being arrested holding a horse's head mask in a carrier bag flashed into my head.

'When I went to the boot to get the last bag, it wasn't there. And the trouble is, Abs, I know I bagged up all the masks because I checked the dustbin bag when I'd bagged them up and it was empty, and then I dropped all the small bags into it and put it into my boot. And then I got rid of the bags and I was missing one.'

'Maybe you put two masks in one bag by mistake?'

Hayley's hair stuck out in little wiggly spikes as she shook her head. 'The thing is, I made myself go back through it all in my head, and that's when I realised that I never saw the pig mask – the one that Jenna wore.'

We stared at each other for a moment as we tried to figure out how much of a problem this was likely to be.

'So... what are you saying... exactly?'

'I'm saying that we must have left it there. We went to all this trouble to remove all the evidence from the cottage and we must have left the pig mask lying there somewhere.'

'That's impossible.' It was my turn to shake my head. 'We checked everywhere more than once. Emma collected up all the masks – we could ask her.'

'No, she'll tell Jenna.'

'Jenna checked the cottage before we left, if it had been there, she would have found it.'

'So where is it? What happened to it?'

'I don't know... Look, Hayles, even if someone found it there, they probably wouldn't think anything of it... I think it's alright... one random animal mask at a cottage... and no one knows what we did anyway...' I crossed my fingers behind my back.

'So you think we can just forget about it?'

'Yes.' I smiled at Hayley's relieved face. 'We won't say anything.' I felt good about making Hayley feel better, but underneath I was worried... Jenna had been so particular about everything and now we had a loose end... one that she was unaware of...

'Did you see on the news?

'About *him*? Yes, Martin even mentioned it. Oh, Hayles, he had a little girl...' I started to sob.

'She wasn't his, at least.'

It took me a moment for Hayley's words to register.

'He was her step dad. They said this morning that they'd only been married for a year, so that's something, I suppose...'

It didn't help, not really, but I pulled myself together enough for us to finish our tea and for Hayley to leave with a slightly lighter step.

That night I received the first message from him.

40

Mad World

Martin had gone out, which was unusual for a Tuesday evening, but Paul had some kind of crisis and the men were meeting for a couple of pints. My mind was so preoccupied that I didn't stop to wonder what Paul's crisis actually was, or how it might relate to Lauren, and I took myself out to the patio with a large glass of wine and scrolled feverishly through the news stories on my phone, searching for anything to do with the missing man and reading every word I could find.

With a second glass of wine, and with something bordering on morbid fascination, I then brought up the Frisky app and signed in. His profile was still there, of course, and I stared at his photo until his features blurred, seeing him as I'd seen him in the flesh, standing fully naked and about to step into the hot tub. My imagination took over for a moment... he stepped into the warm water and took me in his arms, kissing me hungrily as his hands reached for my breasts... I was filled with a painful yearning, but the soft whooping sounds on my phone brought me back to reality, and I put it down on the table to take a large gulp of wine, feeling disgusted at myself.

But... had Martin ever wanted me like that? Certainly not for a long time... he was being nice to me, he just didn't seem to desire me anymore, not in that way... but Night Monster had wanted me... hadn't he? *Yeah, and he'd beaten up Lauren, and I'd killed him, small points, but...* But he'd only wanted me like that in my imagination, hadn't he? The more I pictured him as he'd moved towards me, the more I could see that his desire was fuelled by a different kind of craving, that of hatred, of wanting to do me harm... I shuddered at the thought of what he might have done to me if he hadn't been stopped.

Feeling miserable, I asked myself why Martin didn't want me anymore. What had changed? I couldn't bear it if he'd stopped loving me. Was I so undesirable these days? I thought about the guy who'd messaged me on the app, who was younger than me... he hadn't been able to stop thinking about me, he'd said so in his message... Inexplicably, I tried to remember his name.

Don't even go there, Abigail, I remonstrated with myself as my hand reached for my phone. I could read his messages again, it's not like I was going to do anything, it was just nice to feel desired by someone... and God knows I craved to feel something nice to quash my feelings of utter wretchedness. He'll have moved on to someone else, my inner voice reasoned, after all, you've not shown any further interest... he's young, he wants sex... *So do I though...*

I was surprised at my admission even as I knew it was the truth, I did want sex and my husband didn't... Or did he want sex, just not with me? My mind replayed Jenna's words from the night when Lauren first mentioned being on a dating app – seemingly the catalyst for everything that had happened since. *Can any one of us truly say that our husband has never cheated on us?* I'd been adamant that Martin had never cheated on me, smugly secure in my marital safety net, as I still was, surely...

What was it I'd said? I'd know if Martin was meeting another woman? He hardly got dressed up and disappeared off in the evenings? And then Emma had given me an instant education – *See someone you like, get a match, and hook up for an hour – it was that simple.*

Martin was out tonight... but he was with the lads, he'd explained... He had been out a little more frequently lately though... And what about the night we'd got back from Eynsford? How could he have been with all the lads when Claire and Hayley had both told me they'd spent the evening with their husbands? I shook my head, no, there must have been a mix-up and, honestly, the idea of Martin hooking up with women was absurd, I just had the whole dating apps thing messing with my head. *Really, Abigail, you're trying to convince yourself that your own husband might be cheating on you so that you can justify reading a couple of little messages on an app. Just read them.*

I went back into the kitchen and got myself another glass of wine, deciding that I'd read the messages again, just to feel better about myself, and I sat back down, picking up my phone to search for the message threads, surprised at how many messages I had waiting for me.

Gavin72 was keen, I thought in surprise, a tingle of pride rippling through me as I read his messages, amazed that he hadn't given up on me considering my lack of response for a while. *Well, I did look hot in my profile photo.* Pity I didn't look that good in real life. But hold on... frowning, I scrolled back through the more recent messages. Had I really been that flirtatious? Had I said those things after a few glasses of wine? Surely not. Was it Jenna? Was she still playing at being me? But why? It made no sense. I must have been drunk, I decided a little doubtfully, feeling oddly unsettled. I clicked on his photo and gazed at the blond-haired man, wondering why he was chasing an older woman, and read his last message again which he'd sent only a few minutes ago.

Meet me tonight. Name the time and the place.

I should have deleted my profile and the app, I thought in shock. What was I doing still even having it on my phone? Our mission had been accomplished, I'd served as bait, things had got out of hand in the most horrific way imaginable, of course, and so I had no further need of the

app. But still, I'd take a peek at the other messages first...
and that's when I saw it...

Night Monster had sent me a message.

It took me a few seconds to compute what I was looking
at. *Today* – he'd sent me a new message *today*.
Impossible. Slowly, I moved my finger and clicked on the
message.

*Well, I wasn't expecting things to go that way in the
hot tub, Tipsy Tease, you're full of surprises. Still, it was
fun though, we should do it again some time... I know
what you did...*

I read the message over and over again as my stomach
churned in confusion and disbelief. *He's dead. I killed
him. And we threw his body over the cliff into the sea.*

Had we though? There'd been that moment when we'd
been preparing to swing him over the edge and then we'd
just been holding the black plastic, not sure what had
happened. Oh, for God's sake, of course he'd gone over the
edge, he'd hardly come back to life and walked off, while
we were standing there looking around like a bunch of
idiots, had he?

I tried to picture the scene, feeling ridiculous for even
considering the absurd notion – it had been pitch black in
between the flashes of light from the lighthouse so we'd
effectively been blind... he'd felt heavy, even with us all
holding the plastic... and then, just like that, his weight
was gone and so was he... over the edge of the cliff, surely,
unless... Was it possible, in some kind of fantastical way,
that he had still been alive? That he'd survived being
stabbed repeatedly, survived being wrapped and
transported in plastic, and had somehow crawled away to
safety when we dropped him? But we'd checked, we'd
looked around and been satisfied that he had gone over
the edge. We'd been sure...

But we could have been wrong... and if we were, then
he was out there somewhere taunting me. No, these are

drunk thoughts, I said to myself, as I went to the kitchen and emptied the last of the bottle into my wine glass, he's dead, it's not him, think again, it has to be someone else. Someone who's messing with my head.

So... who'd sent the message then? Despite the warmth of the evening, my skin felt cold and prickly, and I shivered. *Someone else knew what had happened that night...*

I fumbled my way to my contacts and called Jenna. She'd know what to do. After my third attempt, I gave up, leaving a message asking her to call me.

I called Lauren as my desperation grew. I needed to speak to someone who could talk sense to me, except Lauren wasn't answering her phone either.

Next, I tried Emma, letting out a relieved breath when she answered.

'Em, I've got to speak to you, it's about–'

'Abs, I was expecting someone else, look, sorry, I can't talk right now.'

'But, it's about him, I've–'

'Look, the shit's hit the fan, didn't you know? It's all come out. I've got to go.'

What shit? What had come out? Why wouldn't anyone speak to me? With sickening dread, I realised what Emma was talking about. I finished the wine in my glass, walked stoically back indoors and through the lounge to the front window to await the arrival of the police, peering out at the darkness with something like relief. It was over. I'd explain everything, maybe they'd be lenient when they understood it had been a terrible accident.

41

Back To Black
Un-break My Heart

But no one came and after about half an hour I started to wonder if I'd misunderstood Emma. The sound from my phone made me jump in the quiet room, and I clicked on Jenna's message.

Change of plans obvs. We'll meet at mine on Friday.

Why? What was obvious? The sound of Martin's key in the door mobilised me and I walked quickly through the lounge and into the kitchen.

'Abs? Why's the house in darkness?' He switched lights on, dropping his phone and keys on the server as he gave me his now familiar quizzical look.

'I was sitting outside.' I gave a mad, tinkly laugh. 'I didn't realise how dark it had got. How's Paul? Is he alright?'

For a moment, Martin's expression was blank as he stared at me. 'Oh, Paul, yeah, I'm surprised you haven't heard already. Listen, Abs, I'm really tired, I'm going to hit the sack, d'you mind?'

'No, wait.' I ran after him as he went up the stairs. 'What haven't I heard?'

'About him and Emma. Lauren found out and there's a complete shit storm going down. Didn't Jenna tell you?'

'Jenna? No, how does she–? When did you–? Emma and Paul?' *Emma and Paul?* Emma wouldn't do that to Lauren, there had to be some other explanation. Everything was upside down in my head, Lauren having hookups, Paul doing the same – something I was still battling to get my head around – except hookups were with people you didn't know, who you met up with for an hour or two, not one of your wife's best friends. That was the worst betrayal imaginable – there was no forgiveness for that.

And why now? After what we'd all just done? What would happen if our friends started falling out with each other? What would happen if our loyalties were split?

Martin had disappeared into the bedroom, and I walked slowly back outside to retrieve my wine glass. No, none of us would ever speak about what we'd done as a group, we were all implicated, even if I was the one who'd held the knife.

My thoughts brought me back full circle to my own immediate crisis and I stared at the message on my phone again as something bothered me. Whoever had sent that message had to be signed into his app on Frisky… Did that mean they had his phone? But how? And, more to the point, should I reply? Or what?

I scrolled up through the repugnant chat thread, pausing on the photo of me in the hot tub.

Delete. Delete. Delete. The word flashed like a neon sign in my head as my finger hovered over the photo. I hit delete, relieved that it no longer existed, at least on my phone.

Incapable of making any coherent decisions, I exited the app and walked back inside. About to switch off the hall light, I noticed Martin's phone lying on the server. I glanced up the stairs, my earlier suspicions crowding my head, before picking it up and taking it back outside, grabbing my glass and a fresh bottle of wine on the way.

Hating myself, but needing to know, I searched his files, finding the Dare app easily now that I knew where to look, my heart sinking with despair that it existed on his phone. I hesitated for a moment. Did I really want to know? So far it was just in my head – those nights he'd said he'd been out with the lads when it seemed he hadn't, something that I couldn't put my finger on about a couple of comments he'd made when he'd come in from those nights... Scenes played like a film in my head – Martin borrowing my car to meet up with everyone when I'd got back from Eynsford... Martin telling me he'd cleaned out my car the day I'd arrived back from that fateful weekend... when he must have found the boxer shorts in the back seat pocket and done the washing because... *because he'd thought they were his...*

How could he? And in my car? How many of them had there been? Did I want to know or not? I downed half my glass of wine and clicked on the app, expecting to be asked for a password. That would decide it for me – if I needed the password then I'd be forced to give up, I'd be able to stick my head in the sand for a while and not have to face up to the ugly truth of my husband cheating on me.

I'd been sitting right here when I'd first downloaded the Dare app and had played with the idea of setting up an account, when I'd typed in our old shared e-mail address and been told that my password was incorrect... I'd thought nothing of it at the time, but here was the same e-mail address with a row of stars for the password. I should have known then, but I'd been too stupid. I signed in.

No profile picture for Martin, and just numbers for his profile name. I clicked on his chats, finding only one thread, the profile picture a photo of a pinkish-white flower, and the name a row of numbers. Who was she? I clicked on the chat thread, feeling nauseous as I saw today's date on his last message. I scrolled upwards, wanting to see how long it had been going on.

A little over a month, so roundabout the time that Lauren had dropped her bombshell about being on dating apps. And Lauren had been hooking up with someone that night... Lauren? Was it Lauren? I emptied my glass, re-filled it and drank half, enjoying the numbing sensation from the alcohol. Why should it be someone that I knew? It could be anyone. And Lauren would never betray a friendship. Emma had though, said a nasty little voice in my head.

In morbid fascination, I read the messages, looking for clues but finding none. Except... Martin had ended things with whoever she was almost immediately... and she wasn't happy about it. Rephrase that – she was furious about it. I re-filled my glass, gulped some more wine and read the messages again, the words blurring from too much wine and heart break.

How dare you do this to me. You can't reject me, you want me, I know you do. I'll kill you, you bastard, you can't do this to me again, I won't let you. I'll bloody kill you.

Martin's responses to her angry messages were merciless.

I don't want you, I'm not sure if I ever really did. I don't know what I want. That night in Abs' car was the last time. I can't keep doing this. It's all been a huge mistake.

How could he talk about me with such familiarity? How could he even use my name? For a moment that hurt more than the evidence of his cheating.

You don't mean that, we both know it. We're too good together...

Leave him alone, I wanted to shout at her. He doesn't want you.

Stop tempting me... I'm trying to do the right thing. And very funny, hiding my boxers in the seat pocket. She could have found them. You said they'd fallen out of the car.

I allowed myself a moment's satisfaction at the thought of his panic when he'd found what he thought were his own boxer shorts in the seat pocket of my car. *No, Martin, actually those belonged to a dead guy.*

Maybe you ought to join him. The shocking thought came from nowhere. It was almost funny, in a dark kind of way – his betrayed wife, and his spurned lover, mutually wishing him dead. Who knew we'd have something like that in common? But who was she?

I exited the app and dropped his phone on the table, feeling shamed by my thoughts but, more than anything, overwhelmed with the chaos of my life – a killer wife and a cheating husband, what a combination.

I emptied the last of the second bottle of wine into my glass and drank it down, picking up my own phone and clicking on the message from my persistent admirer again in drunken defiance. 'Two can play that game, Martin,' I mumbled, as I stared at the blurred words, trying to focus, my fingers typing a reply.

Baxter's, twenty minutes.

42

Killing Me Softly With His Song

I dropped my phone on the table, staring at it through my drunken haze. He'd either reply right now or it would never happen. My phone gave a little whoop immediately.

I'll be there. Side parking, at the end. Can't wait.

Calmly, considering my alcohol-fuelled state, I booked a taxi and walked through the house, picking up my bag and quietly opening the front door. If Martin asked me where I'd been, I'd tell him it was an emergency with Lauren, I decided recklessly. Drunk Abigail didn't care what he thought.

I watched the cab drive away a short while later and stood peering around in the semi-darkness, the dull sound of pounding music coming from Baxter's a reassuring presence in the background. I began to walk along the side parking, my alcohol buzz still nicely fizzing through my brain and body as I wobbled and held onto a car to balance myself, passing late night drinkers coming and going, their faces illuminated for a split second under the only streetlight as they passed beneath it.

Leaving the streetlight's illumination behind me, I took a couple of steps into the gloom as I saw an arm wave at me, and lifted my own arm to wave in response, moving aside to let the car pass that seemed to be crawling at a snail's pace behind me.

The car didn't pass me, and just as I registering that it was odd that it didn't have its lights on, I heard the owner of the waving arm call out, albeit a little uncertainly.

'Tipsy Tease?'

'Gavin72?' I responded, weaving towards him, trying to focus as I pushed my hair out of my eyes. 'You're not–' I stopped, trying to back away, but bumped into a parked car which blocked my retreat. Blinking rapidly, I tried to clear my swimming head. 'Where's Gavin72? Who are you?'

'I'm Gavin72, darling.' He laughed at my shocked expression. 'You didn't seriously believe that was my real photo, any more than I believed yours was. Come here, let's have a look at you.' He grabbed my arms and pulled me roughly so that I was standing in front of him. 'Blimey, had a heavy night, have you? Yeah...' He squinted, assessing me. 'I can see a bit of a likeness. Pity about the clothes though, I thought you'd have dressed up a bit, made more of an effort, you know?'

I was sobering up rapidly and I stared at the sixty-something, balding stranger mutely, the smell of his long-overdue-for-a-wash denim jacket filling me with revulsion. *What the hell was I thinking?*

'I've got half an hour before the wife starts calling me so we should get on with it.' He pulled me against him, pressing his mouth on mine, his stubble rough on my face, as the car that had crawled along behind me turned on its headlights, and I turned my head blindly towards it in relief.

'Get off me!' Struggling, I whimpered at the blinding headlights, 'Help!'

'What the–?'

I wrestled myself free as he tried to pull me between the parked cars and into the darkness against the side wall of Baxter's, staggering towards the car and watching in confusion as it reversed away from me, its full beam giving me no chance to see the driver or what the car looked like.

'I shouldn't be here. It was a mistake.' Sobbing, I started to run back towards the streetlight and on towards the main parking area, away from the angry words spewing from the man's mouth.

'Fucking cock tease. Prick teasing bitch. You should stop wasting people's time. Fucking Tipsy Tease – trashed bloody trainwreck's more like it.'

Shaking, I kept running until I reached the street and relative safety, the sight of the line of taxies filling me with relief. My breathing was coming in ragged gasps, and I smoothed my hair and dragged a hand across my eyes, ignoring the strange looks from the small group leaving the wine bar. Opening the door of the first taxi, I tumbled in and gave my address.

What had I just done? Sober from shock, I leant back against the car seat and wrapped my arms around myself, my eyes meeting the concerned eyes of the taxi driver in his rearview mirror. My mouth contorted itself into some kind of rictus grin in an attempt to reassure him that I was a rational woman who hadn't just done something completely and utterly reckless and out of character.

'You OK, love?'

'Fine, thank you.' I turned and stared out of the window until he turned into our road, discouraging him from asking me any more questions. 'Here's fine,' I said, handing him a twenty-pound note as he pulled over. 'Keep the change.'

'You're sure? It was only–'

'Keep it.' I closed the door and walked along the pavement until I reached our house, pausing to calm myself for a moment before I walked up the path to the front door, relieved to see the house in darkness.

Quietly locking the door behind me, I crept up the stairs in the dark and undressed in the bathroom, taking my nightie from the hook behind the door and dropping it over my head. I'd got away with it. Martin would never know of my stupidity. My body began to shake with relief and I leant back against the bathroom wall, wrapping my arms around myself and willing it to stop.

Suddenly, all I wanted was to curl up in bed and find oblivion for a few precious hours. But I tossed and turned my way through the night, tormented by my demons, by Martin's affair, by images of the revolting man I'd so stupidly met up with, by my risky behaviour and close shave, and by the message from a dead man.

43

By the time we all met at Jenna's on Friday night, our fingertips must have been worn away from texting each other about the Emma and Paul scandal, with the notable exception of Lauren, who remained silent on the subject, and Emma, who was absent for obvious reasons. I'd desperately wanted to tell someone about the message I'd received, and its implications, but had been somewhat preoccupied with my own problems. Ragged from lack of sleep, my mind had spent the last few days and nights careering between thoughts of Martin's cheating, my own drunken, reckless behaviour and narrow escape, and the disquieting message from a man that I knew, with absolute certainty, was dead.

I arrived at the same time as Claire and Fi, and Jenna roped us in to plate up the snacks for the evening – Claire was tasked with topping bruschetta with cream cheese and smoked salmon, Fi with mashing avocado for the mini pitta breads, and I with slicing chicken fillets and flash-frying them for Fi to add to the pittas.

Jen was in one of her ultra bossy moods. 'Leave the chicken, Abs, and answer the door. And take that clip out of your hair, you really ought to make more of an effort.' She deftly removed my hair clip, fluffing my hair up and smiling into my eyes as her finger stroked my cheek. 'Always be prepared. Haven't I taught you anything? You never know when your picture's going to be taken.' Typical Jen, always concerned with appearances, I thought as I answered the door.

'Is that Hayley? Oh good, can you pour us wine, darling? I'll finish slicing and frying the chicken strips, just leave the knife on the board for me. Claire, pop those bruschetta on a large plate and take them through. Abs, why don't you put some music on in the lounge and we'll move through? Oh, and pop an extra one of those bottles of wine on the small table beside my chair, thanks.' She gave me one of her big smiles as she grabbed a pair of her blue disposable gloves from the box – that was Jen, no getting her hands dirty or messing up her perfect nails.

It felt like some kind of army camp and it was a relief to escape to the lounge. I'd hoped to raise the subject of the chilling message I'd received on the app but the talk was all about the Emma and Paul affair, and poor Lauren. She hadn't appeared, but when one of us asked Jen if she was coming, she assured us that she'd be with us soon.

We passed around the plates of nibbles which, I had to admit, were very tasty – Jen always outdid the rest of us, whether it was food, or looks or pretty much anything.

'Oh, you've got your old photos out!' exclaimed Hayley, picking up a pile of photos from a shoebox on the floor and rifling through them. 'This was when we went to Blackpool, look how young we were. Oh my God, look at my hair, and, Abs, you look crazy, you're grinning like a lunatic while I look scared out of my life.'

'Let me see.' Claire took the photo, grimacing. 'This was our first girls' weekend. I swore I'd never go on another rollercoaster again after that. You can just see me behind Abs, I look like I'm going to throw up all over Jen.'

'Whoah, here's a Jen I haven't seen before.' Fi had reached over and taken a few of the photos from the shoebox. 'Nice school uniform, talk about a short skirt, love, I bet you rolled the waistband over a couple of times, knowing you. And I see you'd started with the signature lippie already. And who's the pimply boy with his arm round you? Boyfriend? That's never Shane.'

'Let me see.' Claire craned her neck. 'Is that Martin? I forgot you went out with him. Wait a minute, who are those girls behind you? Isn't that the poor girl who died? Natalie? Did you know her then?'

'We weren't friends, so no, I didn't really know her.' Jen glanced at the photo and then at me.

'Isn't Emma's maiden name Parker? I never thought about it before, they had the same name. D'you think they were related? No, hold on, that's not right, it was–' Claire's face suddenly blanched. 'Oh God, I'm sorry, Abs, she was your friend, I remember now.'

I flinched at the mention of my best friend, looking helplessly over at Hayley who rifled hurriedly through the remaining photos.

'Here's Shane with Jenna,' she said, holding up a photo of them on his motorbike, triumphantly. 'You two were much better suited.'

I gave Hayley a grateful smile.

'It was your name, Jen, I remember now.' Claire tapped the photo, pleased at her recall.

'Meanwhile, back in Blackpool, here's Jenna and me. That was in front of that terrifying thing that went miles up in the air and then dropped everyone down at top speed to their certain deaths.'

'Hardly miles, Fi, and no one died, just a small point.' I laughed at her usual exaggeration, enjoying the happy memories. 'It was fun, you should have gone on it with Lauren and me.' We all seemed to have conveniently forgotten the horrific event from one week ago, or maybe we were just determined to erase it from our memories.

'I took this of you both when you got off.' Hayley held out another photo towards me, giggling. 'You and Lauren look like twins, you're both in matching outfits.'

At the mention of Lauren, everyone fell silent for a moment.

'What made you look at the old pictures, Jen? Feeling sentimental in your old age?'

'Less of the old, d'you mind.' Jen laughed. 'No, I was just looking for something.'

'Did you find it?' I couldn't stand it when Jen got all cryptic on us.

'I might have done.' She looked at me mysteriously, and I shrugged, deciding to leave whatever it was alone.

'Look at this bloke checking Jenna's bum out.' Fi held out a photo of Jenna licking an ice cream as a man turned to stare at her.

'You're just jealous.' Jen winked at Fi as Claire handed Hayley back the rollercoaster photo.

'There's not one picture of Emma in here, that's odd...' Hayley put the photos back in the box, dropping the one from Claire on top, and reached for the pitta platter. 'Jen, you haven't had any of the pittas, they're delicious, here have one before they all go.' Hayley proffered the plate to Jen, who shook her head.

'I'm not hungry, sweetie, but you go ahead. I'll stick to my wine. Abs, have another one, I know how much you like your food.'

I'd been about to take one, but declined, wondering if Jen had been making a subtle dig about my weight.

Hayley looked from Jen, to the pittas, to the photo box, and then over at me, her mouth opening as if she was about to speak, but then she closed it as if she'd thought better of it.

There seemed to be a division between us – those of us who were in Lauren's camp and those of us in Emma's. The evening was fuelled by too much alcohol which, instead of making it fun, seemed to bring out the worst in us. I was strictly behind Lauren, having made up my mind that she would never betray our friendship by sleeping with Martin, feeling that Emma had betrayed not just their friendship but all of ours as well. Hayley was also in camp Lauren, but Jenna didn't appear to think that Emma and Paul having an affair was that big of a deal, which put her in Emma's camp, together with, surprisingly, Fi.

'How can you support Emma after poor Lauren stayed with you when she was beaten and hurt?' demanded Hayley, as I nodded vehemently.

'Well that was hardly Em's fault, to be fair...'

Fi had a point, but still... I added my own contribution, my hurt at Martin's affair still painfully foremost in my mind.

'It's bad enough that our friend has betrayed one of us, which means she's betrayed us all really, but to stand by her, Fi, it's like you're saying it's just fine to go around jumping into bed with each other's husbands.'

Fi's eyebrows arched comically upwards as she looked at me in disbelief. 'Seriously, Abigail? Have you forgotten why Lauren was all beaten up in the first place?'

'No, I...' Flustered, I looked at Hayley for inspiration.

'That's different, he wasn't one of our husbands.' She gave me a tiny triumphant glance of solidarity.

'Well, I didn't see Abigail complaining when Paul had his hands all over her arse at their barbeque, did you?'

Claire shot me a look of disappointment, as Hayley gasped and gave me a worried look, and I felt my cheeks burning.

'What? You thought no one had noticed?' Jenna's face had that smug look as she looked around the room, enjoying my discomfiture.

'Tell her it's not true, Abs.' Hayley's eyes pleaded with mine.

'It's not true, not the way Jen means it,' I mumbled. 'Paul was drunk and I didn't want to make a scene.'

'Does Emma know?'

'More to the point – Lauren?'

'Does Lauren know what?'

I stared in horror as Lauren walked into the living room.

44

I'll Stand By You

'Oh, did I forget to mention that Lauren was staying with me?' Jenna smiled sweetly, picking up her phone as it gave a soft ping, her eyes unreadable as she stared at the screen.

Lauren moved slowly into the room, her bare feet silent on the carpet, and stopped behind Jenna's chair, glancing down momentarily at Jenna's hands as they fluttered across her phone's screen before looking up at me with a perplexed and anguished expression.

'You as well, Abs? I've had it with everyone, can't anyone be trusted?' Her feeling of betrayal was written all over her face as she looked at me and then walked further into the room to look questioningly at each one of us in turn.

'No, I'm on your side, what happened with Paul was–'

'What happened with Paul.' Lauren mimicked me horribly as she turned from looking at Jenna to sneer at me. 'I think it all went to your head a bit, Abs, once you had a taste of it all on the bloody dating apps. Had a go with anyone else's husband yet? What about Ross? I'm sure Hayley won't mind if you get into him. Or maybe Adrian? Perhaps he's bored with Claire and fancies a change. You could always try your luck with Shane, I'm sure Jenna won't care, she doesn't have a use for him anymore. Do you, Jenna?' She stood, hands on hips, waiting for Jenna's response.

'Shane?' Jenna snorted. 'He wasn't man enough for me, Abigail's welcome to him. Why don't you have another drink, Laur?' She indicated the unopened bottle of wine on the table beside her.

'Stop– I don't– Why are you saying this stuff? I'm married, I don't want someone else's husband, I only want Martin.'

'Well aren't you the faithful little wife.'

At Jen's mocking words, my mind flashed back uncomfortably to my Tuesday night fiasco, and I looked away, feeling flustered.

'But does Martin still want you?' Lauren gave me a pointed look, her face red. She picked up the bottle of Goats do Roam – a South African wine which I remembered Jenna and I both buying by the case based purely on its amusing name – savagely twisted the cap off and began to swig from the bottle.

'This is turning into quite the exciting evening,' Fi drawled, waving her vape in the air.

I nodded, my mind on Martin. *Did he still want me? Was his affair really over?*

'Steady on, Lauren.' Claire frowned at her. 'For what it's worth, Abigail is on your side.'

'Well, she's got a funny way of showing it.' Lauren wasn't to be placated that easily. 'Look, I know what some of you think of me, about the things I've been doing, but I was only doing what Paul was doing.'

'Until he started seeing Emma.'

'Has anyone heard Emma's side of it?'

'No, and I don't bloody well want to, thanks very much. Emma's a deceitful bitch. She must have loved it when I stayed at Fi's and left Paul on his own. She was probably off in my bed every chance she got, screwing your husband.' Lauren was all over the place, glaring at me, swigging repeatedly from the bottle of wine, distracted by Jenna as she tapped something into her phone, her face white with stress, or anger, or whatever as she paced back and forth, correcting herself. 'I mean my husband.'

'God, you need to grow up, Lauren.' Jenna put her phone down with one of her secretive little smiles. 'Why d'you think Shane and I split up? Or Fi and Danny? Or Emma and Craig, for that matter? It's sex, darling, it happens, or it doesn't, and maybe that's the problem.' Jenna let out one of her deep-throated laughs although none of us smiled. 'You're clinging to something that isn't there anymore. Move on, get a life, so what if Emma's with Paul, you didn't want him, did you?'

'But she was my friend, I trusted her, it's got to count for something hasn't it?'

'Yes, it has.' I raised my voice a little. 'Lauren, I swear to you, to all of you, I would never betray any of you, you're my best friends and I'd never do anything to hurt any of you, and if I've upset you somehow, Lauren, then I'm sorry.' I could feel tears welling in my eyes.

Jenna clapped her hands slowly. 'Bravo, Abigail, nice little speech, very moving, a little self-serving considering your current situation and your need for our loyalty, but very moving. Someone pass Abigail a tissue.'

'I think I'm going to leave, this evening is turning out rather unpleasantly, we all need to calm down and take some time to think about how long we've all been friends.' Claire stood up, as I noticed Lauren and Hayley in some kind of whispered huddle at the other end of the room. 'We should all go home. Let's meet up in a few days when we're a bit less hot-headed. I thought we were going to talk about what happened at the weekend and the fact that the police are now looking for him. It's all over the damn news, in case any of you hadn't noticed.'

'Oh relax, Claire, everything's fine, we've covered our tracks, got rid of all the evidence so there's nothing to connect us to what happened. They'll probably never find his body so we've got nothing to worry about. Abigail did the world a favour, and good riddance to him anyway, bloody woman beater. I've got a bottle of fizz in the fridge to toast our successful outcome.' Jenna got up and went into the kitchen as Hayley shot an anxious look in my direction.

I guessed she was concerned about the evidence we'd left behind, contrary to Jen's statement, and I gave a tiny shake of my head at her, the last thing we needed right now was to raise the issue of the missing pig mask – especially as Jenna had been the one wearing it – not when tempers were flying so high.

I looked at Jenna quizzically as she returned with the bottle. 'But it wasn't successful, was it? I mean, it didn't go the way we planned it. He wasn't supposed to end up dead.'

'Wasn't he? Well, we've got you to thank for that, Abs. And who cares, anyway? He had it coming to him. Claire, stay for a toast.'

With a grim nod, Claire sat back down. 'For the sake of our friendship, I'll stay, but not to drink a toast to a successful outcome.'

'To friendship then,' said Jenna, handing round glasses.

'To friendship,' we said, lifting our glasses.

I looked over at Lauren, hoping for a smile, for some indication that she wasn't still angry with me, but she stared at me, her expression inscrutable as she emptied the last of the bottle of wine down her throat and dropped the empty bottle on the floor as if she was making a statement.

I left Jenna's not having told anyone about the message I'd received.

45

Confusion

Lauren called me the next morning, speaking in a hushed, awkward tone which I presumed meant that she was feeling embarrassed about the things she'd said to me the night before, and that Jenna was still sleeping.

'Abs, can we meet up? Are you free? I'm off for my walk in a bit, maybe it'll help clear my head, and I thought you could join me so that we could chat. I need to talk to you. I'm sure it's a mix-up, it's just that Hayley remembered– and well... with what he said, I was right there, I was behind Jenna. It could have just been a coincidence, but... well, anyway, she was going on about that weekend, the first one, and we both thought it was odd, you know, and she was worrying about the photos, and I know it's stupid and there'll be an explanation – I mean you can't be scared but love it at the same time, can you? So why say that? I'm not saying it was a lie, but– oh, I'm sure I'm just adding two and two and making five. People grow out of things, I know that, but the way Martin said it, well, it was as if it's still a thing, so then it doesn't make sense....'

Martin? Photos? A sensation of ants crawling over my skin made me scratch at my arms.

'And, oh, Abs, I can't believe it about that other thing. It's not true, surely? I saw the message on her phone and I thought, I can't bear what happened to me to happen to one of my friends. That's why I got so angry last night. Ignore me, Abs, I shouldn't be saying any of this to you, I should be having it out with Jenna.'

Jenna? I felt cold suddenly.

I waited, listening to her breathing, not sure if I should speak or let her carry on talking.

'And there's something else, Abs,' she whispered. 'I've been trying to go through it all in my head, who was where, why it was there, how it got there, to try to work out what happened that night. You see, at first it didn't make sense, but I think I understand now. I don't want to talk to Jenna, not after what I saw, I mean, if she's got an agenda, then she can't be trusted. We're supposed to be able to trust our friends, aren't we? What utter crap. I trusted Emma, and look how that turned out for me. Did you know?'

It took me a moment to realise that Lauren was waiting for me to respond, and I gave myself a mental shake, trying to dispel the feeling of chill that had slithered through my insides.

'Jenna?' I croaked, my throat dry, not sure if I'd understood. 'Emma?'

'Maybe he didn't even say her name, it's just my stupid imagination taking over with everything that's happening. And even if he did, what does it mean? I could ask Jenna, but I'm just so pissed off with her right now. And Hayley refuses to believe it, any of it – that there was more to it; that it was made up at the time; the cheating; that I even saw it there. But he had the same last name, I realised, and I thought, no, that's crazy, too many coincidences, what with Claire remembering it was Jen's name, before she was married, as well. And then, after what Paul and Emma have done to me, I'm questioning everything, I know that. I'm just feeling over sensitive, I suppose, seeing betrayals and lies everywhere among so-called best friends. Oh, I'm not making any sense, I don't know what to think, my head's all over the place. I'm sure there's an explanation for everything... Maybe I didn't even see it? And d'you know what the worst thing of all is? I don't care, because I'm glad he's dead. Does that make me a bad person?'

Martin? Emma? Jenna? Whose name? What cheating? Didn't see what? Lauren's glad he's dead? I walked into the lounge, my legs leaden, and sat down, feeling shaky, clearing my throat and swallowing, my mouth dry. 'You're not a bad person, Laur, you're just not thinking clearly at the moment that's all.' I needed Lauren to stop talking, she didn't know how dangerous it was.

I thought of the ominous message I'd received from his phone. 'Laur,' I said urgently, 'you can't speak to anyone about this, it's not safe. We don't know who we can trust.' *I didn't know who I could trust.*

'I've only spoken to Hayley. What d'you mean, it's not safe?' She sounded agitated.

'I'll explain when we meet up,' I said, forcing my voice to sound calm, as my body shivered. 'It'll be better to talk in person, and we'll have to include Hayley now. I'm sure there's a good explanation for everything, so you shouldn't worry.' *What exactly had Lauren just tried to tell me? What had she seen? What about Jenna? And what had Martin said?* After everything that Lauren had gone through, I worried that she was becoming unstable, I certainly was. 'You mustn't talk to anyone else until we've met. Do you promise me?'

'Well, sure, I suppose...'

'But it'll have to be Monday if that's alright? Martin and I are out tonight for a special dinner.' I waited for the penny to drop. 'Our wedding anniversary?' As soon as the words were out of my mouth, I realised my mistake, cursing my insensitivity over her current situation. 'Oh God, I'm sorry, Laur, I wasn't thinking, it's just–'

'You and Martin are celebrating your wedding anniversary?' She sounded choked. 'Well, that's nice, I suppose... if you feel like celebrating...'

She had a point...

'Laur, I'm sorry, you know me and my stupid mouth, speaking before I engage my brain. I know we're all still reeling from what happened, but I have to make a show of carrying on as normal. It's no big deal, just dinner, and I'm not sure I even feel like going to be honest.' I felt awkward, not sure if we were speaking at cross purposes.

At that moment, I desperately wanted to confide in Lauren, to tell her what I'd seen on Martin's phone. But once I did that, I'd be making it real and I'd have to face it. Also, my friend had enough in her head already, by the sound of it... and so did I...

'I'm sorry if I've upset you, Abs. I'd better go, don't want to mess my schedule up, you know me, everything like clockwork. At least I've got control over one part of my life.' Lauren gave another bitter laugh.

'Still walking your usual route?'

'Yep. Sure I can't tempt you to join me?'

'No, there's something I have to do,' I said, making a sudden decision. Go, enjoy your walk. So... Monday then?'

'Yeah, Monday... Marks and Sparks café in the Glades? Lunchtime? One o'clock?'

'That sounds great, I'll see you then, and I'll let Hayley know. But we must keep all this between the three of us, not a word to anyone else, Laur, I'll explain why on Monday.'

There was the sound of a door clicking in the background on her phone.

'I've got to go, she's coming. See you Monday.'

Her phone clicked off, and I thought back over what Lauren had said, grabbing my trainers from the shoe cupboard and putting them on, before tying my hair back and transferring the contents from my small handbag into my larger tote, all the while a plan taking shape in my mind. I thought of the evening ahead, dreading it if I was honest with myself, and wondering if I'd be able to carry it off after everything. In my current situation as a murderer attempting to come to terms with the unforgivable, a romantic meal with my husband was the last thing I felt like. If I added to that Martin's lack of interest in me lately, his humiliating rejection of my nocturnal advances just a few weeks ago, and the evidence of his affair, not to mention my own stupid behaviour, then I could honestly say that I'd rather walk naked through Bromley High Street.

I couldn't avoid doing something just because I didn't want to do it, I pep-talked myself. I had to find a way to take control, to fight back. I couldn't just sit back and do nothing, if I did that, I'd lose everything. No, I had to fight for what I wanted. So that's what I would do. I stared at myself in the mirror, jumping as the doorbell rang.

I opened the front door to find a large bouquet of red roses thrust in my face. Thanking the delivery man, I closed the door, breathing in the scent of the flowers as I extricated the envelope from amidst the foliage. Martin was in an extravagant mood, I thought as I slipped the card from the envelope. *Or maybe he was just feeling guilty.*

'Who was that at the door?' Martin came down the stairs, rubbing his hair with a towel after his shower.

I turned and forced a smile. 'Like you don't know. They're beautiful, thank you. Happy anniversary.' I reached up to kiss him.

'Christ, is it today?' He gave me an embarrassed grin as he stepped backwards. 'Sorry, I've just had a lot on my mind lately. Well, er, happy anniversary, Abs.'

'Very funny.' I gave a small laugh. *He hadn't even wanted me to kiss him...* I held up his card to read it. *Happy anniversary to the perfect couple.* 'Oh, they're from Jenna.' I looked at Martin in confusion as his expression darkened.

'Let me see that.' He snatched the card, frowning.

'It's very sweet of her,' I mumbled. He *had* forgotten, some perfect couple we were... Jen's choice of words felt like a cruel jibe...

He dropped the card on the hall table and placed his hands on my shoulders. 'We could go out for a meal tonight if you want? I'm off for a round of golf with the boys but I'll be back in plenty of time.'

'Martin.' I looked up at him, trying to figure out if he was joking. 'We *are* going out for a meal, I booked it ages ago at our usual spot.'

'Oh, of course, yeah, that'll be great.' He walked back upstairs to finish getting dressed, leaving me feeling quite discombobulated, Lauren's cruel question from the night before re-playing in my head. *Does Martin still want you?* I certainly knew the answer to that now, in more ways than one. I felt heartbroken. What had it all been for?

The doorbell rang again and I yanked it open in a fluster to receive another bouquet of roses. *These must be from Martin... he must have been messing around just now... but they were black...* I'd never seen black roses before and I felt a small chill begin to creep along my spine as I pulled the card from the paperclip attached to the cellophane, dropping it in shock as I read the words. *One week since you killed me. Happy Anniversary.*

46

'Someone else at the door?'

I fumbled for the card, standing up and slipping it under the untidy pile of envelopes on the hall table, turning to Martin as he reappeared. 'More flowers.' I laughed falsely, my heart hammering in my chest as he frowned and took the bouquet from me.

'Weird, never seen black roses before. Who are they from?'

'There's no card,' I said quickly. 'Maybe they made a mistake and delivered them to the wrong address.'

'Hmm... there's a clip here for a card... that's odd.'

I took the flowers from him. 'I'll get rid of them, I don't really like them.'

'Shouldn't you ring the florist and get them to pick them up if they delivered them to the wrong person?'

'I don't know which florist it was.' I stood there awkwardly, holding the menacing bouquet as if it might bite me. 'I'll throw them away.'

'Not like you to waste things. Stick them in a vase, might as well enjoy them.'

Enjoy them? When every time I looked at them, I'd be reminded of my murderous act? By someone who had a cruel, unknown as yet, agenda? I took the two bouquets through to the kitchen and found vases, taking Jenna's roses through to the lounge and standing the vase on the mantelpiece with the card leaning against it. Hesitating, I paused for a moment, contemplating the flowers and the card, before taking the vase of black roses to the furthermost corner of the dining room and standing it on a small bookcase virtually out of sight. They'd die without any water and I'd be able to throw them away in a day or two.

Who was doing this? Dead men don't send flowers. Whoever it was, they knew who I was and where I lived... Chaotic thoughts crashed around in my brain – I should tell the others; I shouldn't tell the others; I should look at the Frisky app and see if there were any more messages; I should leave the country; I was in deep trouble; it was my wedding anniversary; my husband had been cheating on me; Lauren had been trying to tell me something important; Martin didn't love me anymore; Jenna, Jenna, Jenna; I had to fight back...

I sent Jenna a hurried text message to thank her for the flowers, adding in how much Martin and I were looking forward to our romantic anniversary meal tonight.

Whatever was going on, whoever had done what and whoever knew what, I only knew one thing – I had to take action. I had to do something if I didn't want my perfect life to implode.

I scrawled a note to Martin, grabbed my bag and left the house, climbing into the car before calling Hayley.

'Abs, I was just about to call you. Happy anniversary!' She sounded terrible. 'I've come down with a bit of a cold.'

'Oh, you poor thing. Thanks, Hayles. Martin and I are off out to our favourite restaurant for a meal tonight. I'm really looking forward to it.'

'You are? Oh, that's good. You lucky things, I can't taste or smell anything at the moment, I'm so bunged up. So, everything's alright then? I told Lauren she'd got it all wrong. She must have imagined what she saw on the phone.'

Well, not exactly... 'Everything's fine, Hayles. Lauren called me, and–' *Lauren had got what wrong? Whose phone?* 'I'm sure it's all a big misunderstanding. We'll sort it out.'

'Oh, I'm so relieved. I felt so bad to even worry about it. I knew I was just being silly and it would all turn out to be some kind of mix up.'

Worry about what? What mix up? I was scared to ask, for fear of what she might tell me. I held the phone away as Hayley had a coughing fit and blew her nose noisily. 'You sound awful. Listen, can you join Lauren and me for lunch on Monday, as long as you're feeling better? Marks and Sparks, one o'clock? We need to talk but, Hayles, you can't speak to anyone else before then. Lauren's really worried and I'm afraid our problems aren't over.'

'Now you're scaring me, Abs. The whole thing just sounds crazy, maybe Lauren imagined it all.'

What did Lauren imagine? Again, I was too scared to ask. 'Hayles, there's something I haven't told you. I haven't actually told anyone yet, because it's too awful.'

'What is it, Abs? You're making me nervous.'

I paused, wondering if I was doing the right thing. 'Someone's got his phone. I got a message from him and it mentioned the hot tub. I don't know who to trust, I didn't even tell Lauren. And then today, I received a bouquet of black roses with a threatening message. I'm terrified, Hayles. Someone from that night is playing a game, a cruel one, and I don't know what they want.' It was a relief to tell someone, finally.

'Someone's got his phone? But how? Abs, we have to tell the others. And black roses? What did the message say?'

'No, we can't tell the others, not yet.' I sounded sharp, and I tried to relax. 'I don't know who it is. Now I've worried you, on top of not feeling well,' I said miserably.

'I'm glad you told me, you know you can tell me anything, Abs. D'you think it's about where Lauren saw the knife? I knew it didn't make sense, I said to her, just because you saw it there, it doesn't mean that–' She stopped to blow her nose again.

The knife? 'Lauren saw the knife?' I whispered.

'Well, she's not sure, of course, because of what happened with Fi and Emma, and Claire was out there, and then you came in to get ready, and Jen was in the kitchen earlier... She just said that it was strange, you know, and saying the name as well...'

'Hayles,' I said, concerned about her laboured breathing, and trying to quell the urge to have a full meltdown in my car. 'I've got a really bad feeling. I don't think it's all over, and until we meet and go over everything, we don't know who we can trust.' I'd never needed Hayley to believe me more than at that moment.

'I wish Ross was here.' She sounded tearful, and the hairs on my neck prickled.

'You absolutely cannot talk to Ross about this, Hayles. Where is he? Are you alone?'

'He's away until Thursday on business.'

My shoulders sagged in relief. 'When you speak to him on the phone, you mustn't worry him about any of this. Will you be alright on your own? I'll drop you off some medicine.'

'I suppose so...'

'We'll talk it through on Monday then, with Lauren, you're the only two I totally trust right now.' I started the car, anxious to get moving, as I checked my rearview mirror and put the car in reverse.

'I don't know how you're coping, Abs. After everything that happened that weekend, to think that Jenna would... and now the message from his phone... and you have to go out for your anniversary, and...'

'Hayles, you mustn't stress, please. Listen, I have to go, but we mustn't go around saying any of this to anyone else. I'll drop off some medicine, but I won't be able to stay. You should have a lie-down, I'm worried about you.'

'But it's wrong, someone needs to tell her that. What if it's not really over? I'll talk to her, maybe tomorrow if I'm up to it, and I'll see you on Monday. Don't worry about me, Abs, it's your anniversary, you should enjoy yourself.'

'No, Hayles, you mustn't talk to her.' The car shot backwards towards the road and I hit the brakes as a car drove past slowly.

'Hayles?' She was gone. I reversed out and drove off, anxious to get on with things, my mind playing something that Hayley had said, on a loop. *To think that Jenna would what?*

47

Never Tear Us Apart

I pulled up outside my favourite health shop, taking deep breaths, as snippets from my conversations with Lauren and Hayley ran through my mind, their oblique references to the knife, Martin, the weekend, and Jenna unsettling me. Closing my eyes for a moment, I rested my head against the headrest, instantly seeing the bouquet of black roses and the message from the unknown sender.

Swallowing hard, as I fought the urge to throw-up, I ticked off the first thing on my mental checklist, my hands shaking as I checked my watch to see how much time I had. I hurried into the shop, grabbed a basket and raced down the first aisle, filled with cooking oils, rice, and noodles, stopping to grab a couple of innocuous cupboard essentials – sesame seed oil and rice. Pausing, I looked around, spying the sign for vitamins, and made for the third aisle to find cough medicine. It would probably taste foul but it would do the job, I decided, choosing a herbal mixture of unpronounceable ingredients. For good measure, I picked up a calming remedy spray for myself – warranted, I felt, after the day I'd had so far, not to mention desperately needed to help me through what lay ahead still – and went to the till, trying not to sigh as the cashier tutted and apologised to the customer in front of me for the slowness of the card machine.

Finally, I placed my shopping bag on the passenger seat and, after sorting through the items, sprayed some of the remedy onto my tongue, before setting off to Hayley's. A promise was a promise.

I looked up and down the road, rang the doorbell again, and walked to the front window, stepping into the flowerbed to peer through, my vision obscured by the net curtain. Grabbing a pen and a piece of paper from my bag, I scrawled a note to Hayley, pushed it through the letterbox and placed the cough medicine on the doorstep, waving at her next door neighbour as she pulled into her driveway. Time was running and I still had shopping to do.

The dress was perfect, I admitted, twirling back and forth in front of the mirror. Deep scarlet, it clung to my curves in all the right places, kindly skimming the others, and the low neckline would look great once I pushed my boobs up with a push-up bra. Swinging the bag containing my dress, I moved on to shoe shopping, mentally ticking off my checklist – *check, check, check*. I found the perfect pair of diamanté-encrusted sandals in the first shop I entered. *Check.*

As far as plans and fighting back went, I hadn't done too badly with my efforts, I decided as I dropped my bags into the boot and headed back home, shaking my driver's mat out onto the drive before I left the car. I should have checked my trainers, I thought, I'd probably left an embarrassing trail of dirt through the shop floors.

Smoothing my dress down with trembling fingers, and spraying a final burst of hairspray over my updo, I appraised myself in the mirror, nodding grimly. I'd gone a little heavy on the eye make-up, and my lips lacked colour. I could have done with Jenna's slutty red, but I couldn't wear it of course, I thought ruefully, rummaging through my make-up bag for something darker than my signature baby pink. Finding a magenta that I'd hardly ever used, I applied the liquid lipstick and pressed my lips together briefly. Perfect. The perfect killer outfit to taunt the man who's been cheating on his wife. 'I'll show you what you threw away, Martin,' I murmured as I spritzed on some perfume, and picked up my bleeping phone, frowning at the unknown number.

'Abs, the cab's here,' Martin called from downstairs.

Hesitating for a second, I clicked on the text message, my skin turning clammy as I read it.

Be careful with those steak knives tonight, you don't want to spill any more blood do you, Abigail? I know what you did.

He, no, someone, had my phone number. I froze. And whoever it was knew that I was going out to dinner tonight. For a second, I was back in the fateful hot tub, blood swirling around me.

'Abs, hurry up.'

I deleted the message and shakily put my phone in my bag as my mind raced through the people I'd mentioned our meal to – Jenna, Lauren, Hayley...

'Coming,' I called as I staggered down the stairs and out to the cab.

'You look– wow, Abs, you look amazing.' Martin's expression was just what I'd been hoping for and I forced a weak smile as my phone dinged in my bag.

'Aren't you going to look at your phone?' Martin glanced pointedly at my bag, gripped between my hands.

'Later, I'll look later,' I whispered, staring out of the window at the passing houses.

'What are you afraid of? That it's an anniversary message?'

That's exactly what I'm afraid of, just not the kind you're thinking of.

'That reminds me, I spoke to Adrian earlier and he and Claire wished us a happy anniversary. He suggested drinks this evening but I told him we were out for dinner. I'm looking forward to it actually, I've got quite an appetite. What about you?'

So Claire knew of our plans as well...

'Reckon I'll have steak for my main, it's always good there. Yep, a nice rare steak, good and bloody.' Martin nodded happily to himself as my stomach churned over. 'It was only Craig, for golf today, Ross is away on business, I'd forgotten. He said he'd seen Paul and that he and Emma feel terrible about the way things have turned out. Maybe we should have them over, show them that we're still friends. I mean, these things happen, don't they?'

I turned my head slowly, staring at Martin in disbelief. 'We're going out for our wedding anniversary and you think it's alright that Emma stole Paul from Lauren? Don't marriage vows mean anything to you, Martin?'

'Well, I didn't mean it like that, of course, but people make mistakes, it happens. Craig's obviously not holding any grudges against Paul for sleeping with his ex, is he? Or against Emma, for that matter, they seem to chat often so I'm guessing they're still friendly. Sometimes you have to forgive a person, Abs.'

'Who exactly are you talking about, Martin?' I looked away, unable to bear the look in his eyes. 'Did you tell Craig we were out for our anniversary tonight?' I kept my face turned to the window.

'I mentioned it, of course. Abs, what's going on, you're acting strange? Can't we at least try to have a pleasant evening?'

So Craig could have told Emma... which only left Fi...

Our cab pulled up outside the restaurant, which got me out of answering, and as soon as we'd been shown to our table, I excused myself for the ladies, locking myself in a cubicle and taking out my phone.

The message was from Fi. She'd spoken to Jen earlier, who'd reminded her about our anniversary. She was sorry she'd forgotten, wished us a happy anniversary and told us to enjoy our meal out tonight.

So that was that, then. Every single one of my friends knew that I was out to dinner with Martin tonight. Every single person that had been there that night – the night I'd stabbed a man to death – knew about our meal, and one of them was using his phone to taunt me. But why? What had changed? We'd agreed that we were all in it together, that it hadn't been my fault, that the knife had somehow got mixed up with the other bits and pieces. We'd agreed that we were all implicated so why was I being singled out?

Unless I wasn't. I couldn't believe that I hadn't thought of that before. I'd told none of the others about the messages purportedly from him, apart from Hayley, so maybe some of the others had received messages too and kept quiet. I needed to get everyone together, I decided, to see if I could flush out whoever it was, but first I had Monday lunch organised with Lauren and Hayley, and before that I had an anniversary meal to get through with Martin.

48

Don't You Want Me

It was a disaster. I spilt my wine, soaking the tablecloth and seeing blood spreading across the table in my mind's eye as the red wine seeped into the white linen, sitting dejectedly while the waiter gave a tight smile, clearing our table and laying it with a fresh cloth.

I nibbled at my bruschetta al pomodoro while Martin made a happy mess with his mussels, and toyed with my penne calabrese, fighting down nausea as he plunged his steak knife into his filetto di manzo, the watery blood oozing from his rare steak onto his plate to mix with the vegetables as he smacked his lips appreciatively.

It took an immense effort to restrain myself from reaching over the table, snatching his steak knife from his cheating hand and stabbing it into his cheating heart.

'Pudding?' Martin eyed the plate of tiramisu as it was placed in front of the woman seated at the table next to us.

'I'm full, I'd never manage it.' I wanted to scream at him across the table, 'How can you behave so calmly when you've been cheating on me?'

'I suppose I could give it a miss.' Martin patted his stomach with a wry grin. 'I certainly don't need it any more than you do. I'll get the bill then, and call a cab, shall I?'

I nodded, excusing myself to go to the ladies, and stood in front of the mirror appraising myself. If I lost a few pounds, would that make him love me again? Was it that simple? And even if it was, it was too late, the damage was done. I headed back to our table a couple of minutes later, keen to get home and escape to bed.

'Victoria?'

Desperately, I kept walking, my eyes fixed on our table. *Oh no, not now, please.*

'Victoria Beckingham?'

I turned to the woman speaking, my heart sinking, knowing that I should smile and managing to twist my lips into some kind of ghoulish imitation of one.

'It's Becca.' She gave a tinkly little laugh. 'Becca? From Propshop?'

I risked a glance towards Martin as he thanked the waiter and pushed his chair back. He looked over, a questioning expression on his face, and began to walk towards us with a puzzled smile.

'Becca, of course.'

Martin was getting closer and I could feel myself perspiring in my panic. 'How lovely to see you, but I really must go, I'm so sorry.' I moved away as she placed a hand on my arm.

'I've got a couple of great new properties just come in and I really think they'd be perfect for you. Can I just get your number again? I tried to call you but I think I must have written it down wrong. That's me, bonkers old Becca, always getting in a muddle.' She gave a chuckle, whipping her phone from her handbag and rolling her eyes as she clocked Martin nearing us. 'Is this your husband? He's a bit of alright, lucky old you, Victoria.' She winked as I felt a trickle of sweat run down my side beneath my dress.

Martin stopped, patted his pockets, and turned back towards our table. *I had to escape right now.*

'Becca, I really do have to go, but I'll pop in soon.' I had one of my masterful brainwaves. 'My husband's not feeling well.' I could see Martin leaving the table again, out of the corner of my eye.

Becca was instantly sympathetic. 'Oh, poor lamb. Now, you make sure you pop in and see me, Victoria.'

'I will, I promise.' I was home free and I gave Becca a huge smile as I turned to go, waving at Martin to indicate that he should head for the door.

'Oh, Mrs Parker's taken the house off the market, I'm afraid – the first one you viewed. Remember?' She leant in excitedly, grabbing my arm. 'Her husband's gone missing. Can you believe it? Disappeared. Poof! One minute he was there, the next minute he wasn't. They were away in the New Forest, poor things. Must be awful for her, mustn't it?'

By now, I was sure that I'd turned some unbecoming shade of green, and I stared at Becca mutely. 'That's... that's terrible,' I finally said, forcing the words out from between my uncooperative lips.

'Missing Madrid?' Becca's voice was all chirpy as she looked over my shoulder, and I turned in dread to find Martin behind me.

In desperation, I enveloped Becca in a hug. 'It's been so lovely to see you, I'll call you, I promise. We really have to go, bye.' I grabbed Martin's arm and gave the confused Becca a mad wave as I led him away.

'You get that poor husband of yours home, Victoria. I hope you feel better soon, Mr Beckingham,' she called, as I hurried Martin out of the restaurant.

'Who the hell was that? And why do I need to feel better soon? Did she just call me Mr Beckingham?'

'Did you forget something at the table?' I tried to distract him.

'What? Oh, thought I'd left my phone but it was in my jacket pocket. Who *was* that woman? Did I hear her right about Madrid? And why did she call you Victoria?'

I gave a manic little laugh. 'I honestly have no idea. I think she confused me with someone else but it was getting a little embarrassing, she was so insistent.'

'You chatted to her for long enough.' Martin opened the door of our waiting cab and I climbed gratefully in.

'You know me, I don't like to make a scene. I'll just close my eyes if you don't mind, I've got a bit of a headache.'

I sensed, rather than heard, Martin sigh beside me. 'I thought you seemed a bit out of sorts. You'd best take some tablets and get to bed then, that'll sort you out.'

Absolutely nothing in the whole world would sort me out ever again, but I gave a little murmur of agreement as I rested my head back and tried to calm my frazzled nerves.

I used the headache excuse as a reason to stay in bed most of Sunday, following a sleepless night, relieved when Martin said he was going out for a couple of pints and would grab something to eat at the pub, and clambered out only to have a shower and make myself some beans on toast as an impromptu dinner that evening.

I cobbled my ragged self together somehow on Monday in time to show up for lunch with Lauren and Hayley.

Except they didn't show.

I sat in the café in Marks and Spencer, checking my watch, and finally called Lauren when they were almost an hour late. No answer. Her phone clicked off no matter how many times I called it. I tried Hayley's number next, sending her a text when I received no answer, to say that I guessed she was still unwell as she hadn't turned up for our lunch and that I hoped she was feeling better soon. I got myself a sandwich and a cup of tea, and then went home, wondering if I should try to contact Lauren again but not wanting to go overboard.

I was tidying the bedroom, collecting Martin's discarded clothes from the chair where he'd dropped them the night before, when Jen called

'Hi, Abs, how was your anniversary? Did the lovey-doveys have a romantic dinner? How was your pasta? Was it a hot night of passion to remember?' Jen's voice was loud and chirpy, and I grimaced into my phone.

'Hardly, just dinner and bed with a headache.' I frowned, noticing the missing metal button on Martin's pale blue shirt.

'Don't tell me Martin's using that old excuse.'

I waited for her to finish laughing. 'No, it was me, actually. Thanks for the roses, Jen, they're beautiful, it was sweet of you to remember.'

'Like I could ever forget the anniversary of the perfect little couple, even if I wasn't there the day you tied the knot all those years ago.'

'I'm not sure about the perfect little couple bit, Jen,' I said without thinking.

'What, you and Marty? Unless he's having his fun somewhere else...' Jen was silent for a second, oblivious to how hurtful her throwaway comment had been. 'Abs, are you alright? You sound a little fed-up. Is anything bothering you?'

Chaotic thoughts crashed around in my head – er, we left the pig's head mask at the scene of the crime – the one *you* were wearing, Jan... I received a message from a dead man on the Frisky app referring to the hot tub and saying we should do it again some time... someone sent me black roses to mark the one-week anniversary of his murder... I've found out that Martin's been having an affair... I don't think he loves me anymore... I got drunk and went on a hook up, found out he was nothing like his profile and had a narrow escape... I went to Night Monster's house about a week before I killed him... I received a taunting text from his phone about knives... and my cover was almost blown by bubbly Becca from Propshop on Saturday night... Is that enough for you?

'Everything's fine.' I gave a tinkly laugh, reminiscent of Becca.

'Are you sure? Listen, Fi's coming round for a drink tonight. You're welcome to join us.'

'Thanks, I don't know, maybe. Are you at home? Is Lauren with you?'

'Lauren? No, didn't you know?'

'Know what?'

'She's gone away for a few days according to the text I got from her. She said she needed some time alone to do some thinking. It's weird though, all her stuff's still here at mine, it doesn't even look like she took any clothes with her.'

'But...' I paused for a moment. 'Thinking about what?'

'I don't know, Paul, I suppose...'

'I was supposed to meet her for lunch today. Why didn't she tell me?'

'Well, don't ask *me*, ask her.'

'I tried to call her and she didn't answer her phone.'

'Maybe she's still upset with you, Abs, give her some time.'

'But when did she leave? Where's she gone?'

'God, I'm not her keeper, Abs, she's a grown woman. She's probably still pissed off with you about Paul having his hands all over your bum at her barbeque. And maybe she hasn't forgiven you for your little performance in the hot tub – it has rather dropped us all in it.' Jenna was still laughing when I rang off.

I looked at Martin's shirt again, feeling sick. The button hadn't fallen off, it had been torn off, there was a small piece of fabric missing. Which could only mean one thing.

49

Unchained Melody

I sat on the bed for a while, staring at his torn shirt as I imagined him in the throes of passion with another woman. Who was it? The same woman from the dating app? The one he'd told it was over? Well it obviously wasn't. He must have been with her yesterday while I lay in bed with my stupid headache excuse because my life was spiralling out of control and I didn't know how to get a handle on things.

I pictured her hands tearing at his shirt as they kissed, pulling it from his shoulders and off his arms before those same hands reached for his flies... Throwing his shirt on the floor, I rushed into the bathroom and flung the toilet seat up, retching noisily.

Splashing cold water on my face, I went downstairs and filled a glass with tap water, drinking it down in one go.

I'd told Jen nothing about the messages I'd received, or the black roses, and something was niggling away in my head from my conversation with Lauren. I'd known most of what she was talking about, but what exactly had she been saying about Jenna?

She'd said she was right there, behind her. She'd been behind her as they'd charged to the hot tub, I could picture the pig mask and the chimp mask, as he'd spoken his last words... but she'd also been behind Jenna's chair on Friday night when she'd been so angry – angry at me. Or had she been angry at Jenna too? I tried to picture the scene – Lauren looking down as Jenna read something on her phone; Lauren glaring at me as she swigged from the bottle of wine; Lauren saying something about sleeping with your husband, as she'd looked from Jenna's phone towards me, and then correcting herself.

And then, when she'd called me, she'd said Hayley didn't believe it about the cheating. And when I'd spoken to Hayley she'd been so relieved that everything was alright. Alright with me and Martin? They'd been discussing my husband's affair. Did that mean they'd both known who she was?

Was it Jenna? Had Martin cheated on me with Jenna? Never. Not her. Martin didn't even like her being around these days. He'd liked her once, a taunting voice chirped in my head. But he'd chosen me, I silently responded. And Jenna was my friend...

Maybe it had been one of the others, after all, Lauren had been all over the place that night, striding around the lounge and spitting out stuff, and she'd probably stood behind everyone at some point. She'd been so angry, she could have misunderstood anything.

I was being ridiculous, I told myself, trying to picture which of my friends had been screwing my husband.

How did Jenna know that you had pasta on Saturday night? I froze, a loud ringing sound in my ears. I hadn't told her, which left... Martin... Martin and Jenna...

I sat for ages, torturing myself with images of the two of them together, until I shook myself out of it. I had no proof, only suspicions, and if I had to prioritise then right now the issue of who was sending me the messages had to take precedence. Time enough to deal with Jenna and Martin later...

I picked up my phone again, re-reading the message that I'd received from Hayley's phone earlier, apologising for missing lunch. Once I'd sent a quick reply saying that I hoped she felt better soon and that she'd found the cough medicine I'd left for her on the doorstep, I sent a message to Lauren's phone.

Hi, Laur. Jenna said you've gone away for a little while. I'm sorry we missed our lunch date. Let me know when you get back. Stay safe. xx

Pushing my worries about Martin to the back of my mind with difficulty, I forced myself to concentrate on what Lauren and Hayley had said to me on the phone – Lauren had been indirectly talking about the knife, Hayley had confirmed that. What I needed to find out was whether either of them had spoken to anyone else, and if they had, what had they told them? It did, after all, directly affect me as it had been my hand holding the knife.

I called Claire first.

'Abs, hi, how are you, love? Did you have a nice anniversary meal with Martin?' Without waiting for my reply, she carried on talking. 'Did you hear from Lauren? I got a message saying she needed some time to think, that she'd gone away for a few days.'

'That's what Jenna said too. We were supposed to meet for lunch today but she didn't show. Have you spoken to her at all?'

'Nope, just the text message. I hope she's alright. And poor Hayley's sick as a dog apparently. Fi had a text from her.'

'I know, I left her some medicine on Saturday, I think she must have been asleep, poor thing. So you didn't speak to her? What about Fi? Did she speak to Hayles? Have you spoken to any of the others?'

'Calm down, Abs. What's going on? You sound like you're in a terrible state.'

Where to begin? Oh, yeah, only that Lauren told Hayley that she saw the knife, which meant she remembered something odd about the night I'd killed a man, and I was receiving messages and bouquets of black roses from him even though he was dead. Oh, and let's not forget about my husband's affair... Don't think about that.

'Can I call you back? I'm just trying to figure something out. I need to speak to Fi.'

Fi answered her phone after what felt like a hundred hours. 'Abs, what's up, babes?'

'Oh, Fi, hi. Um, did you hear from Lauren? Jen said she's gone away for a few days, and–'

'I just spoke to Jen,' Fi interrupted. 'Typical Lauren, drama queen as always. She just took off. I suppose this whole thing with Emma and Paul has really screwed with her head. Oh, how was your meal with Martin?'

'It was good, thanks.' *Well that was a lie.* 'Listen, Fi, so, you didn't speak to Lauren at all? She didn't call you?'

'No, why?'

'I'm just worried. What about Hayley? Did she call you? You know she's not well?'

'Yes, poor love, she's got a bad cold, she sent me a message but I didn't speak to her. I told her to let me know if she needed anything but she hasn't got back to me. Maybe I should check in on her.'

'No, no, that's OK, we shouldn't disturb her. So neither you nor Claire have spoken to Lauren or Hayley? What about Emma? D'you think she might have spoken to either one of them?'

'Emma? Well, this is getting interesting... No, I think we can pretty much assume that Lauren and Emma aren't talking, don't you? And Hayley wasn't exactly sympathetic to the situation so I doubt that she and Emma have been having nice little chats back and forth.'

'I know, I know, but, well, have you spoken to Emma?'

'Abs, if this is some kind of militant defender of friendship call about Lauren and our allegiances, I can assure you that, although I don't give a damn about who sleeps with who in the scheme of things, I'm not having cosy chats with Emma behind Lauren's back.'

'We all need to meet up, Emma as well,' I said, making a decision. 'There's something I need to talk to you all about.'

'Hmm, how mysterious. And Emma, too? Lauren won't like that... Oh, she's not here so she won't know, cunning... and if Hayley's not well, she won't know either... So that'll be you, me, Jen, Claire and the prodigal Emma – welcomed back into the fold. I'll call Em if you like? Why don't we all meet at Jenna's tonight? I'm already going round to hers for a drink, I'll just tell her the rest of you are coming. I'll pick up some snacky bits from M&S, how's that?'

'Thanks, Fi, that's great. Tonight then, if everyone can make it, it is kind of urgent. I'll call the others and let them know.

So, what's your big, urgent announcement then? You're leaving Martin and running off with someone you met on the dating app?'

'That's not funny, Fi,' I said over the sound of her laughter, cringing inwardly as images of my drunken stupidity of a few nights earlier filled my head.

'It's funny because it's the last thing you would ever do in your sweet, innocent, little life, Abs. I'm teasing you, babes, you know that.'

'I know.' I smiled into the phone as we rang off, knowing that being at Jenna's would offer me an opportunity to look for, and hopefully acquire, something important.

50

Don't Let It Bring You Down

I walked into Jen's kitchen as Fi took quiches from the oven and placed them on the counter.

'Oh, hi, Abs, no mini nibbles left so I had to get large quiches, but they smell good.' Fi gave me a quick hug before reaching into the oven again for baguettes which she put on a bread board for slicing. 'And bread and cheese. You could unwrap the cheeses and put them on a plate. Jen, where's your bread knife?'

Claire appeared behind me and gave me a squeeze. 'I'll get it, she keeps it in here. Where is she?'

'I'm here.'

I jumped as Jen's voice sounded right behind me.

'What's wrong, Abs? You're a little jumpy. Got things on your mind?'

I forced myself to smile at my traitorous friend. *Just a few.* 'I'm fine, Jen.' My hands trembled as I dropped my bag on the floor in the corner, and began to unwrap the cheeses, my vision blurred by sudden tears.

'I'll slice the quiches,' Jen said, reaching for her obligatory blue hygiene gloves. 'Blast, I'm out, sorry hands.' She squashed the empty box, throwing it in the bin, picked up a large knife and began to cut the quiches into slices, finishing just as the doorbell rang. 'That'll be Emma, I'll go.'

I watched her drop the knife on the board and walk past me as I washed my hands, looking through the door to the hallway as I heard her and Emma murmuring softly before they moved into the lounge. 'I'm just going to the loo,' I said to Claire and Fi as I scuttled from the kitchen and rushed up the stairs. Pausing to listen for a second, I pushed the door to Jenna's bedroom open and switched on the light, staring at her bed in despair as I pictured her and Martin holding each other as they kissed, as they pulled each other's clothes off...

Breathlessly, I pulled back the duvet, smoothing my hands over the sheet and under the pillows in search of his missing button. Carefully smoothing the duvet back in place, I knelt down and felt under the bed, peering awkwardly, before checking beneath the bedside cabinets. Nothing. My eyes scanned the carpet. Again, nothing. Under the chair in the corner. Nothing.

Jenna's voice reached my ears and I froze awkwardly on all fours as I looked under the chest of drawers.

'I'll take the wine through to the lounge, the glasses are already in there. Where's Abigail?'

'In the loo.' Claire's voice was muffled. 'Where do you want the food put?'

I scraped my hands over the carpet beneath the chest of drawers and admitted defeat. The button wasn't here. Switching off the light, I hurried into the bathroom, shutting the door and leaning against it for a moment before moving to stand in front of the vanity unit.

I stared at my flushed reflection, trying to smooth my hair and calm down before going back downstairs. As I turned from the mirror a small glint on the floor beside the bath caught my eye. Slowly, I reached down, picking up Martin's missing button with trembling fingers, and stroked the tiny piece of pale blue fabric attached to it. So it was true. I had the proof in my hand.

I turned to stare at the face of a betrayed wife in the mirror, drawing a deep breath as I carefully pushed the button into the pocket of my jeans. Jenna's messy basket of accessories was beside the basin and I picked up a crumpled pair of blue disposable gloves, feeling something hard wrapped in them. Opening them up, I found her ridiculous chandelier earrings with their cheap, rainbow-coloured gemstones sparkling on fake gold chains, and I watched numbly as one of them fell to lie amidst the other pieces of garish costume jewellery thrown in her basket.

'Oh, sorry, Abs, the door wasn't locked.' Fi's face appeared behind me in the mirror and I shoved the gloves and earring into my pocket as I turned to give her some kind of psychotic grin.

'That's OK, I'm finished.' My feet felt leaden as I descended the stairs, my hand dragging down the banister that Martin had probably touched as he rushed up the stairs to take Jenna to bed. The sounds of voices, and glasses clinking, reached my ears from behind the lounge door, and I walked quietly past into the kitchen.

Keeping an ear tuned for anyone coming, I opened my bag, slipping my collected items into it and carefully zipping it closed. I looked around, frowning at the dirty chopping board with quiche crumbs all over it, and took it to the bin where I brushed the crumbs off before washing it up at the sink.

'Abs?'

Startled, I looked at Fi's enquiring face at the door.

'Why are you washing up? Aren't you going to come and tell us why you gathered us all together?'

Martin and Jenna would have to wait, it was time to figure out who had the phone and was taunting me... Picking up my bag, I followed Fi into the lounge.

I had to tread carefully – someone here was dangerous, I reminded myself as I looked around at the expectant faces gathered in Jen's living room. Taking a large gulp of wine for Dutch courage, I swallowed and cleared my throat.

'Thanks for coming, everyone, and you, Emma.' I nodded at Emma, giving her a small smile. 'Something bad has happened. I should have told you all earlier but there was a lot going on, what with Emma and Paul, and...' I gave Emma an apologetic glance. 'Well, the thing is, I've had a message from him. More than one actually. And I received a bouquet of roses from him.' I looked quickly from face to face, hoping to catch a look that gave it away, but they all just looked at me non-plussed.

'From... Martin? For your anniversary?' Claire's brow was creased in confusion. 'That's a good thing, isn't it?' She flapped her blouse, her face flushed. 'This heat is unbearable, is it going to storm?'

It would have been, if my husband had remembered it was our anniversary, and if he wasn't cheating on me with someone else... with Jenna... 'No, not Martin. *Him.* Night Monster.'

'The dead guy?' Jen leant forward in her chair. 'You've been getting messages from a dead man, Abs? He must be really keen to get his hands on you.' She laughed loudly as Claire frowned at her.

'What are you talking about? They can't be from him.'

'Someone's winding you up, Abs.' Fi stood and opened the sliding doors to the patio to let in some air.

'Yes? And who would do that?' I looked challengingly back at Fi. 'Who, apart from us, and Lauren and Hayley of course, knew what happened that night?'

'You think it's one of us? Well, here, Abs, here's my phone, have a look and see if it was me.' Emma thrust her phone in my face. 'I want to forget all about that terrible night, not play around sending messages about it.'

'That's not what she's saying.' Fi studied my face for a moment. 'If it was from one of our phones she would know, wouldn't she? Were they text messages? What was the phone number?'

'I deleted the text message,' I whispered, my heart sinking. 'But the first one came via the dating app.'

'So someone used his account? That could be anyone, couldn't it?'

'But who would be able to sign into his account? They'd have to know his password, or–'

'Or have his phone...' Claire's eyes widened. 'What did happen to his phone? Does anyone know?' She looked around the room.

'And the flowers came to my home – a bouquet of black roses – with a message saying it was one week since I killed him. Don't you see?' I looked around in panic, trying to read my friends' faces. 'Whoever it is, they know my real name, my address and my phone number.'

'Let me see your phone, if you deleted the text message it might still be there. What?' Fi's hand dropped. 'You don't trust me now, Abs?'

Jen had been silent, but now she drained her glass and spoke. 'Why you? Is there something you're not telling us?'

Is there something you're not telling me, Jen? Focus. 'What? No, of course not, that's why I wanted us to get together, to see if anyone else had received any messages or anything. Well, have you?'

No one else had, it was established quickly.

'You are the one who stabbed him to death, Abs. Maybe someone's upset about that.'

'God, Jen, what a terrible thing to say.'

I looked gratefully at Claire. 'I had the knife in my hand, yes, but I don't know where it came from, it was just... there...' My eyes welled up as I looked desperately at Claire.

'Oh, Abs, come here.' She enveloped me in a hug, looking around at the others. 'Let's not forget we're all in this together, whatever happened that night, it wasn't Abigail's fault. It was a tragic accident and we all helped cover it up.'

I pulled away from Claire's embrace to blow my nose.

'Can we see the message on the dating app?' Jenna held out her hand. 'Let's clear this up.'

I brought up the app, my fingers fumbling as I clicked on the message thread, scrolling down to find the last message. 'It's gone,' I whispered. 'It's gone. It was there, I saw it. It said something about him not expecting it to go that way in the hot tub, and we should do it again some time, or something like that. I don't understand it...'

'So, let's get this straight. You received a message from him on the app but it's gone, and you received a text message from him but it's gone. I suppose you're going to tell us that you threw the bouquet of roses away as well?' Jen's tone and expression mocked me as she looked at me.

'No, the roses are in my lounge, Martin wouldn't let me throw them away when I said they must have been delivered by mistake, he said it was a waste. But I hid the card from him and threw it away.' Remembering what Fi had said, I searched my deleted messages, clicking on the one purporting to be from him triumphantly. 'Here's his text message. See?' I waved my phone around, letting them read the message.

'Shit.' Fi picked up her own phone. 'Read out the number for me, Abs.'

'You're not going to call it?' I looked at her aghast.

'No, stupid, I'm going to look it up online to see if I can find out anything.'

We watched, mesmerised, as Fi's long nails clicked on her keypad.

'The phone number belongs to Matthew Parker, freelance design consultant. Fuck. Is that him? Does anyone know his bloody surname?' Flinging her phone down on the side table, Fi grabbed her vape, sucking on it furiously.

'It was on the news, but I can't remember,' said Claire.

Emma looked over at Jenna. 'You had his wallet. Did you look inside it? What did you do with it?'

We all stared at Jenna, watching her as she stood and walked to a cabinet and unlocked a small drawer. She threw a dark object at Em, who jumped out of the way.

'I'm not touching it. Why did you keep it?'

'You said you were going to dispose of it.'

Smiling grimly, Jenna retrieved the wallet and opened it. 'I must have forgotten. His name was Matthew Parker.'

Matthew Parker – dead, deceased, not breathing, stabbed to death with a kitchen knife by yours truly, a corpse floating around somewhere in the English Channel... Matthew Parker who could not possibly be using his mobile phone because he probably didn't have any fingers left, because the fish had probably eaten them, because he was fish food, because he was DEAD.

51

This was proof that it wasn't just someone accessing his dating apps and playing cruel games, this was someone in possession of his phone – his phone that he'd had with him when he came to his appointment with death in a hot tub.

Everyone looked as horrified as me as I looked round at my friends' faces, except– I looked back at Jenna. Had that been a glint of malice there for a second? Suddenly, I was picturing her with Martin again. She must be loving the mess I was in as she stole my husband from under my nose. My mind ran riot, trying to make sense of the madness that my life had become, and I pulled myself back to the conversation playing out in the room, with difficulty.

'Is there anything that anyone's not telling us? If someone's been playing a joke on Abs then now's the time to come clean. It's not funny, guys, this is serious.' Fi strode back and forth, running her hand over her scalp in agitation before stopping, hands on her hips. 'Where was his phone? Did anyone see it?'

'It's not one of us, that's ridiculous. It has to be someone else.'

'So someone else knows that we killed a man in the hot tub and threw his body off a cliff? Then why haven't they gone to the police? Why aren't we all in prison?'

'No one else could know, we were completely alone in the middle of bloody nowhere.'

'What about the people staying in the lighthouse cottage?'

'How would they have got hold of his phone?'

'Could it have dropped out when we carried him?'

'He was in the nude, for God's sake.'

'Are we sure he's dead?'

The room fell quiet as a rumble of thunder sounded in the distance.

'You're not serious?'

'We never actually saw his body go over the cliff, did we? We dropped him.'

'And then he was gone...'

'So, let me get this straight.' Fi dropped down into her seat. 'Abs stabbed him in the hot tub, and he died. Sorry, Abs, I know you didn't mean to do it.' She blew me a kiss. 'We wrapped his naked body up in plastic, drove him to the coast and carried him to the cliff, where the plastic tore open and he fell out. He then came back to life, crept off under cover of darkness, still in the nude, and somehow still had his phone which he is now using to taunt Abs, rather than going straight to the police to tell them what we did. Have I missed anything? Oh, and he's currently running around naked, living on wild berries somewhere in the New Forest while being listed as a missing person.'

Fi's sarcastic summation relieved the tension in the room, and we smiled around at each other, realising how crazy the whole thing sounded.

'So who's doing it then? Who's got his phone if it's not him?' Emma's question undid that moment of relief.

'One of us...' Claire picked up her bag, looked inside, then threw it on the floor. 'I could really do with a smoke right now. Where's Lauren when you need her?'

'I've got some.' Fi dropped her vape on the coffee table and reached for her bag. 'Come on, I'll join you.'

'Sod it, smoke inside, I'm sure we can put up with it. Hayley's not here so we don't need to worry about her asthma. It looks like it's going to storm, anyway.'

'Flowers,' I said as they lit their cigarettes. 'I meant to send Hayley some flowers. I'll do it now and say they're from all of us.' I brought up a flower site, clicked on an arrangement, and typed a get well message as they nodded and thanked me. 'There, all done. I chose one with all pretty pinks and whites, she'll love it, and it will cheer her up.' I held my phone out to show them the photo.

'Gorgeous, that's sweet of you, Abs. I dropped a card in at the weekend but I didn't think of flowers, a great idea, babe, thanks.'

I smiled at Fi, feeling pleased with myself.

'Did I see your car parked in Hayley's road on Saturday?'

My head spun round to see who Emma was asking, but she was looking at Jen.

'No, I don't think so...' Jen reached for a bottle of wine and topped up her glass. 'Oh, hold on, maybe I did drive down it, yes, I pulled in somewhere to answer a call, might have been around there.'

'I was there on Saturday as well, I took her some medicine but she didn't answer her door. I had to put a note through the letterbox. She was probably sleeping.'

'You should have let yourself in the back door, she's got that stupid, secret key rock thing, hasn't she?'

'Oh, I forgot about that.'

'So, what's all this about Lauren going away to clear her head or whatever?'

'We can't really– not with Emma here.' I shrugged, feeling awkward, as I looked from Claire to Emma.

'Lauren's gone away?' Emma put her glass down. 'Where's she gone?'

'Well, the thing is, Em, we shouldn't talk about Lauren with you, not after everything... you know...'

Sighing, Emma accepted a refill from Fi. 'Paul said he was going away as well.' She smiled, her eyes suspiciously bright. 'It hasn't turned out quite so well.' She sounded bitter as she gave a brittle laugh. 'I've lost one of my best friends, and the joke is that they'll probably end up getting back together. He's probably with her now. I've been really stupid, loneliness, I suppose.'

For a moment, I felt filled with sympathy for Emma, but then I reminded myself that she'd done the unforgivable – she'd stolen a friend's husband, and I hardened my heart.

'Can we get back to the phone, please?' I pleaded. 'We need to think back to what happened after I– once he was–'

'Yes, let's focus on that.' Jen's expression was inscrutable. 'What do we remember? He walked out onto the deck, saw Abs, then he took his clothes off...'

'No, not then,' I interjected. 'After. That's what's important – what happened after?'

'I took the knife from your hand, then we pulled you out.'

'I got you a blanket because you were shivering,' added Claire.

'From shock,' contributed Jen. 'You poor thing.'

Why did it always feel like Jen said one thing but meant something else?

'Well it wasn't from the cold, was it? It was stifling that night.' Ironically, Fi shivered as she spoke.

A clear image entered my head of the moments directly after I'd spluttered my way up from the water in the hot tub – Jen's hands, blue with cold as they removed the pig's head mask – except it hadn't been cold... and neither had her hands... She'd been wearing a pair of her disposable gloves. Why? I blinked, unable to think straight, aware that everyone was still talking. Should I say something? No, now wasn't the time... besides, she'd only been protecting her stupid nails, no doubt... still... I filed the fact away under useful information.

'You went inside, Claire. Why did you do that?'

'She was turning the music off.'

'Someone folded his clothes.'

'That was Jen.'

'Are you saying I took his phone when I folded his clothes up?'

'I don't know, did you?'

'This is ridiculous.'

'Abs was sick, and I was with her,' said Claire.

'Jen, you stormed off inside after you and Fi were shouting.'

'I needed a moment, is that such a surprise? Someone had to come up with a plan.'

'Where did you go, Emma? You also left the deck.'

'I've got no idea, maybe I also needed a minute. And what about Fi? Who were you talking to Fi? I heard your voice coming from somewhere.'

'I was probably trying to talk myself out of having a full meltdown. What? You think I was on the phone to someone? Maybe I was using his phone, is that it? Maybe I phoned his wife and told her that her husband was dead, then met up with her secretly, gave her his phone, told her Abigail's phone number and address and told her to start sending her threatening messages. Yeah, that all makes perfect sense – in an insane world.' Fi lit another cigarette.

'Lauren went down into the garden, I think.'

'Yes, and Jen told Hayley to grab bags and things from the kitchen, but so what? None of this proves anything.'

'Who put his clothes in the bag? Was it you, Jen?'

'No, Lauren, I think.'

'But you folded them. Was his phone in the pocket of his jeans?'

'Emma, you wore them to drive his car.'

'There was no phone in the pocket.'

'Maybe his phone was still in his car?'

'Did anyone check? Unbelievable. We probably parked his car back and left his phone in there. Why didn't anyone think of that?'

'That's it, Fi, chuck accusations around. If I recall, I was the only one doing any thinking at all. It's thanks to me that we've got through this.'

'Got through it?' I cried. 'I'm being threatened by someone. And that affects all of us,' I reminded them. 'Not to mention there's a photo of me in the hot tub on the dating app on his phone.'

'I remember now.' Emma sat up straight. 'I looked for his car keys in his pockets and they weren't there, and there was definitely no phone, not in his jeans and not in his car, I checked that his car was clear.

'We've only got your word for that, Emma. Maybe you took it. Because someone did. He must have had it on him when he arrived, he'd sent a message to Abs to say he was on his way.'

The rest of us looked from Jen to Emma.

'You're eager to pin this on me, Jen, when, actually, pretty much everyone was missing at some point or another. Any one of us could have gone to his car and taken his phone – he'd left it unlocked, and like I said, it wasn't there when I drove it to the pub. It could have been you, me – except it wasn't, Claire, Lauren, Fi or Hayley. The only person it couldn't have been is Abs as she didn't move or leave the deck.'

'Unless you just missed it.'

'Even if Em had missed it, how the hell would whoever had found it know what had happened to him? No, it's one of us. Leaving Abs out of the equation, one of the six of us has his phone and is hiding the fact.'

Heads swivelled left and right as everyone looked awkwardly at everyone else.

Emma's phone rang, sounding shrill in the sudden silence as we contemplated the fact that someone was lying.

Slowly, our brains registered that something was wrong – Emma's one-word questions of when, where and how, asked in a strained voice, alerting us to the fact.

We watched her place her phone gently on the side table and take a deep, shuddering breath, as another rumble of thunder sounded, this time much closer.

'What is it, Em? What's wrong? You're white as a sheet.' Claire stubbed her cigarette out carelessly, a thin trickle of smoke continuing to dance upwards from the ashtray.

'That was Paul. Oh God. Lauren's dead.'

52

Beautiful Girl

'Lauren can't be dead, it's not possible.' Claire picked up the packet of cigarettes with trembling fingers, as lightning flashed.

'She drowned. Paul just identified her body.' Emma's voice sounded strange as she looked around at us all with staring eyes.

'She's gone away for a few days, she told me.'

'Did anyone actually speak to her?'

'She sent me a text.'

'Me too.'

'I spoke to her on Saturday morning and we arranged to meet for lunch today, but she never turned up.' I looked around at my friends wild-eyed.

'And she didn't say anything to you about going away, Abs?'

'Maybe she just suddenly decided?'

'Where the hell did she drown, for God's sake? We all know Lauren can't swim... couldn't swim, so she certainly wasn't taking a dip somewhere. Oh God, is it really true?'

My eyes met Jen's for a moment, and she looked away. Had that been a look of something like fear in her eyes? Fear of what?

'When I spoke to Lauren on Saturday, she said that she was going for a walk,' I said, keeping my eyes on Jen, not sure how much of Lauren's side of the conversation she'd heard.

'Where? Where was she going walking? Did she say?' Claire stood up and sat down again. 'Keston Ponds, she told us once that she liked to walk at Keston Ponds. She must have gone there.'

'Well, she can't have drowned in bloody Keston Ponds, can she?' Fi paced the room.

'Jen, were you there when Lauren called me on Saturday?' I asked.

'What? Of course I wasn't. Why? What difference does it make?' She sounded defensive.

'Because someone was,' I said softly. 'I heard a door click in the background, and she said something like, she's coming, I have to go.'

The others looked at Jen, waiting for her to say something.

'Jen?' I asked warily, wanting to push her, but feeling afraid suddenly, not sure how much I wanted to hear.

'Well, she was in my bloody house, wasn't she? So what if I was there? I didn't hear anything, and she certainly didn't say anything about Keston Ponds.' This time the look that Jen gave me was definitely off.

'So you were there?'

'Why did you say you weren't?'

'What does any of this matter?' Claire asked miserably. 'Our friend is dead.'

'It was an accident, wasn't it? It wasn't...?'

'It wasn't what? What else could it have been?'

My eyes met Jen's again and I had to stop myself from shrinking back into my chair. I tried to recall Lauren's words from our conversation – she'd talked about that weekend, she'd mentioned Martin, and Jenna, she'd referred indirectly to seeing the knife, and she'd said quite clearly that she'd discussed everything with Hayley... Had Jen heard every word, and if she had, what did that mean? And I was still no closer to figuring out who had his phone...

'Why aren't any of us crying?' Claire asked the silent room.

'Because it doesn't feel real,' Emma said softly, reaching for a tissue from the box on the side table.

I could feel my shoulders start to shake as the full impact of a life without Lauren began to hit me, and tears ran down my face.

'Look, it was an accident, alright? A terrible accident, nothing more, after all, why would anyone want to do away with Laur? That's what you're saying, isn't it? That she could have been murdered?' Fi blew her nose noisily.

'The police might wonder, especially once they find out about Paul and Emma.'

'I can't believe you just said that.' Emma glared at Jenna and stood up. 'I'm going, I don't even know why I came, all this talk about a dead man not being dead and someone using his phone to send threats, and now you're suggesting that Lauren was murdered, it's all bullshit. I need to speak to Paul, he's probably at home by now and he needs my support.'

We looked at each other as the front door slammed behind Emma.

'All I was going to say was that we might be asked where we were when Lauren died.' Jen shrugged her shoulders.

'Like an alibi, d'you mean? A fucking alibi?' Fi's voice had risen with every word. 'Why, in God's name, would any of us need an alibi? She was our friend.'

'Unless it's connected to someone having his phone,' I said, glancing covertly at Jenna. 'And what happened that weekend...' I forced myself to breathe as I considered the danger of what I'd just put out there.

'We don't even know when she died.'

Nodding, we agreed with Claire.

'We need more information. D'you think it's on the news?'

Fi switched the television on and found a news channel, but after a few minutes with no mention of Lauren, she turned it off.

'Someone should tell Hayley, I'll call her.'

We watched as Claire tapped on her phone and waited, finally ending the call when there was no answer.

'She's probably asleep. She'll be asleep, don't you think?'

'Well, she's not bloody dead, is she? We know she's not well so, yes, she's probably in bed. We need to stop with the crazy ideas, OK? Maybe we should call it a night, we've all had a shock, and I for one have had just about as much as I can take of blokes being accidentally stabbed in hot tubs, and being dead but not being dead, conspiracy theories and accusations about dead men's phones being used to send threats, and friends going missing and turning up dead.' A flash of lightning was followed by a crash of thunder, and heavy drops of rain began to fall, splashing lazily in through the open patio doors.

Fi had summed things up pretty succinctly, for the second time.

'Shit, here comes the rain, you're all going to get soaked, and no one's touched the food.'

'Getting soaked and not eating are the least of our worries right now,' said Claire, as she hugged Jen. 'I'm going, I should be with Adrian, he probably doesn't know about Lauren yet.' She rubbed Jen's bare shoulders. 'I always meant to ask you about your tattoo. It's a hawthorn flower, isn't it? I don't know why I'm asking you that now. Weird, the things we say when we're in shock.'

I watched everyone gather their things and hug each other as they said their goodbyes, promising to let each other know of any news about Lauren, feeling disembodied from the situation.

Hawthorn was my surname. Hawthorn was my husband's surname. And Jenna had a tattoo of a hawthorn flower – five white petals, tinged with pale pink – just like the flower on her profile picture on the dating app. All this time, her tattoo had been mocking me, and I hadn't realised.

I held my tote bag in front of my body, clutching it awkwardly so that I could get away with a mumbled goodbye as Jenna turned to me. I avoided eye contact, afraid that if she looked into my eyes she'd read my mind and know everything that was in it – the main emotion at that moment being pure hatred.

I drove home slowly as the rainfall intensified, aware that I'd had a couple of glasses of wine, and that I was only holding my ragged self together by some miracle as I grappled with taunts from beyond the grave, betrayal by a best friend, and by a husband, and the tragic loss of a dear friend, looking out anxiously as lightning flashed ahead of me. Don't think about Lauren, I told myself sternly, knowing it was too much for my head to cope with. Instead, I forced myself to replay the last few hours in my head as I searched for clues as to what was happening. A crash of thunder made me jump as I pulled into our driveway. The message I'd received on the Frisky app, why hadn't it been there? Because someone had deleted it before I could show it to anyone...

I switched off the engine and pulled my phone from my bag, glancing at the curtains pulled closed over the front windows, and knowing that Martin wouldn't have heard me arrive home above the sound of the thunder and rain. Maybe I'd missed it in my panic to prove to my friends that what I was telling them was true.

I couldn't access the app.

After five attempts I had to concede that the password was, indeed, incorrect – in other words, someone had changed it. Someone had changed it in the last couple of hours. Frantically, I tried to sign into the other apps, with the same results. I was locked out of all the apps and unable to see any of the messages I'd supposedly sent or received. Which meant that I was unable to delete everything, something I should have done long ago.

Someone now had the proof of my assignation with a man who'd ended up dead, as well as all my other messages – and my drunken almost assignation the previous week – which made me look like the worst kind of cheating wife, and there was nothing I could do about it. But who?

Jenna? She was the obvious choice. She'd set the apps up on my phone, after all. But why would she change the password now?

I tried to remember who else had been there when Jenna had given me the sign-in details for the apps. We'd been at Fi's... I'd been given my makeover for the profile photo... some of the girls had gone outside for a smoke, I recalled, so that would be Claire, Fi, and... Lauren...

I could picture Hayley sitting there smiling encouragingly as I was shown how to use the app, but of course it wasn't my sweet friend Hayley. That left Emma... Emma who'd been cheating with Paul behind Lauren's back... Emma who... An image appeared in my head of the day of the barbeque, the moment when I'd got away from Paul's drunken embrace and had grinned at Emma in embarrassment. Only she hadn't grinned back, had she? She'd given me a look that could have turned me to stone. The more I thought about it, the more I realised that Emma must have been jealous at that moment, jealous of me dancing with Paul, of him grabbing hold of my bottom.

But it served Emma nothing to lock me out of the apps, whereas Jenna, on the other hand... Jenna held power over me now. She could show everything to Martin. Except she couldn't, surely, because she'd risk him recognising the man in the profile picture as the missing man on the news. Which could prompt awkward questions for all of us... *actually, no, Abigail, only awkward questions for you, there was no indication that anyone else was ever involved...*

Had I been set up? How was that even possible? With shocking clarity, I remembered Jenna casually asking me for my bank card to book the cottage. Had she known more than she was letting on?

Would the others all back Jenna, if push came to shove, and deny having been there? Or could I convince them that we needed to stick together against Jenna? I quailed at the thought of what lay ahead of me, wondering if I was strong enough. *It's that or she takes your husband for good, Abigail, while you go down for murder.*

53

Antmusic

I made a run for the front door, unlocking it just as the sky lit up and another thunderclap sounded close by. Slamming it behind me, I leant against it for a moment, closing my eyes as I tried to find the strength to face Martin.

The hall light switched on suddenly, and I opened my eyes to find Martin in front of me.

'Christ, you look rough.' He picked through the post that had been delivered earlier, as I ran past him and up the stairs.

'Did you eat?' he called from downstairs.

'No,' I said, as I reached the landing.

'I'm making toast, want some?' he called.

'Yes please, thanks.' I shoved my tote bag to the back of my half of the wardrobe, pulled off my jeans and damp shirt, and changed into a T-shirt and some comfy tracksuit bottoms. Who cared what I looked like? Certainly not Martin.

'Any news on Lauren? What's all this about her going away for a few days? Adrian mentioned it down the pub earlier, said she'd sent Claire a text. What d'you want on your toast?' His voice reached me from the kitchen as I walked back down the stairs.

Martin wanted to know about Lauren. He didn't even know that she was dead. I wanted to know who was sending me messages from a dead man's phone. I wanted to know how Martin could have betrayed me with Jenna. Martin wanted to know what I wanted on my toast. And

I didn't have an answer for any of it. Not even about the toast.

'Peanut butter? Marmite?'

I wanted to scream hysterically and roll myself into a ball, but I managed to walk into the kitchen and smile relatively normally. 'Peanut butter, thanks.' *You cheating bastard.* I looked at the slow cooker gathering dust in the corner of the counter, imagining smashing it over Martin's head.

'There's tea brewing. Is that your phone?' He cocked his head to listen. 'You must have left it upstairs, I'll get it.'

'No' I barked, as he turned to leave the kitchen. 'I'll go.'

I pushed past him, ran back up the stairs and retrieved my phone from my tote bag before returning to the kitchen.

'Who was it? Did you say peanut?' His head was in the cupboard as he rummaged around. 'Think I'll have peanut too. What's this? Sesame oil? And here's another one. Ah, and noodles. When did you get these? Thinking of doing a stir fry one night? I can't remember when we last had one, can you? Oh, this one's open.' His head re-appeared from the cupboard. 'When did you— What's up?'

The toast sprang up from the toaster with a loud click, as I stood there, mute. *One more question and I really would scream.*

The knife rasped across the toast as Martin spread butter on the slices.

'Abs? Are you going to say something? What's going on?'

He doesn't know about Lauren. How was I going to tell him? *Plus, he's been sleeping with Jenna. Bastard.*

I watched him twist the lid off the peanut butter and spread it onto the toast, all the time wanting to snatch the knife from him and stab his eyes out for what he'd done to me.

My phone felt like it was burning a hole in my hand, and I touched the screen, looking again at the photo that had just been sent to me. How? How could there be a photo of me in the clutches of the man in the denim jacket outside Baxter's? We looked like we were embracing; we looked like we were kissing; we looked like we were on a hook up. Which we were...

But I didn't do anything, my mind pleaded as a small moan of panic escaped my throat.

'Abs?' Martin gave me a puzzled look. 'Here, take these through, I'll bring the tea.'

'Thanks.' I took the plates from him and walked into the sitting room, my hands trembling and my nerves frayed to breaking point. The car that had slowly followed me in the dark; its blinding headlights; none of it had been by chance. Someone had known where I was going; someone had been keeping track of me on the stupid dating apps; and I had presented them with the perfect opportunity to catch me in an uncompromising situation. *Jenna.* Who else could it be?

I nodded my preoccupied thanks to Martin when he placed a mug of tea in front of me, and tried to concentrate on chewing my mouthful of toast which, for some reason, refused to break down, seeming to swell inside my mouth and stick to it, so that I couldn't swallow. My deranged mind started playing games... *What's that phobia? Something to do with peanut butter... no, any kind of food maybe... fear of it sticking to the roof of your mouth... something phobia, something phobia...* my words played in a singsong voice in my head... *butterophobia... butryphobia... peanutbutterophobia... I almost giggled... nuttybutteryphobia...* I'd ask my cheating husband, he'd know.

I glanced over at Martin to see him engrossed in a brochure of some kind, and, making odd gulping noises, I finally freed and swallowed the masticated mass in my mouth. Taking a swig of tea, I took another small bite of toast, wrinkling my nose as I became aware of the smell of decay in the room.

I put my plate down, stood up and walked towards the vase of black roses, picking it up to throw the hateful things away, as Martin spoke.

'When did you send off for this brochure, Abs? Bliss Cottage, Blissford. Wow, check out the hot tub.'

I turned in shock, my mouth motionless, the piece of toast balanced on my tongue, and stared at a photo of *the* hot tub from *the* cottage.

'Where did you–? I stepped forwards in horror, as the piece of toast shot to the back of my mouth and into my windpipe, letting go of the vase as I fought valiantly for air, my eyes bulging.

Martin jumped up in concern, dropping the brochure onto the coffee table, and rushed to my aid, thumping my back so that the piece of toast dislodged and flew like a projectile to land in a sticky lump on the photo of the hot tub, as dead, black rose petals fluttered onto the carpet around us.

Gasping in air, I staggered through the carpet of death and sank into the chair, my eyes fixated on the brochure.

'I'll get some kitchen towel.'

Martin wiped off the soggy lump of toast and looked over at me. 'What is it, Abs? You look like you've seen a ghost.'

I picked up my tea, trying in vain to stop my hands from shaking, and drank slowly, unable to pull my eyes away from the, now slightly wrinkled, photo of the hot tub within which I'd stabbed a man to death less than two weeks earlier.

'What's that word for when people have a phobia about peanut butter sticking to the roof of their mouth?'

Martin looked at me in confusion. 'Arachibutyrophobia?'

'I knew you'd remember.' I giggled, tried to stifle it, giggled again, and collapsed into paroxysms of laughter as my phone started ringing.

54

Everybody Hurts

We stared at Jenna's name as it flashed relentlessly on my phone screen.

'Are you going to answer it?' Martin held his hands out at me, raising his eyebrows, his eyes guarded.

The ringing finally stopped, and a moment later my phone pinged as a notification appeared on the screen.

A fresh bout of giggling doubled me over, tears streaming down my face. I'd lost it. I was completely out of control.

Martin's phone began to buzz and notifications piled up on his screen, as mine began to do the same, and then Jenna's name began to flash up as she called me again.

Through my hysterical meltdown, it registered that something must have happened. I looked across at Martin as he read his messages, the colour draining from his face to leave him pallid and gaunt-looking. He looked over at me, his expression tortured.

With a trembling hand, I picked up my phone and answered Jen's call.

'Put the news on,' she said in a strangled voice. 'What the fucking hell?' She rang off before I could reply, and I reached for the remote with dread as Martin's tormented eyes followed my every move.

Our small world, contained within the walls of our sitting room, switched to slow motion as we stared at the television screen to be informed that a local man had returned home early from his business trip, having been concerned when his wife had not answered his calls for three days, to find her dead in their home.

A photo of my beautiful, sweet Hayley filled the screen as Martin and I stared at the television in silence.

'Oh God, Hayley.' I doubled over, clutching my stomach as I began to dry-retch, my mouth making strange mewling sounds as tears poured from my eyes.

'Hayley's fucking dead?' Martin shouted, his eyes wild. 'How the fuck is she dead?'

I looked up at him slowly, dragging a hand across my wet face. 'What are they saying?' My voice came out in a hoarse whisper.

The screen changed to an ordinary suburban street and the front of a house that I knew as well as my own. Speaking loudly over the shaky footage, the same reporter breathlessly described the scene, recorded earlier on a neighbour's phone, softening her voice in an attempt to disguise her inappropriate excitement at the shocking news, as she expressed sadness at the tragic death of Hayley Baldwin.

A drumming sound crashed around in my ears and I shook my head, feeling weak, as Ross appeared on camera with a different reporter, snatches of his emotional account making it through the banging in my head.

'She was lying on the lounge carpet, she was just lying there.' He shook his head in bewilderment. 'She must have been trying to get to her asthma spray. Oh God, I should never have left her.' He broke down, covering his face with his hands as his muffled voice shakily continued, 'She had a cold, you see, and she has– she had asthma and a severe allergy. I can't understand it, she always keeps her spray with her, and her epinephrine pen. I can't– I have to go, sorry.' Ross's retreating back was filmed as he staggered slowly back into his house.

Martin's jaw hung open in shock as he stared at the television.

'And in a cruel twist of fate,' a reporter in the studio continued, as the scene changed to parkland and an expanse of water, 'a woman whose body was discovered earlier today at Keston Ponds has been identified as Mrs Lauren Dempsey, a friend of the deceased, Hayley Baldwin. It is believed that Mrs Dempsey, who couldn't swim, drowned when she slipped from the footpath into the pond in an area where the water is relatively deep and weed-filled.'

Martin's jaw dropped even lower, his eyes incredulous as he ran his hands through his hair. 'What?' he yelled at the screen. 'What?'

I watched as images of Hayley and Lauren appeared side by side on the screen, followed by a group photo of smiling women – us, it was a photo of us, – at the Eynsford Manor Hotel, the weekend our lives had begun to fall apart...

We grinned drunkenly at the camera, our arms draped around each other, on the first night of our weekend away – seven excited women, drunk as skunks, having a great time – and now three people were dead...

'Did you know about Lauren?' Martin's voice was squeaky from disbelief.

I nodded as my phone pinged, and my hand reached for it, clicking on the new message, my eyes still half on the TV screen where the newsreader's mouth moved without sound, my ears filled with a loud buzzing.

How many more of your friends are going to die, you bitch?

My head ricocheted from my phone, to the TV, to Martin, and back to my phone, as fear clutched at my body. My phone dinged again.

Two down. How many more to go?

I flung my phone across the room. 'Stop,' I pleaded. 'Please stop.'

'What are you doing? What's going on?' Martin leant forward, reaching for my phone.

'No, no...' I scrambled from my chair, falling to my knees, and crawled desperately to retrieve my phone.

'You're hiding something.' Martin grabbed my phone from my fingers.

'Please, Martin,' I whispered. 'Don't.' His own phone was lying on the coffee table and I snatched it up, backing away from him.

'Don't be stupid, Abigail, give me my phone.' He held his hand out.

'Why? Are you afraid of what I might find if I look at it? Are you hiding something, Martin?'

His shoulders sagged and his body seemed to crumple slightly, as he sighed. 'Here, here's your phone.'

I took my phone, clutching it to my chest, and dropped his phone back on the table, backing away slowly until my back hit the armchair.

The newsreader's voice registered in my head again, and I turned to stare at the latest gallery of horrors addition as the man's impassive voice informed any viewers still watching today's death report that the storms lashing the south west coast had washed up more than just the usual array of flotsam and jetsam, such as plastic bottles and wooden crates.

With increasing enthusiasm, he described how a local dog walker had discovered a man's naked body entwined in a heap of seaweed on a Dorset beach. The body, the now overexcited ghoul continued, had a number of stab wounds on his torso, suggesting that he had died under suspicious circumstances.

You don't say.

I watched in some kind of disassociated way, as if the suggested name of the man meant nothing to me, as if the stab wounds found on his torso had not been administered by my own seemingly murderous hands, with a knife which I'd held. I looked at the photo of his smiling face, his arm around his wife's shoulders, and wanted to howl.

'Well, fuck me,' said Martin. 'Matthew Parker. That's the bloke that went missing when you girls were down in the New Forest.'

Martin could really do with expanding his repertoire of swear words a bit, I thought, as my phone dinged again and I clicked wearily on the message.

Not feeling so lucky now, Abigail? How long before your secrets come out? I know everything, and I'm taking back what's mine.

I deleted the message, not looking at Martin. The threat was clear. And I knew, without a doubt, who was sending the messages.

55

Perfect Day

I couldn't afford to waste any time. I had three allies amongst my four friends, and I had to make them believe what I told them, no matter how crazy it sounded. But we had our grief to deal with, and that gave me an idea. It was fitting, the girls would agree, I was certain – we could honour our dear friends' memories and fulfil a promise we'd all made, albeit too late for Lauren and Hayley – and, most importantly of all, it would bring us all together in the perfect spot.

Claire was at home with Adrian, no doubt still reeling from news of the deaths of Lauren and Hayley, and Jenna was alone – shocked and horrified at what was happening, while Emma was presumably with Paul, comforting him over the loss of his wife, and distraught herself at the loss of both Lauren and Hayley. Fi would be alone, no doubt still up, and in total shock at tonight's news. And of course, all of them would be in a state of complete panic at the announcement that Matthew Parker's body had washed up on the beach.

I, of course, was here with Martin, and couldn't face any more of his questions, not after the evening we'd had. I couldn't face the way he looked at me, what he was hiding, what I was hiding, and I just couldn't face him anymore.

'Shall I make some fresh tea? We could do with it after all this.'

'How are you so calm?' Martin looked at me in astonishment.

'Shock, I think,' I said. 'I don't think I'm feeling anything at the moment. So– tea?'

'Sod that, I need a whisky, a bloody double. You should have one too.'

'Good idea, I'll get them.' I rose, picked up the whisky bottle from the sideboard and took it through to the kitchen as Martin called out.

'I'm going to call Ross, poor bloke, check on how he's doing. Or maybe I should go round and see him?'

'No, it's late, you can't go to his home.' I stuck my head round the door. 'Maybe just give him a call though, and send my love.'

I hurried up the stairs and into our bedroom, pulling open the top drawer and feeling beneath my underwear for the strip of sleeping tablets that Claire had handed me the night Lauren had been attacked. I'd found them in my dressing gown pocket when I'd got home from our weekend in Eynsford and had popped them in with my magpie stash. With shaking fingers, I released four from their blister prisons, and returned to the kitchen, hearing Martin's voice murmuring softly as I passed the lounge door.

I poured two generous measures of whisky into glasses, dropped the tablets into one of them, and stirred the amber liquid briskly with a spoon before adding ice to both. With Martin out for the count it would be easier to take the steps that I needed to, and he'd stop asking me questions that I couldn't answer.

I handed Martin his drink as he was saying goodbye to Ross, and he nodded his thanks.

'God, poor Ross, he's finished.' Martin gulped down half his whisky in one go, gasping as he placed his glass on the coffee table. 'I needed that. What a night.'

We both stared at the muted television as Matthew Parker's image and name was displayed again, with the announcement that police had opened a murder enquiry into his death.

'Wasn't Jenna's name Parker?' Martin asked into the silence.

I nodded, sipping my whisky. *The dots were finally connecting.*

'She had a half-sister and brother, didn't she? Wait a minute–' He picked up his glass and drained it. 'So... your best friend was Natalie Parker... so, don't tell me her mum was Jenna's mum?'

I shook my head. 'Her dad. They shared a father. He got his girlfriend pregnant and she had Natalie, but he stayed with his wife – Jenna's mum – but then his girlfriend got pregnant again, and he left his wife and moved in with them.'

'God.' Martin shook his head. 'So Jenna was left with her mum. That's what she was talking about the night of Lauren and Paul's barbeque.'

I shot him a look of jealousy. *Of course you'd remember every word that ever came out of precious Jenna's scarlet-painted lips.* I nodded slowly as a seed of an idea grew in my mind. 'She must have blamed him for her dad leaving them.'

Martin yawned. 'The kid? It was a boy? The second one? Next you'll be telling me his name was Matthew.'

'Little Matty,' I whispered. 'Little Matty Parker.'

'The boy you saved.' Martin shook his head incredulously. 'Don't tell me he's the bloke who's been murdered.' He yawned again. 'No, that would be too much of a coincidence.' He blinked his eyes sleepily. 'Does he look like him?'

I thought of his eyes, and the small scar on his neck, the hairs on my own neck bristling. Had my nail really scarred him for life when I'd clutched at him while he screamed as Natalie fell to her death? 'He does. It's him.'

I should have felt something as I voiced the shocking truth, but I was numb and devoid of emotion.

'Does she know? Jenna?'

Oh, she knows. 'I doubt she'd have recognised him after all these years.'

'True. I need another whisky.' He stood up slightly unsteadily and went to the kitchen, returning a moment later with the bottle. 'I can't seem to get the lid off.' His fingers fumbled with the bottle, and I reached over, taking it from him and pouring him a generous measure.

'Thanks.' Yawning loudly, Martin sprawled back in his chair. 'What a night, I still can't believe it all.'

I desperately wanted to phone the girls but I needed Martin to go to sleep. 'Why don't you go to bed?'

'Hmm? In a minute. Abs, what went wrong? We were happy, weren't we?' He was slurring his words now – words I didn't want to hear.

I looked over at the television screen as the weather report came on, showing more rain and strong winds for the day ahead.

'I slept with her, more than once, I kept trying to stop, but she's just so– she's got this kind of power... always has...' His glass slipped in his hand, drops of whisky spilling onto his knee.

What was in those sleeping tablets? Some kind of bloody truth serum? 'Shh, I don't need to hear it.'

'It was unfinished business, that's what it was... those lies someone spread about her... not true... at the barbeque... that's when I realised... it's over Abs, it has to be...'

'Martin, please stop,' I pleaded. *What was over? Our marriage? Or his affair?*

His head slumped forward, and I grabbed his glass before it fell to the floor.

'Let me get you up to bed.'

Nodding, Martin let me help him up from the chair and, with difficulty, force his feet to climb the stairs.

I stood over him as he lay on the bed, gently pulling the duvet up and kissing his forehead. 'I love you,' I said softly, before turning and going back downstairs, my heart feeling like it had been torn apart.

56

Set Fire To The Rain

I called Fi.

'Oh, Abs, I'm finished. I can't believe it – Lauren and Hayley, both dead. What the hell is happening? And now they've found his body, it washed up on a beach, did you see on the news? Everyone's in bits, it's like everything's falling apart. I've spoken to Jen and Claire, but Emma's not answering her phone. I suppose she's with Paul.' She broke off, weeping into the phone as my own eyes filled with tears.

'It's too awful to comprehend, Fi,' I sobbed. 'What if it's all connected?'

'What d'you mean?'

'The messages I've been getting, the threats... and now two of our friends found dead...'

'You don't mean–? You're not saying–? What are you saying, exactly?'

'God, Fi, I don't know, but what if we're all in danger? What if none of us are safe?' I waited, letting my words sink in.

'But in danger from who? Am I safe? Alone in my house?' Fi sounded panicked. 'And Jen's alone, is she safe? At least you and Claire have got your husbands at home with you, and Em's safe with Paul.'

'Oh, Fi...' I broke down in fresh tears. 'I don't even know if I've still got a husband...'

'What? What are you saying, Abs? Of course you've got a husband.'

'I think he's been having an affair,' I whispered. 'No, I know he has, he told me. He says it's over but...'

'Where is he now?' Fi was all business, maybe it was the relief of having something other than dead friends, and the risk of being murdered, to think about. 'I'll give him a piece of my bloody mind. Who is she? Do you know?'

I wanted to scream Jenna's name out, but I held it in. 'He's gone to bed,' I said softly, wiping my eyes and sniffing. 'Please don't tell anyone, you're the only person I've told. I don't know who she is, but he did say it was finished. Even still, I can't bear to be in the same house as him, but I've got nowhere else to go.' I took a deep breath. 'But my problems are nothing compared to what's happening– to what's happened, I mean, to Lauren and Hayley... I just feel so alone suddenly...' I began to cry again. 'Sorry.'

'You have to stay strong, Abs. You're not alone, don't ever say that.' She paused. 'Listen, why don't you come over to me? God knows I could do with the company. I've got a bottle of whisky that I'm in danger of finishing all on my own, I could use a hand.'

'D'you really mean that, Fi?'

'Of course I do.'

'You're a good friend, Fi, thanks, I will come over, I just need to have a shower and change my clothes, I just feel, I don't know, unclean or something. Fi,' I began, hesitantly. 'D'you remember how Hayley was talking about that weekend, you know – when we walked from Dover to Deal?'

I could hear the smile in Fi's voice as she answered. 'Of course I do, she and Laur were going on about how much they'd loved it.'

'They were saying how beautiful it was, how it gave them a feeling of peace and freedom...'

'And we promised we'd go back...'

'We never kept our promise.' I grabbed a tissue, wiping my eyes as fresh tears fell. 'And now we never can. I don't suppose we could– no, it's crazy...'

'What is? What, Abs?'

'It's no good, there's no time, not unless we did it straightaway, like tomorrow. There'll be funerals next and loads of arrangements to make, and, oh, I was just thinking how special it would be to just get in the car, the five of us, and just go back there...'

'To remember them... and to help us with our grief... Why not? Why not do it, Abs?' Fi's voice became animated. 'We could drive down tomorrow, it would stop us all moping around at home.'

'We could take flowers and scatter them,' I suggested.

'Like our own special memorial for our friends. That's it, we're doing it. It'll be our own private farewell to our friends, and a fulfilment of a promise we all made to go back.' Fi was fired-up, pleased to have something to concentrate on. 'I'll drive, we can all meet at mine, and we can stay overnight somewhere, I'll have a look online. Right, who's calling who?'

'Could you call Jen? I'll call Claire and try and get hold of Em,' I said. 'Then I'll come over, once I'm ready. And, Fi, please don't say anything to Jenna about Martin's affair, or me coming over to you, I don't think I can bear for anyone else to know right now.'

'I won't say a word, Abs, I'm glad you felt you could confide in me.'

I could tell from her tone that she was pleased that I'd turned to her. I called Claire.

'Abs, I must have called you a million times, I'm in total shock, we all are. How could this have happened? First Lauren, and now Hayley, and she always has her asthma spray with her. I can't bear to think of her struggling to breathe... poor Ross, he's broken, completely broken...'

'Hayley was the sweetest person I knew,' I cried into the phone. 'She didn't deserve this. I can't bear the thought of life without her. And Lauren was always the life and soul, wasn't she? Always up for fun. How can things ever be the same with no Lauren and no Hayley?'

'Why is this happening?' She lowered her voice. 'It's something to do with him, isn't it? Tell me I'm wrong. You said you'd received threatening messages from his phone, but he's dead. God, we know he's dead, the whole world does now that they've found his body. Who is it? Is someone killing us off one by one? What are we going to do? This is a nightmare. It could be me next, or you. We've got to come clean, we've got to stop this.' Her voice was loud and shrill.

'Claire, don't let Adrian hear you, listen to me,' I said urgently. 'We mustn't panic, we have to keep calm. We should think about Lauren and Hayley. I've spoken to Fi, and we've had an idea, it's a way to say our own special goodbye to our friends. That's what we need to focus on at the moment. After that we can talk things through.'

Claire took little convincing, relieved to have something to focus on, and I turned my attention to Emma, which took a little more effort due to the fact that her phone was switched off. With great difficulty, I managed to make a call to Paul, and navigated the process of offering my condolences, expressing my own heartbreak and disbelief, before asking if I could have a quick word with Emma.

She wasn't there, he informed me, she'd spent time with him earlier, but they'd both felt it inappropriate for her to be at his house so soon after Lauren's death. It might never be appropriate, he'd confided, it may have all been a big mistake.

I called Emma's landline persistently, until she answered.

'Em, it's Abs. I had to find out how you are, we're all worried about you. Such devastating news about Hayley, so soon after Lauren.' I sniffed, grabbing a tissue and blowing my nose noisily. 'I can't bear to think about it.'

'It just feels like the end of the world, Abs, you know? None of it makes sense, the more I think about it – from him being killed in the hot tub, to Lauren and Hayley both being found dead. What is it, some kind of revenge?'

I could hear the sound of ice cubes clinking against a glass as she stopped speaking. 'D'you think they're connected?' I whispered.

'Do you?' she countered.

'They must be.'

'What did we start, when we went along with Jenna's stupid revenge plan?' she sobbed.

And there it was. Emma had just put it into words perfectly – Jenna's stupid revenge plan.

'We started a dreadful chain of events – one we could not possibly have envisaged. Em, I'm so sorry that I didn't support you over the whole Paul thing. I don't know why I even got upset about it, I was being stupidly naïve, thinking that marriages were sacred or something, I suppose I just–'

'It's fine, Abs, I understand. I know how strong you and Martin are, and how you feel about marriage and all that. Some of us just aren't as lucky as you.' She gave a bitter laugh. 'I suppose that's why Jenna always calls you lucky Abigail.'

Not feeling that lucky right now, Em.

'Abs, the police told Paul something odd about Lauren's death, he wasn't even supposed to tell me, but... well, the thing is, then he spoke to Ross, and there was something there as well... but d'you know what they didn't find? Her asthma spray or her epinephrine pen.'

My stomach churned at her words, images of Lauren drowning in the pond filling my head, her arms flailing as she struggled to extricate herself from the weeds... Hayley crawling across the carpet, gasping for air, as she tried to reach her bag with her asthma spray inside...

'Stop, I can't bear to think about it, Em,' I pleaded.

'They were murdered, Abs. They were murdered because of something to do with him. I haven't figured it all out yet, but their killer must have dropped those things in the struggle, because they didn't belong to Lauren or Hayley–' Ice clinked again as she took another sip of her drink. 'It must have been a woman...'

I felt a frisson of fear, or excitement. *Was this almost over? Would the police be able to link the evidence to someone?* 'Em, stop, we don't know what happened yet, we mustn't jump to conclusions. There's something we have to focus on first. Once we've done that, we can try to work out what's happening. There's something we'd like to do tomorrow, for Lauren and Hayley. Something special in their honour, before all the arrangements start being made...'

Emma was in, as I'd known she would be. So that left Jenna. As if my phone could read my mind, it dinged with a message from Fi, letting me know that Jenna had agreed to our plan.

With a shaking hand, I dropped my phone in my lap. I wanted to curl up in a ball and give in to hysteria, but I couldn't, not yet. I sent a message back to Fi, telling her that Claire and Emma had agreed, and that I'd be over in about an hour.

My whisky was sitting there, virtually untouched, the ice long since melted, and I picked it up, downing it in one go, in the vain hope that it would help me through what I would forever remember as the worst night of my life.

57

Why Does My Heart Feel So Bad?

Showered, dressed in a clean top and jeans, and wearing my grippy trainers, I picked up Martin's phone, and gathered my things, placing them by the bedroom door. The stupid photos I'd stolen were still in my drawer, I remembered, surprised at my forgetfulness, and I trod softly across the carpet to retrieve them. Looking around one last time, my gaze rested on Martin for a moment, before I turned and walked downstairs.

Accessing the dating app, hidden in his files, the way that Jenna had shown me on my own phone, I opened his message thread, grimacing at the profile photo of the Hawthorn flower, as I read her last exultant message.

'I've got a surprise for you,' I muttered. 'Change of plans, he's not leaving me for you after all.' My fingers were still trembling slightly, and I took a deep breath, before typing out a message from my husband to his lover – make that ex-lover now. I hit send, imagining Jenna's face when she read that Martin wanted nothing more to do with her, that he'd chosen me, that it had always been me. The fact that he was unaware that he'd just ended their affair amused me, in my current somewhat deranged state of mind. I switched his phone off and placed it on the coffee table.

The black rose petals were still strewn across the lounge carpet, and I scooped them up, adding them to the rubbish bag I was carrying, then I remembered the Bliss Cottage brochure, and grabbed that from the coffee table, dropping it in the bag too. I could hear Jenna's voice mocking me as she called me anal Abs and, in defiance, I picked up the whisky bottle and glasses, carrying them to the kitchen and washing and drying the glasses, before putting them back in the cupboard. Lastly, I scrawled a short note for Martin, telling him of our plans, and left it prominently on the kitchen counter.

Switching off the kitchen light, I opened the back door and crept quietly through, closing it gently behind me. I hadn't realised that it was raining heavily again and I was soaked by the time I hurried round the side of the house and got into my car.

I started the car and switched on the wipers, the windscreen fogging up from the combination of my wet clothes and hair, and warm breath. Shivering, I blasted the heater and hurriedly reversed out of the driveway, hitting the brakes in shock as a car drove past, its wheels making the water on the road surface gush upwards either side of it. My car slithered backwards across the road haphazardly as I panicked and tried to regain control.

'Don't lose it now, Abs,' I muttered to myself as I began to drive. I pulled over outside our local parade of convenience shops, grabbed the rubbish bag from the passenger seat and pushed it in amongst the piled-up bags awaiting collection in a few short hours. It was time to put Martin out of my mind and allow myself to fall into grieving friend mode – something I hadn't fully surrendered to in my battle to hold it all together.

Fi almost squeezed the breath out of me when she opened the door, wrapping her strong arms around me and hugging me within an inch of my life.

'I'm so glad you're here,' she said. 'I'm sorry about bloody Martin, but you'll get through it, we all do, one way or another. Come in, I've poured you a drink.'

We sat in her lounge, chinked our glasses, and looked sadly at each other.

'To Lauren and Hayley,' I said.

'Lauren and Hayley.' Fi swallowed a mouthful of whisky. 'We'll never forget you.' She finished the rest of her drink in one go and put her glass down.

'Emma said something worrying...' I began tentatively, as Fi's head jerked up. 'Hayley's asthma spray and epi injection pen were missing. And the police found something there that didn't belong to her, according to Ross, who told Paul.' My hands twisted nervously in my lap as I continued, 'And they found something where they think Lauren fell in the pond.'

Fi's body tensed. 'What did they find? Did she tell you?' She sloshed some whisky into her glass without looking, her eyes fixed on me.

I shook my head. 'She only said that it must mean their killer was a woman.' My hand trembled as I picked up my glass and took a large gulp. 'She's saying they were murdered, isn't she?'

'They were.' Fi cradled her glass as she looked at me, and my stomach churned.

'By who?' I whispered.

'Someone's picking everyone off, one by one, as some kind of retribution for him, maybe?'

'It doesn't make any sense, Fi.' I shook my head. 'Unless, no...'

'Unless what?'

'It was weird, the day that Laur called me from Jen's. She was saying so many strange things, about her having the same name, something about the knife, and, I think– well, I think she was trying to tell me something about Martin's affair... She said she'd spoken to Hayley, and then she said she had to go because she was there.'

'Who? Who was there? Jenna? Well, obviously, if she was calling from her house. Oh God.' Fi slammed her glass down. 'Jenna's maiden name was Parker. How did I not remember that?'

I nodded. 'I wasn't sure if I should say anything or not. Martin reminded me earlier, when he saw the news about the body washing up on the beach.' I tried to stop the bile from rising in my throat at my mention of Martin, as I gasped. 'I forgot to lock the back door when I left.'

Fi was dismissive. 'Martin's a big boy, he can look after himself. So, let me get this straight. Jenna had the same name as the bastard who beat Lauren up; Jenna planned that whole bloody weekend where he ended up dead–'

'Her revenge plan – Emma reminded me that was what she called it, when we spoke earlier,' I contributed helpfully.

'Exactly, her revenge plan. And then Jenna hears Lauren talking to you on the phone, saying stuff about the knife, and Martin's affair, and– oh my God, that she'd spoken to Hayley.' Fi's eyes were huge as she stared wildly at me. 'And then Lauren and Hayley both turn up dead.'

I stared back at Fi, unable to speak.

'Abs, is there any way... you don't think it was Jenna that Martin was having the affair with, do you?'

'I don't know,' I sobbed. 'It could have been, they had a thing when they were young... No,' I said firmly. 'I refuse to believe it of her.' I simply couldn't bring myself to admit to Fi that Jenna had been sleeping with my husband, not right now. 'Anyway, that's over, he told me.'

'That's always been your trouble, Abs, you believe the best of everyone.' Fi gave me a sympathetic look. 'Is there anything else?'

I looked up at the ceiling, as if for inspiration. 'Well, only that when Martin and I were talking about it, we remembered that my friend Natalie, who died, had a little brother, and that's why Jenna's dad left her and her mum – he stayed with them when his girlfriend had Natalie, but when she got pregnant again, he left them for his new family.'

'Was his name Matthew?' Fi was glaring at me, her shoulders tense.

I nodded. 'He was always called Matty.'

'Was it him? Did you recognise him? You must have?'

'It was so many years ago, he was just a little boy,' I cried.

'Think, Abs, think. Was there anything about him that reminded you of him as a kid? His voice, or–?'

'His scar,' I whispered. 'As he walked to the hot tub, his hand touched his neck. I think he lost his leather thong when he– when he took his T-shirt off. I saw a mark on his neck but it meant nothing to me at the time.'

'And?' What about the scar?' Fi's leg was jogging impatiently.

'It might have been from my nail, when I grabbed him and stopped him from going over the balcony...'

At any other time, Fi's expression would have been comical.

'Fi, no,' I pleaded. 'Not Jenna, it can't be, we're making a mistake. It's just a coincidence, it means nothing.'

'Sod that, I'm calling Em. She's all on her own at her house and fuck knows what's going on.'

I listened to Fi as she barked orders at Em, telling her to grab some bits and get herself over to her house in a taxi.

'She'll be here in an hour, tops,' Fi informed me. 'That leaves Claire, but she's with Adrian so she's safe, and she'll be with us in the morning.'

'And Jenna?' I asked, timidly. 'What if we're wrong, and she's in danger?'

Fi drummed her fingers on the arm of her chair. 'Well, let's look at it this way – if the killer is one of us, and three of us are here, and Claire's at home with Adrian, then Jenna's safe, isn't she?'

I couldn't argue with her logic even if it was twisted, and totally bizarre, to be discussing so calmly the fact that one of our remaining group of five was a killer.

By the time that Emma arrived, Fi and I were slurring our words as we talked rubbish to each other, way past the point of making sense of anything, and Emma, who had been drinking at home, was in no better state.

'Abs, I didn't know that you were here.' Em hugged Fi and then me, looking surprised. 'What about Martin?'

I looked at Fi for help.

'They've had a bit of a tiff, and we both needed the company after finding out about, first Lauren, then Hayley, and then that bloody bastard's body turning up on a beach.'

'Damn right.' Emma nodded. 'I'm glad of the company too, I was just mulling over everything continually, sitting at home on my own. Sorry about you and Martin,' she added as an afterthought. 'Not a serious tiff, I hope?'

'Oh no,' I said, forcing a laugh. 'Just a stupid misunderstanding, everything's fine, and Martin understands the shock we're all in. He wanted to get to bed, and I needed the company of a friend... I'm so glad you're here as well, Em.'

We smiled at each other, and I was surprised at my emotions as I realised how much I'd missed her for the short time the whole Emma and Paul affair had encroached on our friendship.

Fi handed Emma a huge glass of whisky and topped our own glasses up as we toasted, yet again, our departed friends.

Emma broke the momentary silence. 'Did Abs tell you about the things they found at the scene of Lauren's and Hayley's deaths? Murders.' She spat the last word out as she looked from me to Fi.

'How do we find out what they were?' Fi asked, as she nodded.

'I already know. Ross told Paul about Hayley, and Paul told me, and about Lauren, right before he said that he needed to be alone, indefinitely, the bastard. Sorry, I don't mean that, not after what's happened.'

'And?' Fi was becoming impatient.

'Close to where they think Lauren supposedly slipped and fell into the pond, they found a lipstick – not just any lipstick – a deep red lipstick in a distinctive gold tube with rhinestones on it.' Emma sat back, waiting for us to absorb the information.

'Bloody fucking hell.' Fi stared at Emma, before turning to me, as I gaped in shock.

'And at Hayley's? What did they find?'

'A hair clip – a hair clip with a scarlet flower on it. One of the petals was broken a bit.'

'Hayley never wore hair clips,' I whispered.

'And Lauren never ever wore red lipstick, she said it was trashy. She was a pink girl, the brighter the better, but never red,' growled Fi. 'And she certainly didn't own any lipsticks in gold tubes with glittery stones stuck on them. But we know who does, don't we?'

'It doesn't mean anything,' I whimpered. 'We can't jump to conclusions because of a lipstick.'

'I bloody can, especially with everything else we know. Hold on a second.' Fi began to scroll frantically through her phone. 'Here, look at this.'

We all peered at my photo.

'Where did you get the flower clip from, Abs?'

'It's Jen's, she fixed it in my hair.'

'Exactly, and if I zoom in like this... Look carefully. See here? The tip of this petal is missing. I rest my case.' She sat back triumphantly, her arms folded, her eyes gleaming.

'What case? What the hell are you saying?' Emma looked confused as she turned from Fi to me.

'Sit back and listen to this.' Fi took Em through our crazy thought process about Jenna, as I sat mutely, my input unnecessary.

'If you're right, d'you realise what this means?' Em shifted in her chair to face me. 'It means you didn't stab him in the hot tub. It means you didn't kill him, Abs.'

58

Suddenly I See

'I didn't kill him... all this time, I thought...' I slumped in my chair, covering my face with my hands.

'Think, Abs, think hard. When do you remember having the knife in your hand?' Fi leant forward intently.

'I don't know, I can't...' I shook my head in frustration. 'I've tried so hard to block it out. I remember hitting him... our hands all bumping against each other... then I was under the water... I felt like I was drowning and I grabbed for anything to pull myself up with...'

'That's it – that's when she put the knife in your hand, it must be. And then I grabbed your wrist and got you to drop it.' Fi jumped up and began circling the room.

'I remember Jen's hands being blue... I thought she was cold...'

'She was wearing her bloody disposable gloves, and none of us noticed. She must have taken the knife from the kitchen earlier...'

'But when? The only person I saw with a knife was you, Fi, remember? Are you sure you didn't have it with you when we–'

Fi stared at Emma. 'Now it was me who had the knife? I was trying to open a bottle of vodka – the lid was stuck. You can't seriously think–'

'I'm not thinking anything, I'm just trying to figure out how someone took a knife without any of us noticing.' Emma picked up her glass, and walked to stand in front of the window, staring out at the rain.

'I've already told you, it was Jenna.' Fi lit a cigarette, inhaling heavily as she paced.

'Jenna was in the kitchen when I was unloading the dishwasher, there was all the cutlery...'

They both ignored me as they faced off against each other.

'I cut my hand. D'you think I would have done something that stupid if I was planning on stabbing the bloke? Anyway, you were there too, maybe you took the knife.'

'All I'm saying is, you're so keen to tell me that Jenna had the knife, but you can't be sure. Wait, I remember now – you actually said maybe we should cut him up a bit.'

'For God's sake, we were all talking shit, we were nervous, we didn't know what we were doing.'

'Stop,' I pleaded. 'Everyone was in and out of the kitchen, it's pointless arguing about who took a knife, it could have been any one of us. Even Claire was walking in and out from the kitchen to the hot tub.'

'Exactly, thank you, Abigail.' Fi smiled grimly. 'Except not any one of us did, Jenna did. Jenna planned the whole thing, she wore her blue gloves, she stabbed him and made us think Abs did it.'

'But why? Why set Abs up?' Emma's question stopped Fi in her tracks.

'Because she's been having an affair with Martin,' I whispered. The time felt right to tell them.

Fi and Em stared at me, as Fi broke the silence.

'Why didn't you tell me it was Jen? You said you weren't sure.'

'I couldn't. If I told you, it made it real. I only found out tonight.' I let out a huge juddering sigh. 'It's Jen who's been sending me the messages from Matthew Parker's phone. She sent me more last night.' The relief to have finally told Fi and Em the whole story was immense. I remembered one more detail. 'She used my bank card to book the cottage – it was booked in my name.'

'Oh my God.' Emma's eyes widened. 'She must have recognised him right from the start, from Eynsford, when she found him on the dating app.'

'She came up with her revenge plan, as she called it, but it wasn't for Lauren, it was for herself – she wanted to kill the man she held responsible for breaking up her family when she was a girl.' Fi's voice was loud with excitement. 'She booked the cottage in Abs' name, killed him and made it look like it was Abs...'

'And took his phone. She must have taken it from his car when she didn't find it in his jeans. Don't you remember? She disappeared off while we were all in shock.'

Fi nodded at Em, as I let them piece everything together between them. 'Which she then used to freak out Abs by sending her taunting messages as if they were from him.'

'Why, though?' Em's head tilted as she looked confused. 'Why bother to torment Abs like that?'

They both turned their attention to me.

'Because she hated me,' I said, surprised to realise the truth. 'All these years I thought she was my friend, but she hated me. She must have blamed me for taking Martin from her, when I didn't even know her at the time. She was screwing with me, making me lose my mind, and killing us off one by one, all the time holding the murder of Matthew Parker over me. I think she was threatening to kill more if I didn't give Martin up, and it felt like she might expose me as a murderer at any time. She didn't exactly say that, but she said she was taking back what was hers.'

'Except Martin gave her up. She's not going to like that one little bit,' said Fi, her voice fierce. 'That bitch killed our two friends because she thought they were going to tell Abs about her affair with Martin, and because she thought they'd worked out that she'd taken the knife, and that it was her, not Abs, who killed Matthew Parker. Well, news flash, Jenna, we know everything.'

'She's locked me out of the dating apps,' I added, sounding panicked. 'She could use them to show Martin and make him think that I was cheating on him.' I couldn't tell them about the photo, I was too ashamed.

'He'll never believe it,' said Em, supportively.

'If you ask me, she's mad, bloody bonkers. And who knows what she'll do next? OK, listen, she killed Lauren because she overheard her on the phone telling Abs something she'd remembered about the knife, and hinting at Martin's affair, and she killed Hayley because she heard Lauren tell Abs that she'd spoken to her, right?'

Emma and I nodded dutifully.

'At the moment, she doesn't know the rest of us have any idea, right? She can't be sure that you've guessed it's her, can she?'

I shook my head.

'So the rest of us are safe, for now.'

'Yes, but hold on, how could Jenna ever falsely expose Abs as the woman who stabbed Matthew Parker to death in the hot tub without implicating the rest of us, which would include herself?'

Emma had made a good point and our addled brains took a moment to consider the problem.

'She could if we were all dead,' Fi said slowly.

Emma let out a crazed laugh, her eyes staring around the room wildly as if Jenna was about to jump out from behind the curtains wielding a large knife.

'No,' I responded. 'She wouldn't want to kill her friends for no reason, I'm sure of that.'

'You're still too trusting, Abs, even after everything that she's done to you. When are you going to toughen up?' Fi glared at me, but in a well-meaning way.

'We have to think like her,' I said. 'If I was Jenna, I'd try to get you all on my side, try to turn you against her – well, me – by telling you a pack of lies about me. I'd– I don't know– I'd get us all to say something like – we were staying at the cottage but we went out that night, except she stayed behind on her own because she said she had a headache, or something. That way, as long as we stuck to our story, we could never be implicated.'

'That's genius.' Fi clapped her hands, as she and Em looked at me admiringly.

I basked in her praise, feeling chuffed.

'We could turn the tables on her.'

'What do you mean?' Fi and I turned to stare at Em.

'We only need to get Claire on board, which will be easy enough once we tell her what Jenna's done, and it'll be our collective word against Jenna's. We can stop this – we can tell the police what we suspect. Let them piece it all together, they've got all the evidence they need to figure it all out.'

'But no evidence that Matthew Parker was ever at the cottage, or that Jenna killed him.'

I shook my head. 'That's not strictly true, Fi...' I picked up my phone and my fingers fumblingly opened my photo gallery, searching for the photo I'd moved back from my deleted files. I passed my phone to Fi.

'Wow,' Fi breathed as she stared at the photo of Jenna in the hot tub, resplendent in her pig's mask. 'What made you take this? Jenna was so hardcore about us not taking any photos. Our little Abs has a teeny tiny little bit of the rebel in her after all.' She looked at me proudly.

'It proves she was there, but that's all,' sighed Emma. 'What about him?'

I looked over at Fi, waiting to see if she would remember.

'Abs, you said he lost his necklace when he took his T-shirt off. Some leather thong?'

'It must have fallen through the deck, it's probably lying there underneath it.' I paused for effect. 'And that's not the only thing left behind.'

'Well, spit it out, Abs, the suspense is killing me.'

'When Hayley–' I stopped, swallowing hard at the mention of my dead friend. 'When Hayley disposed of all the masks in rubbish bins in different towns, she told me, in secret, that the pig mask wasn't there. We didn't dare tell Jenna.'

'So what happened to it then? We definitely didn't leave it lying on the deck, I think one of us would have noticed it.'

'I wasn't really in my right mind straight after I got out of the hot tub, obviously, but I remember bits and pieces, weird images... I remember Lauren kind of howling, and then she threw something off the deck... It was pink... I think she picked up the pig's mask and threw it, and it must have fallen into the bushes. It must still be there. It had a bloody handprint on it, I remember seeing it when I was in the hot tub – he must have clawed at her mask...'

'Well, we've got her.' Fi was loud in her excitement. 'Remember when we were throwing back Tequila shots? We'd tried on the masks and we'd been laughing at each other about how mad we looked?'

Emma took over. 'And we laughed at Jenna because she got her hair stuck in the mask when she pulled it off.'

'Jenna's hair in a pig mask – with his fingerprints on it in his own blood, lying in the bushes at Bliss Cottage, Matthew Parker's leather thong and pendant lying underneath the deck, Jenna's lipstick found at the scene where Lauren drowned, and her hair clip found at Hayley's after the poor girl suffocated to death... Add that to all the other stuff – her hatred of him since his very existence broke her family up – and we've got everything we need to go to the police and tell them about Jenna.' Fi tilted the whisky bottle, shrugged, and sloshed some more into each of our glasses.

'Except we couldn't possibly know about the pig mask, could we? And aren't the police going to ask how on earth she disposed of his body in the sea all on her own? Not to mention getting his car back to the pub car park.' Emma's comments brought us back down to earth.

'We've got Abs' photo, we'll find a way to use it. Hell, we'll just say that she brought it with her and we had no idea why. We could even throw in something about her having hook ups, to get them thinking along those lines. And why should we care how she got rid of his body? We didn't know he existed, did we? That's the police's problem. As for his car – maybe she just picked him up from the pub. Maybe we went out in Em's car and she took Abs' car. See? There's an answer for everything.'

Our story was coming together nicely, and we picked up our glasses, downing the whisky.

'What about the dating app? I'm on it, there's a message thread with him, it's got everything, even the rendezvous, and I can't get into it since she changed the password.'

'Uninstall it. Remove it from your phone, Abs. Here, I'll do it.' Fi held her hand out for my phone. It'll be like it never existed. If the police ever ask you, you just say that you know nothing about it. By that time they'll be quite open to the idea that Jenna used your photo to set up a fake profile to lure him in.'

I watched Fi as she expertly worked on my phone, removing all evidence of my involvement with the dead man, or any other men.

'What about his phone?' I said as my mind still raced through any obstacles we hadn't thought of. 'Wouldn't it be better to somehow get hold of it and destroy it? Don't forget, she's been sending me those messages.'

'If she's keeping it with her, we'll find a way to look in her bag. I know – when we go for our memorial walk I'll suggest that we lock our bags in the boot. One of us will have to get back to the car before the rest of us, and have a look. If it's there, we'll take it and get rid of it somewhere.'

'This is all well and good, but we still have to get Claire on board don't forget. How do we do that? We're meeting her and Jenna here in–' Emma looked at her watch. 'In less than five hours.'

Tiredness hit me, at Emma's words, and I yawned loudly. I was drunk, stressed out, exhausted, heartbroken from loss, and my brain felt completely overwhelmed with the effort of trying to juggle so many stories. If I was to get through tomorrow successfully I desperately needed some sleep.

'We should all try to get some sleep.' Fi appeared to have read my mind. She yawned, followed swiftly by Emma.

'What if I walk on with Jenna, ahead of you three? You could hang back with Claire and fill her in.' I looked from Fi to Emma.

'Are you sure you can handle it, Abs? You'll have to stay calm and not give anything away.'

'I can handle it,' I assured them. 'The most important thing tomorrow – today, I mean – is that we come together and remember our friends. Once we've done that, we can deal with Jenna.'

'Oh, we'll deal with her alright.' Fi's voice was harsh as she stood up and collected our empty glasses. 'Our lovely friend Jenna is about to go down for the murder of Matthew Parker, Lauren Dempsey and Hayley Baldwin. Her little revenge plan against Matthew Parker, and against Abs, is about to backfire on her. We've got ourselves our own revenge plan, ladies, and this time it's against Jenna.

60

'It's straight down the M20, it'll only take us about an hour and a half.' Fi turned round awkwardly in the driver's seat. 'Everyone alright in the back there?' Her eyes locked with mine for a second – a secret message, just for me. I could see her concern at how the seating had ended up – me sandwiched between Claire and Jenna.

I smiled wanly, nodding. 'Fine.'

''Of course we're fine, aren't we Abs?' Jenna put her arm around me, and I tried not to shudder as I pictured her arms around Martin, his around hers... Her cloyingly sweet perfume filled my nostrils and I fought the urge to gag. Leaning forward to dislodge her arm, I looked out of the front windscreen. 'At least it's not raining.'

'The sun's trying to come through,' said Claire, sniffing as she screwed up a tissue and bent down to shove it into her handbag. 'That's nice.'

'Abs suggested that we get some flowers and scatter them from the cliff,' said Emma. 'We'll look for a florist once we get to Dover.'

'Well, aren't you just the sweetest person, Abs? Roses would be nice, don't you think?'

'Yes,' I replied, looking down at Jenna's feet. In typical Jenna style, she'd chosen vanity over practicality, as I'd known she would. Her platform fashion trainers were covered in pink glitter and purple sequins, and the soles were almost completely smooth. I glanced at Claire's feet, pleased to see that she'd been sensible and worn flat shoes with a sturdy, ridged sole.

Claire saw me looking at her feet and shifted slightly, squashing me against Jenna as she looked at my own footwear. 'It'll be muddy on the path after all that rain, at least we've both got the right shoes on, but I'll probably still struggle, you know me. Oh dear, you'll be in trouble with Fi.' She nudged me, indicating the crumbled, dried mud that my trainers had dropped all over Fi's rear footwell. 'Oh well, we'll all be adding to that soon enough, I suppose.'

'We'll take it slow,' said Em, from the front passenger seat. 'You can hold onto me and Fi, can't she, Fi?'

'Absolutely.' Fi nodded as they successfully set the scene to separate Jenna and me from them and Claire.

We fell silent for a while, each with our private thoughts, and I jumped when Jenna spoke loudly.

'Had any more mysterious messages from the dead man's phone, Abs? Anything you want to tell us about?'

'No.' I wasn't about to give her the pleasure of knowing how much she'd freaked me out with her taunting messages, or the dreaded photo.

'How's Marty? He must have been upset about Lauren and Hayley.'

I swallowed desperately, hating my husband's diminutive name coming from her scarlet-painted lips. 'Of course he was upset, like we all are.'

'Did you tell him about our plans today?'

'I left him a note, he was asleep when I left.'

Fi adjusted the rearview mirror and gave me an approving nod. 'Did you tell Adrian what we were doing today, Claire?'

'Oh yes, he thought it was such a nice thing to do, the perfect way for us to say our own private goodbyes before the... before the funerals... Oh God, I can't bear to think about it...'

'Shall I give Marty a call? Tell him we're on the road?' Jenna reached for her bag, and I pulled my shoulders up, turning towards her slightly.

'I told you he was asleep. He wouldn't want you disturbing him, Jenna. In fact, before we went up to bed last night, he turned his phone off, he said he'd been having some bothersome calls from an annoying person and he was sick of it. He said it was so tiresome when people kept pushing for something you weren't interested in. I suppose it was some cheap, tacky salesperson trying to force him to sign up for something he didn't want, you know what they can be like, not taking no for an answer.' I paused for effect, and smiled as I continued, injecting warmth into my voice, 'He was such a comfort to me last night, I was just in pieces, and he held me until I fell asleep. He even said we should go away for a romantic weekend together once we get through all this.' *Take that, bitch.*

Fi gave me a warning look in the mirror before adjusting it back, and I reeled myself in, feeling Jenna bristling beside me. I'd hit a nerve and it felt good.

'Martin's a real treasure, Abs, you're a lucky girl. Mind you, Adrian's not so bad, bless his cotton socks. He certainly kept me in cups of tea last night – his version of offering comfort.'

'She's lucky Abigail, Claire, remember?' Jenna leant across me to smile at Claire before turning her eyes to meet mine for a second.

'I never really knew why you called Abs that…'

'Nor did I, come to think of it.' Em turned round to look at me, giving me an encouraging smile.

I wriggled uncomfortably in the sudden silence as everyone waited for Jenna to explain her nickname for me.

'Oh, well, you've only got to look at Abigail's life, haven't you? The way everything's always worked out for her? She hooked the perfect boyfriend, her mum died which meant she didn't have to move away and lose him, and then she married him, and they're still happily married all these years later. Like I say, lucky little Abigail.'

I gasped, wanting to claw her eyes out. 'Lucky? My best friend dies and I'm lucky? And my mum too?' *And happily married? After you seduced my husband?*

'Really, Jenna, I don't know what's come over you.' Claire spoke in her mumsy voice.

But Jenna was relentless and on a roll. 'Not only that, she even managed to stab a bloke to death in a hot tub and have us all feeling sorry for her, and as if that wasn't enough, she—'

'Stop it!' I sobbed.

'Jenna, for God's sake.' Fi was furious. 'Shut up. In case you've forgotten, today is about Lauren and Hayley.'

'I swear, Jenna, if you say one more word...' Emma very rarely lost her cool, but she turned and gave Jenna a death stare before reaching her hand back to squeeze my knee in solidarity.

'Sorry,' Claire whispered in my ear, as Jenna laughed and stared out of the side window shaking her head.

61

Angels

'We should listen to some of our favourite tunes, don't you think?' Emma said into the awkward silence that had fallen over us all. 'We can remember Laur and Hayles, and so many happy times.' She fiddled with her phone and we fell silent as the first gentle piano chords sounded in our ears.

'Lauren loved Robbie,' said Claire, reaching for another tissue.

'So did Hayley, I think she played Angels about a hundred times at her fortieth. D'you remember?'

Slowly, we began to join in, each with our own private thoughts and memories of our friends. Claire passed me a tissue and I wiped my streaming eyes, the full impact of a life without Lauren and Hayley hitting me anew.

I must have dozed off, and I shifted my head from Claire's shoulder, blinking as Emma's voice suddenly barked out loudly.

'Pull in, pull in! There's one, over there on the right.'

Fi swerved, parking the car in one smooth movement, and turned off the engine as we looked in the direction that Emma was pointing. 'Perfect timing, it looks like they've just opened up,' Fi said as we watched a green-aproned man carry buckets of flowers out to the display stand.

'Shall we all go, or is that overkill?' asked Emma as we winced at her choice of word.

'Let's all go, we could do with stretching our legs anyway.' Claire opened her door and climbed out as I gratefully shuffled across the seat away from Jenna.

We stood in the small florist's shop, looking around at the displays.

'Roses,' said Claire. 'We'd like to buy some roses. Red ones, I think, don't you?' She looked around, waiting for us to agree.

'And maybe some yellow ones?' I suggested.

'White would be nice too,' added Emma.

'Let's get a few of each,' Fi said.

'Do you have any black roses?'

I froze at Jenna's question. She was goading me, I knew it, but I kept calm.

The man whistled. 'I can organise you some, but I'd need a bit of time. It'd be a special order, we have to dye them, you see.'

'It doesn't matter, it was just an idea.' Jenna smiled at him, and I noticed his eyes flicker with that familiar indication of interest as they glanced from her face to her body, and back to her eyes.

'So, it's decided then, we'll take six of each, that's the red, yellow and white. Everybody happy with that?'

We mumbled and nodded our agreement, completed our purchase, and Claire carried the wrapped flowers back to the car.

'I could do with the loo,' Claire said as we hovered around the car.

'Me too, and maybe a coffee?'

'A cup of tea would be nice.'

'That looks like a coffee shop up there.'

Refreshed, and relieved, a little later, we returned to the car and drove to the parking area from where we would begin our memorial walk.

'We'll lock our bags in the car,' instructed Fi, opening the boot and dropping her own bag in, as Emma did the same, catching my eye.

'Here, Claire, I'll take it.' Fi placed Claire's handbag in alongside the other two, and I turned to Jen, holding out my hand.

I put my own bag in and stood Jenna's beside it, and Fi slammed the boot closed.

We began to walk, and I tutted, turning to Fi. 'I forgot my phone, I might take a photo or two, and I meant to grab a packet of tissues. Can I have the keys? Keep going and I'll catch you all up.'

I hurried back to the car, opened the boot and reached into my bag, grabbing some tissues while I kept an eye on their progress, my hand trembling as I fumbled and dropped things. Finally, holding my phone, I slammed the boot and rushed to catch up with the others, handing Fi back her keys.

We began the steep climb, the gravel path crunching beneath our feet until it became a dirt path, and we slowed as we walked on along the muddy path.

'Can we take a breather?' Claire was red-faced and puffing, and we stopped for a moment to take in the view. 'Couldn't we do it here?' The wind had picked up, and the clouds were darkening ominously. 'It looks like it's going to rain.'

'We should go a bit further,' I said. 'There's a perfect spot where it levels out, and we can stand on the edge so that we can scatter the roses. I think I remember where it is, we all stood there together the last time.'

I began to walk on as Jen fell into step beside me. I glanced back at Fi, who took the hint, holding Claire's arm for a second as she asked her for a tissue.

'I've got one, hold on.' Em made a show of searching her pockets, and Jen and I moved further ahead as their soft voices fell behind.

Jen's feet slipped in the mud, and I forced myself to grab her arm as she righted herself.

'Come on, it's not much further.'

'Looks like I wore the wrong shoes,' she said ruefully as she laughed. 'I suppose I'm just not like you, Abs, you're always so prepared, aren't you? Everything thought out so that it all goes perfectly. Little anal Abs.'

I ignored her mocking tone. 'I thought I was lucky Abigail?'

'Well, you have been so far, haven't you? But luck always runs out, Abs, maybe yours is about to.'

It was a clear threat, and I checked behind me, seeing Fi, Em and Claire huddled close together as they walked slowly, their mouths moving rapidly, arms waving around frantically, the wind now taking away all sound of their voices.

The path was getting muddier by the minute, and I pushed on, enjoying the sight of Jenna's sparkly footwear being ruined. 'Hold on to me, we're almost there.'

'He doesn't want you anymore, Abs.'

I thought I'd imagined her words for a second, as the wind whistled around us.

'Give him up and you can keep on being lucky Abigail. Everything can stop, it's enough now, surely? Too many people have died. It's a fair deal. Otherwise...'

Otherwise, what?

'Not now.' I stopped suddenly, so that Jenna slipped again, the mud squelching up around her shoes. Pushing down my panic at her threatening words, I said, 'This is where we all stood, all seven of us, looking across to France.' I stepped closer to the cliff edge, gazing out.

'And now there are only five of us...' Jenna dropped my arm as she looked out across the channel, her hair flying in a tangled mass about her face.

'We need to remember Lauren and Hayley now,' I said sadly.

The others had almost caught up with us.

'Tell me it's over and give him back to me,' Jenna hissed. 'Otherwise the whole world will know you're a murderer.'

62

'It's not over, not quite,' I said to her, my voice cold. 'And you got it wrong – you're the murderer, not me.'

I turned away from her bewildered expression, smiling at Claire as she reached my side. 'We made it,' I said, hugging her. 'Are you alright?'

'Thanks to Fi and Em.' Claire looked me in the eyes, nodding, and I knew they'd brought her up to scratch and that she believed us.

Fi squeezed my shoulder as she came to stand beside me, small droplets of drizzle beginning to dampen the air.

We stood in a line, steadying ourselves against the wind buffeting us from behind, staring out across the Dover Strait as Emma began to pass along the roses, the water of the channel turning a threatening shade of grey as the wind licked up angry white waves, and the drizzle intensified.

'Let's do this.' Fi dropped a rose from the cliff, her legs splayed to prevent herself from slipping. 'This is for you, Hayles, our sweet girl, and Lauren, our crazy babe.' Her voice caught in a sob as she let another rose fall.

'For you, Laur, for bringing such joy into our lives.' I dropped a rose, watching it fall, the wind catching it and carrying it further out to sea. 'And for you, my precious Hayley, my gentle friend. I love you both.' I forced my fingers to let go of another rose.

Jen silently dropped her roses, her eyes following their descent, before turning to look at me with dark eyes.

'Oh, Laur, Hayles, how are we ever going to manage without you both?' Claire burst into tears as she let her roses fall from her hands, and I felt tears prick my eyes.

'I'll love you both forever. I never meant to hurt you, Laur.' Emma's fingers relinquished her roses as she began to cry.

I bent down as one of her roses landed in the mud, picking it up and dropping it over the edge.

Fi took my hand and we dropped the last of the roses.

'To Lauren and Hayley,' sobbed Fi.

'Lauren and Hayley.' Our words were carried out to sea by the wind, and we stepped forward collectively, holding onto one another to look down at the steely water as we tried desperately to catch a glimpse of the scattered memories of our friends through the droplets of rain now falling steadily.

Turning, we looked at one another through our tears and nodded.

'We should head back,' Em shouted above the intensifying wind and rain. 'Claire, hold onto me.' They turned and began to walk away from the cliff edge as Fi gave me another nod and turned to walk behind them, all three of their bodies bent slightly against the wind as they began their slow progress.

I reached out and grabbed Jen's arm as she turned to follow them. 'Wait,' I said, just loudly enough for her to hear. 'We need to talk – alone.'

Her eyes narrowed as she pushed her damp hair back from her face. 'Fine, it's about bloody time. You could have picked better weather though.' She looked over at the retreating backs of Em, Claire and Fi, as Fi turned to look back at us. 'We'll catch you up!' she shouted at Fi, who acknowledged my reassuring nod with anxious eyes and turned to follow Em and Claire.

'So, talk.' Jenna stood confidently, a gleam in her eyes. 'What do you want to say? You want to beg me to give

Martin up, is that it? Forget it. Either you give him up or I expose you for what you really are – a cold-blooded killer. Your luck's about to run out. No more lucky little Abigail for you. You lose.' She laughed in my face.

63

The Show

I laughed back, enjoying her look of surprise. 'No, you lose, Jenna. How about I expose you as a killer?' I gripped her arms, yelling in her face. 'It was your revenge plan; you recognised your long-lost half-brother in the photo of him as a grown man, after he'd beaten Lauren black and blue; you blamed him for breaking up your family. Natalie being your half-sister was one thing, your dad still stayed with you and your mum, but when Matthew came along your dad left you both for his new family. You recognised him in the photo and planned your revenge; you booked the cottage with my credit card; you put the knife in my hand after you'd stabbed him to make it look like I'd done it.'

'What? What are you talking about?' she cried, her feet slipping as she tried to shake off my hands. 'That's a lie. I never even met him as a kid. The closest I ever got to seeing him was a grainy photo in the paper, so how the fuck could I have recognised him? I hated him, but why would I have wanted him dead, then or now?' She pushed me hard and I fell backwards, taking her with me so that she straddled me, staring into my face. 'You recognised him...' Her eyes glinted. 'I knew there was something about the way you looked at his photo... But it wasn't until he said her name as he walked towards you – Nats – that I began to wonder. And then I asked myself – why say her name?'

I heaved myself up, managing to topple Jenna so that I now straddled her. 'You took his phone from his car –

you've been sending me messages – you wanted to taunt me, to send me over the edge.'

'I took his phone and wallet to confirm my suspicions, once you'd killed him. I wanted to freak you out. I wanted you to know that I knew what you'd done.'

'To blackmail me,' I spat.

'To make you give up Martin. You stole him from me,' Jenna screamed up at my face. 'You spread lies about me, and Martin believed them. I know it was you, I finally worked it out. Natalie wanted to meet me that day, she said she had something important to tell me, but she never made it, did she? Because you pushed her off the balcony. Is that what happened? Did she tell you that she knew what you'd done?'

Images of my best friend's terrified face filled my head and I let go of Jenna's arms, staggering to a standing position as she pulled herself up and faced me warily.

'Natalie was too earnest, too honest. She was going to ruin everything for me,' I sobbed.

Jenna stared at me with wild eyes, pushing her wet hair from her face and leaving a trail of mud. 'God, you did do it, didn't you? You killed her, and when her little brother flew at you in a rage you tried to chuck him off the balcony too, so that he couldn't tell anyone that you'd just killed his sister.'

'Except his mum came running, and I had to make it look like I was trying to save him. That's why he had a scar on his neck, it was from my nail. He should have stayed abroad. Why did he have to come back?' I wailed, as we circled each other. 'Why did he make me kill him?'

'You thought you'd seen the back of him, didn't you? But then there he was, Lauren's attacker and your worst nightmare. No one believed his stories at the time, he was just a kid, but he was back, all grown up, the one person who knew the truth about what you'd done. And we were planning our revenge plan. You were terrified of him recognising you, even after all this time, and spoiling your perfect little life.'

'What perfect life?' I screamed, lunging at Jenna. 'You've been fucking my husband. How could you do that to me?'

We grappled to hold onto each other's arms as the wind did its best to blow us over.

'You took him from me and I loved him.' Jenna clawed at my face. 'He couldn't wait to comfort poor little Abigail, so distraught at the loss of her best friend.'

'Martin chose me. You were a little slut, you were never good enough for him.' I grabbed hold of Jenna's hair, pulling it hard, as the rain lashed down around us.

Jenna stopped struggling for a moment as she stared into my eyes. 'Your family was going to move away after it happened, you and Martin would have broken up and he'd have come back to me.' She gasped. 'You killed your mother. You pushed your own bloody mother from the ladder, didn't you?' For the first time there was a hint of fear in her eyes. 'You're a monster.'

I pushed her backwards, holding onto her hair and her arm. 'I had to, I couldn't lose Martin, Don't you see? He was my world.'

'Not anymore, he's my world again now, Abs. He's leaving you. I'll show him the photo of you kissing that bloke outside Baxter's. And once he knows you're a murderer he'll hate your guts, he'll be repulsed by you. You're a fucking deranged serial killer.'

We spun around, dangerously close to the cliff edge, and I caught sight of Fi in the distance, partially obscured by the rain, as she made her way back along the path in our direction.

Jenna slammed me to the ground, clambering onto me so that she looked down at me, her face wild. 'You're fucking sick, Abigail. And you killed Lauren and Hayley, I know it. Their deaths weren't accidents were they, you sick freak? They were your friends. They loved you. Why did you do it? Because Lauren was confused about the photos of our first weekend away together, and your lies about being afraid of heights? She didn't know anything, she didn't even know what she was saying about the knife, she was never going to figure it out. I was the only one who'd guessed the truth. And she told Hayley, and sealed both their death warrants. How did you do it? What did you do to them?' She was screaming, her spit landing on my face in globules to mix with the rain as it ran down my skin.

'You killed them, Jenna,' I screamed back at her, twisting my neck to see how close Fi was getting to us. 'That's what everyone's going to believe. The girls already believe it. You dropped your lipstick when you smashed Lauren's head with a rock and pushed her from the path and into the pond. And when you gave Hayley cough medicine mixed with sesame oil, and took her epinephrine and asthma spray, you lost your hair clip – the scarlet flower one. The police will figure it all out.'

'You set me up? You took my things, you sick bloody bitch? You're mad. No one will believe that, it's a crazy fucking lie. I would never have hurt a hair on either of their heads. You smashed Lauren's head in with a rock? How could you? And you watched poor Hayley gasping for breath until she collapsed and died? You're pure evil.' Her eyes glinted. 'You took their phones and sent us the texts.'

I grinned up at her, panting. 'No, wrong again. You took their phones, Jenna. They're in your bag in Fi's car. I put them there when I deleted the photo from your phone.'

She gasped, her eyes huge in her white face as she said desperately, 'Give me back Martin, and I won't tell anyone the truth. Abs, no one needs to know, I'll help you cover it up. I'll get rid of the phones. We'll say I gave Lauren the lipstick and Hayley borrowed my hair clip. I'll delete all that dating app stuff, I won't tell anyone.'

I let my body go limp and Jenna released her grip on me. 'You won't tell anyone?' I said, as we both stood, gasping from our exertions, oblivious to the heavy rain thundering down around us.

Jenna reached out, holding onto my arms as she stared triumphantly into my face. 'It's over, Abs. This is your only way out. I win, you lose.' She grinned, her eyes widening as I suddenly gripped her arms, swinging her round as I saw Fi beginning to run towards us, her mouth opening and closing silently, her words drowned out by the wind and rain.

'You want Martin?' I screamed. 'Too bad he's dead, isn't it?'

'What are you talking about?' Her foot slipped dangerously close to the cliff edge, and I held her steady as her fingers gripped painfully into my flesh.

I looked triumphantly into her scared eyes. 'I told you once, if I can't have him, no one can.'

'You killed him?' Her voice was shaky, and I could smell her fear.

'No,' I said gently, smiling. 'You did, Jenna, with the knife I took from your house last night that has your fingerprints on it, after he rejected you to stay with me. You also left one of your trashy earrings in my bedroom, next to his body, just in case the police have any doubts. I was at Fi's, with Em, all night. You must have gone to my house to have it out with him. The message was a nice touch, I thought, didn't you?'

Screaming hysterically, she struggled against me. 'It's not true. It's not true, you insane cow.'

I looked into her eyes. 'I win, you lose. I'm lucky Abigail, remember? But it's not by chance, I make my own luck.' I gave her a gentle shove, falling to my knees as she began to fall backwards, her feet teetering on the edge for a moment as her horrified eyes met mine. Her hands clutched uselessly at nothing, and then she was gone.

'Jenna!' I screamed, looking over the edge of the cliff on all fours. 'No, Jenna, no...' I wailed, my hand reaching out desperately. 'Oh God... Jenna...'

I felt Fi's hands pull me back from the edge, her arms cradling me as I sobbed. 'I t– t– tried to save her... she tried to k– kill me...'

'Shh... it's OK... you're safe...' Fi gripped me protectively as she slowly edged us away from danger. 'It's alright.'

'Oh God, Jenna...' I moaned, burying my face into Fi's shoulder. 'She tried to push me, she said...'

'Don't try to talk.' Fi rocked me gently as I cried. 'Oh, Abs, you poor thing...'

I realised that Fi was crying too, and I lifted my head to look at her. 'What have I done?' I wailed.

'You haven't done anything, Abs. Shh...'

My phone was ringing in the pocket of my jacket, but Fi stopped me as my hand reached for it.

'Don't answer it, let's get you back to the car. We need to call the police.'

'But what if it's Martin?' I asked tremulously.

A shadow passed over Fi's face. 'Come on, let's go. Can you walk? Lean on me.'

We began to stagger along the path, me leaning heavily on Fi.

'What are we going to tell the police, Fi?'

'The fucking truth. Well, some of it. God, you could have been her next victim.'

'She slipped... She said I was dead, and she tried to push me but she slipped in the mud. I tried to grab her but it was so muddy... She was saying such awful things... She said– she said something about Martin...'

'Come on, keep walking, that's it, nearly there. Don't try to talk.' Fi marched me along the path, and eventually we began our descent towards the car park.

'Where's Jenna?' Claire and Emma jumped from the car, ignoring the rain, as we arrived.

'Oh my God, Abs, what happened? Are you alright?' Claire looked at my mud-caked clothes, grabbing tissues from her pocket as she held my hands and tried fruitlessly to remove the worst of the mud from them and from underneath my nails. She gently wiped my face before taking me in her arms as she looked from me to Fi, who was shaking her head.

I allowed Claire to smother me in her motherly arms as they murmured quietly, feeling her body stiffen in shock as Fi told them about Jenna.

I continued to cry, adding in a few shakes and moans, as I heard their shocked voices take in what Fi was telling them about Jenna's attempt on my life.

'We have to tell her,' hissed Emma.

'Tell me what?' I pulled away from Claire and looked around at them. 'What do you have to tell me?'

Fi shook her head again. 'Only that we found Matthew Parker's phone in Jenna's bag. And that's not all, she had some photos of him. We were right – she'd clearly planned the whole thing, right from the beginning. She had Lauren's and Hayley's phones in her bag as well.'

My phone rang again and I pulled it from my pocket.

'No!' Claire's voice was sharp. 'Give it to me.' She grabbed my phone, looking at Fi for direction.

'Abs, why don't you sit down in the car.' Fi sighed heavily. 'There's something we have to tell you, it's about Martin...'

AFTER

One
Don't Stop Me Now

Jenna wasn't charged with any of the murders, or my attempted murder, of course, because she was dead.

Fi, Claire, Emma and I were all interviewed separately by the police, and gave the same stories, and, with a little help, the press did a magnificent job of revealing the overwhelming evidence surrounding the deaths of Matthew Parker, Lauren Dempsey, Hayley Baldwin and Martin Hawthorn, so that in the court of public opinion, Jenna was a mass murderer who had got what she deserved.

I declined to comment publicly on Jenna's attempt on my life, not wanting to push my luck, but was gratified to read the public messages of sympathy beneath the online accounts, especially the comments saying that she'd got what she deserved.

I was discharged from hospital into the care of Fi, just in time for the funerals of our two friends, which were heartbreaking to attend. Just because I killed them didn't mean I didn't feel the pain. And I missed them terribly.

A few days after that we held Martin's funeral. I played the part of the grieving widow perfectly, it wasn't difficult, I *was* grieving. I'd lost the love of my life. But he'd cheated on me. And as I'd told them, what felt like a lifetime ago, when Lauren had first mentioned the dating apps – if he cheated on me, I'd off him and his dirty little bit on the side in one second. No one messes with my life.

And then it was Jenna's funeral.

'Should we go?' Claire had asked, as we'd sat together at Fi's the night before.

'I don't know if I can stand it.' Fi was still filled with anger.

'If she wasn't already dead, I'd kill her myself.' Em topped our wine glasses up as she glared at us all.

They all looked at me, as if waiting for direction.

'She was our friend... I feel like we should be there, we loved her once,' I said softly, feeling noble.

'God, you're so forgiving, Abs, that's always been your problem. I've told you a million times, you need to toughen up.'

I smiled sadly at Fi. 'I can't help it, it's just the way I am, I suppose. Maybe it would help give us closure?'

'Oh, it'll give us closure alright. I'll cheer when that bitch is lowered into the ground.'

I silently applauded Fi's fierceness. I couldn't have put it better myself.

'Let's do it,' Claire said. 'We'll be able to lay our ghosts to rest and move on.'

And so, dressed in black once again, we gathered at Jenna's grave with the tiny group of mourners who felt it their duty to be there, each dropping our small handful of earth onto her coffin once it was lowered into the ground.

As I let go of my handful of soil the thought occurred to me that Jen and I had been the same in many ways, both determined to get what we wanted at all costs. I suppose we both lost. Except she's gone, and I'm still here. So there's that.

Claire had appointed herself my protector, and she wrapped her arm around me as we walked away, tutting as she held up my hand and studied my dirty nails from picking up the soil.

'I can't believe it was only two weeks ago that we were at Fi's looking at the old photos of us all on our first ever weekend away together. You grinning like a mad thing on that rollercoaster...' Her grip on my hand lessened, and I felt her stiffen slightly beside me.

'But you were scared of heights, Abs...' She looked at my hand again. 'That night at the cottage, before he came... there was dirt under your nails... I found you by the hot tub... you had your hand in the plant pot... as if you'd just put something...' She dropped my hand, her eyes suddenly wary, and I knew she'd figured it out.

Oh, Claire... Why couldn't you leave it alone? I can't let you spoil everything now... not when I've got away with murder, as I always do. I'm lucky Abigail, remember?

THANK YOU

I had huge fun writing this book and getting to know the characters as they developed throughout the story. Thanks for reading – I hope you laughed, I hope you gasped, but more than anything, I hope you enjoyed it! As always, if you are able to leave a few kind words in a review in any of the usual places, or share on your socials or in your book groups, it will be much appreciated.

ABOUT THE AUTHOR

Linzi Carlisle grew up in Dartford, Kent, in the UK, on a diet of Agatha Christie and Ruth Rendell, before moving to South Africa where she met her husband. They lived in Zambia for many years before settling in South Africa in the beautiful town of George, part of the Garden Route, nestled between the Outeniqua Mountains and the Indian Ocean – the perfect spot for writing her books. They share their home with their two beautiful cats.

Also by Linzi Carlisle – The Sasha Blue Mystery Series:

Village Lies
Graphic Lies
Old Lies
Nocturnal Lies

linzicarlisle.blogspot.com
instagram.com/linzicarlisleauthor
facebook.com/linzicarlisleauthor
goodreads.com/linzicarlisle